THE

CATALYST

BY

LYNN WOOD

Cover Design: Consuelo Parra

Follow Lynn on her Blog and website: WritersBlockNot.com

Twitter.com/eternallynow

TITLES BY LYNN WOOD

FICTION:

ROMANTIC SUSPENSE:
DESTINY BECKONS COLLECTION:
THE CATALYST
THE YOUNG MADONNA

HISTORICAL ROMANCE:
NORMAN BRIDES SERIES:
KEEPER OF THE STONE
FINDERS KEEPERS
THE PROMISE KEEPER

THE COMPLETE KEEPER TRILOGY

ALSO BY L. M. WOOD

AWAKENING SERIES:
AWAKENING
CHOOSE

THE FIRSTBORN SERIES:
MICHAEL, BELOVED OF GOD
DANCING WITH THE DEVIL

NON-FICTION:
LESSONS IN ILLUMINATION
    ...A BEGINNER'S GUIDE TO THE ETERNAL WAY

YOGA BEHIND THE VEIL
    ...A JOURNEY OF SELF-DISCOVERY

PROLOGUE...

The new gendarme whiled away the hours of his first official assignment flirting with the pretty young cashier who occasionally paused to assist a tourist with his or her purchases. Though the assignment of keeping watch for suspicious activity among the visitors to the historic site was not exactly what he'd anticipated when in a burst of patriotic enthusiasm following a terrorist attack on his beloved Paris he'd joined the ranks of the gendarme, he accepted the drawn out boredom of his first placement as part of his initiation into the service. With the increased threat of terrorism around the world, France's military police had been called upon to play a more visible and active role in protecting her country's national treasures.

Certainly, the ancient abbey that was Mont Saint Michel qualified as one of those. Dating back to the early eighth century, the abbey had survived not a few threats to its continued existence, the Hundred Years War, numerous fires, the French Revolution and two World Wars, to name but a few. So Jean was not particularly concerned about the prospect of an imminent terrorist attack, particularly since Mont Saint Michel was located on a remote island a four-hour drive from heavily populated Paris.

While the lovely Marie's attention was currently focused on assisting a tourist with her selections, Jean looked about him, concluding after a brief examination of his surroundings that there was no discernible threat for him to worry about. His glance fell on a young girl standing before the statue of Saint Michael in the alcove near the exit. The statue was the plaster model for the depiction of the archangel that crowned the structure's fleche and stood almost fifteen feet high, towering over the child. The girl's long dark curls fell almost to her waist and when she turned around to assure herself her mother was still close by, he could see even across the distance separating them that her eyes were an astonishing, piercing blue.

Her mother collected her purchases and strode towards the exit to where her daughter now stood staring intently up into the face of the statue. When her mother took her hand to lead her away, the child shook her head in denial, turning to look up at her mother to presumably explain her reluctance to leave just yet. Whatever she said to her mother apparently surprised the woman, because her eyes widened and she cast an apologetic look to those in earshot of her conversation with her young daughter, who were all wearing indulgent smiles at the child's declaration. Curious, Jean stepped closer to the pair so he could eavesdrop on their exchange.

"It's true, Mommy, Lord Michael is angry," the child insisted.

Jean felt his own lips curving in an amused smile at the girl's claim as he watched her mother kneel down so she was face-to-face with her young daughter. "Who is the archangel angry with, Noelle?" She inquired patiently in the voice of an adult indulging a child's imagination.

"France." The child replied without hesitation, bringing amused chuckles to the lips of the bystanders who, like Jean, had drawn nearer to listen in on the conversation between mother and child.

Jean noticed the mother cast another apologetic look in the direction of their amused audience before returning her attention to her earnest, very young daughter. "Why is the angel angry at France?"

"Because they took it away. They have to give it back," the young girl insisted.

"They took what away?" Her mother asked, as confused as the eavesdroppers of the couple's conversation.

"His home. It's supposed to be a house devoted to God. He said so. What does devoted mean, Mommy?"

Sighing, perplexed, the woman explained, "It means loving service."

"Oh. France has to give his house back. Michael said so."

Jean noticed no one was laughing now and the crowd around the young mother and child was growing larger with each fantastic proclamation out of the young Noelle's innocent lips.

"I don't understand, Noelle." Her mother gave voice to the confusion they were all feeling.

The little girl turned her focus back to the statue of the archangel, then swung her arm wide in a gesture encompassing everything in sight. "This, Mommy. This place is one of his homes on earth. France took it away and now Michael wants it back."

The young mother looked at a loss as to how to answer her daughter. She stood and gripped her daughter's hand, only just becoming aware of the amount of attention they were attracting. "I'm certain if the Archangel Michael wants his home back he won't have any difficulty in retrieving it."

The woman's frustrated comment brought fresh amusement to the expressions of those witnessing their exchange. The young Noelle, however, seemed not to hear her mother's response. She suddenly lifted her gaze to the ceiling and spun around in a slow circle, then stopped and reached for her mother's hand, attempting to pull her in the direction of the exit.

"We need to leave now, Mommy. He's coming. Lord Michael's coming. He's going to show them what they did."

"Noelle, what are you talking about?"

The young girl tugged harder on her mother's resisting hand. Jean felt the tension in the crowd surrounding them ramp up in response to the desperation in her childish voice.

"Mommy, please. He's coming. He's coming now. We have to leave."

At the same instant as the girl's desperate plea to her mother, a loud crack split the undercurrent of voices among the observers surrounding them, silencing them as everyone looked around in fear, seeking the source of the loud noise that still reverberated around the room. Young Noelle covered her ears and hid her face against her mother's legs. The woman bent down to lift her shaking, slender form into her arms even as the prior amused witnesses to their odd exchange froze in place. In the next instant, the head of the statue of Michael separated itself from the rest of his body and fell with a loud crash to the floor. Still intact, the head rolled a few feet from where it landed and came to rest at the feet of the mother holding her terrified child in her arms.

"See what they did, Mommy?" The child cried out, staring for a moment down into the vacant eyes of the decapitated head.

"Noelle, sweetheart, no one did anything." The woman clutched her daughter close and spoke in soothing tones in an attempt to relieve her fear, but the girl was beyond comfort. She clenched her eyes tightly closed and once more raised her small hands to cover her ears.

"I don't want to see anymore. I don't want him to tell me anymore. Make it stop, Mommy. Make him stop...."

Jean was too stunned to do anything but watch as the young mother still clutching her daughter close against her chest, hurried through the exit. He turned his astonished gaze to the head of the angel resting on the floor, the little girl's words replaying through his thoughts. Looking down at the archangel's decapitated head he couldn't help but recall the defacement of the religious statues that occurred during the French Revolution. Mont Saint Michel had been converted into a prison for the use of the revolutionaries, but only after the monks in residence had been evicted and the oppression of the church and clergy had begun.

....PROLOGUE

The middle aged man paused in his perusal of the contract in front of him, removed his glasses and slid his office chair away from his desk. Rather than rise immediately he first bent down to remove his shoes and socks. Then barefoot, he rose from his chair and crossed the few steps to the small sink installed in the cabinetry behind his desk. He washed his face, hands and feet and then removed his prayer mat from the cabinet beneath the sink. He stepped around his desk to the open area in front of it and carefully aligned his sajjada so that it faced the Ka'ba Shrine in Mecca, before mid-day Salat.

After he completed his mid-day prayers, he returned to his desk and to his work. His people were under increasing pressure and scrutiny all over the world, but they were no more closely scrutinized than in Paris, where recent terrorist activity had understandably alarmed the citizenry and galvanized the far right. Abdul had been somewhat surprised by the group's recent defeat in the presidential election, particularly given the American president's stunning election and the decision by British citizens to exit the European Union.

Still, there was no denying something needed to be done about the growing backlash against Islam and its adherents throughout the world. His father, flush with youthful idealism, and lured by the seemingly endless opportunities in Europe had move to Paris as a young man where he met and married a French citizen and set out to build a new life for himself in the west. The result being that Abdul was raised both French and Muslim; a difficult combination in the current political environment in France. Still, he clung to his father's optimism. His upbringing at the hands of two, often-clashing cultures had led him to an outlook on life that was out of step with the populist movements sweeping the globe. In his view, the world had shrunk to such a degree that it was senseless for its citizens to attempt to adhere to ancient hatreds and ideologies that fostered national boundaries drawn around religious practice and/or ethnic origin. After all, the price of waging war in defense of these ideologies was approaching apocalyptic consequences for the continued existence of mankind.

He paused momentarily in his review of the papers in front of him, recognizing that he could not recall any of the content he'd read in the past several minutes. He sighed heavily at his distracted thoughts. Though he still retained his optimistic view of the world, there was no denying that diplomacy did not appear to be making much headway in world affairs and that his people were bearing the brunt of the consequences of those failures. France seemed to be the flashpoint for terrorist attacks by Islamic extremists, while at the same time, millions of Syrian refugees, the majority of them Muslim, were stuck in camps on the outskirts of a Europe that no longer welcomed them, despite the promise of free movement of its citizens among member countries.

Admittedly, the majority of the refugees were not from European Union countries and Turkey had grown justifiably tired of being the recipient of so many desperate souls fleeing conflict in the Middle East in the hopes of creating a better life for themselves and for their children in Europe. The political situation in Turkey, along with several European Union members was growing increasingly unpredictable as member nations had begun following the American President's promise of '*America First*', in their own national discourse.

The citizens of wealthy nations were tired of feeding the world's poor, repressed, and desperate and fighting battles for those unable to lift a weapon in their own defense. Abdul was still hopeful of a diplomatic solution, but just in case his hope failed him in the end, he and those of a similar mind, had a contingency plan in place.

She was the key. He was certain of it. Noelle Dominique was the natural heir of her father's legacy. They had been patient for decades waiting for her to grow up. She was an adult now and yet she still had not returned to her father's homeland to claim her inheritance. She would at some point. She had too. They needed the location of the key. Information her father had gone to his death in order to protect. Still,

Abdul was certain Michel Dominique had found a way to pass that information along to his daughter prior to his death. Or given her tender age at the time, he would have taken precautions to ensure the location of the key was preserved until she was old enough to take possession of it. The duke's legacy demanded that his successor continue to safeguard the key. Noelle Dominique was the last of her line. That knowledge would pass to her. When it did, the Brotherhood would finally have the power it needed to upset the balance of power in the world and compel its own ends. He fervently hoped Noelle Dominique would not attempt to thwart their aims the way her father had. He was not anxious to add the death of an innocent young woman to the debit side of his eternal ledger, but nor would he shrink from his sacred duty.

CHAPTER ONE

Noelle breathed a sigh of relief as the wheels of the jet touched down on the runway. She'd been happy to snag one of the few remaining seats on a direct flight to Paris, but her good fortune had not come without price. A middle seat in the middle row had been her penance for her procrastination, but she was soon to be released from her self-imposed purgatory. She dutifully waited while the plane taxied to the gate and the seat belt sign was turned off before bending down to gather her belongings from beneath the seat in front of her.

Her feelings of relief soon gave way to the pressure of the anxiety making itself felt in the pit of her stomach. She was actually doing this. She was returning to the place where it all began more than two decades earlier, when she was just a little girl, wide-eyed and excited to discover the possibilities this new life had to offer her. In the intervening years, that excitement had been winnowed with a healthy dose of caution and skepticism. She'd learned to keep her own counsel and to swallow the urge to share her secrets with anyone...even her mother.

Not that her mother would instantly assume she was imagining things if she revealed her closely guarded secrets. No, the few times she'd broached the subject of her visions, it was the fear and not disbelief she read in her mother's eyes that had kept Noelle from continuing. That same fear had sealed Noelle's lips since she'd been old enough to recognize it for what it was. Her mother's unease wasn't for her own safety. It was for Noelle's.

So she had done her best to suppress the visions and close her ears to the occasional voice of her angelic visitor instructing her in the night, when she was alone and there were no distractions at hand to drown out the sound of his urgings. It was easier to deny him when she was still a little girl. With each passing year, her denial had grown more difficult to sustain, her excuses sounding weak even to her own younger ears.

1

Until one day, he stopped asking. A few weeks ago, just shy of her twenty-fourth birthday, and only months away from the twentieth anniversary of when she'd first heard his voice in her head; Michael had ordered her to return.

For all Noelle told herself that Michael couldn't make her go back to Mont Saint Michel she was not as certain of her attempts to reassure herself as she pretended to be. The fact that she remembered all too well her terror of that morning twenty years earlier made her unwilling to put her resolve to the test. She'd run out of excuses. She was no longer the child she'd been, dependent on an adult to take her where she wished to go. She couldn't even use the convenient excuse she lacked the funds to make such a journey on her own. At twenty-one, the first installment of the trust fund she'd been left under the terms of her father's will had come under her control.

Although she was grateful for the generosity of the father she barely remembered, a part of her had dreaded the approach of that pivotal birthday. Her friends couldn't understand her reluctance to assume control of her financial destiny and the resulting freedom they could only dream of. How could they? She'd never confided in them. Because of her reluctance to do so, most of her friendships were largely surface in nature. Another loss. Another consequence of that day.

As the plane emptied, she stood up but remained hunched beneath the low ceiling while she made her way to the aisle. Once there she reached into the overhead bin to retrieve her carry-on. She noticed her hand trembled slightly as she gripped the handle and wheeled it behind her down the aisle. She very deliberately stilled its shaking. There was no reason for her to be afraid anymore. She was doing what he wanted. She was back in France.

She wasn't doing a very good job convincing herself not to be afraid, but at least she could take comfort in the realization that she was no longer fighting against the implacable will driving her towards what she very much feared was her destiny. Where it was leading her, she had no notion. What it would demand of her, she was too scared to ask, but at least she'd taken the first step. The coming weeks would either free her from the burden she'd silently carried over the course of her entire life, or trap her deeper beneath its weight. She wasn't even particularly committed to one outcome or the other. She just wanted it to end.

Though she believed she was still technically a French citizen, she traveled on her American passport. She'd never inquired into the status of her French citizenship, as the topic seemed to distress her mother. Like everything else regarding her father's homeland, she'd simply let it go. Until now. Her mother had merely nodded and wished her a pleasant visit when Noelle informed her she was traveling to France to visit her grandmother.

It was as if they both understood she could no longer prevent her from returning and her mother had resigned herself to the fact Noelle would one day go back. She thought her mother had finally come to peace with her efforts to protect her only daughter from the consequences of such a decision. Noelle could take her own contentment from knowing she'd given her mother the time she needed. She hid from her the price at which that peace had been purchased.

Drawn from her musings by the emptying of her row of fellow travelers, she took her place in line and breathed a sigh of relief as she exited the plane. Customs was as painless as it could be. The customs official welcomed her to France, asked her a few questions about the nature of her visit, scanned and stamped her passport and then sent her on her way.

Her grandmother was waiting for her at the exit for international flights. Noelle had feared she wouldn't recognize her, but she realized now it was a foolish worry on her part. Even without the recent selfies the two had exchanged a few days earlier, Noelle knew she would have recognized the older woman from the deep well of love mirrored in her expression watching anxiously for her arrival.

"Grand'Mere Michel," Noelle called and waved as she approached. She watched the older woman's lined face fill with a mixture of relief, abiding love and the shimmer of unshed tears.

"Noelle," her grandmother whispered against her hair as the two embraced. Noelle felt her arms, frailer she thought than their last visit the previous Christmas break in New York, draw her close. She pulled back and smiled widely, her gaze roaming over Noelle's grinning face,

"Let me look at you. I swear you grow more beautiful each time I see you…and so like your father."

Noelle laughed away her extravagant compliment and looked admiringly at her perfectly fashioned grandmother. "You are the one who grows more beautiful each time I see you. Maybe we could spend some of our time together shopping. I think it's time I abandoned the coed look and acquired a more polished and grown-up wardrobe. Obviously, you are far more versed in the mysteries of feminine fashion than I am. I would appreciate your guidance."

Her grandmother laughed and exclaimed, "Oh, yes. I was hoping you wouldn't mind staying in Paris for a few nights and I am not so old I have stopped keeping up with the latest fashions. I had Bernard open the town house in the hopes I could persuade you to stay more than the few days we usually spend together."

Noelle took one of her grandmother's hands and gave it a gentle squeeze in response to the anxiety the older woman was unable to disguise. With Noelle's father's death, she guessed her grandmother had been lonely for family over the years. The uncomfortable thought was accompanied by a sting of guilt that she hadn't made the effort to return sooner. "I plan on staying so long you'll be wondering if you're ever going to get rid of me," she joked.

She watched the astonishment register at her surprise and her own eyes filled with tears at her grandmother's almost awed joy at her announcement. "Truly? You are not just here for a long weekend?"

"No, Meme, if you think you can stand me for that long, I thought I'd stay for the summer. Perhaps longer."

"Oh, Noelle what a wonderful surprise. I'm so happy you've finally come home."

Yes, Noelle supposed that's what she'd done. Though she'd spent her entire life in the states, somehow she too felt as though she'd finally come home.

CHAPTER TWO

Captain Jean Martin, immersed in the seemingly unending stack of papers on his desk, the lifeblood apparently of every government everywhere, caught only a glimpse out of the corner of his eye of the fresh alert as it flashed across his computer monitor. Distracted, disbelieving, he double-checked, then triple-checked the alert trailing across the bottom of the screen. He was certain there had to be some mistake, a not uncommon occurrence in the bureaucratic world he'd chosen to wed his life to.

With a click of his mouse, the photograph of a young woman filled his monitor. He knew then there was no mistake. He'd never forgotten that face. He didn't think he'd ever forget those compelling blue eyes. She'd come back. The little girl who'd warned of an archangel's wrath upon his homeland had finally returned.

He'd been expecting her to for the past twenty years. The fact that she'd remained beyond the borders of her father's homeland had given rise to a variety of emotions in Jean over the years...surprise...curiosity...even insult. But the one he buried deepest, and the one he was most reluctant to admit to, was... fear. It was as if the young Mademoiselle Dominique knew something the rest of them did not and she didn't want to be anywhere near his beloved France when the promised consequences of defying an archangel's will burst over their unsuspecting heads.

Now she was back. To what purpose, he couldn't begin to guess, but he would keep a close eye on the presumed heir to the Duchess of Dominique. Yes, he'd been curious enough to track her down twenty years earlier, despite her mother's desperate attempt to spirit her away. Noelle Michel Dominique, daughter of the man who'd died shortly after he inherited his father's title. Now the young American would presumably inherit her grandmother's wealth and the glorious chateau near St. Malo overlooking the channel. Would she return to Mont Saint Michel? He'd bet his pension on it.

It seemed to Jean as if the world nearby had lain suspended for the past twenty years awaiting the little, dark-haired girl's return. She'd had the look of an angel then with her long curls, fair flawless skin and huge blue eyes staring in awe at the statue of Saint Michael. Jean's eyes returned to the photo in front of him. The young, angelic girl had grown into a devastatingly beautiful woman.

He found it interesting that she had made the trip back to her father's homeland alone. He chose not to speculate on the consequences of such an observation. His long years of public service had squelched in him any attempt to predict the future or to try to guess an individual's motives for their actions. He long ago recognized his theories and speculations would not in any way impact the end result.

Still, it was with undeniable anxiety creeping along his reach that he retrieved the key from his pocket of the only drawer in his office he kept locked. From it, he withdrew the file he'd amassed over the years on the mysterious events that had been occurring almost annually, and more often than not, on the very anniversary of the young Mademoiselle Dominque's visit to the ancient structure that bore the Archangel Michael's name. A place, he apparently still claimed as one of his homes on earth.

CHAPTER THREE

Noelle couldn't contain her delighted gasp when her grandmother's driver pulled into the gated entrance to what her grandmother had casually referred to as the 'town house'. Turning to meet her anxious expression, Noelle grinned and parroted, "Town house? Really, Meme this is way over the top. If Bernard had to open up the town house, where do you live the rest of the time?"

Noelle was delighted to see the slight blush staining her grandmother's cheeks when she admitted, "At Chateau Dominique."

"Ah, of course, Chateau Dominique," Noelle repeated with a laugh.

"Didn't your mother explain to you about your heritage?"

Noelle shrugged. "Maybe you'd better fill me in. Mom didn't talk much about my father. Only that he was a wonderful man she fell madly in love with and then eloped with after an all too brief acquaintance. She still misses him. I think that's why she's never remarried even though she was widowed so young. I don't think any other man could ever measure up to him in her eyes."

Her grandmother reached over and squeezed her hand. "Thank you for telling me that. I always wondered. I'm sure you know by now that your mother and I are not close. Not that I don't believe we could have been given time, but as you said, Michel died so soon after they were married. We'd barely been introduced to his new wife, were thrilled when he called to tell us we were going to be grandparents. There was so little time for your grandfather to get to know you before he died. Then before we had a chance to recover from his death, your father was lost to us as well. It all seemed to pass in a blur. In a second, he was gone."

"I'm sorry I didn't have the chance to know him," Noelle confessed, reaching for and squeezing her grandmother's hand.

"So am I, Noelle. He was so proud of you. So enthralled by everything you said or did. He was as madly in love with you as he was with your mother."

Tears in her eyes, Noelle whispered, "I'm sorry, Meme. I should have come sooner. I understand why my Mom didn't or couldn't, but that's no excuse for me."

Her grandmother patted her hand. "It doesn't matter, Noelle. You're here now. Let the past remain buried where it belongs, and let us simply enjoy our time together."

"I'll drink to that," Noelle quipped to relieve the tension and was rewarded with her grandmother's laughter.

"And so we shall. Chateau Dominique has its own label. Private now. The vineyards were your grandfather's passion. I never shared it. I saved my love for him and for the gardens. I can't wait for you to see them."

"Me too. Right now though, I'm hoping for a taste of my grandfather's passion. A private label? I think maybe I got off at the wrong stop and I've fallen into the pages of a fairytale with chateaus and town houses disguised as Parisian mansions and private labels from the family vineyards."

"As long as I get to play the role of fairy godmother and not the wicked stepmother, I like the sound of that. You, of course, are the beautiful princess. We must begin looking around for your Prince Charming."

Laughing, Noelle climbed out of the seat and passed through the door being held open for her by her grandmother's driver. She waited for her grandmother to join her on the drive before laughingly responding to her comment. "No, no, definitely no Prince Charmings for me. I'm just looking forward to a nice long visit with my grandmother and learning more about the father I never knew."

Linking her arm through Noelle's, her grandmother responded with a smile, "I don't see any reason why we can't do both, Noelle, dear."

CHAPTER FOUR

Raphael Lucien regarded his reflection with a critical eye, finding no fault with his appearance. He knew his dark hair and sculpted features were set off to advantage by the stark black suit. The white dress shirt and knotted tie at his throat provided a perfect foil for his swarthy complexion, compliments of his Italian ancestry, which gave him the appearance of having spent long hours in the sun even though the majority of his time now was spent behind a desk in his office.

He was relieved to be able to assure himself that the excesses of his fading youth were not yet evident in his face. The few wrinkles around his mouth and eyes gave his appearance a maturity he found quite useful in negotiating the shark-infested waters of international commerce where he made his living. No, it was not his appearance *per se* he took fault with, it was the fact that he was there at all...in the spacious bath adjoining his suite of rooms overlooking the Paris skyline in one of the family properties he chose to make his home.

He'd had plans for the evening. Plans that did not entail a command performance at the townhome of the reclusive Duchess of Dominique so that he might be introduced to and dance attendance on the former's half-American granddaughter. Rafe was unable to comprehend how his grandfather managed to have them all dancing to his dictatorial tune whenever he waved an imperious hand in the direction of one of his progeny.

Yet here he was a grown man, of independent means, answering the older man's summons, as if he was still a boy in awe of the larger than life figure who held the title of Duke of Lucien. The title, like most in France, was a mostly ceremonial one in French society, given the fate of the nobility during the time of the French Revolution. Still the title had passed, along with the glorious family chateau in Normandy from father to son in an uninterrupted line of succession from medieval times, when his ancestors had fought along the Norman Duke who was

9

destined to become the King of England. That same title that would one day pass to Rafe if the old man didn't out live both his son and grandson, a possibility Rafe did not lightly dismiss.

At eighty-two, his grandfather showed no signs of slowing down. Though he'd passed the responsibility of running the day-to-day operation of the family's far-ranging business interests to his only son and heir a decade earlier, he still knew exactly what was going on in the family enterprises. Nor was he the least bit shy about voicing his opinions on his son's and increasingly now, grandson's decisions, whenever the mood struck him.

Turning away from the mirror, and casting a fleeting glance of regret at his empty bed as he passed through his suite towards the long hallway that led to the entry foyer, Rafe found his lips curving in an admiring grin at his grandfather's tactics. He only hoped he would follow the old man's example and be just as intimidating to his grandsons when and if the time ever came.

He doubted old Ari would be particularly concerned if Rafe shared with him the source of his regret about the plans for the evening he was forced to forego in light of his grandfather's autocratic summons. Those plans had revolved around a delightfully lovely young runway model who Rafe occasionally kept company with when they both conveniently found themselves in the same city. Now he would very likely be sleeping alone in his bed that could comfortably accommodate a feminine companion or two, perhaps even three, though he'd never put the latter speculation to the test.

City traffic being what it was, Rafe sighed his frustration as he settled behind the wheel of the Maserati and started the engine. It would probably be faster to walk to his destination, he mused, before setting off with a sense of resigned acceptance of his fate, turning into the heavy traffic and instantly reigning in the powerful engine against the red stream of brake lights ahead of him. In spite of the delay, he clung to the hope that he might be able to extricate himself early from the evening's festivities and salvage his plans for the evening with the inventive and energetic Giselle.

CHAPTER FIVE

Noelle swallowed nervously as she regarded her reflection in the mirror. When her grandmother had mentioned the dinner party to introduce her to her friends, Noelle's immediate instinct was to try to talk her out of it. Then she reminded herself of how Bernard had only the day before confided in her that he hadn't seen her grandmother so happy in years. He'd gone on to express how glad he was that Noelle planned an extended visit.

Noelle had realized then how lonely her grandmother must have been with no family in her life, so when the proposed dinner party had come up the previous week, she'd swallowed her reluctance and endorsed the idea with somewhat feigned enthusiasm. Besides, the excuse of the party gave her a few more days to prepare for the true purpose of her visit and to decide whether or not she should confide in her grandmother.

Bracing herself for an evening spent among strangers, most of them drawn from the remnants of the French aristocracy, Noelle turned an appraising eye to her appearance, seeking any flaws. She so wanted her grandmother to be proud of her tonight. Likely, there was a great deal of curiosity among her grandmother's friends in regards to Noelle in light of her extended absence from France.

She noticed her deep blue eyes held a trace of telling anxiety, but she could find no other fault with her appearance. The lighter ash brown hair of her childhood had deepened over the years into the color of a rich French Roast. Her flawless complexion and classic feminine features she guessed she could thank her father's noble ancestry for. She did not indulge in false modesty and accepted her physical beauty with a sense of deep gratitude for the gift that it was, but she gave it little thought beyond that. She had always believed a beautiful spirit was a far more worthy goal to strive for, and an infinitely more challenging one to achieve. She was doing her best with the latter, but at the moment, it was another character trait she wished she'd inherited in greater measure from her father.

Noelle didn't consider herself particularly brave. She didn't know if her encounter with even the imagined voice of an archangel had forged her tendency towards timidity when she was only four, or if she was just naturally shy, but there was no denying she lacked the devil may care bravado her father had been known for in his youth. Though she'd joked with her grandmother about being unaware of her heritage, as a young teen Noelle had voraciously consumed every scrap of information she could find on the Internet about her dead father.

Her mother's reluctance to talk about him only forged a deeper need to learn as much as she could. During her dramatic adolescent years, she'd convinced herself that her mother was hiding some dark family secret about the late, dashing Duke of Dominique, but Noelle had been unable to find any trace of confirming evidence of it online. She could summon a wistful smile now for her teenage conspiracy theories that had concluded her father's death was not caused by the tragic accident everyone assumed it had been, but was actually the result of unknown enemies who had made his death appear to be an accident for their own nefarious purposes.

Fortunately, that obsession had lasted only a few months before it had faded away from a lack of any actual support for her dramatic theory. In the end, Noelle was forced to accept it was grief over her devastating loss rather than a desire to protect Noelle from the consequences of some terrible family secret that accounted for her mother's reluctance to discuss her dead husband with his only child.

She held her own glance in the mirror for a few moments longer, realizing one of the reasons she was so nervous about the night ahead stemmed not only from a need to make her grandmother proud. It was also a product of her hope that her father, wherever he was, would be proud of the woman his young daughter had grown into.

Squaring her shoulders, Noelle gave herself a bracing lecture as she prepared to face the lion's den and turned away from her reflection in the mirror. Smiling a little at her tendency to dramatize, she reminded herself that the people whose voices she could hear even now beginning to fill the main salon, as her grandmother referred to the huge foyer at the entrance to the stone mansion, were her grandmother's closest friends. They were no doubt curious about Noelle's sudden appearance after so long an absence, but they had no reason to dislike her.

At least she needn't be concerned about the language barrier. Her mother might not speak about her dead husband, but perhaps because of her own reticence and her refusal to allow Noelle to return to France after the incident at Mont Saint Michel, she'd felt a deep sense of responsibility to pass along her husband's French heritage to Noelle. Even before that fateful day at Mont Saint Michel, Noelle had been enrolled in a French pre-school. When her formal schooling began, it was at the French immersion school in the city.

Though her mother had grown up in a small town in the Midwest, and Noelle suspected she missed the slower pace such a life afforded, they had remained in the nation's capital after her father's death. Noelle spent her early years in the Georgetown townhome her father had purchased for their use while his extensive business interests kept him in the area, with the result being Noelle spoke French as easily as she did English. Her written skills were actually better in French and she sometimes noticed the thoughts circling around her head did so in French, and not her mother's native English.

Noelle suspected her mother's need to pass along her husband's heritage to his only child had created a distance between them that a shared culture would have lessened. The proof of her presumption was the ease with which she understood her grandmother and the pleasure they took in each other's company. To an outsider, seeing the three women together, Noelle thought one might conclude that she'd been raised in France by her grandmother and not in America under her mother's careful tutelage.

Additional proof of her mother's need to honor her husband's memory was her insistence that Noelle be raised in his Catholic faith. Her mother was a Christian but not Catholic. It had been her father's wish and the couple's agreement when they wed that their children would be raised Catholic. Noelle's mother had upheld that agreement even though when it was made she'd had no expectation of having to be the one to take Noelle to Mass every weekend and see to it that she attended catechism classes and received the sacraments.

Sometimes Noelle wondered if the price they'd paid for keeping her father's memory alive was worth the sacrifice of the closer relationship she and her mother might have forged if she had been raised in a manner her mother was more comfortable and familiar with.

"Noelle, I was just wondering if I should come up to check on you." Her grandmother's voice from the doorway drew her from her musings.

"Sorry, Meme, it took me longer than I anticipated to figure out how to work the straps of these shoes," Noelle joked, lifting an ankle to reveal the complicated straps of the high-heeled dress sandals they'd bought on their shopping expedition the previous week. The designer gown she was wearing had come from the same shopping trip.

Her grandmother laughed, and stepped into the room to take in Noelle's appearance with an experienced and measuring eye. She nodded her satisfaction at the sight of Noelle in the cream gown, with the fitted bodice and feminine skirt that fell to just below her knees. "I don't believe we will have any difficulty attracting any number of Prince Charmings for you to choose from. After this evening, I predict they will be lining up on our door step with the quintessential glass slipper in hand."

Noelle laughed at her grandmother's teasing, seriously doubting that there would be any candidates for Prince Charming in attendance among her grandmother's close, and likely, similarly aged friends.

CHAPTER SIX

With a muttered curse escaping in a whispered breath only he could hear, Rafe allowed his eyes to linger on the source of his frustration. They'd been introduced earlier in the evening. The young Mademoiselle Dominique appeared as charming as she was beautiful, though a little shy to his mind. Because he enjoyed the company of a beautiful woman as much as the next man he'd made an effort to tease a smile to her lips and watched the enjoyment dance in her eyes at an amusing anecdote he'd recalled for her benefit. The attentive duchess seemed pleased with his efforts, which would earn him a gold star for his performance from his grandfather.

All in all, after the duchess had drawn the lovely Noelle away from his side for no doubt additional introductions to her inner circle, Rafe had been satisfied his family obligation to the granddaughter of one his grandfather's closest friends had been fulfilled. At the same time, he'd begun to plot his escape from the affair, deciding optimistically there was still time for him to salvage his previous plans for the evening when he was distracted by the echo of Noelle's laughter drifting across the room.

She really was a beauty, he acknowledged without rancor. Old Ari was clearly making his own efforts to charm the lovely Noelle. From the light in her eyes and the feminine laughter reaching him, it was obvious his grandfather's efforts were not without effect. Realizing he was staring, Rafe drew his attention away from her shimmering beauty, only to surrender brief moments later to the temptation to look his fill.

He couldn't fault his masculine inclination. Noelle Dominique would tempt the resolve of even the most committed celibate. Rafe's lips curved in an amused smile at his own joke. He found the idea of any man voluntarily choosing a celibate existence a baffling mystery. The sight of the duchess' granddaughter's luminous beauty only reaffirmed his confusion.

Her dark hair, the length of which he could only guess at, was fashioned in a severe knot at the base of her neck and served to emphasize a perfect, feminine profile and a slender, elegant neck. Full lips framed a hesitant smile, but it was her eyes that captivated him. Even though he knew them to be an inherited Dominique trait, they were no less compelling when they had shyly met his in response to their initial introduction.

Rafe reminded himself he was no longer a man easily impressed by feminine beauty. So it was all the more irritating to realize he was quickly and most inconveniently becoming fascinated with the lovely Noelle. Inconvenient because of the close ties their families shared. Irritating because those very ties would likely prevent him from acting on his fascination.

From a young age, Rafe had liberally indulged his ease with which he attracted feminine companionship. Because he was in no hurry to confine his attentions to just one, he knew he would do well to avoid the lovely Noelle. Yes, the wisest course of action on his part would be to limit himself to his usual uncomplicated relationships with runway models and ambitious career women who were not averse to having their names linked with his. The Lucien name remained an influential one in France, and in all of Europe. He took no exception to his feminine companions using his name and connections to their own advantage. He considered their rather mercenary motives an even exchange for their delightful company on his arm and in his bed.

He watched Noelle disengage herself from her grandmother's side and slip through the glass doors leading out to the deserted terrace. Chiding himself for his recklessness, Rafe set off across the room, intent on catching her alone.

CHAPTER SEVEN

Noelle drew in a deep breath of the fragrant air where she sought a few moments refuge on the quiet terrace. Wisteria grew along the iron trellis fashioned into the stone walls. Potted plants lined the hand painted stone floor and crowded around the pillars. The fragile shoots were just starting to bud in the uncertain warmth of the late spring evening and softened the harshness of the stark iron and stone. Noelle felt the tension she'd been carrying for most of the evening begin to drain from her shoulders. Relaxing in the welcome solitude, she drew a deep, cleansing breath.

She thought she was holding her own among her grandmother's guests. At least her grandmother seemed pleased with how the evening was going. She could smile at the memory of her introduction to her grandmother's close friend, Ari (short for Ariel) Lucien, the patriarch of the Lucien family. He had charmed her with his smiling claim that Lucien was actually a derivative of the family's true surname- Lucifer.

Apparently, the older man had confided in a conspiratorial whisper with a twinkle in his eye, somewhere in the family's noble past, one of the Lucien patriarchs had concluded the surname of Lucifer might one day present too great a temptation for the church to resist. In the superstitious times in which he lived, with the power the Catholic Church historically wielded in France, the Lucien ancestor feared an ambitious bishop might avail himself of the opportunity to confiscate the family's lands and extensive wealth. So to prevent such a catastrophe he'd adopted the more French sounding Lucien, which could arguably be a tribute to Saint Luke rather than the devil himself.

Still the family hadn't been completely successful in erasing their connection to the reputed ruler of hell. Some of the legends Ari regaled her with claimed the Lucien clan were actual descendants of the fallen dark angel.

The old charmer had gone on to relate the details of the legend. How on one of his earthly visits Lucifer had taken advantage of the innocence of a lovely, nobly born, virgin daughter of a somewhat impoverished Italian count. The count was quite put out when he discovered his presumably innocent daughter was pregnant, particularly when he'd thought to use her beauty and innocence to restore the family's finances and position among the Italian nobility.

In compensation to the family, Lucifer had seen to it that the girl was improbably accepted into a wealthy convent where she gave birth to a son. The child, who she named Lucas, presumably after his father, was given to his grandfather to raise. Lucas grew up to become the one single-handedly credited with propelling the family into the forefront of Italian nobility, and by the time he'd passed from this mortal plain, he'd become a force to be reckoned with throughout Europe.

Noelle caught herself smiling at the memory of Ari Lucien's outrageous recitation. Clearly, he enjoyed the idea of being the devil's descendant. While she enjoyed the older man's attempts to charm her considerably, Noelle was careful to avoid dwelling too long on her introduction to his grandson, Raphael, or the more familiar, Rafe, as he insisted she call him when they were introduced. Now there was a man who she had little trouble believing was a direct descendant of the prince of darkness. The force of his attraction had slammed into her with all the subtlety of a punch in the gut.

She decided Raphael Lucien was one of those men who should be required to go around wearing a sign the same way fallen women in New England had been forced to wear the letter A around their necks proclaiming to the world their sin of adultery. The former's sign would proclaim to any female who chanced to encounter him that it would be wise for them to run in the opposite direction. Unless of course the idea of being seduced by the devil's descendent appealed to one. Noelle was honest enough to admit that under other circumstances she would have been tempted to respond to the masculine challenge she'd read in Raphael Lucien's frankly admiring gaze when it rested upon her earlier.

She wasn't certain if she was relieved or disappointed that her reasons for being in France precluded such extracurricular activities on her part. Her lips curved upward at the thought of Michael's reaction to any further delay on her part to return to Mont Saint Michel being attributed to his fallen brother's reputed descendent.

She could only be grateful for the mixed feelings she sensed on Raphael Lucien's part at the prospect of his pursuing her. Noelle couldn't remember ever experiencing such an intense reaction to any other man. She'd managed to escape his unsettling presence as soon as courtesy allowed, but throughout the evening, she'd felt his glance on her, even when she was successfully resisting the temptation to locate him in the crowded room.

Just to prove she was imagining things, she would occasionally cautiously swing her attention in his direction and their eyes would invariably meet. His would be filled with amused acknowledgment of their awareness of each other. She had no doubt hers appeared more like that of a startled doe confronted with a predator in the woods who'd already had his fill of meat for the day. Awed and grateful at her own luck she could only scamper off in the opposite direction as fast as her high-heeled strappy sandals would carry her.

"Forgive me for intruding on your privacy. It seems we both had the same idea."

Noelle didn't have to turn around to know it was him. His voice matched his looks, intrinsically masculine and compelling.

She drew a bracing breath, at the same time chiding herself to stop being an idiot…. that Raphael Lucien wasn't the first attractive man she'd ever encountered. She turned to face him, hoping the sound of her heart thudding in her chest was audible only to her. After an awkward pause she reached back into her faltering memory for the conversational lead he'd cast in her direction and responded as courtesy demanded, "No apology necessary. I was just enjoying the beautiful evening."

"And the solitude?" He mocked her so gently she couldn't be certain he was truly mocking her at all.

She shrugged slightly. "Perhaps. I'm not overly fond of parties."

"No? That is a great pity, since your beauty adds considerably to the appeal of this one."

The compliment rolled off his lips with such ease she all but gawked in admiration. "That was really smoothly done. Do you have a store of similar lines memorized for every possible social occasion or do they just pop into your head at the appropriate moment?"

He laughed at her candid response and allowed his gaze to roam over her flushed face before returning to capture hers. "It depends. Admittedly, sometimes I am unable to summon the effort for the kind of compliment women seem to expect as a matter of course. In those rare moments, I am careful to keep a ready supply at my disposal. In your case though, I can't imagine any man having to resort to memorized platitudes."

Noelle's lips twitched at his outrageous confession. After a moment of struggling with her own amusement, she gave in to the urge to laugh. "I guess French women learn at a young age not to take such extravagant compliments seriously. Even though my mother did her best to see that I learned as much as I could about my father's homeland, clearly my education has been lacking in a few critical areas."

He grinned along with her and replied easily, "Your mother's efforts were not without a share of success. Your French is impeccable."

"Thank you. I do have my mother to thank for that. She enrolled me in a French immersion school when I was three and I completed my primary and secondary schooling in similar programs."

"They did their job well," he told her, then asked curious, "What else do they teach in an American French immersion program?"

Noelle shrugged. "History, art, literature, a feel for the culture."

"And yet you rarely visited."

It was a statement, not a conjecture and Noelle realized their families were close enough he would know of her failure to visit.

"Yes, that's true. Not since I was a little girl."

"Why? I imagine your mother's relationship with her husband's mother was not a close one, given the circumstances surrounding their marriage, but in light of your mother's considerable efforts to provide you with a foundation in your father's heritage, it seems odd she wouldn't have made certain you visited his mother and only surviving relative."

"She had her reasons. My grandmother understood."

His dark brow arched in surprise at her evasive explanation and Noelle feared she'd roused his curiosity. Not good. The last thing she needed was for Raphael Lucien to be wondering about the reason prompting her return to France. "We should go back inside."

He hesitated a moment, as if he wanted to question her more closely, then nodded his assent. "As you wish. We certainly wouldn't want to give rise to speculation about why we sought the privacy afforded us on this secluded terrace."

Noelle rolled her eyes at his outrageous inference. "Ha, ha." Then a thought struck her and she asked, "Are you married?"

This time his laughter filled the small terrace, his white teeth flashing in the dim light. "No, why do you ask?"

Noelle felt the fierce blush climbing her cheeks. "Sorry. It's none of my business; I don't know why I asked that." She stumbled through her apology and then fled back to the safety of the crowded party.

She didn't flee fast enough. Rafe followed her through the double doors. She felt his hand on her arm preventing her escape. To a casual observer the two of them might have been returning to the gathering from exactly the kind of intimate interlude he'd hinted at.

Annoyed, and suspecting his motives for delaying her, Noelle attempted to pull her arm away, but he refused to release her. Short of engaging in a tug-of-war for her arm in the kind of display that would attract the very attention she was trying to avoid, she was forced to content herself with rebuking him fiercely beneath her breath. "Will you let go? Everyone's staring at us."

"I would think a beautiful woman is used to being stared at."

Noelle's breath emerged in an audible sigh. "This isn't funny. My grandmother is intent on finding me a Prince Charming to sweep me into his arms and carry me off to his castle in France where we can live happily ever after. So unless you want to put ideas into her head and encourage her ambition, I suggest you let go and stay away from me for the rest of the night."

Chuckling he bent to whisper in her ear, "Can you not envision me as your Prince Charming?"

Exasperated she turned to face him. That was a mistake. Because in her five inch heels they were eye to eye and barely a breath apart. She quickly drew in hers and forgot all about pulling away.

His lips curved in a slow smile at her confusion. "I've never been a big believer in fairy tales, but in your case, my sweet Noelle, I might be willing to make an exception."

Noelle could almost feel the weight of the interested eyes in the room boring into her back. Dropping her gaze before his laughing one she ignored his ridiculous endearment and instead pleaded earnestly, "Please let me go. Why are you doing this? I was so hoping to make a good impression on my grandmother's friends. I don't want them to get the idea that I'm using tonight's introduction as an opportunity to cash in on my grandmother's close friendship with your family."

"What?! Don't be ridiculous." His shock at her fear was genuine and enough for him to loosen his grip.

Noelle seized her chance and pulled her arm free of his grip, intent on putting some distance between them. She'd barely managed a single step before his fingers clenched around her arm in a grip that was just short of painful. He swung her around to face him.

"Noelle, darling, I was just looking for you. I wanted to introduce you to a friend of mine who has only just arrived."

Noelle could only be relieved when Rafe had no option but to release his grip on her arm. Without daring to meet his glance, she meekly allowed herself to be led away by her grandmother. She could feel his eyes watching her retreat, but she didn't give in to the urge to turn around and confirm her suspicion.

"I should have perhaps warned you about Raphael." Her grandmother was speaking softly next to Noelle's ear as she led them across the room. "Like all Lucien males he's charming and devastatingly handsome, but I can't imagine even the most dedicated optimist casting him in the role of Prince Charming."

Noelle did not miss the very real concern veiled in her grandmother's less than subtle warning. "Meme, I assure you I am not the least bit interested in Raphael Lucien. I mentioned your comment about wanting to find me a Prince Charming while I was in France and he apparently decided it would be a great joke to let everyone think he was interested in me. Don't worry. I am not about to fall victim to his charm and devastating good looks. I am well aware he's out of my league."

Seemingly relieved, her grandmother laughed at her vehement protest. "Undoubtedly out of your league in the realm of experience, Noelle dear, but definitely not in charm and good looks."

"What made you come looking for me anyway? Is there really someone I haven't met yet or did I appear so desperately in need of rescuing?"

"Perhaps not desperate, but definitely on the verge of going under for the third time," her grandmother replied with a wicked smile.

Grinning, Noelle replied, "Thanks for pulling me out. I wasn't having much success rescuing myself. Your Raphael can be very persistent."

Her grandmother's laughter was filled with keen amusement. "He's not my Raphael. Though there was some speculation in the distant past he might have been."

"What?!" Noelle demanded, turning a shocked glance in her grandmother's direction.

Her grandmother lifted one elegant shoulder in an understated shrug. "I almost ran off with his grandfather when I was a bit younger than you, so I can attest from personal experience as to the force of the Lucien charm. Fortunately, I came to my senses before succumbing to the temptation. Of course finding Ari in the arms of my best friend was enough of a shock to jolt me back to my senses."

"Oh. Ouch. That must have been awful," Noelle sympathized.

"There are no words to describe how devastated I was. When people say a heart cannot actually break it's only because theirs has never been broken."

Noelle was having trouble imagining her perfectly coiffed and confident grandmother as a young woman with a broken heart, but her warning hit home. She had absolutely no intention of allowing herself to end up nursing a similar wound inflicted by another Lucien male. She stole a glance over her shoulder to where she'd left Rafe, only to find him still standing where she'd left him, watching her.

He nodded his head in a mocking salute, even as his glance captured hers and refused to let go. Noelle felt the telling blush creep up her cheeks, and with an effort returned her attention to where her grandmother was on the verge of introducing her to yet another old friend. Even as she forced an appropriate response to her lips, Noelle could feel Rafe's eyes following her with that hint of speculation in his glance she found so unnerving.

CHAPTER EIGHT

He dreamt of her. The unpleasant realization pierced his thoughts even as part of him wanted to sink back into his dreams and into her soft, waiting arms. Cursing mildly beneath his breath, Rafe rolled over in his empty bed before dawn had even begun to threaten the complete blackness of the night sky. He thrust a hand through his thick hair and sat up enough to lean his weight against a pillow propped in front of the antique, hardwood headboard at his back, accepting with annoyed frustration that sleep would likely elude him for the remainder of the night.

Having spent the night alone in the generously proportioned bed, his mood was already black. Memories of his dreams of the lovely Noelle Dominique did nothing to improve it. The fact that those dreams were erotic in nature and had left him aroused and wanting irritated him. The young Noelle was undeniably beautiful, but he was not some randy teenager, a slave to his hormones who was left panting at the sight of a beautiful woman.

The truth was he couldn't remember ever having actually been left panting over a woman. Since the time he was old enough to understand the very appealing differences between the male and female anatomies, women had fallen into his hands like so much ripe fruit from a low hanging branch. The previous evening it had actually amused him to discover Noelle Dominique was determined not to become one of them. He imagined the duchess had something to do with that determination, though he was not so convinced of his own appeal he wasn't aware that his family's wealth and position in the highest echelons of society did not play a role in his legendary success with the fairer sex. The fact the lovely presumed heir to the Duchess of Dominique was likely not in need of his family's wealth nor his social connections served nicely to even the playing field between them.

His lips curved at the memory of the wariness in Noelle's gorgeous eyes that the duchess might mistake him for her very own Prince Charming. Not likely. He had understood the duchess' warning, even if Noelle had been oblivious to it. The older woman had not come right out and ordered him to stay away from her young granddaughter, but the message had been there in the steel in her expression when her eyes met his over Noelle's embarrassed head.

All in all, he accepted the smartest tactic for him to adopt towards the very appealing Noelle Dominique was to stay as far away as possible. It would not be difficult. The woman herself obviously had no intention of seeking him out. Contrary to her fear her grandmother would get the wrong idea about his interest in her, Rafe had no doubt the duchess would be dismayed to learn he was pursuing her granddaughter. Such an event would no doubt entail a concerned call to his grandfather, and a subsequent uncomfortable interview with the old autocrat for Rafe.

No, clearly he would do well to keep his distance. Though the challenge he read in Noelle's hesitant glance intrigued him, there were any number of less complicated relationships he could pursue. It wasn't as though the mantle of Prince Charming would settle easily around his shoulders, anyway.

CHAPTER NINE

She dreamt of him. Noelle lifted trembling hands to her flushed face when she came fully awake and realized where her dreams had taken her. She was surprised at the intensity of the contest she was forced to wage with herself against the temptation to simply slide back into sleep and into Raphael Lucien's waiting arms. When she sighed her relief at having triumphed in the initial skirmish, she could almost hear the whisper of Rafe's deep voice taunting her over her cowardice. Forcing herself to sit up in bed she closed her eyes and leaned back against the pillows she propped against the antique, hardwood headboard.

Raphael Lucien was a complication she could do without. Not that he wasn't just as charming and devastatingly handsome as her grandmother had pointed out, but she had enough on her mind at the moment.

On a sigh, she reached over to retrieve her diary from the drawer in the nightstand next to the bed, thinking the reminder of her true purpose in France would keep her errant thoughts at bay. She kept the lock to the small leather notebook on the charm bracelet she rarely removed. The little gold key looked like just another charm on the bracelet full of mementos from her childhood. Her mother had never noticed its addition. She unhooked the bracelet, inserted the key into the lock, and turned back the cover. Leafing through the pages, she noted the swiftly passing years were evidenced by the sight of the older pages written in her own child's hand.

As soon as she was old enough to learn the basics of conducting research online, Noelle began keeping the diary. The realization that her mother was disinclined to help her with anything that touched on the fateful events at Mont Saint Michel that pivotal morning had compelled her to take matters into her own hands. At first, she used the compact notebook merely as a place to store her collected research. Some of the earlier posts detailed the legends surrounding Bishop Aubert of Avranches who was credited with building the monastery on the remote site. She let her eyes drift down to the first page and read the article pasted there.

"...Mont Saint Michel was built on a site originally known as Mont Tomb where two earlier sanctuaries were built by Christian hermits in the sixth century. These two sanctuaries were dedicated to Saint Stephen, the first Christian martyr and another early martyr, Saint Symphorian of Autun.

The archangel Michael did not become associated with the site until the year 708 when Bishop Aubert dreamt that the archangel had come to him in his sleep and demanded he build a church in his honor at the site. Aubert convinced himself he was imagining the archangel's visit, which forced Michael to return on three separate occasions to repeat his demand. On his final visit, in order to convince the bishop he was real, Michael drilled a hole in the bishop's head with the tip of his finger. Finally convinced, Bishop Aubert built a chapel on the site using a replica of Monte Gargano, a shrine in Southern Italy where it was believed Saint Michael had appeared in the year 492.

Having embarked on his course to build the chapel dedicated to the archangel, the bishop sent two of his clerics to Italy in search of relics for the chapel. They returned with part of the stone on which Saint Michael reputedly stood, and a fragment of red cloth the archangel was believed to have left on the altar at Monte Gargano. Worshippers travelled to the remote site in increasing numbers to seek the protection of the archangel and soon Mont Saint Michel became one of the leading pilgrimage sites in Medieval Europe.

In the 11th and 12th centuries, the Benedictine monks built a Romanesque abbey on the summit of the rock and a complex of monastic buildings for both the monks use and to provide lodging for the pilgrims. Additional buildings were added over the centuries. In 1204, to atone for the sin of setting fire to Mont Saint Michel, the king of France contributed generously to the rebuilding. The La Merveille was built in record time on the north side of the church and additional buildings were added in subsequent centuries, though the last major construction project was completed in 1450.

Noelle had read the article dozens of times over the years since her only visit to Mont Saint Michel when she was a child, but no new inspiration leapt out at her from reading it again. She could almost recite the article from memory by now. Her diary entries had been the beginnings of her rather stuttering attempts to understand what had happened to her that morning on the medieval site. After reading the story of Bishop Aubert, Noelle had been so relieved to learn she wasn't the only one in recorded history the archangel had spoken to, she'd printed the article and pasted it to the first page. To her younger self, the bishop's experience had confirmed what she'd always known...that she hadn't imagined his voice in her head that day.

Sadly, she'd learned little in the intervening decades, despite her years of study and research. She supposed she should be grateful Michael hadn't seen fit to put the tip of his finger through her skull to get his point across, but she'd been just a little girl.

In the beginning, he'd been patient with her, accepting her excuses over the years for her failure to return. As the years passed, she sensed his patience with her was running thin. When she turned twenty-one and gained access to the trust fund her father had left her, she ran out of excuses. Her mother no longer controlled her financial destiny. Nor did she require parental permission to leave the country. When she graduated from college, she fully intended to return to France that summer, but she changed her mind at the last minute.

She knew Michael had not been pleased with her cowardice but he had refrained from retaliating. Or so she convinced herself at the time. The following spring a historic super-tide submerged the new bridge built by the French government to provide more reliable access to the site and protect the three million tourists that flocked to the island each year. Prior to its opening the tides surrounding the island routinely cut off access to the site, trapping visitors on the island until the tides receded.

But by then Noelle could not easily return to France. She was in the middle of a graduate program at Georgetown University. She'd taken up residence in the townhome her parents were living in when she was born. Over Noelle's objections, her mother had deeded the house to her as soon as she learned of Noelle's plans to return to the east coast.

They both understood without the need for words being exchanged between them that Noelle was slowly making her way back to where her destiny was calling her. Though they had never discussed it, both women understood her mother would never return to the home she shared with her husband at the time of the accident that claimed his life and devastated their small family.

Noelle had dreaded the approach of the anniversary that summer, but apparently, Michael had forgiven her delaying tactics because the havoc at the site had been relatively mild. She was very much afraid the residents of the island would not be so lucky this year.

She turned to the final page in the slim notebook she held and let her glance fall on the crude impression she'd recorded there. It was the image before her that had finally compelled her to stop fighting against the inevitable and book her flight to Paris. She'd made the drawing from the memories of her dreams. She was no artist but in this case, she didn't need to be. The ancient structure she'd visited only once, but one she'd seen hundreds, perhaps thousands, of times online with its soaring spires and impenetrable fortress-like stone walls, lay in ruins, the dead scattered like so much refuse amidst the rubble.

The statue of the archangel that had been so painstakingly returned to its original state the year following her initial visit now stood undamaged, and unfathomably had been moved to block the gated entrance. It was her own imagination rather than any artistic ability on her part that was responsible for the mocking smile on the archangel's lips and the satisfied gleam in his eyes. Despite her lack of talent in her attempt to recapture the memory of what she'd witnessed in a dream, Noelle harbored no doubts that her rough depiction represented the monastery's fate unless she could somehow figure out a way to thwart the will of an archangel.

CHAPTER TEN

Paris in springtime. Rafe decided the morning might very well represent the kind of perfect spring day the familiar adage referred to. He was stopped at a traffic light with the top down in his convertible, but the delay did not dampen his mood. He looked around him, content with his lot in life and reflected on the simple joys of a sunny day, a light breeze and the busy streets teeming with beautiful women. He knew he was in the minority of Parisian residents when it came to anticipating the arrival of the millions of tourists that would flock to the city each spring. At least half of those tourists would be women, he reasoned, and with the warmer temperatures, the majority of those would be clothed in little more than short skirts and tops, baring long, feminine limbs. More than adequate compensation, to Rafe's way of thinking, for the inconvenience of some additional traffic on the city streets.

The temperature outside had tipped in the hours since dawn from chilly to just the right side of warm. Sunlight glittered off metal cars, iron fences, and post lights, sending tourists and natives alike in search of the sunglasses they hadn't needed for most of the long, dreary winter. On this perfect day, the sky was so blue photographers were out in droves, both amateur and professional alike, seeking to capture the city's most famous venues.

A sterling example of the reason behind his particular fondness for the season was standing not far from where he sat in traffic, using her phone to capture a personal memory of the iconic Eiffel Tower. Her back was to him so he couldn't see her face, but the parts of her he could see sent every masculine nerve ending to its knees in gratitude. A meter of espresso-colored hair fell to her hips and swayed in the gentle breeze.

She wore one of those carefree spring dresses that made a man send up a prayer of thanksgiving to his God. The flowing skirt fell just above her knees and provided him an ample view of bare, fair legs. He would have preferred those long legs to be set off by the kind of intricate, high-heeled sandals most women seemed to delight in, incomprehensible to the male of the species as their preference might be, but acknowledged the ballet flats the young mademoiselle wore were a more sensible option for a day of sight-seeing. Besides even the sensible, yet regrettable shoes could do little to detract from her feminine beauty.

For perhaps the first time in his life, Rafe was actually grateful to be stuck in the gridlocked traffic near the heavily visited tourist attraction. Ironically, he found himself hoping it would take him a few more turns of the light to get through the intersection, long enough at least for the brunette beauty to lower her camera and turn her head so he could catch a glimpse of her profile, if not her full face. Likely, it was a foolish aspiration on his part, since so rarely did a face live up to the perfection hinted at by the view he was enjoying. Still, hope sprang eternal in the male heart. Besides, hadn't his pessimistic conclusion been proven wrong just a few weeks earlier when familial duty had drawn him into the orbit of the beautiful and somewhat mysterious Noelle Dominique?

He'd stayed away from her, despite his grandfather's urging that the young Noelle would no doubt appreciate some company closer to her own age to show her around the city. While his grandfather was encouraging Rafe to offer his close friend's granddaughter a friendly welcome, old Ari was at the same time making it clear that the friendly welcome was not to become too friendly. His grandfather had no desire to find himself on the receiving end of a verbal thrashing at the hands of his close friend, Michel Dominique, about his grandson's breaking her young granddaughter's foolish heart. Since Rafe had recognized almost immediately the lovely Noelle might very well prove too great a temptation for him to resist talking her into his bed, he'd acted the gentleman, risking his grandfather's ire, and kept his distance.

His thoughts drifted back to that night. There was no doubt Noelle was beautiful in every sense of the word. Every little movement on her part was intrinsically feminine. She was obviously sincerely concerned about making a good impression on her grandmother's friends. Her concern about the impression she was making was puzzling considering she'd stayed away from France for the past twenty years. She'd told him her grandmother understood her reasons, but she hadn't bothered to grant him the courtesy of satisfying his curiosity over the seeming inconsistency in her behavior.

He'd seen the two Dominique women together. They were obviously very close and devoted to each other, which only made Noelle's puzzling absence in her grandmother's life all the more inexplicable. Perhaps her mother had forbidden her to return to France or to have any contact with her late husband's family. Rafe immediately dismissed his rather dramatic speculation. Had that been the case, he would have heard of the injustice done to the duchess by her American daughter-in-law through the family grapevine. The Dominique and Lucien families had been intertwined for generations through friendship, business dealings and the occasional intermarriage.

He noticed the traffic begin to inch forward just as he caught a glimpse out of the corner of his eye of the lovely object of his attention lowering her camera and turning away from the crowded walkway so the other tourists surrounding her could make their own memories. Sighing, he shook his head when he saw her face through the throngs.

He should have known. He should have realized by the way he'd been drawn to her, singling her out from the dozens of women lining the sidewalk, his focus immediately captured and held enthralled by her. Cursing under his breath at his own susceptibility, he drew audible curses from his fellow drivers as he turned his concentration to skillfully working his way through the stalled traffic. He managed to make it to the right lane of traffic just a few feet ahead of where Noelle was stowing her phone in her purse, before pulling to a stop, drawing more irate horns from the line of cars he was blocking behind him.

At the commotion, Noelle looked up to determine its cause. Their eyes met across the distance separating them while more determined honking and loudly expressed profanities in various languages rained down around them. Rafe grinned at the startled, wary look that appeared in Noelle's eyes as soon as she recognized him. Shaking his head slightly, he inwardly mocked his futile efforts to stay away from her. He would never be able to maintain his distance. Why waste energy fighting against his inevitable capitulation? "Get in," he called out over the noise.

Noelle immediately shook her head, bringing an amused grin to his lips as she launched into some obviously made-up, frivolous excuse as to why she couldn't join him.

He waved his hand in dismissal, cutting off her objections, and motioned with his head to the traffic stalled behind him. "The drivers behind me would be grateful if you would get in so they could be on their way."

As he'd known she would, Noelle cast a guilty look in the direction of the long line of cars forming behind him. After a brief moment of indecision, she cast him a disgruntled look and began weaving through the parked cars between them until she reached his. Before she had a chance to open the door, Rafe put the car in park and jumped out of his seat to hurry around to hold it open for her. She rolled her eyes at his exaggerated courtesy given the circumstances, and with obvious reluctance allowed herself to be settled into the passenger seat.

Waving his hand in the direction of the thoroughly annoyed drivers behind them, Rafe strolled back around to the driver's side, settled himself back into the low seat and put the car in gear. Unfortunately, by the time he'd accomplished his objective and had Noelle safely tucked beside him in the close confines of the convertible, the traffic light had once again changed back to red. He was only able to move up a few feet along the crowded street before being forced to obey the signal, gaining him another round of frustrated honking and screaming curses from those stuck behind them.

Noelle stole a worried look over her shoulder, obviously fearing the noisy confrontation might escalate to violence. She turned back to catch Rafe grinning in her direction, and simply shook her head in awe at the depths of his unconcern. "Did you follow me here?"

Rafe laughed at her confusion. "No, I had other plans for the morning, but it appears the universe is intent on throwing us together. When I caught sight of your shimmering beauty in the midst of this incredible spring morning, I was compelled to stop."

Noelle waved off his praise with an airy gesture. "Don't let me keep you from your plans. You can just drop me off at the next corner...in the parking lane...not the middle of the street."

"Ah, well, that is no longer possible. I am so dazzled by your beauty, *Mon amour*, my previous plans for the morning escape me."

"I am not your amour," Noelle protested, trying to subtly smooth her short skirt further down her legs, in a vain attempt to cover up as much bare skin as possible. Fresh amusement leapt into his glance.

Rafe congratulated himself on the charming distraction he'd procured to his otherwise ordinary morning. After they navigated the heavy traffic near the Eifel Tower, Noelle didn't bother voicing the protest he could see forming on her lips when he failed to slow at an open curb to allow for her escape. She had apparently already figured out that he had no intention of allowing her to leave him until he was good and ready.

Noelle sighed audibly and bit down on what would no doubt prove to be a futile protest over Rafe's highhanded tactics. She'd never encountered anyone like him in her life, and had discovered rather belatedly that she was woefully unequipped to deal with his breathtaking arrogance. He wore self-assurance much like he sported the custom tailored trousers and open collared shirt he'd donned for wherever his morning plans were taking him before he waylaid her.

Noelle thought Rafe's self-assurance would be a helpful commodity in her current predicament. Not that she deluded herself that Michael would be inclined to appreciate any false arrogance on her part, no matter how smoothly she wore it. She briefly considered confiding her troubles to Rafe, and then quickly discarded the idea. Although she had no intention of becoming any more involved with him than she already was, she didn't want him to conclude she was unstable and inform her grandmother that she was in need of psychiatric help.

If she were completely honest with herself, she would admit that it wasn't only her grandmother's opinion that concerned her. She didn't want Rafe to think less of her. She enjoyed his company, and foolish as they were, she enjoyed being on the receiving end of his ridiculous compliments.

She stole a glance at Rafe's profile. Sometime in the past few moments when she had allowed herself to become preoccupied with her thoughts, he'd led them away from the heart of the tourist area and was in the process of taking an exit to the highway that would lead them away from the city. "Where are we going?"

"To the country. It's too beautiful a day to waste in the city. We'll have lunch at one of the vineyards along the way where I can ply you with questions over wine and cheese and chocolates."

Since Noelle couldn't come up with any objection to his proposed plan, she didn't bother giving voice to any. It sounded like much more fun than her own half-hearted plans to visit a few more of the tourist attractions on the list she'd compiled for her visit, but the part about plying her with questions over wine had her a little worried. "Questions about what?"

In response, Rafe merely turned his head and winked in her direction. Realizing she wasn't going to get an answer, Noelle sighed audibly and leaned back in her seat. As if sensing her surrender, the powerful convertible accelerated as they reached the highway and within moments had her long hair whipping every which way. She reached up to restrain it, wishing she'd thought to tuck a spare hair tie into her purse. Since conversation was virtually impossible at the speed they were travelling, Noelle forced herself to relax and take in the scenery as they left the densely populated city behind.

After a few moments, the smooth rhythm of gliding along the highway in Rafe's luxurious car lulled her to let down her guard she instinctively raised whenever she found herself in his presence. All of the excitement of seeing her grandmother again and her growing anxiety as she began mentally ticking off the days until the next anniversary of her visit to Mont Saint Michel had kept her on edge for months. The worries circling around her head began to slow as the miles sped passed and she let her lids close even as she chided herself not to fall asleep.

CHAPTER ELEVEN

With Noelle safely asleep at his side, Rafe allowed himself the indulgence of looking his full at his lovely passenger. She really was exquisite, with her pale, flawless skin, perfect features and the Dominique eyes, closed now in sleep. Her death grip on her long hair loosened as she relaxed and the long strands were beginning to escape her slackened grip. He reached over to capture the silk tail before the wind whipped it across her face and woke its owner.

He puzzled over his deepening attraction to her even as he acknowledged that his legendary familiarity with feminine beauty had done little, in Noelle's case anyway, to lessen his susceptibility to it. He was a man who appreciated beauty in all forms, but there was no denying the feminine version of it was the one he found most appealing. He was struck by Noelle's stunning femininity every time he encountered her, but it hadn't been the appealing sight of her in the little flowy dress that had driven him to abandon his admittedly rather boring plans for the morning. No, the cause had been the wary look in her eyes when their glances met across the stalled traffic, and the way she attempted to keep a safe distance from him, as if she suspected, despite their families' long friendship, that he would somehow prove to be a threat to her.

Though he was reasonably certain she recognized he would never pose any kind of physical threat, he could not fault her defensive instincts. At the basest level, he was male, and therefore a natural predator. She was female, and appealing enough to recognize, likely from experience, that she was in danger of becoming his prey. He'd convinced himself the safest thing for him, for both of them, was to stay away from her. So far his rational side was winning the contest over his more primitive instincts, but there was no arguing his conviction was losing ground against the part of him that wondered how soft her skin was, how she would look with those magnificent eyes of hers dazed with passion.

37

Shaking his head in disgust at the predictable direction of his thoughts, he drew his gaze away from Noelle and returned his concentration to the road, wondering how in hell he'd ended up on a highway, headed in the direction of a small vineyard where they offered an intimate lunch and tasting, with a woman he'd sworn to himself he would keep his distance from asleep in his passenger seat.

By the time he'd covered the more than two hundred kilometers to the small vineyard in the Loire Valley, his mood had soured considerably. While Noelle had slept the morning away, he'd called his office and instructed his assistant to rearrange his tight schedule for the remainder of the day, thus ensuring the rest of his workweek would be accompanied by the stress of juggling two appointments into a single time slot, the way Americans routinely managed. He admired the work ethic of his American counterparts, but he had no wish to replicate their stressful, legendary workweeks in his own life. Balance was the key to a contented, satisfying life. He had no compunction in blaming Noelle for disrupting his own.

He stole a glance over at his still sleeping companion. Somehow, he couldn't imagine Noelle fitting into his easygoing lifestyle. No, some deeply engrained part of him recognized Noelle Dominique represented a true threat to the carefree bachelor's life he'd carved out for himself. Well, he reasoned with a smile, he'd never been one to back down from a challenge and this one promised to prove more interesting than most.

Still smiling, he reached over to gently slide his knuckles along the soft skin of her cheek. Noelle stirred but didn't wake. In sleep, at least, she trusted him enough not to shy away from his every advance, but tempted as he was to discover the limits of that trust, he was not one to take advantage of a defenseless woman. Gripping her shoulder, he gently shook her awake. "Noelle, we're here."

Heavy lids lifted over eyes so blue they still had the power to shock him, even when they were disoriented from her long nap as they were now. "Where's here?"

"*Moulon Bleu.*"

"The blue windmill?" She echoed, her disorientation turning to confusion.

Rafe pointed to the large blue windmill standing watch over the small vineyard. "Yes. *Moulon Bleu* is the name of the vineyard."

Noelle mentally shook herself out of the sense of disorientation of waking up beneath Rafe's probing glance. In an effort to regain her equilibrium and put some distance between them, she reached for the door handle and hurriedly climbed out of the close confines of the front seat before Rafe had a chance to perform the courtesy for her. He joined her on the walk leading to the entrance to the vineyard, clasping her hand as if he feared she might try to run from him. Looking down at their joined hands, Noelle looked askance at Rafe, who merely flashed a devastating grin at her uncertainty and gave her hand a reassuring squeeze. Noelle let it go, deciding she would do well to conserve her strength for when Rafe began plying her with the dreaded questions he hinted at earlier.

The owner of the vineyard, a middle aged, surprisingly plump woman, given her French heritage, wore a friendly smile on her sun-leathered face and greeted Rafe like a long lost son. Upon Rafe's introduction, Noelle was relieved to note their host was inclined to include Noelle in her friendly greeting and happily consented to give them a personal tour of the vineyard.

Though Noelle couldn't see any signs of grapes on the vines, the view from the hilltop vineyard was spectacular, all green, rolling hills covered with vines. Noelle received an education in winemaking and learned an amusing bit of trivia to take back home to the states when their host related the history of how all of the French vines had died in a blight at the turn of the previous century. The only way the French winemaking industry survived was through the assistance of California vine growers who sent seedlings across the Atlantic so the French could graft their dying plants onto the Americans' gifts. Thus, the vineyard owner pointed out with a twinkle in her eye, as a result of the scourge, there were no longer any purely French wines. They were all hybrids, courtesy of American generosity. Noelle shared their host's amusement. Given the French devotion to wine and winemaking, she couldn't imagine many French vineyard owners being so humble and gracious about sharing a story of how their American counterparts had saved their passion along with their livelihoods.

After the tour, their host led them to a private table beneath the tent set up for public tastings and encouraged them to sample a selection of the wines the vineyard produced. After she left them alone Noelle let her gaze dwell on the scenery, even as she allowed the wine Rafe poured into her glass to linger on her tongue. She was a bit surprised to realize how much she was enjoying herself. Rafe was proving to be an interesting and attentive companion, who appeared remarkably well informed about wines and the ins and outs of operating a vineyard.

"My grandmother tells me Chateau Dominique has its own private label. Is it possible Chateau Lucien does as well?"

Rafe seemed to hesitate before admitting, "The family actually owns and operates a number of vineyards throughout France."

"Under the Lucien label?" Noelle asked curiously, thinking she would be sure to stop and purchase a few bottles to try out her new education by sampling some of Rafe's family's wines.

"No, actually the labelling of wines in France is closely regulated but all of the family wines are offered under the umbrella of the *Diable* Elixir.

Noelle laughed. "I suppose the devil isn't offended by the idea of his descendants profiting from his moniker."

"Apparently not, as the family enjoys an almost legendary reputation for being quite skilled when it comes to the pursuit of profits." Rafe concurred with a smile and a shrug, while at the same time he reached over to refill her nearly empty glass from the carafe that sat between them on the table.

"Oh, no more, I'm not used to the French custom of wine with every meal. My head's already spinning."

Rafe brushed off her weak protest with a dismissive gesture. "If you spend much time in France you will no doubt soon grow accustomed to our ways."

"No doubt," Noelle agreed on a sigh, taking a sip of the fresh wine. It really was delicious and somehow adventurous to be sipping wine with Rafe at a small iron table beneath a tent in the warming mid-afternoon sun, a plate of French cheeses, and freshly baked breads, and olives and tapenade artfully arranged on a colorful hand-fired plate between them. She helped herself to another slice of bread and soft, but strongly flavored cheese, and then washed down the offering with another swallow of wine.

"So, now that you have completely disrupted my work day, you can compensate me by solving a little mystery that's been puzzling me since the evening we met."

"You cannot seriously be attempting to blame me for interrupting your day," Noelle protested. "You all but kidnapped me off the street and set off without my permission on this little jaunt of yours."

"Are you not enjoying the day?"

Even though she knew it was for her benefit, Noelle couldn't help but be affected by Rafe's wounded expression. She managed to swallow her instinctive leap to reassure him, as she guessed he guessed she would feel compelled to do and instead asked suspiciously, "What little mystery do you want me to solve for you?"

"It is obvious to even the most casual observer that you and your grandmother are close."

"Yes." She could guess where this was heading. In the last direction she wished him to pursue and one in which she had few answers to offer him in order to appease his curiosity.

"One cannot help but wonder what has kept you from visiting all of these years."

Noelle sighed. "It's not that we haven't seen each other."

"I know, but you've never visited your grandmother at her home in France."

"That's not exactly true."

"Really? When did you last visit?"

Noelle fell silent, searching for an answer that would not set off another round of questions. She never for a moment actually considered confessing the truth to him.

"Noelle?"

She reluctantly lifted her glance to meet his probing one. "My mother preferred my grandmother visit us in the states."

"Why? I cannot believe there was any financial constraint that would warrant such a condition on your mother's part. Did your mother

41

and grandmother have some kind of argument the last time you visited? When was that by the way?"

Realizing Rafe wasn't going to let the matter drop until she satisfied his curiosity, she reluctantly admitted, "When I was four."

"And you are now?"

"Twenty four."

"So what happened between your mother and grandmother that kept you away from France for decades? Even more curious, what has suddenly propelled you to end your self-imposed exile?"

She could see the deep vein of suspicion in the dark eyes that followed her every expression and attempt at evasion she mustered against him. Sighing audibly, she assured him, "It's not what you're thinking."

"You have no idea what I'm thinking."

"Yes I do. You're concerned I'm somehow trying to take advantage of my grandmother's loneliness and her love for me." Her lips curved in an appreciative smile at Rafe's protective poster on her grandmother's behalf. "It's sweet that you're trying to protect her, but I would never do anything to hurt her."

"Yes, I would like to believe that, hence my curiosity as to your motives for this sudden visit after staying away for so long."

"Okay, I can see how that might look from an outsider's perspective," she conceded.

"Our families have been close for centuries. I am hardly an outsider."

Rafe was right, which answered one niggling worry. Either her mother had never confided in her grandmother what had happened that day at Mont Saint Michel, or her grandmother had never confided in her close friends, the Luciens. She looked beyond Rafe's shoulder, wondering how much to tell him. Maybe he could give her some advice as to how to proceed. She really didn't want to bother her grandmother with her fears. They were having such a wonderful time together.

"Noelle." Rafe reached across the table and covered her hand, gently urging her to ease the death grip she'd unconsciously clenched around the fragile stem of her wine glass.

She risked meeting his glance. Could she trust him? Or would he laugh at her? Conclude she was unbalanced?

"Noelle."

"My mother was trying to protect me," she admitted softly.

Rafe strained to hear her whispered confession. "From your grandmother?"

"No, of course not."

"Then who was she trying to protect you from?"

Noelle could tell from his tone and his expression that Rafe was ready to jump in and eliminate any potential threat to her wellbeing. He really did have a few things in common with the mythical Prince Charming despite his rather questionable connection with the ruler of hell. "Not who…well not exactly."

Rafe leaned back in his chair, dragging the hand he held with him. "Maybe you'd better start at the beginning."

"It's a long story."

"We have plenty of time," he assured her. As if sensing she might appreciate a little boost to her hesitant courage, he reached over to refill her glass again.

When he replaced the nearly empty carafe in the cooler their host had courteously provided, Noelle afforded herself of even the false bravado the wine offered. "All right, here goes," she began, straightening in her chair and bracing her shoulders. "I told you the last time I was in France I was a little girl."

"Yes."

"My mother took me to visit Mont Saint Michel. She'd always wanted to visit. I guess we must have been staying at Chateau Dominique. That's not far from the site is it?"

"No, it's only about an hour drive from the estate."

"I don't really remember much about those kinds of details from that day…you know, like where we were staying, or how we got there."

When she failed to continue with her recitation, Rafe prompted her, "Something happened the day you visited Mont Saint Michel?"

"Yes."

Seeing she was reluctant to trust him, he squeezed the hand he still held reassuringly. "Noelle." Rafe didn't want to risk pushing her too hard now that she was on the brink of confiding in him, but the truth was they weren't leaving until Noelle explained the source of the troubled expression she was still wearing twenty years after the events in question would have occurred.

"Like I said, I don't really remember the details of our visit that day, what we saw, or the layout of the abbey. I've seen pictures of it since so I know what it looks like."

When her eyes took on a faraway expression, Rafe pulled her back to the present. "But you remember something else about that day that's kept you away from France and the grandmother you love for most of your life." She drew herself back from wherever her memories had led her and met his glance. He was struck by the lost look in hers, as if she was still the little girl she'd been that day. "Tell me."

Noelle's lips curved upward slightly at his persistence. She could imagine exactly the look that would come into his eyes when she confessed the truth to him. First, it would be relief that it was just a childhood fantasy that had kept her away, followed quickly by amusement that such a small event in a child's life had such a profound effect on her. Then there would be anger that the same trivial event had kept her grandmother's only granddaughter away from her father's home for twenty years. She couldn't risk telling him the rest....that it hadn't ended that day...that it was still going on.

"We were getting ready to leave. My mom was at the cash register buying me a gift...a little stuffed replica of the Archangel Michael, and being a mom, a few children's books about the history of Mont Saint Michel." She paused and added, "I told you I was enrolled in a French immersion program even then."

"Yes."

"I was waiting for her in the alcove that houses the replica of the fleche', you know, the statue of the Archangel Michael."

"Yes, I know it." He confirmed, and then clearly alarmed by her continued hesitation, demanded, "Did someone hurt you?"

"No."

Her voice had taken on that faraway quality again. "Noelle..."

She finally raised her eyes to his. "He spoke to me."

"Who spoke to you?"

"Michael…his statue…whatever…"

She held his glance as she confessed her deepest secret to him. She needed to see his reaction. If this was just the first of many such confessions, she needed to prepare herself for people's reactions.

"I don't think I understand."

Confusion. She could understand why that would be number one before relief took over at what he would no doubt conclude had been a young child's imagination.

"He said they had to give it back."

His brow furrowed. Noelle could tell he was preoccupied searching his thoughts for the missing pieces of their conversation. "Give what back?"

"Mont Saint Michel. He said they had to give it back."

"I still don't understand. Who had to give what back?"

She could tell Rafe was trying valiantly to keep up with her revelations, but the effort was not without cost to him. His grip on her hand was becoming almost painful.

"Michael said the secular world had proven an unreliable steward. He wanted the government to restore his home on earth to the stewardship of the church."

It was easier than she thought it would be. In some ways, it was a relief to just say the words aloud to someone who would listen. Whenever she tried to speak about that day to her mother, she would always cut her off before Noelle could even get the words out…telling her not to think about it…it was just a dream…her mind was playing tricks on her.

Now it was Rafe who was desperately trying to wrap his mind around her incredible confession. Next, she guessed would be disbelief, followed by pity that she was turning out to be delusional. He was probably already trying to figure out how to break the disheartening news to her grandmother. She couldn't suppress the giggle that rose to her lips at the thought.

His eyes pierced hers. "What's so funny?"

"Sorry, your expression. You're trying so hard not to offend me but at the same time you're wondering how you're going to break the news to my grandmother that her only grandchild is unbalanced."

"You're not unbalanced." He protested half-heartedly.

"Delusional?" She offered in its place.

"For God's sake Noelle, you were just a little girl. You wouldn't be the first child to have a conversation with an imaginary friend."

"That's generous of you."

She was feeling lighthearted all of a sudden. The dread that had been weighing her down blessedly absent for the moment.

"What aren't you telling me? I can't believe a child's imagination was enough to make your mother keep you away from France for the past twenty years."

"I guess you had to be there," Noelle quipped grinning. She could feel the laughter bubbling up inside her. She quickly raised her hand to her lips to suppress it and then at the doubtful expression on Rafe's face, in the next moment she found herself all but doubled over with laughter. She laughed so hard tears streamed down her face. Seeing Rafe's disapproving expression, she tried to regain control, but one look at his face set her off again.

"I fail to see the humor in this situation," he remarked.

With an effort, Noelle swallowed the last of her laughter, reached up to wipe the lingering tears from her eyes, and replied with a grin, "No, I imagine not."

"Noelle…"

She was growing accustomed to his intimidating tactics. "You're used to getting your own way, aren't you?"

"Stop trying to distract me. It won't work. Why did your mother keep you away from France?"

Noelle shrugged. "I guess my therapist convinced her."

"Your therapist?" Rafe echoed appalled.

"Well, you can't really blame her. When your only child is convinced she had a conversation with an archangel a child therapist seems like an appropriate response. That was the thing, you see. She kept telling me I was imagining his voice speaking to me, but I wouldn't listen… I wouldn't back down. I know what he told me that day. She figured removing me from the scene of my delusions would make everything go away."

"But it didn't?"

"Unfortunately not. Hence the child psychologist. Dr. Adams meant well. My mother was careful to hire a Catholic therapist. You know, considering my fantasy involved an angel. I'm sure my father would have approved. She didn't want my therapist to be someone who was predisposed not to believe me. I think that was the hardest part for my mom. There was a part of her that almost believed me, or at least was willing to allow for the possibility that Michael really did speak to me that day. That's why she wouldn't let me come back."

Rafe sat back in his seat, his eyes never leaving her face. "I'm not certain I understand. If your mother was open to the idea that the Archangel Michael might have actually spoken to you, why would that compel her to keep you away from France? It seems to me the opposite reaction for a person of faith."

"Like I said, you had to be there. In one moment, she's standing at the cash register paying for her purchases and the next thing she knew there was a crowd of people gathered around her four-year-old daughter. The same daughter who was staring as if mesmerized by the statue in the alcove and who suddenly covered her ears and started screaming, "Give it back. Give it back. He says they have to give it back."

"Does your grandmother know about this?"

"I don't know. We've never discussed it."

"You're going back to Mont Saint Michel."

She was surprised by his insight. "Yes. I'm sure Dr. Adams would approve. I think she would agree it was time for me to find closure after all these years."

"I'll take you."

Noelle was taken aback by Rafe's offer. Though he'd flung it at her in his usual casual manner, she had no doubt he would take her back to the scene of the crime, so to speak, if she made the request of him. As much as she tried to maintain her distance by dismissing him as just the grandson of her grandmother's close friend, he kept surprising her. There was a genuineness to Rafe she couldn't deny. His concern for her grandmother when he thought Noelle might be taking advantage of her was heartwarming.

Whenever she least expected it, he slipped behind, around, or beneath the defenses she'd hastily erected against him, leaving her wide open to the legendary Lucien charm and devastating good looks. "Thank you for that, but when the time comes, I think I need to go alone. You know...just to prove to myself I can."

"There's no reason for you to go alone, Noelle. If you won't allow me to accompany you, then confide in your grandmother. If she doesn't know what has kept you away all these years, I think she'd be relieved to hear your story."

Noelle considered his advice "Maybe," she hedged, and then added hesitantly, "Can I ask you a question?"

"Of course."

"Do you believe me?"

He hesitated, obviously considering how to frame his response so as not to offend her. "I believe you believe he spoke to you that day."

"Diplomatic."

"What about you, Noelle? Do you still believe the Archangel Michael spoke to you at Mont Saint Michel when you were a little girl?"

"No, I don't believe it." Noelle took note of his obvious relief at her admission before she added softly, "I know it with certainty."

Rafe's glance probed hers, testing her claim. "I really don't think you should return to Mont Saint Michel alone. You obviously experienced a traumatic event there when you were a very young child. You cannot be certain how you'll react to being there again."

"Well, we can agree on that at least." She raised her glass in a mock toast and downed the rest of her wine in a single swallow. She couldn't help but notice Rafe failed to mimic her act of bravado.

Silence fell between them. This one seemed more uncomfortable to her and in stark contrast to their earlier ease in each other's company. She rushed to fill it. "We should go. I think I've taken up all of the time allotted to the granddaughter of a close friend of the family. Especially now that I've satisfied your curiosity about my reasons for staying away for so long."

"And you believe those were the only reasons I whisked you off for a day in the country?"

"I think it would be wise for us both to pretend those were the only reasons for today," Noelle replied softly.

"Why is that?"

Noelle rolled her eyes at his challenge. "Our families, as you pointed out, have been close for centuries. If we were to become involved, my grandmother would worry that you'll break my heart, and your grandfather would worry your carelessness with said heart would come between him and his very close friend."

"I would never be careless with your heart, Noelle."

He sounded so sincere she almost believed him. Then she reminded herself he was a man who kept a store of memorized platitudes for exactly these kinds of occasions. "Trust me. I would never make the mistake of laying it at your feet."

"Is that a challenge?"

"No! No! No!" Noelle protested instantly and vehemently. "I am well aware it would be a colossal error on my part for me to issue any sort of challenge in your direction when it comes to…" Her voice trailed off. She could feel the blush rising in her cheeks. She fidgeted in her seat and dropped her embarrassed gaze beneath his amused one, before she managed to get the words out. "…when it comes to that sort of thing."

He laughed at her discomfort. "That sort of thing? You mean it could become awkward, considering our families' long friendship, if we were to become lovers?"

Noelle sucked in her breath at the casual way he referred to the prospect of them becoming lovers. "To say the least."

"Why is that? We are both consenting adults. There's no reason for anything to become awkward between us."

Noelle wasn't certain if Rafe was teasing her or if he was completely oblivious to the pitfalls of the two of them becoming intimately involved. "Spoken like a man."

"But of course."

Noelle laughed at his mystified expression. One she was quite certain he adopted for her benefit. No one could be that clueless. "Perhaps we should just change the subject. I have no intention of falling into bed with you. I'm just here to catch up with my grandmother and find closure for a traumatic event that occurred in my childhood, as you refer to it. Both of those endeavors are going to be taking up the majority of my time while I'm here. I don't have any left over to indulge in, at best, a questionable affair with you."

"Ah, *mon amour*, you would be wise to refrain from tossing those challenges around so carelessly. I am a man, after all, and therefore somewhat reluctant to overlook them."

"Try," Noelle suggested, bringing a grin and a bark of laughter to Rafe's lips.

He stood with his customary fluid grace and reached for her hand to draw her out of her chair. He raised the hand he held and brushed his lips across her fingertips. "I will do my best, my lovely Noelle. Come; let us be on our way. Your grandmother will be worried if you are not home before dark."

She rolled her eyes again at the way he insinuated she was a child who needed her mother's permission to stay out after dark, but there was no denying her grandmother would likely worry if she wasn't home in time for dinner. She glanced at her watch and then acknowledged Rafe was right. By the time they made it back to Paris, her grandmother probably would be wondering if some mishap had befallen her.

"Why don't you just call her and let her know you'll be home in a few hours," Rafe suggested, seeing her glance at her watch.

"Because then I'll have to explain I spent the day in your company and that will set off all of those awkward questions I'm trying to avoid by not becoming involved with you."

Grinning at her honesty, Rafe led her away from the small table where she'd confessed her most closely guarded secret to him. Surprisingly she'd been able to do so with very little of the unpleasantness she had been anticipating. He hadn't called the men in the white coats to come and take her away. In fact, Rafe seemed less concerned about her confession to having had a conversation with an archangel than he was with her insistence that an affair between them was off the table.

"Some experiences, *mon amour*, are worth the price of a few awkward questions."

"No doubt," Noelle agreed sighing, unable to summon the effort to come up with a more sparkling response to his blatant dare.

When they reached the car, Noelle stood aside and waited for Rafe to open her door so she could slide into the passenger seat. Instead of doing so, he turned her to face him and caged her between his arms, his hands resting on either side of her against the side of the car. Noelle instinctively tried to retreat from his unsettling nearness but was unable to put more than a few inches between them because her back was already plastered up against the side of the car.

"What are you doing?" She had intended her question to come out as an authoritative demand but instead it came out in a voice that more closely resembled breathless anticipation even to her own ears.

"I'm going to make certain both of us have all the facts before we conclude an intimate relationship between us would not be worth the price of a little awkwardness with our relatives."

"I thought you were going to try to resist responding to my unintentional challenges," she reminded him.

"I did and I will, but I've decided first we would be better served finding out what we've both been wondering about since that night on the terrace of your grandmother's home."

Noelle stopped protesting. She actually thought Rafe might have a point. Better to find out if taking the plunge with him would be worth the obvious pitfalls accompanying it. If a simple kiss would resolve the tantalizing temptation floating in the air between them, it was worth the risk. She raised her hesitant glance to Rafe's only to find him staring down at her, his eyes alight with laughter.

"No further objections?" He mocked. When she just stood there staring back at him, he bent his head to make good on his threat.

'A simple kiss?' Had she actually managed to delude herself that anything with Rafe could be simple? For the space of a breath she attempted to keep up with the flood of emotions pulsing through her before she abandoned her brief delusion that she could hold her own against him, and simply let him draw her under to where it was dark and tantalizing and unbelievably sexy.

Her mind dazzled at the depths of her previous misconceptions about passion's true nature and her previous arrogance (and not a little disappointment) that she was immune to its most provocative lures. She had feared she was incapable of responding fully to a man's touch,

51

simply because her rather limited experience with men had left her largely unmoved. She supposed she owed Rafe for stripping her of that absurd anxiety.

She raised limp hands to grip the front of his shirt, both because she needed something solid to hold onto as she was growing dizzy beneath the unrelenting onslaught of feelings she could not control, and because she wanted to touch him, to feel the heat coming off of him.

When his lips slid from hers to brush across her face, her closed eyes, to trail down the long slide of her throat, she couldn't suppress the moan of longing that slipped passed her lips. She leaned back against the car, no longer confident her legs retained enough strength to keep her upright. Surely if a few awkward moments with her grandmother, admitting that she had recklessly allowed herself to fall victim to the legendary Lucien charm was the price of the glorious, languorous, erotic feelings pulsing through her, it was not too high a price for the promised reward he was offering in exchange.

Rafe was aware of Noelle's initial hesitancy to accept the gauntlet he'd thrown down between them. She'd stood stiffly in his arms, as if bracing herself for his kiss. So he'd deliberately gentled his approach, softened his instinctive demand for her surrender to persuasion, tempting, 'come my love, let us play' his lips urged her. For all her luminous beauty Noelle was surprisingly hesitant, and perhaps he presumed wonderingly, charmingly inexperienced. He recognized the exact moment when she abandoned her defensive posture and simply melted against him, all soft and breathless, because every male instinct within him reacted instantly to her surrender, clamoring at him to take what she was so artlessly offering.

With an effort, he resisted their frantic urgings even when her hands reached up to grip the front of his shirt as if she sought a lifeline to keep her from sinking beneath the swirling surface and plunging recklessly in the direction of the beckoning depths below. It wasn't easy fighting both of them, especially when everything inside of him was screaming at him to draw her under, dive together into the darkness wherever greater pleasure, accompanied by a more complete surrender, awaited them both.

She was no longer using her hands braced between them to keep him at a distance, or to merely keep herself upright. No, now her busy fingers were loosening the buttons of his shirt so they could get at the warm flesh beneath. He closed his eyes against the struggle of pulling back, of denying himself, of denying them both, because no matter how he'd attempted to trivialize their families' close connection there was no denying propelling them both head first into a hot, impulsive affair would not prove to be without consequences. Given her gentle nature it was likely, those consequences would weigh more heavily on Noelle.

The kiss had started out as a simple, calculated maneuver on his part, a demonstration of how good they could be together in bed, to make her reconsider and perhaps even regret the ease with which she dismissed him and the possibility of an affair between them. Somehow, she'd managed to turn the tables on him. Somehow, it was Noelle who was showing him just how much she had to offer. Not that he'd ever doubted her appeal.

Hadn't he been drawn to her from the very beginning? Hadn't his eyes followed her across the room, watching her bloom like a rose beneath a warm sun provided by the gracious acceptance of her grandmother's friends to her presence in the duchess' life? Hadn't he followed her when she escaped to the terrace? Hadn't he dreamt of her that night and the intervening nights since, even when he'd woken from one of those erotic dreams next to another woman in his bed?

He drew back, slowly, first gripping her hands and drawing them away from his chest where they danced lightly across his bare flesh. Then he raised his own to encircle her face when he lifted his lips from hers so he could gaze down into her incredible eyes, dazed with passion and longing, causing the sharp blade of regret to bury itself a little deeper into his already bleeding male longings.

"Noelle." Her name whispered alongside a sigh of regret and for a moment, her eyes simply clung to his as she slowly surfaced from the effects of their shared passion.

"God, God…" She whispered, still dazed, bringing a slight smile to his lips. "I know that was a huge miscalculation, at least on my part, but I can't bring myself to regret it."

Rafe couldn't resist the urge to brush his lips against hers in a swift kiss, though he managed to refrain from taking them under again. "Nor can I, but I believe we both have a lot to think about before we take this any further between us."

"Oh no, it can't go any further," Noelle immediately protested, even while her hands still clung to him, her fingertips unconsciously seemingly continuing to caress his naked flesh. "Not that I don't understand why women reputedly throw themselves at your feet."

"But you have no intention of doing so?" Rafe countered her ridiculous protest with growing amusement.

Noelle heaved an audible, and what Rafe hopefully interpreted as a disappointed sigh. "Regrettably not. I told you I don't have time to indulge in an affair with you now. Maybe my next visit..."she offered, then realized how that sounded, added blushing, "I didn't mean to say that....I mean, you'll probably be married by then, or involved with someone. Are you by the way? Involved with someone?"

At the laughter dancing in his eyes, Noelle added swiftly, "Never mind, that's none of my business. Maybe we should just go now. You're right; my grandmother will be worried if I'm not home before dark."

CHAPTER TWELVE

He was back. Invading her dreams. Not Rafe, though she could admit in the silence of her room he'd invaded her dreams more than once since their date, she supposed was not an unreasonable term for it, at the vineyard. Him. Michael was back wondering what excuse she'd come up with this time to explain her delay in responding to his increasingly autocratic summons.

Noelle sat up in bed and brushed her sleep-tangled hair away from her face. The truth was she'd run out of excuses and they both knew it. She had yet to take Rafe's advice to confide in her grandmother about the real reason she'd stayed away all these years. Her grandmother was so happy, seemed to be enjoying their time together so much, Noelle was reluctant to be the one to cast a dark cloud on their sunny reunion.

What choice did she have? She needed to return to Mont Saint Michel. Rafe had informed her that Chateau Dominique was only a short drive away. She supposed she could just suggest to her grandmother they leave the city for a while, that she wanted to see her father's childhood home. Then once there, she could casually mention to her grandmother about her understandable desire to visit Mont Saint Michel. After all, it was one of the most popular tourist destinations in the world, with millions of people from all over the globe making their way to the remote site that had stood for more than thirteen centuries. Would her grandmother accept her innocent suggestion? Was it wrong of Noelle to not be completely forthcoming with her?

Noelle wished she could be certain of whether or not her mother had ever confided in her grandmother about the events of that day. Surely, she must have told her something to explain her refusal to allow Noelle, her grandmother's last remaining tie to her only son, to return to France. Did she know about that day? Were they both simply avoiding bringing up the topic so as not to distress the other?

She didn't know what to do. She supposed she could call her mother and just ask her what excuse she'd given her grandmother about why any visits between them would have to take place anywhere other than France. Unfortunately, that door was closed to her. Noelle knew better than to attempt such a conversation with her mother. It would only upset her and likely throw them back into that time of their relationship where there had been a lot of long, resentful silences on both of their parts.

They'd managed to grow beyond them over the past few years. They'd both made an effort, though the process was often slow and painstaking, to achieve a more normal, and mostly loving relationship between them. Noelle didn't want to risk a return to the dark days of their relationship. She figured her insistence on returning to France had tested their somewhat fragile bond enough, without forcing her mother to both explain and inevitably defend her actions yet again.

With being unwilling to reach out to her mother, Noelle felt sorely how limited her options were. She could either confide in her grandmother or lie about her reasons for wanting to visit Mont Saint Michel. It might be a lie of omission but her grandmother might not see it that way. In fact, if she already knew the truth, she would likely be hurt by Noelle's unwillingness to confide in her. Noelle longed for another voice besides the one in her own head to bounce her worries off of. Unfortunately, her grandmother was the extent of her close acquaintances in France. There was no one else besides her mother, even her girlfriends from school, who knew the truth about that day.

Actually, there was someone else now. Rafe knew about the events of that pivotal morning, but she could hardly ask his advice. Or maybe she could, she reconsidered. He knew the truth. He was a close friend of the family and genuinely cared for her grandmother. Rafe had a way of bringing all of her angst and confusion out of the clouds and putting some much-needed perspective on things.

She let the prospect simmer in her thoughts for a moment. He was a friend after all. She was fairly certain he wouldn't mind if she sought his advice. Hadn't he offered to take her back himself? Just because they hadn't seen each other since that day at the vineyard didn't mean he would revoke the offer if given the opportunity. Besides, she wasn't asking him to take her back to Mont Saint Michel; she just wanted to get his opinion on whether or not he really believed it was in her grandmother's best interest to confide the whole sorry story to her.

"I'm going this time. I just need a few more days to work out the details."

She felt a little ridiculous whispering her rationalization out loud to the invisible will she could feel pressing against her own, but she felt some explanation was warranted. Glancing at the bedside clock, she decided it was a little early to show up on Rafe's doorstep. Then she realized it was Sunday and she had the perfect excuse to take the car her grandmother had left at her disposal for the length of her visit. Since her grandmother was unlikely to be out of bed this early, she could tell Bernard she was going to Mass.

Her plan decided, she jumped out of bed and hurried to the adjoining bath. She was feeling decidedly upbeat now that she had a plan, even if the thought of showing up unannounced on Rafe's doorstep was somewhat intimidating. She paused in the act of stepping into the shower, realizing she had no idea where Rafe lived or even how to get in touch with him.

Bernard would know, she concluded, brushing aside the most obvious obstacle to her rash plan. The Luciens were close friends of her grandmother's. Bernard would have Rafe's address, or at least his grandfather's, though Noelle couldn't imagine having to summon the nerve to reach out to Ariel Lucien and ask him for his grandson's address.

She showered and dressed hurriedly, refusing to allow her nerves to stop her from putting her plan into action. Her only other option was to knock on her grandmother's door and offer a full confession. In the end, she might be left with no other option than to do that anyway, she conceded, but she was willing to risk a little awkwardness with her grandmother's butler to put off that discussion a little while longer.

It wasn't as bad as she anticipated. Bernard responded to her hesitant, blushing inquiry in regards to Rafe's address with merciful efficiency. His expression hadn't betrayed even a hint of the curiosity she was sure he must be feeling when he passed her the paper with Rafe's address neatly printed on it. When he inquired politely if she required directions, she just as politely declined, figuring she could use the app on her phone to find her way and not wanting to prolong the embarrassing situation any longer than necessary.

Rafe's apartment was in the luxurious and aristocratic seventh arrondissement. The uniformed doorman merely nodded in her direction as he held the door open for her. No one at the front desk demanded her destination so she stepped to the elevator and pressed the button for the top floor. The elevator opened into an expansive foyer with only a single door. Apparently, Rafe's apartment occupied the entire floor. Swallowing her nerves and giving herself a bracing lecture beneath her breath, she stepped towards the ornately carved hardwood door and knocked, wondering if Rafe employed his own butler who she would be forced to make her excuses to as to why she was showing up on Monsieur Lucien's doorstep without an invitation.

When the door opened in response to her summons, Noelle couldn't be certain which of them was more surprised at the sight of the other. One thing was certain, the gorgeous woman in the flaming red silk robe, was probably not Rafe's butler.

Noelle tried but couldn't force any words passed the blockage in her throat. She simply stood there for long, silent, shocked moments staring at the gorgeous, voluptuous woman with long, curling ebony hair, olive skin, perfect features, and chocolate brown questioning, but somewhat amused eyes, staring back at where Noelle stood frozen in the doorway. The other woman's professionally shaped brow was lifted not unkindly in askance at Noelle's unannounced appearance on her lover's doorstep.

Her brief robe was carelessly knotted around her small waist with the neckline gaping open to reveal the kind of ample cleavage that made every other woman in the room feel like a twelve-year-old girl wondering when her breasts were ever going to look like that. This was not a woman who was going to look like your best friend's frumpy Italian grandmother in another thirty or forty years. No, this woman understood the blessing of great physical beauty and the wisdom of nourishing that blessing. Likely, she would sail into her seventies collecting and breaking young male hearts and leaving them shattered and discarded at her perfectly pedicured feet.

"May I help you?" She asked in perfect French, but with a slight accent suggesting Italian was her first language.

Before Noelle could frame her lips into something resembling a reasonable response to the woman's surprisingly gracious welcome given the circumstances, Rafe's voice broke through her stunned immobility.

"Carina, *Mon amour*, is someone at the door?"

Noelle frantically turned a pleading glance in the beautiful Carina's direction. She saw amused comprehension reflected there and more than a trace of sympathy enter the other woman's gaze before she thankfully began closing the door in Noelle's face and turning around, no doubt with some hurriedly concocted lie on her beautiful lips about a delivery man showing up at the wrong door. Noelle was just heaving a relieved, appreciative sigh for the other woman's feminine understanding when Carina's good intentions were abruptly upended by Rafe taking control of the door's direction from her manicured fingertips and yanking it wide open.

Noelle couldn't be sure which one of them was more shocked. If she hadn't found herself in the middle of the embarrassingly clichéd drama being played out on his doorstep, she thought she might be able to find humor in the picture of Rafe standing there, his hair still damp and mussed from carelessly running a towel through it after his morning shower. Clearly, he hadn't been expecting morning visitors, as he answered his front door with a less than ample towel wrapped casually around his waist.

Noelle was still young and inexperienced enough to be shocked (and admiring) at the sight of Rafe in all of his masculine glory. She remembered the strength in his muscular shoulders from that afternoon at the vineyard. Noelle refrained from looking any lower than the top edge of the damp towel. To give her eyes and her mind something else to concentrate on she raised her glance to his face.

The shocked, incomprehensibly confused expression Rafe was wearing had hysterical laughter bubbling up in her throat. She desperately restrained it, and chided herself to say something; anything that would initiate the process of extricating herself from what she was quite certain was the most embarrassing moment of her life.

Rafe's own shocked expression was quickly passing to one of amusement at their ridiculous predicament. Noelle felt her face flame even further in response to the laughter she read in his eyes. She opened her mouth in a vain attempt to force words passed her stunned lips. Any words. Anything but to just continue standing there confronting Rafe and his beautiful lover like some poor imitation of a naive ingénue in a romantic drama who just discovered the man of her dreams was cheating on her.

After another excruciatingly long moment of standing still as a statue on Rafe's threshold with her lips parted, hoping to hear sound emerge, Noelle gathered the remnants of her tattered pride and forced a hurried, completely inadequate apology through them. "I'm sorry. I'm so sorry. I don't know what I was thinking showing up like this. Please forgive me. I'll just go now."

Before she had a chance to make good her escape, Rafe's strong grip closed around her arm, preventing her from leaving. How was it possible he wished to prolong her agonizing embarrassment for a single breath longer than absolutely necessary? Wasn't he the slightest bit discomforted at the idea of having to explain her presence to his lover?

"Noelle, this is Carina. Carina... Noelle." She had to hand it to him. He completed the awkward introductions with a casualness that was surreal. The two women exchanged glances; one echoing her host's amusement, Noelle's reflecting her desperation to escape.

"Why don't you come in and we can talk?"

"Talk?" She couldn't suppress the laughter that rose to her lips at Rafe's suggestion. Fortunately, she smothered it almost in time and it came out more like a slight cough, as if she was attempting to clear her throat. Rafe wasn't deceived. His eyes lit with renewed laughter, appreciating her appreciation of the ridiculousness of the situation they found themselves immersed in. She had to admire his nerve. How many men could handle with such unconcern a woman, who a week earlier he'd been attempting to talk into his bed, showing up on his doorstep and discovering his current lover all dishabille, answering his front door?

The former woman in the production being played out on Rafe's doorstep could only thank God she hadn't given in to the urge to sleep with him. Though Noelle supposed she should give credit where credit was due. She was under no illusions that the reason she hadn't succumbed to that temptation was more Rafe's doing than her own. Ironically, she found herself actually feeling grateful towards Rafe that she wasn't stumbling over that particularly, ungodly awful regret at the moment.

She was so busy feeling relieved she hadn't allowed herself to become one of the no doubt legions of lovers he took and discarded with what she was certain was depressing regularity, that it took her a minute to realize the man who could pass for a model of a Roman God in Caesar's palace, was waiting for her to accept his invitation. She raised an apologetic glance in his direction, thinking to offer a more heartfelt apology for disturbing him, but her words froze on her lips.

It was hard to describe the emotion lurking beneath the polite façade he was regarding her with. It wasn't quite anger. No anger would be understandable and forgivable given her unannounced intrusion. No, what she saw was so much worse. Anger at least implied some depth of feeling.

She decided the emotion she was having difficulty putting a name to was a mixture of curiosity at her motives for seeking him out without an invitation on his part, and a somewhat bored irritation at the inconvenience of having to deal with her in his home…in his private space. She had known he had no serious interest in her as a woman. She could only be grateful she'd avoided the massive mistake of falling in love with him, but she'd let herself believe they were on their way to becoming friends, to further cementing the bonds between their two families.

She had convinced herself that he regarded her with some fondness, but seeing the careless indifference in his glance made her realize the magnitude of the mistake she'd almost made, thinking maybe Rafe was the one she could confide the whole truth to…that maybe he would help her decide what to do next. She should be grateful she found out before it was too late. She should be thanking the almost too-perfect-to- be-real beautiful woman who stood regarding her with sympathetic kindness rather than a perfectly reasonable indignation at Noelle's interruption of her cozy *tete-a-tete* with her lover.

"Noelle?" She heard Rafe's voice, recognized the steel behind his polite insistence and in the grip on her arm, and knew she had to get it together if she was going to escape. She searched frantically to come up with a believable excuse for showing up the way she had.

She didn't bother tugging on her arm, knowing how stubborn he was and that he wasn't about to release her until he got the answers he wanted. She launched into another desperate apology, anything to just get away.

"No, no, let's not make this silly situation any more embarrassing than it already is. I'm sorry for showing up like this. I don't know what I was thinking." She couldn't resist the urge to tug a little on her arm, just to see if there was any give in his grasp, but wasn't really surprised to discover there was none.

"What were you thinking? I believe you owe me some explanation for what brought you here this morning."

It was hard to argue with Rafe when he was being reasonable, so she decided a little bit of truth would be the best way to satisfy his curiosity. "I wanted to ask your advice about something. It has to do with my grandmother (not a complete lie). I didn't know who else to turn to, (also not a complete lie, but she figured garnering a little sympathy by confessing how pathetically alone she was in the world would only serve her cause), but clearly now is not the time. (After all, they could hardly discuss family secrets in his lover's presence). So, maybe another time... or not. I shouldn't have come here. I don't know what I was thinking. I'm really sorry."

Rafe thought he could guess what was responsible for Noelle's unannounced visit, but he recognized the tears shimmering behind her pleading expression were real. He thrust an impatient, frustrated hand through his hair. "This isn't over," he warned her, growing even more impatient at the relief that leapt to her eyes at the evidence of his willingness to release her.

Noelle didn't wait to give Rafe a chance to change his mind. She merely nodded at his warning, pulled her arm from his slackened grip, and turned and ran, unconcerned about the pathetic picture her fleeing back gave rise to. Unwilling to risk waiting for the elevator, she found the exit door at the end of the hall leading off the foyer and dashed down the numerous flights of stairs, not pausing until she sat behind the wheel of the little sports car her grandmother had provided for her use while she was in France.

After a few moments, she gave up trying to fit the key into the ignition with her hands trembling so violently and instead leaned her head back against the seat. 'God, God what was she supposed to do now?' She forced her breathing to slow as she contemplated her options. They were pitifully few. Actually, they were one. She would have to confide in her grandmother. As reluctant as she was to drop her own fears in her grandmother's lap and risk the same reaction she received from her mother, Noelle accepted she had no other choice. She needed help. Her grandmother was in a position to offer it and Noelle acknowledged with a little twinge of guilt troubling her intent, that her grandmother loved her enough to do anything to help her.

Not that her mother didn't love her. Noelle recognized it was love for her that had driven her mother to shelter her daughter from whatever was happening to her. When it all started, she'd been an innocent child. Noelle realized she probably would have done the same thing in her mother's position. Taken her only child and run as far away as she could get from the source of any perceived threat to her daughter's wellbeing.

Not that there was any overt threat to her that Noelle could see. More likely if she went public with her story, the damage would be to her reputation and to her family's reputation. She could already hear the lamenting voices dancing around inside her head. 'What a shame the duke's daughter had turned out to be mentally unbalanced. The poor Duchess of Dominique was forced to suffer through one family tragedy after another and now this.' Deciding there was no other help for it, and recognizing she needed her grandmother's help, Noelle drew a steadying breath and with fresh resolve turned the key in the ignition.

A dozen stories above her, Rafe turned away from the wall of windows he'd watched Noelle's undignified retreat from and faced his long-time friend and lover, who understanding him better than any other living human being, had waited silently, not intruding on his thoughts, for him to return his focus to her. He detected no condemnation or rebuke in her glance at the events of the morning. A resentment that would not have been unreasonable considering how they'd spent the morning and that they'd been interrupted by a younger, beautiful ingénue like Noelle showing up on his doorstep when they had not yet had a chance to dress after those morning activities.

"My apologies. Obviously I was not expecting company this morning."

Carina lifted one shoulder in an elegant, philosophical shrug. "Not your usual type if I still know your tastes. A little younger and considerably more naïve than your normal preference."

"Noelle and I are not lovers. She is the granddaughter of Michel Dominique. My grandfather requested I keep an eye on her during her visit."

"Ah, that makes sense. Part of me thought she looked familiar. Now I realize it was her eyes. Noelle Dominique. I heard she had returned to France. Is she in the running to become the future Duchess of Lucien?"

Rafe's amusement at his lover's less than subtle tactic escaped in a harsh bark of laughter. "No, not that my grandfather has not hinted he wouldn't be opposed to his good friend's granddaughter in the role."

Carina nodded her understanding of everything he left unsaid, before assuring him, "You needn't feel guilty. She's not in love with you. Finding me here did not shatter her young heart."

Rafe's eyes probed her slightly amused ones, grateful to her for dispelling the worry before he'd even had a chance to give birth to it in his thoughts. "Then what the hell was she doing here?"

"I think she's in trouble and alone. I don't think she was lying about that, but I think the problem has less to do with her grandmother than it does her unwillingness to confide the source of what's troubling her to her grandmother."

Rafe considered and nodded his agreement, and felt both inexplicably guilty and understandably irritated at Noelle for having cast him in the role of her rescuer and problem solver. Because she had apparently already figured out, despite his reputation to the contrary, that he would do whatever he could to both rescue her from the source of her

64

troubles and solve whatever problem it was she was unwilling to go to her grandmother with. That it was a source of worry of seemingly insurmountable proportions in Noelle's mind, he had little doubt, because he was quite certain nothing short of an overwhelming burden would have driven Noelle to his doorstep this morning.

He suspected, whatever it was, it had something to do with the events at Mont Saint Michel twenty years earlier. He had a feeling Noelle had been less than completely forthcoming when she'd relayed the story to him. He very much feared the Archangel Michael was not done with her yet.

"Hell," he muttered beneath his breath, bringing an understanding chuckle to his lover's lips. "Sorry," he added with another hand thrust through his still damp hair. Then he turned aside from his half formed plans for the morning, none of which involved chasing after the naïve granddaughter of a close family friend, and unravelling whatever tangled web she'd knotted herself into.

CHAPTER THIRTEEN

"Noelle darling, Bernard informed me you'd gone out this morning. Did you go to Mass? I would have attended with you," her grandmother proclaimed when she saw Noelle standing somewhat hesitantly in the doorway of the morning salon.

Noelle blushed guiltily and admitted, "No, Meme. The opposite."

Her grandmother laughed at Noelle's dramatic response. "Well, that sounds interesting. I've never considered what the opposite of Mass might be and I'm very curious to learn what it is but there's no reason for the discomfort I sense such an admission brings you. Your relationship with the Almighty is none of my business, and don't think my own is in such wonderful shape that I would presume to judge anyone else's."

"Thanks for that, at least," Noelle replied before entering the room and joining her grandmother around the small table where she sat enjoying her morning croissant and espresso.

Her grandmother's amused grin only widened at Noelle's resigned expression of gratitude. "So now you've aroused my curiosity, don't leave me hanging, dear. I'm not trying to intrude, but I have to confess the direction of my speculations are probably much worse than the truth you are so obviously reluctant to confide in me."

"I wouldn't be too sure of that," Noelle protested, and then admitted with a sigh, "I was at Rafe's." The silence that greeted her admission had a fierce blush staining her cheeks. "It's not what you think."

"I'm not sure what I think," her grandmother admitted with a smile. "Not that I would be surprised if it was not exactly what you're implying. I am reasonably confident Rafe's enviable reputation with women is not without reason. Remember, I fell victim to the Lucien charm myself at your age."

Noelle helped herself to a croissant from the tray in the center of the table, broke off a piece, and placed it in her mouth. Not because she was hungry, but because she needed a minute to gather herself after her disastrous morning and to decide how much of it she was going to share with her grandmother. She heaved another audible sigh then abruptly launched into her rambling confession. "Oh, Meme, it was awful and so embarrassing. I went to Rafe's because I thought I could confide in him and ask for his help with this problem I had...not that I didn't know you would help me, but I didn't want to burden you."

"And Rafe was unwilling to help you with whatever this problem is you didn't want to burden me with? You surprise me."

"No, it wasn't that he was unwilling. I never really gave him the chance. I completely misread our relationship." At the renewed speculation in her grandmother's glance, Noelle added quickly, "No, no, I knew he wasn't interested in me in that way, well not seriously...but I thought we were at least friends... but I was so wrong. I misinterpreted everything. His grandfather asked Rafe to well, not be my friend, but to be friendly, right? To look after me while I was here? Did you ask him too?"

"No, Noelle dear, though I don't doubt your suspicion about Ari asking Rafe to keep an eye on you. The Lucien men are protective by nature. Ari would naturally take that responsibility even more seriously for my granddaughter, particularly as you have no father or brother or other male relative to assume that role in your life."

"Great, so Rafe was merely doing his grandfather a favor by showing any interest in me. Like I said, I misinterpreted everything. Which only makes me feel like an even bigger fool for seeking him out this morning."

Grinning at her dramatic confession, her grandmother prompted, "Don't leave me in suspense. Tell me what happened."

"Exactly what you no doubt suspect happened. I showed up on Rafe's doorstep only to have said door answered by some Italian bombshell in a loosely knotted silk robe that made it very clear how she and the owner of said door had spent the morning."

"Oh, dear. How embarrassing," her grandmother remarked sympathetically, trying unsuccessfully to hide the amusement dancing in her eyes.

"Totally mortifying, but I was the only one who seemed embarrassed. I tried to escape before confronting Rafe, but just as I was on the verge of doing so he flung his front door open wearing nothing but an inadequate towel."

Her grandmother gave in to the urge to laugh she'd valiantly suppressed up until Noelle's latest confession. She laughed so hard tears ran down her cheeks. It took her several moments to regain control over her amusement. Then becoming aware of Noelle's dejected expression, she swiftly apologized, "Oh, Noelle dear, I'm sorry. I hope you know I'm not laughing at you. But I can just picture you standing at the door and the look on your face, just like a scene out of a bad novel."

"Yes, that was exactly what it felt like, that I'd been cast in the role of the young ingénue discovering her worthless lover's infidelity in some predictable romance." Then she added swiftly before she planted any more seeds in her grandmother's fertile mind. "No, I never slept with Rafe." Then quickly added in a burst of honesty, "not that I wasn't tempted, which would have only made this morning so much worse."

"Perhaps, dear, but the experience itself would no doubt have had its own compensations for a few moments embarrassment."

"Meme!" Noelle exclaimed shocked, and then gave in to the urge to laugh. When she was able to speak again, she acknowledged, not without a little incipient regret, "Perhaps you're right, but that ship has sailed. I can't afford to indulge the time and energy in an affair with Rafe at the moment."

"Ah, I believe we're returning to the problem you went to speak to him about that you didn't want to burden me with."

"Yes."

"Are we by any chance referring to the events that took place twenty years ago at Mont Saint Michel?"

Noelle sighed. "Yes, how did you know?"

"I didn't of course, but I remember how upset your mother was over what happened that day and her refusal to allow you to return to France."

"I wasn't sure she told you about that day. I'm running out of time. I need to go back."

"Then I will accompany you. Chateau Dominique is not far from Mont Saint Michel."

Noelle stared nonplussed at her grandmother's beloved face. Just like that. She would go with her. No demands for explanations. No trying to dissuade her or to convince her it would be a mistake to return to the ancient monastery. Of course, she didn't know the full story. Noelle decided to wait on that confession until they were on their way. She turned her attention back to her grandmother. "Can we leave today?"

"Yes, now if you wish. I'll let Bernard know and then you can tell me the problem that sent you dashing off to Rafe's this morning. I hope, Noelle, you know there is nothing I wouldn't do for you, no problem I wouldn't help you resolve, or threat to you I wouldn't give my life to overcome."

At her grandmother's fierce declaration, Noelle popped up out of her chair and knelt in front of her grandmother's, clasping her frailer hands between her own. "Even though we've spent so much of our lives apart, I never doubted your love for me. Why do you think I reached out to you now and asked if I could come for a visit? I didn't want to drag you into any of this, but I knew you would help me. I knew I could trust you."

"You would have encountered more difficulty keeping me from anything that disturbs your peace of mind. Contrary to your conclusion you are dragging me anywhere, I'm so happy you trust me enough to finally confide in me."

Upset by her grandmother's conclusion she hadn't trusted her enough to confide in her earlier, Noelle opened her mouth on a protest only to close it again at her grandmother's dismissive gesture. Nodding, Noelle said simply, "Thank you." For the first time in a lifetime of fear, she felt a blessed relief from the terror that had been her constant companion since she was a little girl. "Give me ten minutes to pack."

Before Noelle had a chance to hurry out the door and up the wide center staircase to gather her things, she was greeted at the salon door by Bernard, informing her that M. Raphael Lucien was in the day salon and wished to speak with her.

At the older man's announcement, Noelle sighed and turned back to exchange a resigned glance with her grandmother. "You start packing; I'll catch up after I get rid of Rafe."

Laughing at Noelle's assumption the latter could be so easily achieved, her grandmother cautioned, "In my experience, dear, Lucien men are not so easily dispatched. They can be inconveniently stubborn at times."

"I know. I've already figured that out from personal experience," Noelle confirmed and pausing at the door to draw in a bracing breath, she straightened her shoulders and went out to face the devil's namesake, and possibly his descendant.

For a moment, she stood at the entrance to the day salon and stared at his back where Rafe stood near the window gazing out into the formal garden. As if sensing his solitude had been violated, he swung around and their eyes clashed momentarily. Noelle felt immediately the force of his compelling attraction.

She'd made such a fool of herself over Rafe, she acknowledged, not without a dent to her pride. She wasn't sure she could keep up with the extent of her misconceptions. It was all right now though, she told herself. As soon as this interview was over, they would be leaving for Chateau Dominique. There was really no reason for her to ever again be alone in Rafe's company. She just had to get through the next few minutes and then she would be free of this maddening impulse she felt to throw herself into his arms whenever their paths happened to cross.

'It was just a crush, Noelle', she silently assured herself. Perhaps, a juvenile, embarrassing crush but no harm done. She'd hadn't made the incredibly stupid mistake of falling in love with him. Certainly, she couldn't fault her tastes. No, her feminine instincts were working just fine, thank you very much.

Distracted by her musings, she missed the successive expressions passing through Rafe's eyes…curiosity, genuine concern, bemusement at his own susceptibility to her innocence, and then resigned amusement that the lovely granddaughter of his grandfather's closest friend would be the source of such consternation.

"Noelle. Why don't we have that talk now?" He suggested from where he remained near the windows.

She entered the room, barely, being careful to keep as much distance between them as possible. "Rafe, you didn't need to interrupt your…ah, morning to come chasing after me. I shouldn't have bothered you. I'm really sorry. I decided to speak with my grandmother, after all."

"So, it is as I suspected. Your appearance at my door this morning had something to do with the events that occurred at Mont Saint Michel when you were a child."

"Yes, though not about the events *per se*, more about whether you thought it was fair of me to burden my grandmother with them." She let out a brief laugh and added, "Funny. I didn't particularly worry about burdening you... a man I barely know. I guess it's because you seem so incredibly competent. I figured you could take care of my little problem without breaking a sweat, but that didn't give me the right to show up at your door on a whim. I'm really sorry."

"You have already apologized a dozen times. Once was sufficient. There's no reason to burden your grandmother if you are reluctant to share the truth with her. I'm happy to escort you back to Mont Saint Michel so that you might find the closure you seek."

"Thank you. That's a very generous offer, but my grandmother already knows about what happened that day. My mother apparently told her at some point. You'll be relieved to know we're leaving Paris this morning. We're going to stay at Chateau Dominique for a while so you won't have to worry about me showing up at your home unannounced again. Please convey my apologies to your friend. She seems very nice. Goodbye, Rafe."

After she delivered her little speech, Rafe just stood there staring at her with one autocratic brow raised, his piercing gaze probing hers. Noelle struggled to hold his glance, to show him she meant what she said, but she gave up after a moment or two and dropped her own to where her hands were clasped in front of her. She hadn't needed her grandmother's warning to know Rafe wouldn't be so easily dismissed.

He'd hurt her. He could see it in the bruised expression in her blue eyes and the way her voice quavered when she delivered her rehearsed little speech intent on getting rid of him. Carina had assured him Noelle wasn't in love with him, but clearly, he'd somehow managed to offend her. He just wasn't certain how. One thing was clear. Whatever perceived difficulty that had driven her to his door this morning, she no longer had any intention of confiding its contents to him. He suspected there was more to it than her desire to find closure from a trauma she had suffered as a young child.

He should be relieved. Noelle was leaving Paris. He would be rid of the source of the disruption to his peace of mind and in her absence, hopefully get over his near obsession with her, an obsession on his part she thankfully appeared completely oblivious of. He should just let it go. She was obviously hoping he would.

If it was only embarrassment prompting the barely concealed panic in her voice and in the glance she refused to raise to his, he would gladly do so, but the fear she was so desperately trying to hide from him made that impossible. He was a Lucien and it had been ingrained in him since birth never to abandon a damsel in distress. The fact that this particular distressed damsel was the granddaughter of one of his grandfather's closest friends made his retreat that much more impossible.

Sighing, his lips curving in amusement at the frantic look in Noelle's eyes when she finally gathered the courage to meet his resigned glance again, he suggested courteously, "Why don't we sit down and discuss this problem of yours?"

Noelle threaded her fingers through her hair and sent him a baffled look. "Did you hear anything I just said? I don't need your help anymore. Though I really appreciate your willingness to offer it, especially since we barely know each other."

When he just stood there staring at her and made no move to leave, Noelle abandoned her place near the door and strode across the room towards him. She met his dark eyes and confessed, "Trust me; you don't want to get in the middle of this. My life's a mess. I came here to straighten it out."

His eyes narrowed at her frank confession and she could see her pitiful admission was having the opposite of its intended effect. "Okay, that came out wrong, but rest assured I didn't return to France to take advantage of my grandmother's generosity, at least not financially."

Rafe's expression had grown from merely disapproving to one of near disgust. She was making a mess of things, and why she felt the need to explain herself to Rafe was a complete mystery to her. He strode purposefully across the room, closed the door, then returned to her side, grasped her hand in a less than gentle grip and led her, despite her half-hearted resistance, to the sofa, pulling her down beside him. "Start explaining."

One glance into his forbidding expression made Noelle realize she wasn't getting out of there without some sort of explanation. Since the truth would only re-inforce the dark conclusions she could see already circling through his thoughts, that she was trying to take advantage of her grandmother's loneliness and love for her, she wasn't certain where to begin.

"Noelle?"

She suppressed the urge to pour out the whole ridiculous story at his expensively shod feet. About how the visions hadn't stopped…about the events that had been occurring regularly on the anniversary of her visit twenty years ago…about the last catastrophic vision and Michael's insistence she return…about her terrified suspicion that even if she did everything he told her, it wouldn't prevent him from destroying Mont Saint Michel.

"I was only delaying the inevitable by coming to you for advice. I know what I have to do. It wasn't fair of me to drag you into any of this. We're leaving today. My grandmother will go with me back to Mont Saint Michel and it will be over. I'll be able to put my childhood trauma behind me and get on with my life." She held Rafe's searching glance for long, silent moments then almost fell off the sofa in relief when he merely nodded and stood from his place next to her.

"I believe you made the right decision to confide in your grandmother. I know she would do anything to assist you. I won't intrude further on your privacy."

Noelle ignored his little dig about intruding on her privacy the way she had so ignominiously intruded on his that morning. Releasing an inward sigh, she rose from the sofa. They were just inches apart, but he made no move to touch her. Instead, his glance searched hers for a long moment before he bent to whisper in her ear, his lips brushing her skin, "This still isn't over."

CHAPTER FOURTEEN

Bernard drove them. That left Noelle and her grandmother in the back of the luxurious car with plenty of time to talk and no distractions to disturb them. It wasn't until she settled into the seat in the rear of the limo next to her grandmother that she released the relieved sigh she'd been holding since she managed to escape Rafe's relentless questioning.

"Well dear, you don't look any worse for having done battle with the devil."

"He makes me nervous," Noelle admitted reluctantly.

"Hardly surprising. The Lucien men make most people nervous and they're not averse to pressing that advantage home whenever they feel the occasion warrants it."

"Well, that's a relief. I thought it was just me. Now that I think of it, Rafe does appear to have a lot of experience intimidating people to get them to do what they want."

At her grandmother's speculative look, Noelle added, "I didn't mean it that way. He just doesn't seem to have a lot of experience taking no for an answer." When her grandmother only raised one brow in query, Noelle shook her head, dismissing her understandable conclusion. "He knows about what happened that day twenty years ago at Mont Saint Michel. He thinks I imagined the Archangel Michael speaking to me. He told me I wasn't the first child to have an imaginary friend." When her grandmother failed to respond, Noelle turned and met her frank glance. "Did Mom tell you about that day?"

"Yes, but I wouldn't mind hearing your recollections if you still recall anything?"

Recall anything of that day? Noelle echoed silently in her mind. The events were indelibly imprinted on her memory. There'd never been a time when she could escape her memories, no matter how hard she tried. "I remember, but before I start, I just want to ask you a question first."

"Of course."

"Did you believe her? When she told you about what happened. Did you believe her?"

Noelle felt the warmth of her grandmother's hand close around her own now icy ones clasped together in her lap. "Yes, Noelle. I never for a moment doubted your mother's account of what happened that day."

"I think it scared my Mom. You know that's why she never let me come back, don't you? It wasn't anything to do with you."

"Yes, Noelle. I could have wished she trusted me more, but she was your mother and I had no right to interfere. I hope you understand that was the only reason I wasn't more insistent about you returning to France. Surely you know how much I missed you and how anxious I was to see you more often and be a larger part of your life."

Noelle moved to squeeze the hand grasping hers. "I know, Meme. Thank you for not forcing Mom. It wouldn't have made any difference. She was doing what she thought was best." She expelled a deep sigh and admitted, "Maybe it was for the best. I'm floundering now to deal with all of this. Certainly it was worse when I was younger, but at least I could pretend, or we could both pretend I was safe so far away from France."

"Tell me what happened that day," her grandmother urged.

"We were leaving. My Mom bought me a toy. It was a little replica of St. Michael, with wings. I was waiting near the exit; staring up at the statue... you know the one that's a replica of the fleche?" At her grandmother's confirming nod, she continued, "He spoke to me. First, I thought the statue was talking. You know as a kid, you don't instantly dismiss such a silly conclusion as impossible. Then I realized no one else seemed to notice he was speaking. That's when I realized his voice was inside my head. I was fascinated and excited. I drew closer. I remember standing there looking up at him. I didn't understand a lot of what he told me that day, but now I understand more...at least the meaning of the words he used....He said that the secular world had proven an unreliable steward. He wanted the French government to return Mont Saint Michel to the stewardship of the church." Noelle turned to meet her grandmother's shocked expression. "Of course back then with a child's understanding, it seemed to me a simple thing to do. Just give it back."

Her grandmother smiled at the innocence of her former self and squeezed her hand. Noelle continued, "He said that Mont Saint Michel was one of his dwelling places on earth and it was unacceptable to him for it to remain in the hands of the faithless." Noelle drew a deep breath and then added softly, "He said if they didn't give it back, he would destroy it."

"What?!"

Noelle nodded in response to her grandmother's stunned exclamation. "I think we're running out of time."

"Why do you say that?"

"Each year, on the anniversary of that day, something happens on Mont Saint Michel. I think the events were meant as warnings, but no one seems to be paying attention. Is it really possible I'm the only one who's connected the events on the anniversary to his warning that day?"

"I never noticed the timing," her grandmother's admission, muttered beneath her breath, shocked Noelle. Had her grandmother been keeping track of the events at Mont Saint Michel all this time? "I admit I wondered when I heard of some tragedy or another happening at the site, but I never put the dates together. You're saying these events, the flooding, the foundation shifting, even the plague-like infestations have all occurred on the anniversary of your visit that day?"

"Yes."

"You were so young. How did you possibly make the connection on the dates?"

"Because Michael warned me in advance what he was going to do. When I was still too young to understand what was happening, I would tell my Mom about his warnings. She became so upset. I didn't realize it was because when I told her something was going to happen in advance the events I warned her about actually did end up happening. She just kept trying to convince me to forget about that day. That it was just a child's imagination. After a few years, I stopped telling her. I knew I wasn't imagining things. When I was old enough I began doing my own research. I never told Mom. There was nothing she could do. She'd already tried taking me away- even moving us to the west coast, and the visions never stopped. I never stopped hearing his voice, or taking note of his warning. It came at the same time every year, a few months before the anniversary date."

"Oh Noelle, I wish you could have confided in me sooner. You must have felt so alone."

"I thought about reaching out to you, but then I realized that there wasn't anything you could do either. I mean it's not like the French government is simply going to hand over Mont Saint Michel to the Catholic Church."

"No, I don't see that happening."

"He's going to destroy it, Meme. And I don't think he's particularly concerned about how many lives are lost in the process. He's given man ample warning of his intentions." She fell silent, and then added the source of her greatest fear. "If people die, it will be my fault."

"Oh, no Noelle."

"But I haven't told anyone that Michael's the one behind all of the events at Mont Saint Michel since that day. They don't know it's not over. I don't know what to do. Even if I wanted to tell someone, I don't know who to confide in. No one will believe me. Certainly the government isn't about to just turn over Mont Saint Michel to the church or close off the island completely. They'll think I'm some kind of nut. I'm so sorry to dump all of this on you. I just don't know what to do. I need your advice. I need to know what to do."

CHAPTER FIFTEEN

She had finally returned. She didn't know what she was expecting when she finally answered his summons, a hallelujah chorus from the heavenly hosts, perhaps? But she never expected the occasion to be so ordinary, as if she and her grandmother were no different from their fellow tourists filing down the aisle to the bus exit, near the end of the bridge at the entrance to the site. Noelle drew a steadying breath as her eyes took in the magnificence that was Mont Saint Michel.

Once upon a time, the crowds of people walking along the paved bridge to the entrance to the monastery would not have come to gawk. In earlier centuries, Mont Saint Michel had been a place of pilgrimage for the faithful. They believed the site had been blessed by the Archangel Michael and that if they were faithful enough, if their prayers devoted enough, he would intervene on their behalf before God's high altar in heaven and grant them the intercession they sought. Their journey to the site would not have been on paved roads and via air-conditioned cars and buses. They would not have approached the site across concrete sidewalks complete with coffee and gift shops.

No, the travel would have been long and treacherous to the remote location. They would arrive by boat. They would have to be wary of the tides and travel with an experienced guide familiar with the tidal swings and the quicksand surrounding the island. To this day, the treacherous beaches would still occasionally swallow the imprudent traveler who thought to walk across the patch of sand revealed when the tides receded, despite the signs posted warning of the dangers of such an attempt.

Noelle turned her focus away from the imposing structure that dominated the skyline. Her eyes swept out to the water surrounding the island. In her mind's eye, she could envision the exhausted pilgrims as they finally arrived at the sacred site, their eyes wide with wonder at its magnificence rising up out of the water like some ancient beast of the sea set on consuming them.

Her lips curving in a reminiscent smile, she was unaware of her right hand reaching up to make the sign of the cross, and the whisper of a prayer that passed her lips that he would look kindly on her plea and grant her the miracle she sought. For nothing less than divine intervention would save her from their plans for her...marriage to a man old enough to be her father and one with a cruel streak she'd heard the servants whispering about after the betrothal was announced. She recognized it was not merely idle gossip on their parts when she saw the compassion reflected in their eyes when they chanced to meet her glance magnified in the fear her mother so desperately tried to hide from her whenever she spoke of her upcoming marriage.

Noelle had done her best to hide her terror from her mother. Funny, she had been Noelle then as well. What could her mother do after all to save her from her fate? She too had been bartered to her father in a business exchange between two powerful Norman families. Marriage vows might have been the currency of the transaction but everyone party to the exchange understood her mother had been sold to her father. She was no less his property, no less a slave to her new husband because her position was accompanied by a fancy title and expensive gowns.

Noelle had not bothered pleading with her father to set aside his carefully negotiated plans for her own marriage. She knew well her pleas would fall on deaf ears. So in a last desperate effort to escape her dreaded fate she had come to the ancient monastery, the one that was reputed to have been constructed after the Archangel Michael visited the bishop in his sleep and compelled him to build the prince of the legions of heaven a place of worship on the site.

Noelle finally turned away from the channel bay to face the imposing structure. It was not gentle in appearance. Nor did it call to mind the beauty of heaven awaiting the faithful when their earthly sojourn was complete. Instead, the structure had been built along masculine lines with its soaring towers and wide stone walls. It was as much a fortress as a place of devotion with little of the graceful lines and intricate detailing of the magnificent cathedrals of Rome she'd witnessed on her only visit there.

Noelle cared less about its appearance than she did the good will of its benefactor. She had no real notion as to how to go about procuring his good will. What did she know about the biblical Michael, after all? That he had defended heaven against the assault of his older brother, Lucifer? That he had astonishingly defeated his brother and succeeded in banishing him and his followers from heaven? Michael was known as the protector of the innocent.

At least she could still claim that particular virtue for the few remaining months prior to her marriage. She had no doubt her betrothed husband would live up to his reputation for cruelty when he took hers. Hadn't she seen the lust in his eyes when they swept over her? But it wasn't his masculine lust she feared, for wouldn't their union be blessed by the holy church? No, it was the speculation she saw in his gaze when his eyes fell upon her when he thought no one was watching him, as if he wondered just how far he could push the limits of her obedience without doing her any lasting harm.

At least until she produced the legitimate heir every lord in his position so desperately desired. She might even be spared the deepest brunt of his dark evil until she had given him a second son. Times were uncertain after all and there was no guarantee a son, no matter how well cared for and jealously guarded, would live to see adulthood. It was always best to have a contingency heir in place, just in case the world proved more inhospitable than the best laid plans accounted for.

Noelle felt the terror rise up inside of her until it all but choked off her ability to breathe. Most of the time she could hold it at bay. Most of the time she could manage to convince herself it wouldn't come to that. Surely, her father would not give his youngest daughter to an evil man. He must surely value her more than that. Was it possible he could be unaware of the rumors surrounding the baron....of the evil emanating from him? She couldn't delude herself that the latter was possible. If she an innocent, who had been sheltered her entire life from the brutal realities that existed outside the thick walls of her father's main seat was aware of the danger her future husband represented to her, how could her father be ignorant of it?

The last question brought tears to her eyes. For she suspected her father, despite his professed fondness for her, was aware of her betrothed's reputation and that he valued the benefits such a connection would bring to his esteem in the eyes of his peers more than he valued his daughter's life, or certainly, her happiness. There were times she hated him…not the baron, but her father. Wasn't it his duty to protect her? She swallowed her complaints before ever giving voice to them. She knew by now her mother would merely shake her head in wonder that Noelle had somehow managed to cling to her fairy tales and glossy illusions for so long.

Noelle lifted her glance to the very peak of the spires and then let her glance fall to the wall that opened up onto the upper levels. Even now she could see other pilgrims, some no doubt in as desperate circumstances as she was, looking out over the bay and pondering their options. How many helpless, desperate souls sought the Archangel's intercession in their bleak lives? And how many left this sacred place dejected after their long journey, their final hope dashed under the weight of the crushing blow of silence, the only response they no doubt received to their prayers?

Noelle prayed silently she would have the courage to carry out her plan if God's holy messenger failed her. It was a sinful prayer and one that would no doubt not be looked kindly upon by her maker. If his angelic servant failed her, she would not be returning to her father's estate to become a ritual sacrifice to satisfy his greed. She considered herself a dutiful daughter but if both her earthly father and her heavenly father's messenger failed her, she would take her chances in hell, the reputed domain of Michael's older brother, Lucifer. Which, according to church teachings, was the eternal destination of the damned soul who thwarted God's holy will by taking her own life.

"Noelle? Are you certain you want to go through with this?"

The familiar, feminine voice drew her from her deep well of … memories? Fantasies? With an effort, Noelle shook herself free of their clinging tendrils and turned in the direction of the voice. It took her a moment for her to put an identity to the older woman's concerned features. She had been expecting a different face, a different voice…one belonging to her companion from another life on a previous visit.

"Yes, Meme, I'm certain. I just needed a moment to gather my thoughts, but I'm ready now."

Her grandmother gave her hand a reassuring squeeze and together they turned towards the gates leading to the entrance and followed their fellow pilgrims…no…tourists, Noelle silently corrected herself. If Michael was to be believed there were too few pilgrims left in this world for him to even bother maintaining a home here.

They climbed the winding, and sometimes, steep path to the top of the monastery at their own meandering pace, stopping now and then to rest and to gaze in wonder at the magnificence of a structure that had been constructed more than a millennia earlier without the aid of large earth moving equipment and tools. How had men armed with little more than iron tools and shovels fashioned this monument that had stood against invading armies, fierce storms, and always, the relentless tides nipping at its foundations, as treacherous and cunning as the devil's sword had no doubt been in his contest with his brother.

But light had won that battle with evil an uncounted millennia earlier and its representative, in the form of the monastery, still stood as a witness to the eternal contest between good and evil. But apparently, the Archangel Michael, the embodiment of all that was light and good, was ready to abandon this holy place and destroy it rather than see the faithless profit from it.

They were near the top now and circling the garden where in earlier times the monks could sit in peace and solitude for meditation. It was a clear day and the sun shone brightly on the green grass, which struck Noelle as being out of place surrounded as it was by so much carved stone and thick columns. When they climbed the final stairs to the level of the terrace open to the sky Noelle turned an apologetic look in her grandmother's direction and motioned in the direction across the stone to the opening in the wall where she could look out over the waters below. Her grandmother squeezed her hand again and indicated she would sit on one of the benches. "Take your time, Noelle. I know this must be incredibly difficult for you."

Noelle shook her head. "Not difficult so much as disorienting. It's as if everything else but this place is fading away and no longer has the slightest claim on me."

Noelle was aware of the look of concern that entered her grandmother's eyes at her odd claim, but she ignored it as she turned and crossed the distance to the outer walls. The sea was calling her. She could hear the echo of the gulls' cries and watched them circling overhead. There was no crash of waves against the structure. They were in the bay and therefore spared the full force of the ocean. The water surrounding them was gentle. She noticed it barely lapped against the walls beneath her as she reached an opening in the stone and gazed downward.

She wondered if her former self had taken that deadly leap into the release only death could offer her, or if her prayers had been answered that fateful day. Maybe that's why she was chosen for whatever this was. Perhaps her former self owed a debt to the benefactor of this place for rescuing her from a fate she had decided in her previous innocence would be worse than the eternal flames of hell.

"There is as of yet no evil in this world to compare to the agonies of my brother's domain. The darkness in men's hearts can at worst threaten only the physical shell a spirit occupies in this world. My brother's power is infinitely greater and poses a much darker threat to a man's soul."

"Did you save me that day?"

"Does it matter now?" He challenged.

Noelle released a deep sigh and acknowledged, "I suppose not."

Silence fell between them; one Noelle was no longer tempted to break. Instead, she turned to stare out at the horizon, likely from the very spot she had taken the same stance centuries earlier, but this time she couldn't help but wonder if the shoe was on the other foot, so to speak. This time she thought maybe Michael had a request to make of her.

"There is the small matter of a debt to be settled between us." At Noelle's startled reaction, he added, "And I do not refer only to the request you made of me that day."

Somehow, Noelle wasn't surprised to discover she was beholden to Michael. She wondered how many times he had come to her aid in the past. In how many lifetimes had she visited this sacred place and begged for his intercession? No wonder she was so drawn to it. Even now, she was aware of a growing reluctance to return to the life waiting for her outside the shelter of its protective embrace.

"It wouldn't prevent what is coming. They would find you. Staying here would only make it easier for them to do so and hasten the coming devastation."

"I don't understand," Noelle protested.

"You understand enough. Why did you delay?"

She didn't pretend not to understand what he was asking her. "I was afraid."

"Are you less afraid now?"

She ignored the mockery he couldn't quite disguise in his blunt question and admitted with a sigh. "No."

"That at least gives me hope. Your delay in returning, in taking your place as your father's heir, has only made you more vulnerable to those who destroyed him. Your father's death delayed them as he knew it would, but you have failed to take advantage of the time his sacrifice purchased for you."

Stunned by his disclosure, Noelle couldn't help but lift her head and look frantically around for the source of the voice she understood only she could hear, even knowing there was nothing for her to see but other tourists who had been drawn to the site that day. Tears filled her eyes. "What are you saying?" She screamed inside her head. "What does my father have to do with any of this?"

"You would do better to ask your grandmother for that explanation."

Noelle didn't think she could stand any more revelations. She felt confused and betrayed by the one person she hoped could help her. For long moments, she stared unseeing at the sea beneath her, at the little island only a hundred yards or so away, fronting the monastery, that had housed the English forces intent on conquering Mont Saint Michel. The monks and the resident knights had incredulously held off the determined assault of the English. She wondered idly if Michael had had a hand in that. She thought he would not take kindly to enemy forces lobbing cannon balls at his precious home.

Her gaze was vacant when she turned in response to her grandmother's concerned greeting. Seeing her white face, and fearing what had precipitated it; her grandmother reached for her hand and led Noelle away from the wall.

"Noelle?"

Noelle met her grandmother's anxious expression and shook her head. In denial of the questions she saw behind the concern in her grandmother's eyes, or of her own devastating suspicion that her grandmother had betrayed her, she couldn't be certain which. She only knew she had to leave this place now. The odd sense of welcome she'd felt earlier accompanied by the strange urge to remain in the monastery forever had been supplanted by an urgent need to escape its isolated confines. They would find her. On the isolated isle, there would be no place for her to hide. She had to get away before they knew she was here.

Noelle raised her glance to meet her grandmother's. Was it possible the love and concern reflected in them was all an act? No, Noelle refused to believe that. Hadn't Michael told her she would be better off asking her grandmother for an explanation? The secret that her grandmother had likely hoped by maintaining her silence would protect her son's only child?

Was it possible her father hadn't died in an accident? Did Michael really imply her father had been a part of this…whatever this was…and that he had been murdered or sacrificed himself, in order to buy her time? Buy her time for what? To grow up?

Did her grandmother know what her son had done? Was she aware he was part of the events unfolding at Mont Saint Michel? Noelle suspected not. If she had known, surely she would have confided in Noelle's mother. Or maybe she had. Maybe that's why her mother was so adamant about keeping Noelle away from France. It helped to explain her mother's rather over-the-top reaction to an incident that most people would have, like Rafe, put down to a child's imagination.

Or maybe it wasn't her grandmother who'd confided the truth to her mother. Maybe Noelle's father had said something to her before he died so suddenly. Maybe something to the effect that if anything strange happened at Mont Saint Michel she should take their daughter and run as fast and as far away as she could get. But, if Noelle's father really had confided in her mother, why would her mother have brought Noelle to the site that day? It didn't make sense. None of it made any sense. Maybe she really was just imagining things.

Realizing her grandmother was regarding her with increasing concern; Noelle clasped her hand and said, "We have to talk. Not here. We need to go. It's not safe here."

"What do you mean it's not safe here?"

Noelle didn't respond to her grandmother's stunned challenge. "Not here, Meme. We need to leave now. I'll tell you what he said when we get back to Chateau Dominique."

Visibly gathering herself, her grandmother nodded and allowed Noelle to lead her back down the steep descent to the exit. Noelle paused a moment as they exited the gift shop in front of the shining statue of the Archangel Michael, his sword held aloft. She met his empty gaze as it stared out at the trespassers of his domain, but no words of his formed inside her head. She guessed he'd already delivered his message.

Aware of her grandmother's tense stance at her side, Noelle turned to meet her questioning glance, shook her head in denial of her unspoken questions and then led her over the uneven pavement towards the exit. They passed shops and cafés along their descent, but Noelle was not inclined to linger. Realizing belatedly her grandmother would likely welcome a chance to rest, Noelle turned to her, an apology forming on her lips.

As if reading her thoughts, her grandmother shook her head. "No, Noelle, let us leave this place. I am very anxious to hear what Michael told you and you were correct when you said such a conversation should not take place in public, even beneath his watchful eyes."

CHAPTER SIXTEEN

Chateau Dominique rose out of the flat coastal landscape near the walled city of St. Malo in Brittany overlooking the English Channel and stood unapologetic in all of its Renaissance glory recalling that majestic period in French history. In such times a nobleman's residence was built as much to serve as a defensive fortress as an elegant residence, hence the evidence of the thick stone wall and now empty moat that once surrounded the grand structure with its cross layout and soaring cylindrical towers at the corners. The chateau had been a country estate of a Norman noble at its birth and had stood for centuries both dominating and surveying the now serene landscape surrounding it.

There was a large staff in residence to maintain the nearly two hundred-room structure, and an additional separate staff to maintain the acres of formal gardens surrounding the chateau. The vineyard was attached to the estate, her grandfather's love, but it was set some distance from the chateau.

Though it was a beautiful day, her grandmother led her into her private office rather than the open-air terrace overlooking the formal gardens. Noelle understood her grandmother's choice of venue for the discussion they were about to engage in was motivated by her desire for privacy. She didn't want to risk their conversation being overheard.

They waited in silence until her grandmother's housekeeper delivered the requested tea and lunch. When the older woman left them alone, Noelle reached for a plate and filled it with a selection of offerings from the tray between them, largely to give her hands something to do. She realized her grandmother was no more anxious to break the silence that had fallen between them on the long ride to the estate than she was. Or perhaps it was more a case of neither knowing where to begin. Noelle had used the time afforded her along the drive back to the chateau to compose herself and to decide what she was and was not willing to share with her grandmother.

She had already made the decision to leave out Michael's claim that her father may have been killed because of his involvement in whatever was going on at Mont Saint Michel. She would not distress her grandmother in such a cruel way without any discernible proof to back up Michael's fantastic claim. Even if her father had been murdered for whatever his part had been in all of this, there was nothing to be gained now by such a revelation. Besides, if her father had truly died attempting to protect her, wouldn't he have left something, some note, some record to guide her on her way?

She had come into her inheritance from her father at the age of twenty-one. There had been no personal legacy attached to the legal and financial documents she was required to sign to take control of the trust he left her. No, Noelle was forced to conclude that even if it had been her father's intention to explain his part in whatever was going on at Mont Saint Michel, he never had the chance. Whether his death was a result of an accident or murder, it had apparently happened so suddenly, he didn't have the opportunity to pass along anything to help her resolve her current impasse.

"Noelle?"

She turned at her grandmother's gentle probing and with a slight smile accepted the teacup her grandmother was holding out to her. She took a small sip then placed the fragile cup into the saucer provided.

"You should try and eat something," her grandmother urged in the same gentle voice, as if she feared startling her. She motioned to the tea sandwiches and cheese and fruit Noelle had filled her plate with but had made no move to place in her mouth.

Noelle concluded she must appear as fragile as the fine porcelain teacup sitting between them. Her grandmother seemed intent on treating her with equal care. As much to prove to herself as her grandmother that she was not about to shatter at the first sign of trouble, she selected a cucumber and goat cheese sandwich from her plate and raised it to her mouth. The heavy silence continued between them for the duration of their midday meal. At its conclusion, it was Noelle who abruptly broke it.

"He asked why I had waited so long to come back, that my delay had only made things worse."

"Made what things worse?" Her grandmother zeroed in on her rather evasive description.

Noelle shrugged. "I don't know."

"Perhaps your mother was right. Perhaps the best thing for you to do is to leave France and never return."

Noelle raised her shocked glance to her grandmother's concerned expression. Concern for her, no matter the cost to herself. All doubts of her grandmother having kept secrets from her, of having betrayed her, were washed away by the tears filming her eyes. Noelle reached across the distance of the small table between them to clasp one of her grandmother's frail hands. "No. I can't spend the rest of my life running and I won't let fear keep me, keep us, from having the relationship we deserve."

"Just promise me you'll let this go at the first sign of danger," her grandmother pleaded with her, squeezing the hand holding hers. "I can't lose you, too."

CHAPTER SEVENTEEN

Rafe stood across the stone floor on the highest level of the ancient abbey and watched Noelle. Telling himself he was behaving like some lovesick idiot, he had nevertheless succumbed to the urging of his usually reliable instincts and followed her to St. Malo. When he'd arrived at the duchess' doorstep earlier that morning, thinking to corner Noelle into finally providing the answers he sought, the duchess confided that Noelle had returned to Mont Saint Michel that morning and had insisted on visiting alone. Rafe saw his own concern for his elusive quarry reflected in her grandmother's eyes.

"What's going on?" He'd demanded, hoping the duchess would be more forthcoming and less suspicious than her granddaughter.

"I don't know. I don't think Noelle knows either, but I'm worried about her...about her being there alone." Their eyes had met and held. Rafe guessed the older woman knew more than she was willing to admit to him, but there was no disguising the anxiety in her expression. An anxiety she made no effort to hide from him.

"I am going to catch up with Noelle, and when I do, I am going to get some answers out of her."

Rather than be alarmed at his less than subtle threat, the duchess seemed relieved. He wasn't certain how he felt about that. If she knew more about the situation Noelle was tangled up in than he did, and that knowledge was responsible for the near panic he'd read in her expression when she answered her own door upon his arrival, it meant his own feelings of unease were not without reason. He turned his focus now to the object of that unease.

Noelle stood staring out between the parapets facing the sea. He couldn't detect any sign of her angelic confidant, but he did not fail to notice the very visible presence of the uniformed gendarmes standing nearby. Their positions near Noelle, while seemingly keeping a watch out for any suspicious activity, almost gave the impression that they were deliberately flanking her. He dismissed his foolish conclusion, deciding it was likely the recent spike in terrorist activity that was responsible for the visible military presence, when he couldn't recall ever seeing soldiers at the site before.

Just when he'd decided he'd waited long enough for his answers and would have approached Noelle, the two gendarmes, as if by some pre-arranged signal between them turned to each other and then together approached her, cutting her off from his line of vision.

Noelle was lost in her thoughts. She was no closer to unravelling the mystery she'd stumbled into than she'd been twenty years earlier when she was a little girl. She wished Michael would just tell her what he wanted her to do, so she could do it and get whatever it was over with. It was for this reason she'd insisted on returning to the site alone that morning, despite her grandmother's objections and the very real panic she could see in her expression at the thought. Unfortunately, Michael did not appear inclined to fall in line with her plan. He had been oddly silent this visit.

"*Pardon Mademoiselle*, you must come with us now."

Puzzled, assuming the masculine voice must be addressing someone else, she turned away from her contemplation of the scenery spread out before her and looked into the faces of the two uniformed men standing in front of her. They were positioned, whether deliberately or coincidentally, to block her escape. A chill ran up her spine at the sight of the menacing weapons they wore slung over their shoulders.

"I'm sorry, were you speaking to me?" She confirmed confused, aware of the adrenaline spiking through her system as her fear coalesced into an icy knot in the pit of her stomach.

"Yes, *Mademoiselle*, please come this way." One of the men reached for her arm. Noelle's initial confusion and unease immediately turned to terror.

"RUN!!"

The command, when it came, ringing inside her head after his extended absence, shocked her more than the presence of the two armed men demanding she accompany them. But there was no hesitation on

94

her part. She responded instantly to his command. Fortunately, her sudden movement freed her arm from the one man's grasp and she took off at a run, ignoring their forceful command to halt.

She fled towards the exit, with the two guards in hot pursuit. Rafe inexplicably appeared at her side. He took one look at her terrified expression, and darting a quick glance over her shoulder at her pursuers, grasped her hand and carved a way through the throng of shocked tourists towards the exit. Down the ramps, the stone steps, through the sometimes-narrow passageways they fled. When Noelle stumbled and would have fallen, Rafe dragged her back to her feet, barely breaking stride.

They gained ground on their pursuers in the narrow descent lined by gift shops and cafes. The street was crowded with tourists. Rafe never broke stride. He shouted a warning and the sea of flesh parted for them to pass through and then quickly closed again, forcing the two men following them, still several strides behind, to force their own way through the gawking crowds.

When the street opened up at the main entrance, Noelle risked a glance behind her. She could see the two uniformed men, but they were twenty or so feet behind them now. Rafe all but threw her on the back of a convenient scooter, turned the key and roared off over the bridge to the main part of town where they'd left their cars. Since the noise of their borrowed vehicle precluded any conversation between them, Noelle merely wrapped her arms around Rafe's waist and hung on for dear life.

They ditched the scooter at the entrance to the parking lot when it became apparent they'd lost their pursuers, but Rafe wasn't taking any chances. He pulled her along to where his Maserati was parked, all but tossed her into the front seat and set off at a furious pace, weaving through the parking exit and then gave the powerful engine its head as they took off up the straightaway.

She saw Rafe glance in the rear-view mirror more than once to be certain no one was following them, but even so, he never slowed his pace until they passed through a set of large iron gates that swung open magically, it seemed to Noelle upon their arrival, and then swung shut again after they'd passed through. Noelle was wondering where the tree lined drive was leading them, when she caught a glimpse of the huge Chateau coming into view. She gasped audibly at the sight. If Chateau Dominique was one of the last remaining remnants of the glorious Louis XIV period in France's long history than this home must surely be a national monument every bit as treasured as Notre Dame and Mont Saint Michel. Why would Rafe bring her here? Wouldn't the men pursuing them find them more easily at another tourist destination? Perhaps he thought to lose them in the presumed crowds. Funny though, she didn't see any tourists or any signs indicating where they were.

She turned to Rafe seeking an explanation at the same time he pulled the car to a stop at the front of the imposing main entrance. Noelle could feel the waves of tension rolling off of him. She had been so relieved at the sight of him earlier it hadn't occurred to her until now to wonder what he was doing at Mont Saint Michel that morning and how he'd managed to find her amidst the throngs. She presumed it was a safe bet his presence there wasn't a coincidence. When she opened her mouth to ask him why he had followed her, the burning fury in his expression made her think better of the idea and she closed her lips again.

She'd never seen Rafe in such a rage. Usually he tended to regard her with all the familiarity and mild irritation he might use to interact with a young niece or cousin. Of course, that was when he wasn't flirting with her or throwing outrageous compliments in her direction or interrogating her about her motives for returning to France. Right now though, there was no mistaking his mood. He appeared to be having trouble keeping his hands from wrapping around her throat and shaking some sense into her.

Noelle concluded it would be best to let him calm down a little before she starting pestering him with the questions piling up inside her head. Questions about what he was doing at Mont Saint Michel that day, who were those two men who had accosted her, where were they intent on taking her, and where, by the way were they? What were they doing in this magnificent setting? Why hadn't he taken her back to Chateau Dominique? Her grandmother would be worried if she didn't return soon.

"No more evasions. No more half-truths. You are going to tell me exactly what is going on. I want to know who those men were and what they wanted with you."

Apparently, Rafe had his own questions he wanted answers to. Noelle thought she would do well to placate him with a few answers, at least until he calmed down a little. "I don't know who they were and what they wanted. I thought they were with the police."

"If you believed they were with the police, then why did you run?"

In retrospect, it was a reasonable question. Noelle, hesitated, not sure if she should tell him the truth and then decided he deserved it, for his part in rescuing her. "He told me to."

"Who told you to?"

"Michael. As soon as that man grabbed my arm, he told me to run. I wasn't taking any chances. I ran."

Rafe's still red-hot glance searched hers and then he thrust a hand through his hair in a visible gesture of frustration. "Michael told you to run." He echoed his disbelief just on the edge of mockery.

Noelle sighed. "I know you don't believe me. I really appreciate your help back there, but I should probably be getting back to Chateau Dominique. I don't want my grandmother to worry. Where are we by the way?"

Before Rafe had a chance to answer her question, the front door of the magnificent chateau was flung open and the Lucien patriarch approached where they sat arguing in his driveway. "Raphael, was I expecting you? Ah, Noelle, what a charming surprise. Are the two of you going to sit in the car all afternoon? Won't you come in?"

"M. Lucien…" Noelle began when it was obvious Rafe was in no hurry to explain their presence to his grandfather. Then her hastily summoned greeting trailed off for lack of inspiration as to how she could possibly explain her uninvited presence at his home. She seemed to be making a habit of showing up uninvited at the home of one Lucien male or another. She turned an accusing glare in Rafe's direction for putting her in this position.

Rafe merely shrugged in response and turned to answer his grandfather's curiosity. "Forgive us, *Grandpere'* for showing up unannounced. Noelle has stumbled into some sort of trouble and was accosted by two armed gendarmes at Mont Saint Michel. I thought it would be best to bring her here until we could unravel this mess."

At Noelle's outraged gasp, Ari turned his shocked eyes from his grandson to her. Noelle blushed profusely at the forbidding expression on his face. "It's not what you think…" she protested, then turned back to Rafe. "Say something. Your grandfather thinks I'm some sort of thief or worse."

"What *would* you like me to tell him?" Rafe demanded, no longer attempting to disguise his sarcasm.

Losing patience with their exchange, Ari Lucien waved his hand in a dismissive gesture and commanded, "Enough. Let us at least move this discussion inside. You were right to bring Noelle here, Raphael. There is no point in upsetting Michel over this minor inconvenience."

"Of course," Rafe agreed, turning a triumphant glance in Noelle's direction.

Accepting there was no escape, Noelle sent Rafe another fuming glance, and then climbed out of his car with as much grace as she could muster under the circumstances, uncomfortably aware of his grandfather's disapproving glance following her every move. "It's not what you think," she whispered as she passed by him on her way to his impressive doorstep.

"I will reserve judgment until I hear the whole story. Let us go inside and be more comfortable and you may explain why armed gendarmes would attempt to accost you."

Sighing, resigned to another confession she was quite certain the Lucien patriarch wouldn't believe, she followed Rafe through the door. She took a moment to be awed by the entrance foyer decorated with priceless antiques from the Renaissance and the Louis the XIV era. Then couldn't help but notice, what she was quite certain were original works of art from some of the most famous artists of their day. Pushing aside her distraction, she sighed and meekly followed Rafe into a purely masculine domain along one of the halls leading off the entry. A domain, she presumed was his grandfather's personal office.

"Sit, please," Ari commanded as Noelle hovered uncertainly in the doorway, unintentionally blocking his own entry.

"Madame Blanc," the older man called to someone out of Noelle's line of sight. "Refreshments, please, for our guests."

Noelle turned to protest the idea of refreshments, but at the look in Ariel Lucien's eyes, she swallowed her words. This wasn't exactly a social call. Besides, she thought she might choke if she tried to put anything in her mouth. Yet that didn't prevent her from obeying Rafe's rather sharp demand, a few minutes later when he pushed a wine goblet into her hand and ordered her to drink it, pointing out with little noticeable concern that she was as white as a ghost.

"Not surprising, I suppose, under the circumstances," he tacked on, a glimmer of a smile lifting the corners of his lips.

"Ha. Ha," Noelle countered before taking a healthy swallow of the truly delicious wine.

"Let us not become sidetracked with the squabbling again," Ari interrupted the start-up of renewed hostilities between her and Rafe, before adding with a speculative glance at them both, "I didn't realize the two of you were on such familiar terms."

Noelle blushed at his implication, took another sip of wine, but wisely kept her mouth closed. Let Rafe deal with his grandfather. She couldn't imagine with their two strong personalities clashing against each other over the course of their lives that they hadn't engaged in their own squabbles from time to time. More likely, she concluded at the rising tension in the room, their contests of wills were in the form of knockdown, drag-out battles to near death.

After an extended silence, that neither Noelle nor Rafe made any effort to fill, Ari Lucien persisted dryly, "Is someone going to tell me what is going on?"

"Noelle?" Rafe suggested.

"Why don't you explain?" Noelle suggested in response. She was getting a little tired of telling people about her experiences with Michael and seeing that look come into their eyes.

"I would gladly do so, but I'm not certain what exactly it is you wish me to explain."

Noelle caught onto his teasing, refused to rise to the bait and remained stubbornly silent as the weight of Ari Lucien's growing impatience hung heavily around her.

"Raphael. Explain." His grandfather's order settled in her favor the outcome of their little standoff.

"As you wish. Noelle's mother kept her away from France for the past twenty years because of an incident that occurred at Mont Saint Michel when she was a child."

"Yes, I'm aware of that. Michel was of course devastated by her daughter-in-law's decision to keep her only granddaughter from returning to France, but she respected her right to do so. What does that have to do with Noelle being accosted by two armed gendarmes today?"

"You knew?" Noelle asked, exchanging an astonished glance with Rafe.

"Yes, of course. Michel called me that day when your mother returned to Chateau Dominique in a panic and insisted on leaving France immediately and taking you with her. Of course Michel had no way of knowing your mother would use the childish incident as an excuse to keep you from returning to France forever."

Noelle was aware of the simmering anger in Rafe's grandfather's accusation and felt compelled to defend her mother. "It wasn't only that day."

"What?!" Rafe demanded.

His grandfather waved off his grandson's astonishment. "Explain."

Sighing, threading her fingers through her long hair in a nervous gesture, she asked quietly, "Haven't you noticed the signs? The events that have been occurring almost annually at Mont Saint Michel since that day?"

"What signs? What are you talking about?" Rafe interjected again, further irritating his grandfather.

"Let us allow Noelle to tell her story in her own way, without interruption," Ari rebuked.

"Do you remember about twenty years ago, actually, it was nineteen, the fire that occurred at Mont Saint Michel? The one that caused the site to be closed to visitors for several weeks?"

"Vaguely. What does that have to do with any of this?" Ari demanded.

"The fire occurred on the anniversary of my visit the previous year. Michael told me there was going to be a fire that day. I told my mother.

100

She told me I was imagining things. Later that same week she took me to see a child therapist. What I didn't learn until I was old enough to do my own research was that there was a fire at Mont Saint Michel on the anniversary of my visit that year, just as Michael told me there would be."

Noelle saw Ari and Rafe exchange uncomfortable, disbelieving glances over her head. "You didn't tell me that part," Rafe chastised her.

"No, I never told anyone. After the first few years, I stopped even telling my mother. She never asked. When something happened at Mont Saint Michel on the anniversary of our visit, she never asked if Michael had told me about it in advance. She obviously hoped that I'd forgotten all about it... that Dr. Adams had done her job and turned me back into a normal little girl again. I guess we both pretended for the other's sake. That was why my mother wouldn't allow me to return to France. We even moved away from the townhome in Washington, D.C. where we were living when my father died. I guess she hoped if we moved across the country and put another three thousand miles between me and France, they would stop."

"You mean she hoped your visions would stop?" Rafe clarified, his glance holding hers.

Noelle dropped her glance beneath his probing one and admitted softly, "That too, but I think what she was really hoping was that the incidents would stop."

"But they didn't?"

"No, sometimes he would skip a year or even two and I would let myself believe that it was over, that he'd given up on trying to get me to come back...and maybe even that he'd changed his mind about his plans for Mont Saint Michel. Then it would happen again and he would remind me that time was growing short...that I was no longer a little girl. The year I turned eighteen and was no longer legally under my mother's direction was the year the scaffolding collapsed killing those people. The year after I turned twenty-one and gained access to my trust fund from my father, was the year the super tide occurred washing out the new bridge. It was my fault. If I'd returned to Mont Saint Michel when he insisted, those people would still be alive."

"Don't be ridiculous, Noelle. You cannot possibly blame yourself for a construction accident at the site," Rafe protested, incredulous at her claim of being responsible for the deaths of those people.

"It wasn't an accident. He was angry with me for defying him. Most people look forward to the advent of summer. I can't remember ever feeling anything but dread at its approach."

"Does Michel know any of this?" Rafe's grandfather demanded.

"I explained some of it the day we left Paris for Mont Saint Michel. She agreed to accompany me back to the site. He told me my delay in returning had only made matters worse. I didn't tell her the rest," she added, unaware of the tears filling her eyes and spilling down her cheeks. "I couldn't tell her the rest."

"What is the rest?" It was Ari Lucien who demanded the entire truth. She supposed Rafe was still reeling from what she'd confessed so far.

She raised her eyes to the older man's, unaware of the devastation reflected in her bruised glance. "He said I had wasted the time my father's sacrifice had purchased for me. Something about being his heir…I can't remember exactly what he said. I was too stunned by his implication that my father had been involved in all of this and that his death may not have been an accident. When I asked him what he was talking about, he suggested I should go to my grandmother for an explanation, but I couldn't. I couldn't add to her pain…not without some proof that my father's death was anything but the accident everyone believed it was. I can't drag her any deeper into this. Not if there's a chance my father was killed because of it."

Silence fell heavily between them. Each busied themselves with their own thoughts. Noelle couldn't tell what her companions were thinking. At this point, she was too empty inside to worry overly much if they came to the understandable conclusion that she was dangerously deranged. Maybe if they saw to it she was locked up somewhere, Michael would find someone else to carry out whatever task he obviously expected her to see to.

After long minutes, Ari sighed audibly and stood from his place behind his antique hardwood desk. He walked across the room, pressed a button concealed beneath the painting of a man, who from the way he

102

was dressed and his resemblance to the two men in the room, Noelle concluded was an ancestor of theirs, and revealed the hidden wall safe. Noelle turned to Rafe with a questioning, troubled look. He merely shrugged in response, as if suggesting she should wait to see what his grandfather was planning rather than locking onto one of the fantastic conclusions that were running through her thoughts.

The older man retrieved a legal sized padded envelope from the safe before closing the heavy door, resetting the lock, and concealing the hidden safe once more behind the painting. He turned back to them, and then crossed the room, coming to a stop in front of Noelle. He stood there regarding her with a serious expression before he explained what he held in his hand.

"This envelope was given to me by your father's attorney a year to the day after his death. It was accompanied by a note written in your father's hand asking that I pass it along to you when you gained your twenty first birthday."

"But I'm twenty four," Noelle reminded him in a barely audible whisper.

"I know. I didn't think you were worthy of whatever legacy your father had entrusted to me if you couldn't even bother to return to France to visit your grandmother. I was wrong. You've been trying to protect her all these years."

Tears in her eyes, Noelle shook her head, denying his conclusion. "I'm not sure if I was trying to protect her or if I understood all along there was nothing she could do to resolve Michael's demands. Knowing that, it would have been selfish on my part to burden her with any of this. After all, it wasn't like even the Duchess of Dominique would be able to convince the French government to return Mont Saint Michel to the stewardship of the Catholic Church."

"What are you saying?" Arial Lucien asked.

"Oh, did I leave that part out? Twenty years ago, Michael told me that they had to give it back. He said the secular world had proven an unreliable steward and that he would destroy Mont Saint Michel rather than allow it to remain in the hands of the faithless."

"You believe him," Rafe remarked.

"Yes. I think we've run out of time. The anniversary of my first visit is only weeks away. Michael showed me what he was going to do. I'm no artist, but I drew a picture of it. That's what finally convinced me to return. He's not fooling around anymore. He's going to destroy Mont Saint Michel and I have no idea how to stop him."

An even heavier silence descended on the occupants of the room after Noelle finally revealed the full extent of Michael's threats. "I should go. My grandmother will be getting worried. She wasn't happy when I insisted on going back to the site alone today."

When she would have risen from her chair, Ari gently pushed her back down into it. "I will call your grandmother and inform her that Raphael brought you for a visit and that the two of you are staying for dinner." At Noelle's anxious expression, he added, "And no, I will not tell her about your father's legacy or Michael's implication that his death might not have been an accident. You are not alone anymore, Noelle," he assured her gently, then gesturing to the envelope Noelle had almost forgotten about, he added, "Why don't we see what your father has to say about all of this?"

Noelle looked down at the legacy he referred to she was holding clasped between her trembling hands. "Thank you, but you don't have to do this."

"Do you have some objection to our assistance?" He asked, one autocratic brow raised over his piercing dark eyes.

"No, no of course not," she rushed to assure him. "I'm really grateful for it. Do you actually believe me?" She tacked on incredulously.

When the older man merely responded with, "Why don't we see what your father has to say?" Noelle guessed she had her answer.

Nodding, dejected, she turned the envelope over in her hand. Seeing it was sealed closed, she tore open the seal and looked with some trepidation at the contents. Inside was a small box, large enough to hold a ring or earrings perhaps. Disappointed that there wasn't a handwritten note accompanying it, Noelle assumed the box likely held a piece of family jewelry her father wanted to pass to her personally, rather than trust his estate attorneys with the contents of the box.

She wished he'd left a note to go along with it, but accepted that unless her father folded up the paper he'd written it on into a tiny square and slipped it inside the box; she would be left guessing as to his part in the growing mystery she'd fallen into, and to the true manner of his death. Discouraged at the thought, she reached into the envelope and removed the box. Inside, rather than the jewelry she was expecting, she found a velvet pouch. Puzzled, she lifted her glance to Rafe's, and at his silent encouragement, she untied the silk ties and emptied the contents of the pouch into the palm of her hand.

Not a ring, or earrings or some other family heirloom. Her father had left her a key. She suspected it was a key to a safe deposit box. Maybe if they found the safe deposit box, Noelle would get the explanation she sought from her father after all. She held the key out for Ariel Lucien's inspection.

"I think it's a safe deposit box key, but there's no indication on it about what bank it belongs to. The box could be anywhere, France, the United States, or any other place in the world." At the older man's continued silence, Noelle tacked on anxiously, "Do you think it has something to do with all of this?"

"There's no way of knowing, but I can't help but wonder why your father chose me as the steward of his legacy to his only child, rather than your mother or grandmother," the older man mused.

"Yes, that seems rather odd to me too. Were you two close?" Noelle wondered.

"I have always been close to his mother. Your grandfather and I were more rivals for your grandmother's affections in our younger days, than we were friends. So no. Your father and I were not close, but he would have known that I would do anything to keep his mother safe, and that my protection would naturally extend to her only granddaughter."

"So how do we go about finding the bank?" Noelle wondered.

"I have an idea about that. Let me take a few photos and send them off to Jacobs. I imagine he'll be able to track down the bank for us, if not the branch," Rafe interjected.

"Yes, I believe that's an excellent plan." Ari concurred.

"Who's Jacobs?" Noelle wanted to know

"The head of Lucien security."

"Oh." Since she couldn't fault Rafe's plan, Noelle couldn't come up with anything more scintillating to contribute in response.

"There's just one more thing that concerns me that we haven't discussed," Rafe added when she fell silent once more.

"Agreed," his grandfather concurred succinctly.

The two men seemed to be speaking in code. Mystified, Noelle asked, "What is it?"

"The two gendarmes. Why would they approach you and why would Michael tell you to run from them?" Rafe explained.

Noelle had almost forgotten about the two armed men who had chased her and Rafe through the narrow streets, but at the reminder, she felt her earlier unease begin to claw at her insides again. "I don't know who they were or what they wanted."

"What did they say to you?" Rafe asked.

"I wasn't even aware of them standing there until one of them gripped my arm and said something like, "You must come with us now, Mademoiselle." Before I had a chance to ask for an explanation, Michael told me to run. I ran." She turned to Rafe. "What were you doing there? How did you just happen to be there when those two men tried to get me to go with them?"

"Well, it was certainly not because I was in league with them, if that's what you're implying."

Noelle had the grace to blush at his direct challenge. She couldn't help it. Lately she had become suspicious of her own shadow. Heaving a disgusted sigh in her direction, Rafe added by way of explanation, "I suspected there was more to the story about the events at Mont Saint Michel than you shared with me at the vineyard that day. I stopped by Chateau Dominique this morning to offer to escort you back to the monastery. Your grandmother informed me that you had insisted on returning to the site alone. She seemed very concerned about your decision. I followed you there."

"Oh," Noelle replied, but left unspoken her thoughts that it was odd that Rafe happened to show up just in time to rescue her from those two men.

"Well it's easy enough to discover what the gendarmes wanted with Noelle," Ari Lucien inserted into the silence.

106

"It is?" Noelle turned to him, mystified.

"Of course. I shall simply call their commanding officer and demand to know what they were about accosting a guest of mine."

Rafe sent his grandfather an admiring look. "No doubt leaving out the part about this guest of yours being the granddaughter of the Duchess of Dominique."

"The identity of my guest is none of their concern," Ari replied with a dismissive gesture of his right hand. "My call will also serve another purpose."

"What is that?" Noelle wanted to know.

It was Rafe who answered. "You're putting whoever was behind this on notice that she's under our protection now."

"Yes," Ari confirmed.

Noelle's glance swung from one to the other, noticing the similarity between the two men and how their faces were set in identical expressions. She suspected the looks on their faces gave their adversaries pause when they were confronted with them across the width of a conference table in a boardroom. Those same looks would give even the most hardened criminal pause if one happened to be confronted with them in a dark alley in an unsavory part of town.

"Thank you," Noelle offered. "I know you feel responsible for me because of my grandmother, but that doesn't lessen my gratitude for your assistance with this. But what do you think I should do about Michael?"

The expressions on the men's faces became hooded. Noelle was not blind to the look they exchanged over her head. She sighed, defeated, her earlier appreciation and hopefulness effectively deflated. They didn't believe her about Michael. How was she going to convince the authorities to close Mont Saint Michel to visitors if her closest acquaintances in France thought she was imagining things? "You don't believe me, do you?"

The two men turned as one to regard her, but it was Ari who replied, "It's not that we don't believe you, Noelle, but you were a very young child when the events at Mont Saint Michel occurred. You had lost your father just months earlier. Don't you think it's possible you could have imagined that the archangel spoke to you? Michael, after all, is a powerful, protective figure. How much more so would he appear to a young girl who just lost her father?"

"I didn't think of that," Rafe commented, his voice filled with relief that there was such a logical explanation for her delusions.

Noelle hesitated only briefly, then decided she needed all the help she could get and she was unlikely to come across more effective assistance than the Luciens could provide. "I have proof." The two men's focus became laser sharp and honed in on her instantly at her astonishing claim.

"What proof?" Rafe demanded, his glance raking hers.

Noelle held it. "I've kept a diary about the events at Mont Saint Michel. Ever since I was a little girl, I wrote down whenever Michael told me something was going to happen at the site. Then as I grew older, I would print out the stories from the Internet and paste them into the book."

"You didn't mention the diary earlier," Rafe reminded her.

"No," Noelle admitted sadly. "I never told anyone about it. I guess I thought if something happened to me, maybe my mother would find it and give it to my grandmother. I thought someone should know what he was going to do. I don't want to be responsible for the deaths of thousands of people when the day comes and Michael carries out his threat."

"Where is this diary?" Ari demanded, at the same time Rafe insisted, "Noelle, nothing that has happened or will happen at Mont Saint Michel is your fault. You are no longer alone. We are going to get to the bottom of this."

Noelle nodded, a slight smile curving her lips at the idea that she was no longer alone. If anyone could take on an archangel, it was the Luciens. "Thank you."

"The diary?" Ari reminded her.

Noelle nodded. "It's at Chateau Dominique."

"Your grandmother doesn't know of it?"

Noelle shook her head. "No. I never told anyone, not even my mother. I was afraid she would throw it away or destroy it." At the look the two men exchanged, she added in defense of her mother, "She was worried about me. She's my mother. Maybe the reason she was so worried was because she knew or suspected something about my father's death."

Rafe crossed the small distance separating them. When she refused to raise her glance to his, he squatted before her chair and reached out a gentle hand to lift her chin from where she sat staring dejectedly down at her hands clasped in her lap. "Noelle, you are no longer alone. We are going to find out the truth about your father's death. We are going to find what he left you in that safe deposit box and we are going to find out what's going on at Mont Saint Michel and who those two men were that tried to make you accompany them and why."

Noelle nodded, tears shimmering in her eyes. When she opened her mouth to ask about the singular part of the mystery he'd neglected to address, he ran his thumb over her lips and added, "And we are going to find out why Michael chose a little girl to warn France of the consequences of removing all that is sacred from his home on earth."

The tears that hovered on her lashes spilled over and trailed down her cheeks. She held Rafe's glance through the glimmer of her tears. "I think that's what bothers him the most. It used to be a monastery. The magnificent halls echoed with prayer and hymns day and night. There were gardens and smaller chapels for meditation and quiet communion with the Lord. You're right. There was a sacred aura that encompassed the entire island, as if it was indeed a home for the divine, or one of his most faithful servants and beloved sons. That's almost all gone now. You can feel it slipping away, seeping through every passageway filled with loud voices and the evidence of commerce being conducted. They sell t-shirts now…the shops lining the streets. There's so little left… a small order, but even their presence can only slow the stripping away of what was once a place of pilgrimage for the devout. A place where they sought his intercession with their earthly worries. I don't really blame him for being angry at the affront offered him at the desecration of his home by mankind."

A heavy silence followed her words, until Ari commented dryly; a speculative look in the dark eyes taking in his grandson's stunned expression as he regarded Noelle. "I think perhaps Michael's reasons for choosing Noelle are not as inexplicable as we first assumed."

Ignoring his grandfather's sarcasm, Rafe returned his focus to Noelle. "You and I are going to be spending a lot of time together until we know what those two men were after."

Before Noelle could protest, Ari interjected, "Well, that at least is one mystery we should be able to resolve fairly quickly. If you will excuse me, I will make a few calls."

Rafe nodded and helped Noelle to her feet and led her back out into the grand entry. "When was the last time you ate?"

"I don't remember."

His lips tilted slightly at her bemused admission, and reaching for her hand, he led her out onto the stone patio overlooking the formal gardens. If she hadn't been staying at Chateau Dominique, Noelle would have sworn the view was like something straight out of a celebrity magazine spread featuring the country home of a head of state or someone equally important. She supposed the Luciens qualified on both fronts. The gardens alone would encompass several city blocks spread out before them in acre after acre of manicured green. There were flower gardens, shrubbery gardens and vegetable gardens all displaying their early summer offerings. Wildflowers grew in the fields beyond the more formal setting. "It's stunning. It's hard to believe that this place is one family's home."

"Home and heritage," Rafe corrected with obvious pride in his voice. "The chateau and surrounding lands have been in the Lucien family for over a thousand years, though the structure itself was built and re-built over the course of centuries."

Noelle smiled slightly at the picture of an older Rafe one day ruling over all her eyes could see. That he would take his responsibilities seriously, she had no doubt, as his grandfather obviously did. The perfectly manicured gardens, the exquisite art and furnishings that graced the chateau itself, the elegance and grace on quiet display all spoke to the loving care afforded the lands, the house itself, as well as its contents.

She couldn't begin to hazard a guess at how much money it took to keep an estate this size going. She was aware that many noble progeny turned their inheritances into tourist destinations or sold off all but a few acres of land surrounding the chateau just to be able to afford the upkeep on the property. She couldn't imagine Rafe or his grandfather parting with even a remote foot of ground, or a single piece of art that made up the Lucien legacy, which implied the family was possessed of a very reliable and very generous flow of income, one that would require more than simply what they could make from the family vineyards. Hadn't Rafe admitted that the Lucien's were known for their ability to turn a profit? She had to give credit where credit was due. At least part of those profits had been spent to maintain the beauty spread out before her. She turned to Rafe and said, teasing, "I can picture you in your ancestors of centuries past and in your descendants' centuries into the future, standing on this very overlook, surveying your domain as far as the eye can see, and ruling it with an iron hand."

Rafe's lips curved in response to her teasing, but his reply, when it came, though cloaked beneath his own lighthearted teasing, was wrapped in the iron will she spoke of when he proclaimed, "I intend to do so in hopefully not more than a century hence."

Noelle laughed. "You are perfectly typecast for the role."

"And why not? I have been raised since birth to assume it."

"Do you think it was the same for my father?" Noelle asked curiously.

"I barely remember him but I cannot imagine it was any different for him. You share his legacy, Noelle. You are the last of the Dominique line."

Noelle nodded and something about his comment about being her father's heir jogged her memory. "Michael said something about that…about my father's legacy…but it's all fuzzy now. That's why I started keeping the diary. When I would try to remember what he told me a few days, or even a few hours later, I could never remember it clearly. I always got the impression it was frustrating for him dealing with my mortal limitations."

Noelle turned away from the look in Rafe's eyes. She was growing accustomed to it even though it hurt to know he didn't believe her. She used to be more careful about letting anyone get too close, about confiding in anyone about Michael, but the walls she'd erected around herself when she realized her mother didn't want to believe her, didn't want her to be who she was, were becoming harder to hide behind now that she was back. It was happening more and more often, she realized. The memories were starting to seep through.

She turned in on herself, her attention captured by the scene unfolding there. She looked around, trying to orient herself. She was in Mother Superior's cell. It was larger than the novitiates. She had been summoned there by Sister Regina. The older sister told her Mother Superior asked for her to come to her. Marie could tell Sister Regina was not happy about the Revered Mother's request, but she could hardly deny it, or her own superior. The Reverend Mother was dying. Marie would genuinely mourn the older women. She was the closest thing to a mother Marie had any memory of.

She'd been left on the convent steps as an infant. Abandoned like so many others. No one knew who her family had been or why they left her on the convent steps. Mother Superior had taken her in. When she was old enough Marie had worked in the gardens, then the laundry, and then in the kitchens until she'd taken her initial vows the previous year.

The Reverend Mother had been the gentle guiding light of her life. She knelt beside the simple cot the older woman rested upon and reached for her frail hand, understanding when she clasped it and felt the warmth draining from it, why she'd been summoned. Mother wanted to say goodbye.

In the candlelight, the older woman's skin looked like the fine parchment paper Marie had seen in her office whenever Mother received an official communication from Rome. The convent was a wealthy one, attached to the monastery at Mont Saint Michel.

"Marie?"

Marie gently squeezed the frail hand in hers and answered in a quiet voice. "Mother?"

"There's something I must tell you, Marie, before I am called from this world. I promised the one who entrusted you into my care that I would never reveal her secret as long as I lived, but I cannot go to my Lord with this sin of omission on my conscience."

"No, Mother, you must not speak so," Marie protested urgently, unshed tears forming a knot in her throat. "I believe your cough is so much better today. I have prayed and prayed to our Lord to spare you to us. What will we do without you?"

"Marie, you must listen, for my time grows short."

Marie winced when the older woman grasped her hand with all of her remaining strength. Tears streaming down her cheeks, she leaned forward so Reverend Mother wouldn't have to strain herself.

"Closer child. I cannot risk anyone else hearing what I have to tell you."

"Yes, Mother," Marie whispered and bent over the dying woman until her ear was all but pressed up against her lips.

"You are not an orphan, Marie. They told him you were dead, that you were stillborn, and then your mother secreted you here. She feared her husband, your father, for he was an evil man, and I'm sorry to say your brother is reputed to be little better. She wanted you to grow up protected by the church. For surely behind these holy walls is the one place he cannot defile. Open the top draw of my chest and pull out the small box in the back."

Reeling, Marie stumbled towards the chest and did as she was instructed. Inside the top drawer was the box the Reverend Mother referred to. She pulled it out and returned to the bed with it.

"Open it. Inside you'll find a pouch that contains a key."

Marie did so and allowed the old iron key to drop into her palm.

Sighing, the Reverend Mother leaned back against the linens covering her small cot. "Take it with you. Tell no one about its existence. Your mother tasked me with its stewardship for the length of my life. I have fulfilled my promise and paid my debt to her."

"What promise, Mother? What debt? What does the key open?" Marie asked desperately.

But there was no answer from the dying woman. She had paid her debt. Her Lord had rewarded her faithfulness and granted her release from her pain in this world.

CHAPTER EIGHTEEN

"Noelle, Noelle." Strong hands gripped her arms and shook her briskly until her head lobbed back and forth on her neck. Marie sought frantically to hide the key on her person before the stranger could steal it from her.

"No, no, you can't have it!" She cried, struggling desperately against the hands that refused to release her.

"Noelle!"

He shook her again, then gripped her chin and made her meet his dark, concerned glance. Confusion gripped her. His eyes looked familiar, but how could that be? She'd lived in the secluded convent her entire life. She had only seen a few men in all of that time, most of them priests and certainly none who had ever touched her so familiarly. None who were possessed of the blazing dark eyes staring down at her.

"Noelle, answer me."

"Why do you keep calling me, Noelle? That's not my name," She whispered in a voice that seemed to come from far away.

"Then what is your name?" The stranger asked, his hands and voice gentle now.

"Sister Marie. How did you get in here?" But even as the words left her lips, the small cell with the bare stone walls fell away and she was back in the present, staring up into Rafe's anxious expression.

She stopped fighting against his grip and reached up to clasp her head between her hands. "I don't understand what's happening to me. Maybe my mother was right. Perhaps I shouldn't have come back to France. This is where it all happened before."

"Where what happened before?" Rafe wanted to know.

Noelle shook her head, denying his urgent question. "I need to sit down." At the moment, she was trying desperately not to either throw up all over Rafe's finely tailored trousers or faint at his Italian-leather-shod feet.

115

Rafe put his arm around her and led her to a nearby chaise. When Noelle just continued staring up at him with a puzzled look on her face, he gently pushed her down into it. For a moment, Noelle leaned back against the chaise, her eyes closed, then her memories returned and she began frantically searching her pockets. "Where did it go? Did you take it?" She demanded, staring accusingly up at Rafe.

"Did I take what?"

"The key. Mother Superior gave me a key."

"Noelle, look at me," Rafe commanded, his voice still gentle, as if he was addressing a small child. His hands reached for both of hers and squeezed them gently to still their panicked search.

Noelle raised her glance to his and the rest of her disorientation receded.

"What just happened?" Rafe asked, his gaze holding hers, as if he was afraid to release her, in case she slid back to wherever she'd fallen into a few moments earlier.

Noelle shook her head in an attempt to clear it. "I was a novitiate summoned to Mother Superior's cell. She was dying. She was the only mother I'd ever known. She told me there was something she needed to tell me. That even though she promised to take the secret to her grave, she didn't want to die with it on her soul. She said it would be a sin of omission. I always believed I was an orphan, but she said my father was an evil man and my mother told him I was stillborn and then smuggled me to the convent. She gave me a key. She told me I could never let anyone know about it."

"What did the key open?"

"I don't know. Mother Superior died as soon as she gave it to me." Noelle fell silent, then added, "It's funny, isn't it?

"What's funny?"

"That my father's legacy to me in this life was also a key."

"Have you ever had this type of vision before?"

Noelle shook her head.

"No, you've never had a similar experience before?" Rafe sought clarification of her silent answer to his query.

"No, I didn't mean that. It wasn't a vision. It was a memory and I remember now. The order I was a novitiate in was the one attached to Mont Saint Michel."

"How can you possibly know that?" Rafe demanded, his frustration evident.

"I remember," Noelle said softly. "It's all beginning to make sense now. It's something Michael told me. I think he chose me because I'm indebted to him somehow."

"You do realize how crazy that sounds?" Rafe asked, desperately trying to regain control over their conversation.

"Yes, but whatever this is, I'm beginning to think it didn't start twenty years ago. It goes back much further, not decades, but lifetimes, centuries. That's why he keeps showing me little snatches of other lifetimes. I think they're significant. I think they have something to do with why he chose a four-year girl for whatever it is I'm supposed to do. He was letting me know even then, this was it. He was tired of waiting. I suppose even an archangel eventually runs out of patience. I have to find that key. If my father really was part of this, maybe that's what's inside the safe deposit box. At all costs, it cannot be allowed to fall into the wrong hands."

"And how do you know whose hands are the wrong ones?" Rafe thrust both hands through his nearly shoulder length hair in a gesture Noelle was beginning to recognize meant he was nearing the end of his rope.

"He knows," she insisted, ignoring Rafe's disbelief. "I think those two gendarmes at the monastery were the wrong hands. That's why he told me to run."

"They were not gendarmes." Rafe's grandfather's voice inserted itself into the silence that fell between them. Rafe was apparently so far beyond his comfort zone by that point; he was at a loss for further conversation.

"What are you saying?" Rafe demanded harshly, turning to his grandfather.

"I just got off the phone with the head of security at Mont Saint Michel. There are no gendarmes stationed there at this time. When they have additional security assigned to them from the state police, they are usually plain clothes and in response to a specific threat of terrorism activity aimed at the site."

Noelle felt the color drain from her face. "I can't go back to my grandmother's. They'll find me. I don't want her in the middle of this."

Ari stepped closer to where Noelle sat huddled on the chaise; her hands shaking in reaction to his disclosure that two strange men had attempted to kidnap her. Somehow when she believed they were with the police the idea was less frightening...as if it was all some big misunderstanding that would be quickly straightened out.

"I agree. You will stay here. Michel is on her way." Ari announced.

"No, I can't stay here," Noelle instantly protested.

At the same time, Rafe echoed dryly, "Michel is on her way?"

Noelle turned accusing eyes in the direction of Rafe's grandfather. "You told her?"

He lifted one shoulder in a Gallic shrug. "Yes. Trust me; your grandmother would not have been put off by any lie we concocted to explain why you would not be returning to Chateau Dominique. It is better if she is on her guard. I am going to try to persuade her to return to Paris while we attempt to unravel whatever is going on here."

"You're right. She'll be safer in Paris," Noelle sighed, both relieved and alarmed that she had to consider her grandmother's safety.

"How do you suggest we begin to unravel whatever is going on here?" Rafe demanded, his grandfather apparently not exempt from his sarcasm. It was obvious to Noelle he wasn't completely convinced anything was going on. If it hadn't been for the two men that had chased them off the island today, she was quite certain Rafe would have put down all of her revelations to the fantasies of an unbalanced mind.

"I think our first step is to find the safe deposit box Michel Dominique left for his daughter. At the same time, we try to discover the identity of the two men from Mont Saint Michel. Can either of you describe them?"

Rafe shrugged. "Only in the most general of terms, but I will say their uniforms appeared genuine and I can attest to the fact that their weapons were not merely toys meant to frighten a young woman into complying with their demands."

"I would recognize them again," Noelle announced softly. "I've seen their type before."

"Their type?" Rafe echoed, no longer bothering to hide his disbelief.

"Yes," Noelle confirmed, ignoring his frustration. "They're fanatics. Their eyes burned with the kind of fever only a true fanatic understands."

"And when have you encountered fanatics before that you recognize them so easily?" Rafe demanded, making no effort to disguise his sarcasm.

"I think I should leave. It was wrong of me to involve you, either of you, and especially my grandmother. My mother was right to keep me away from France, but at least I know she's safe. If you'll give me the key my father left me, I'll take it from here."

"Don't be ridiculous! Just where do you think you'll be taking anything? Had I not been there this afternoon you would already be at the mercy of those two men and whoever they were working for."

Ariel Lucien was once again forced to insert himself into their budding argument. He stepped forward and bent down before where Noelle sat on the chaise, so they were eye to eye. He reached out, clasped her icy hands in his, and gave them a gentle squeeze. "You are no longer alone in carrying this burden, Noelle. You will allow us to help you."

"He thinks I'm delusional or unbalanced or deliberately lying to take advantage of your generosity and your friendship with my grandmother," Noelle whispered, motioning her head in Rafe's direction.

"Perhaps," Ari conceded, surprising Noelle, before adding, "But eventually he's going to realize there is no reason for you to go to such lengths in order to accomplish whatever my grandson believes your nefarious purpose is, as there is nothing on this earth your grandmother would deny you if it is within her power to give you, which means there is very little I would deny you as well."

Noelle held his concerned glance and pleaded with him. "I don't want her to know what Michael said about my father. I don't want her to know that part, at least not until we have some proof there's a chance it could be true."

"I believe we already have the proof you speak of, but I will agree to your request to keep this secret, if you will share the contents of your diary with me."

"Yes, all right, though I don't see how that will help. It's just a record of his warnings over the years and the Internet stories I printed out when they invariably came true."

"And there's nothing else you kept in your diary?" Ari confirmed.

Noelle shrugged. "I kept a record of the research I'd done on Mont Saint Michel...even the old legends. You know the ones about Bishop Aubert and Michael putting his finger through his skull. It made me feel better to know I wasn't the only one he'd spoken to. I was grateful he never put his finger through my head. When I was little I remember being afraid for a long time to fall asleep, just in case he decided to do the same thing to me for disobeying him."

Ari smiled at her confession, but it was a gentle smile, without the mockery his grandson's usually held when she made such an admission to him. "And how did you disobey him?"

"I didn't come back," Noelle whispered.

"You were just a little girl. How were you supposed to come back if your mother refused to bring you?"

"I think that's why he didn't...you know...punish me for my defiance. When I grew up, I could tell he was growing impatient with me. I was afraid to stay away any longer. I was afraid of what he would do. I didn't know how I was going to explain a hole in my head." Noelle bent her head dropping her glance beneath his gentle expression. "Is that why you called my grandmother? Are you going to tell her I need to be institutionalized?"

"No, of course not. Something is clearly going on, Noelle. Are you forgetting those two men who attempted to force you to accompany them today?"

Noelle sighed, "Yes, I guess I was. Who do you think they were? What could they possibly want with me? How did they know I was part of this? Surely, they haven't been waiting around for me to return for the past twenty years. They weren't that old, maybe in their late twenties or early thirties. Why did they focus in on me? How did they know I would be there today?"

Ari sighed, and then turned to Rafe with his brow raised in query. "Perhaps you have some ideas to explain Noelle's very excellent questions? Unless you believe she was somehow in league with those two men and she had somehow deduced you would follow her to Mont Saint Michel today so you would be conveniently nearby for them to stage their little scene and you would be forced to come to her rescue?"

Noelle hadn't thought about the earlier incident in quite those terms. As ominous as Ariel Lucien's recitation sounded, it did make Rafe's conclusion that she was imagining things seem a little ridiculous when one examined all of the evidence.

"Ari!" The single word echoed sharply from inside the house.

"Ah, I believe Michel has arrived. She must have driven herself. Bernard would have been at least another half an hour."

Noelle's grandmother appeared in the glass doorway leading onto the terrace just as Ari concluded his dry sentiment. Her grandmother didn't say anything. Her eyes did a sweep of the terrace, then seeing Noelle seated there, apparently unharmed, relief replaced the crushing anxiety in her gaze. She raised a shaking hand to brush back a wisp of hair from her face. Noelle saw the color flood back into her white face and she jumped up from her seat and rushed to take her grandmother's hands in hers and lead her back to the chaise she had just vacated.

"Oh, Meme, I'm so sorry I worried you. The last thing I wanted was to involve you in this mess."

Her grandmother brushed off Noelle's apology. "I am already involved. Ari at least had the good sense not to attempt to keep me in the dark. Tell me what happened today. Did two men actually try to kidnap you? They were dressed as gendarmes?"

"Yes, fortunately Rafe showed up in the nick of time and rescued me."

"I don't understand any of this." Her grandmother echoed the confusion they were all feeling.

"We believe it would be best if Noelle remains here as my guest until this situation is resolved," Ari proposed.

Noelle was surprised by her grandmother's immediate, vehement reaction. "You are not keeping me out of whatever this situation is. Noelle is the only family I have left. I will not be shuttled aside like a child while you big, strong Lucien males take over."

Noelle grinned, and then couldn't resist the urge to giggle. "Go, Meme," she said softly into the tense silence.

Her grandmother turned in her direction. "It is not that I am ungrateful for Rafe's assistance today, but I have had decades of dealing with the Lucien arrogance. I rarely complain, because I admit it has its moments. This is not one of them," she tacked on, shooting a warning glance in Ari's direction.

"Perhaps we should discuss this privately," Ari suggested in a soothing voice.

"Stop it!" Michel demanded, waving her hand in a dismissive gesture, and then turning her attention back to Noelle. "Now, Noelle dear, I suspected there were things you failed to confide in me. I was willing to respect your privacy, but after today's events, I think you'd better tell me everything."

Noelle sighed and anxiously met Rafe's watchful, slightly amused glance over her grandmother's head. "Apparently Daddy left me something in a safe deposit box."

"What are you talking about?" White-faced, her grandmother's glance swung between the three of them.

"Michel…" Ari began, and then stopped abruptly, apparently deciding to let Noelle explain in her own way.

"Daddy left the key with Rafe's grandfather and asked him to give it to me when I turned twenty-one."

Her grandmother's piercing gaze looked first at Noelle before settling on her dear friend. "So are you telling me Ari informed you of your inheritance from your father three years ago on your twenty first birthday and you are only now informing me of it?"

"Not exactly," Noelle admitted, a little intimidated by her grandmother's tone, one she'd never heard before.

"Then what exactly are you telling me?"

Noelle caught Rafe's grin at her grandmother's autocratic tone. She had to admit it sounded very similar to Rafe's grandfather's tone when he was demanding an explanation earlier. Sighing, she confirmed what her grandmother no doubt already suspected. "Rafe's grandfather didn't tell me about the envelope Daddy's attorney left with him until this afternoon."

"God dammit, Ari, how dare you!"

Michel jumped up from where she sat facing Noelle and turned on her closest friend, advancing on him with a menacing look on her face.

"I believe this is where Noelle and I make our excuses. I'll take her to dinner. That should give the two of you enough time to work this out."

Neither of their grandparents acknowledged Rafe's suggestion. They were too preoccupied at the moment with the coming argument. Noelle's anxious glance darted from one to the other, even as Rafe took her hand and pulled her out of the line of fire. With a warning finger to his lips he led Noelle back through the terrace doors, across the grand foyer and out onto the front porch, where she could see her grandmother's car parked behind Rafe's Maserati.

"Is it safe to leave the two of them alone?" Noelle asked in a hushed voice.

Rafe laughed. "I don't believe there will be any resulting bodily injury despite all evidence to the contrary, but I believe they would prefer to conduct their discussion without an audience."

"I've never seen my grandmother in such a rage," Noelle confided, awed.

"No, I don't believe I have either. It was quite an impressive display. I believe even my grandfather was shocked. He probably assumed he would sweet-talk your grandmother into bed and all would be forgiven. I believe this is one of those rare instances when he has badly miscalculated his adversary."

Noelle waved a hand in front of her face to clear the stunned shock she knew her expression must be wearing. "What are you saying? Your grandfather believed he could talk my grandmother into bed? That's absurd."

Rafe laughed right in her face. "Surely, sweet Noelle, you are aware our grandparents are lovers?"

Noelle was still reeling from the shock of Rafe's casual disclosure about their grandparents' sex lives. "Don't...don't use the words our grandparents and lovers in the same sentence. And I am not your sweet Noelle. You think I'm delusional, remember?"

"Not delusional exactly. Perhaps a little confused, though I'm forced to admit my grandfather had a point."

"Oh, good. Please share it with me. I would hate to think I missed something important in my confused brain."

Rafe's lips twitched at her sarcasm. He took her arm and began leading her down the steps to his car. "We'll talk about my grandfather's point over dinner. Then I believe we'll swing by Chateau Dominique so we can retrieve your diary."

"Fine, as it turns out I'm starving. I had no idea my fantasies of getting chased by two men who might start shooting at us at any moment would work up such an appetite. Perhaps I should track down Dr. Adams and ask her what it all means."

Rafe's teeth flashed in a wide grin at her sarcasm. "*Touche'*, my young adversary. I believe we've circled back to good old Ari's point. Something is indeed going on and you have managed to land yourself right in the middle of it. Perhaps it has something to do with this mysterious inheritance your father left you. The sooner we discover what is in that safe deposit box the better."

"This whole thing just keeps getting more complicated, and at the same time more crazy, if that's even possible. I don't understand my father's role in any of this. Surely, given the fact he was French and the head of a wealthy and influential family, if he knew what Michael was planning, wouldn't he have said something to somebody?"

"You believe the French government would have been any more receptive to the idea of turning Mont Saint Michel over to the Catholic Church if the suggestion had come from your father rather than you?"

Nicole released an audible sigh. "All right, I guess you have a point. My father was likely even more loathe to leave himself open to the idea that he was having fantasies of conversations with archangels than I am, given the fact that he was the head of a wealthy and influential family and all."

"Likely," Rafe agreed, amusement dancing in his expressive eyes. Then he steered the conversation along more serious lines. "Do you know any of the details surrounding your father's accident?"

Noelle shook her head. "Very few. Only what I read years later on the Internet. My mom never spoke of it. I can't really blame her. It had to have come as a terrible shock. She would have been my age when it happened. I was three years old. They eloped before my mom even graduated college. I can't imagine finding myself alone in the world as a single parent."

"She was not alone," Rafe reminded her.

Noelle shrugged. "Perhaps not, but I'm sure my grandmother could not have been thrilled by her only son's very sudden marriage to an American college student. I imagine my mother was painfully aware of her mother-in-law's feelings on the subject of her only son's marriage."

"I'll concede that the circumstances of your parents' marriage were not ideal for the development of a close relationship between your mother and grandmother, but that's no excuse for keeping you away from your heritage for twenty years."

"That wasn't the reason. I'm quite certain the purpose of that visit when I was four was to make certain I was given a chance to begin to understand the other half of my heritage."

"And then Michael intervened," Rafe commented in as neutral a tone as he was likely capable of.

Noelle rolled her eyes in Rafe's direction and then sat back in her seat, closing them. "Can we not talk about this anymore today? I swear my head's going to explode if I have to go through it all again."

Rafe grinned at her dramatic turn of phrase. "Fine, we will let it go for now."

Noelle peeked out from beneath her lashes, trying to decide if she could trust him to keep his word. If he was going to use the opportunity given him to grill her over dinner, she'd just as soon skip it. Rafe turned to catch her staring at him with the speculative look in her eyes and grinned back at her.

"You really think our grandparents are...involved?" Noelle asked, changing the subject back to the incredible one she'd somehow managed to push to the rear of her reeling brain.

"That shocks you?"

"Of course it shocks me. I mean, I knew they were close friends...I just never thought...I never considered the idea that they could be...involved." Noelle refused to use the word lovers in the same sentence as her grandmother.

"Because of their age?"

"Partly, I guess. I don't know, I never thought about what sex would be like in my seventies."

"Eighties," Rafe inserted grinning, "At least in my grandfather's case."

"Eighties?" Noelle echoed, and then added without thinking, "Well, that's impressive."

Rafe laughed. "And what is the other reason you find the idea of our grandparents involved in an intimate relationship so difficult to believe?"

Noelle hesitated, unsure if Rafe knew the details of their grandparents' past. Then assuming he must, she relayed, "Because he broke her heart."

Rafe turned his attention away from the road for a moment to raise a questioning brow in her direction. "What do you mean?"

"She told me there was once talk of marriage between them, but then she found your grandfather with another woman...her best friend...and congratulated herself on her narrow escape. She was madly in love with him. He broke her heart."

Noelle waited for Rafe to say something, to confirm she hadn't violated her grandmother's confidence and that the story was well known in the annals of their family history. "I never heard that. Is that why you were so adamant that laying your own heart at my feet would be such a colossal mistake on your part?"

Noelle was unprepared for the swift change in the direction of their conversation. She tried to shrug it off with a lightness she was far from feeling. "That and the Italian bombshell that opened your door dressed in nothing but a scanty silk robe."

"What does Carina have to do with us?"

"There is no us, Rafe. Clearly, I'm not your type. I don't even own a scanty silk robe."

He grinned wickedly. "I would be happy to purchase one for you."

"No, thank you."

Apparently, he wasn't done teasing her yet. "Carina asked me if you were in the running to become the future Duchess of Lucien."

"Ha, ha," Noelle deflected breathlessly.

"As she is well aware our relationship is not destined to end in marriage. We are friends, Noelle."

"It's none of my business," Noelle countered desperately.

"On that at least we can agree, but I feel it's only fair to warn you that you are quite wrong about your naïve conclusion about not being my type. Truth be told I have had to exert considerable effort to stay away from you. I can assure you it is only our families' long histories that has persuaded me to do so until now, but I admit my self-discipline where you are concerned erodes just a little bit more with each encounter between us."

"You can't be serious," Noelle protested, disbelieving.

"Oh, I assure, *Mon amour*, I am quite serious."

"I am not your amour and how can you claim to be attracted to me? You think I'm some kind of nut."

"Perhaps," Rafe conceded thoughtfully, causing an outraged gasp to emerge from between Noelle's lips. Ignoring it, he continued in a considering tone, "Though I would not use the term nut. As I indicated earlier, I believe you are somewhat confused and prone to dramatics, but you would be surprised what a man in the throes of a sexual attraction is able to overlook in a prospective mate."

Noelle laughed. She couldn't help it. Rafe's outrageous confession convinced her he was just teasing her. "Thanks, but I think I'll pass."

"That would no doubt be the wisest course of action for both of us. You will let me know if you change your mind."

Grinning, Noelle told him, "Don't hold your breath."

"Ah, Noelle, I do believe I warned you about tossing those challenges around."

Reminded, chastised, Noelle retreated into a safe silence.

CHAPTER NINETEEN

After dinner, Rafe drove them to Chateau Dominique so Noelle could retrieve her diary. She was almost sorry to see the evening come to an end. It had been so normal to sit there and have dinner with Rafe. Of course she'd spent the early part of the meal looking around the crowded restaurant for any sign of their two assailants that day. Until Rafe, seeing her anxiety, reached across the table for her hand, and squeezing it, admonished her, "They're not here. Stop worrying. I'm certain they've retreated to reconsider the wisdom of trying to approach you in such a public place and the repercussions of involving the Lucien family."

She met his glance, saw the certainty contained within it and his commitment to not let anything happen to her, and forced herself to relax and enjoy the evening in his company. Rafe went to considerable effort to put her at ease. She spent the remainder of their time at the restaurant laughing at one amusing anecdote after another he related about their shared family history. Noelle was actually sorry when it came time for them to leave.

When he pulled the car to a stop in front of the entrance to her grandmother's home, Noelle intended to jump out of the car to keep Rafe from accompanying her inside. "I'll just be a few minutes."

Rafe gripped her arm before she managed to escape. "I think not. Considering this morning's events, I believe we should go in together."

"But Bernard is here," Noelle protested, "and the rest of the staff."

"Nevertheless," Rafe responded and Noelle, resigned, recognized the steel in his voice.

"Fine, but you're not coming up to my bedroom," she informed him less than graciously. "It's bad enough there's speculation concerning our grandparents' relationship. We're not giving anyone any reason to speculate on the nature of ours." When Rafe merely grinned in response to her admonition, Noelle added, "I mean it."

She hadn't been certain Rafe would remain in the foyer where she left him when she dashed up the wide marble staircase to her rooms. Thankfully, he'd remained behind in conversation with Bernard when she'd fled at the earliest opportunity.

She flicked on the overhead light to her room and crossed the distance to the closet where her empty suitcases were stowed beneath the luggage racks. She drew out her carry-on bag and unzipped the inner pocket where she'd been keeping her diary since they'd arrived at Chateau Dominique. She didn't want one of the maids who cleaned her room to get curious about its contents if she found it in a drawer in the end table beside her bed. She knew she was being overly cautious, but she felt better knowing the household staff had no reason to go into her luggage once it had been unpacked.

She reached inside the carry-on bag and felt around the inner pocket. Nothing. Chiding herself over her growing panic, she pulled the small bag onto her lap and searched every pocket inside and out. She was still sitting there clutching the empty bag on her lap, wearing a dazed expression on her face, when Rafe found her there several minutes later.

"Noelle?"

She didn't turn to meet his glance. She could already see the disbelief in his eyes when she told him the diary was missing. He would assume she'd made up its existence, given that she was prone to dramatics and all.

"Noelle, what's wrong?"

She carefully zipped the pockets of the bag closed, then returned the suitcase to its place behind the luggage rack and scrambled to her feet. Bracing herself against his anticipated disdain, she admitted, "It's gone."

"The diary's gone?" He confirmed.

"Yes." She felt the tears stinging her eyes and held up her charm bracelet for his inspection. Reaching for the tiny key, she told him, "This is the key. I always keep the notebook locked. I was worried my mother would find it and realize I hadn't forgotten about that day. I pretended I had. We never spoke of it. Just like she never spoke about my dad. Every once in a while we'd be somewhere or be doing something like walking along the beach and she would retreat to some place I couldn't reach and say things like, "Your father loved the beach. Do you remember that time we took you to the ocean and he bought you that enormous pink kite shaped like an Octopus? He tried so hard to get it up in the air for you, but it wasn't a very windy day. You cried. I thought your father was going to cry to." But of course, I didn't remember. I didn't make it up. It was here. I swear, I didn't make it up."

Rafe held her tearful glance and swiftly crossed the room to where she stood standing there holding the key up as proof of the diary's existence. He gently took her hand and raised it to his lips, then pulled her with infinite tenderness into his arms. When she just stood stiffly within their loose circle, he pushed her head down on his shoulder. "I believe you, Noelle. I swear we are going to find out what's behind all of this, and then you will truly find the closure you sought in returning to France."

Despite her misgivings as to the wisdom of it, Noelle let herself lean into Rafe's strength. She hid her face against the side of his neck and let the tears fall. "Why would anyone take my diary?" She whispered between her tears. "There wasn't anything valuable inside."

"Except proof that Michael warned you in advance about the events at Mont Saint Michel," Rafe pointed out.

"I don't think it proved anything. You would have had no trouble dismissing it as an elaborate ruse of an unbalanced psyche."

He pulled back and regarding her sternly, shook her gently. "Stop it. I don't believe you're unbalanced. We're going to get to the bottom of this, I promise."

She nodded and couldn't resist the urge to lean against him for a few more precious moments. He let her cling to him, his hand stroking her back in a soothing gesture beneath her hair, until she reluctantly drew away from him. "I suppose we have to go back."

"Yes, I believe that would be wise," he agreed, then smiling he teased, "You know how difficult it is for me to be in the same room with you, with a bed so conveniently at hand, and not test your resolve where I am concerned."

Noelle laughed, for once grateful for his teasing. "Do you think one of the staff took it?"

"I don't know. Bernard or your grandmother will know if there have been any recent additions to the household staff."

"I suppose my grandmother's going to have to know about this."

"I believe she made her feelings on the matter of being kept in the dark very clear earlier this evening, but I can't tell you what to do."

"Really? What would you call your role in this entire affair until now, except you telling me what to do?"

He smiled, but offered no defense on his own behalf, and taking her arm, led her out of the room, with only a single regretful glance back at the beckoning bed.

Later that night, back at Chateau Lucien as Noelle settled into bed in the luxurious suite of rooms provided her; she almost wished Rafe was with her. She couldn't help but wonder if her grandmother was sleeping alone. And thanks so much Rafe for planting that picture in my head. And what did that say about her own love life that her seventy eight year old grandmother's sex life was more exciting than her own?

Rolling over on her side, Noelle allowed an admiring smile to curve her lips, "Go Meme!" she whispered softly into the night. She couldn't help but hope she would be just like her grandmother when she grew up.

CHAPTER TWENTY

"Aren't we going to have to come up with some explanation as to why the two of us are spending so much time together?" Noelle directed her question in Rafe's direction where the four of them were gathered around the breakfast table, discussing their plans. Noelle hadn't had a chance yet to speak to her grandmother in private or to disclose to her and Rafe's grandfather that her diary was missing.

She couldn't help but wonder if Ari Lucien had been able to 'sweet-talk' her grandmother into his bed the previous evening. At the same time, she was trying hard not to notice the older couple seemed on remarkably good terms this morning, particularly after the intense argument brewing between them when she and Rafe left the scene. Squelching the thought instantly, she realized belatedly no one had responded to her question about Rafe and her spending so much time in each other's company. Curious she looked around the table and noticed the amused, knowing looks passing over her head.

"What? What am I missing?"

Rafe merely grinned at her disgruntled tone. It was her grandmother who took pity on her and explained gently, "I don't believe any explanation on our parts will be necessary. I imagine anyone who takes notice of the amount of time the two of you are seen in each other's company will very likely conclude that you are being considered for the role of the future Duchess of Lucien."

Noelle rolled her eyes at the laughter she saw reflected on the faces of her companions. "Carina will be devastated."

Michel bit back an amused laugh at the same time Ari asked, sending a piercing glance in Rafe's direction, "Who is Carina?"

Rafe threw Noelle an irritated look before turning to respond to his grandfather's inquiry. "A friend."

Noelle was quite certain Ari had no trouble interpreting Rafe's brief response, but he was obviously puzzled under what circumstances

Noelle, and apparently her grandmother, had made the mysterious Carina's acquaintance.

Rafe didn't waste any time exacting his revenge for her little dig, "I believe I know just the occasion for Noelle to make her debut on my arm." Noelle cast him a suspicious look, before he added grinning, "The President's Dinner honoring Bastille Day."

"Excellent, yes that will serve nicely," Ari agreed.

"That is this weekend, is it not? " At Rafe's confirming nod, her grandmother continued, "Then Noelle, dear, I believe we'd better return to Paris this morning. We'll need to go shopping."

"I thought we agreed Noelle would remain at Chateau Lucien until we understood what we were dealing with."

"No, you decreed Noelle would remain here," her grandmother corrected, "but obviously that is impossible. If Noelle is to attend the dinner at the presidential mansion, she will need an appropriate gown to wear. We'll leave immediately following breakfast." Before either Ari or Rafe could protest, she added, cutting them off with an imperious wave of her hand, "I will ask Bernard to arrange for additional security at the townhome."

"And just what does Bernard know about arranging for additional security?" Ari barked nastily.

Rafe interrupted their budding argument, "Perhaps, you will allow me to speak with Bernard in regards to the security arrangements. I will have to brief our head of security about the details of our plans. I believe it would make sense to coordinate our arrangements and to bring as few people as possible into our confidence."

"As you wish. Thank you."

They were back at her grandmother's home in Paris that afternoon The following morning Noelle found herself standing on a carpeted platform modeling evening gowns for her grandmother's approval. The designer, who went only by the single name of Louis, appeared awed by her grandmother's presence in his small salon. He'd greeted them at the door, exclaimed over Noelle's beauty, and profusely expressed his gratitude to her grandmother for her condescension in allowing him to offer his humble services to her lovely granddaughter. Then the compact proprietor had discreetly turned the open sign on his front door around to the closed side, apparently assuring that his attention and that of his small staff would not be distracted while the duchess was patronizing his establishment.

"No, I don't think so," her grandmother was saying in response to the current gown Noelle was modeling. "It's stunning," she acknowledged, turning to a hovering Louis, "but it's not right for Noelle. She is so striking in her own right that any embellishment only serves to detract from her natural femininity. Do you have anything with simpler lines? We are not trying to hide a too ample waist, or too little on top. We are trying to emphasize perfection."

"Meme," Noelle protested shocked.

"*Non. Non.* The duchess is right, of course, and her eye most discerning. Yes, I believe I have exactly the perfect gown. It is not finished yet, but if you wish, we can try it on and if you approve, do the fitting now so the gown will be ready for Saturday night."

"Yes, please, let us see it."

Noelle was beginning to feel as though her presence in the smart salon could have been replaced with a model sporting similar measurements for all the notice anyone was taking of her, but when Louis returned, reverently carrying a deep blue, silk gown, a few shades darker than her eyes, she had to admit she was curious. Her initial impression when Louis held the partially finished gown up for her inspection was vague disappointment, but she smiled genially, genuinely grateful the man was going to so much trouble for her, and anxious to ease his obvious anxiety to please her grandmother.

Once Louis had pulled the gown over her head and pinned it in place, then turned her around to face the mirror, she could understand why no one bothered seeking her opinion earlier. Obviously, she did not have her grandmother's discerning eye or instinct for fashion. She hardly recognized the gorgeous woman staring back at her from out of the depths of the three-way mirror.

"Oh Noelle," her grandmother exclaimed with tears in her eyes, before turning to a proud and relieved Louis. Noelle thought she detected a glimmer of tears in his eyes as well.

"*Fantastique! Magnifique!* You will be the most sought after woman at the ball," Louis explained.

"It's perfect," her grandmother confirmed. "Can you have it ready by Saturday morning?"

"Yes, most definitely. And I predict by Sunday morning I will be the most sought after designer in Paris," Louis added with a satisfied smile curving his lips.

"I believe you are correct," her grandmother replied with an equally satisfied smile.

Noelle was barely paying attention to the conversation going on over and around her, as Louis circled the platform, adjusting a pin here and there to perfect the fit of the gown. She didn't consider herself a vain woman, but she had to admit, in this gown, she thought she might give even the lovely Carina a run for her money.

Deceptively simple the skirt fell to mid-calf in the front and brushed the floor behind her in the back. The silk clung to her breasts and hips, fit tightly along her thighs before falling in a graceful skirt. The neckline was daring but not absurdly so and the cut made her neck look long and... elegant... was the only word she could come up with. Elegant. Yes, the description fit perfectly the reflection of the woman staring back at her, her coolly confident glance meeting Noelle's surprised one.

She hadn't been too keen on the idea of attending an important social function with Rafe. She'd known from the beginning he was out of her league, but in this gown, she knew she would at least look the part of a woman the future duke might consider for his future duchess. 'It's just a cover story, Noelle; don't go letting your imagination...fantasies more like, run away with themselves.'

"Noelle?" her grandmother asked, obviously concerned by her long silence.

She turned to her grandmother with a wide smile. "It's perfect, Meme. I feel as though my fairy godmother has just turned me into Cinderella for the ball at the palace."

Her grandmother grinned. "Yes, and I imagine your Prince Charming will be chasing after you just as desperately as Cinderella's did."

"Ha, ha. Did you perchance arrange for another date for me for Saturday night?"

"We shall see, my dear, we shall see. Now let Louis finish the fitting and we'll stop for lunch and then head out in search of the perfect shoes. I already have something in mind for your jewelry."

CHAPTER TWENTY ONE

Saturday night Noelle stood before the mirror in her five inch heels, staring at her reflection. Louis' magnificent creation, caressing every feminine curve, shimmered softly in the light from the chandelier in her dressing room. Her long hair was swept up in a sophisticated, twisting knot, compliments of her grandmother's stylist who had been pleased to attend Noelle in her grandmother's home. After her hair was done, Noelle had succumbed to the man's pleading to allow him to assist her with her make-up. Since Noelle rarely bothered with any, she could only be grateful for his offer.

Examining her reflection in the mirror, she decided that maybe it was time for her to begin paying a little more attention to her wardrobe, and things like foundation and mascara. Paul had been very restrained in his use of the luggage-sized bag of cosmetics he'd pulled out of his bag of tricks. A sweeping of shadow, eyeliner, mascara, and a little blush worked wonders. Combined with foundation, lip-gloss and a finishing powder, and her face appeared almost too perfect to be real. Her eyes looked twice their normal size and gazed out at her in wonder and growing excitement at the prospect of the night ahead. If she was honest with herself, most of her excitement stemmed from the anticipation of spending an adult evening in Rafe's company. A soft knock on her bedroom door interrupted the meandering trail of her thoughts.

"Noelle?"

"Yes. Meme, come in and tell me what you think."

When their eyes met in the mirror, Noelle watched as her grandmother's filled with tears. She swiftly turned and held out her hands. Her grandmother gripped one of hers and squeezing slightly, exclaimed, "Oh Noelle. You are so beautiful. I believe Louis' prediction will come true, and he will find himself tomorrow morning the most sought after designer in Paris. You should know he refused to allow me to pay him for the gown. He said he could have searched the entire world and never found a more perfect model for his genius. He insisted on making a gift of the gown to you."

"Oh, that was so generous of him," Noelle exclaimed, sincerely moved by the man's gesture.

"And I believe I mentioned I had the perfect jewelry in mind to complement your gown."

"Meme," Noelle protested. Then fell silent at the imperious wave of her grandmother's hand.

Her grandmother set the small box down she'd carried into the dressing room, opened it, and carefully lifted out a diamond drop necklace, the diamond the size of a plump, tear-shaped pebble. "I intended to give you this on your twenty first birthday..."

"...but I wasn't here. I'm so sorry. You know why now. And you must know I can't possibly accept such a magnificent gift even from you," Noelle protested, tears in her eyes.

Ignoring her protest, her grandmother placed the necklace around Noelle's neck and secured the clasp, then turned to retrieve the matching earrings from the box. She held them out to her, and with a shaking hand, Noelle accepted them and threaded the posts through her ears. She felt her grandmother's gentle hands descend on her shoulders and turn her unresisting so Noelle once more faced her own reflection in the mirror.

"Now, my dear," she began, with a slight smile curving her lips, "you are ready to take on even the devil himself."

Sighing, lips twitching, Noelle met her grandmother's speculative glance in the mirror, before turning her attention back to admire her own reflection. "Maybe," she agreed, thinking about the night ahead.

CHAPTER TWENTY TWO

Noelle was no expert on Paris city streets but she knew enough to know exactly when Rafe failed to take the turn that would lead them back to her grandmother's townhome. When he turned to regard her with one brow raised, as if daring her to contest his destination, Noelle met his glance, prepared to silence any protest that rose to her lips at her own recklessness. They'd both known where this night would end before Rafe even arrived at her grandmother's doorstep. The two had been exchanging small talk in the grand salon while Rafe followed with his eyes Noelle's hesitant descent down the wide marble staircase. Their eyes had met as she reached the last step. Noelle's breath got trapped in her throat at the promise she read in his.

She'd known then that the little waiting game they'd been playing with each other would end that night. She wouldn't be sleeping in her own bed at her grandmother's home in Paris. Instead, she would be spending the night in Rafe's bed and in his arms. It was a miracle she managed to make it down the stairs without tripping over her own feet. The evening had yet to begin and she was already breathless with anticipation.

Rafe had excused himself from her grandmother's side when he caught sight of her. He crossed the distance between them and held out his hand. She'd placed hers in it, very aware of its warmth and the strength in his fingers when they closed over hers and drew her closer, until they were barely a breath apart. In a romantic gesture that was purely French, he lifted her hand to brush his lips against her fingertips. "For the record, this is not a line," he began in a soft voice only she could hear. "I swear I've never seen a more beautiful woman than you are in this moment."

Tears stung her eyes at the sincerity of his compliment. "Thank you. I didn't want to embarrass you tonight."

He laughed at her anxiety. "There was never a danger of that, my sweet Noelle. Now, I shall no doubt be forced to defend my flanks against encroachers."

"Noelle, dear, you look breathtaking. I knew that gown was perfect for you," her grandmother exclaimed intruding on their whispered exchange.

"Thank you, Meme. I will try my best not to disparage the Dominique name."

"There is no chance of that, my dear. I predict you are about to add another glittering page to the family legend. For tonight at least, try to put all of this behind you and simply enjoy yourself."

As Rafe made the turn into the underground parking garage in his building, Noelle couldn't help but wonder if her grandmother had been giving her tacit approval for the romantic liaison she could no doubt sense was brewing in the air around her. If Rafe was to be believed, her grandmother had a little more experience with the Lucien male than she had let on. Her lips curved in amusement at the thought.

Rafe parked the car, and seeing her smile, asked lightly, "Dare I hope your smile is in anticipation of tonight?"

Noelle grinned, and then gave into the urge to laugh. "You're really never at a loss, are you?"

He grinned back then cut the ignition and climbed out of the driver's seat to walk around the front of the car to open her door. When she placed her hand in his, he drew her skillfully from the car and into his arms. "If you are having second thoughts you'd better give voice to them now while I still retain enough control to allow you to escape."

He whispered the words against her bare flesh along the side of her throat. Noelle barely suppressed a moan of anguish at the thought of depriving herself of this night with Rafe. She forced the breathless words passed her parted lips, "No, no second thoughts."

He shut the car door and leaned her up against it. His eyes, filled with dark promise held hers captive. "Do you have any conception of how much I have longed for this night?" Noelle couldn't look away as he bent his head to brush her lips with his. "I've dreamt of you, *Mon amour*, and woken with a longing in my blood that only you can satisfy."

142

Noelle closed her eyes on a sigh, and leaned back against the car as his lips trailed over her face, her closed eyes, along the curve of her throat. At the same time, his hands slid up her sides along the silk gown to cup her breasts. This time she couldn't suppress her moan of longing. His lips returned to hers, teased, and tantalized until Noelle couldn't take his teasing anymore and she sank her teeth into his bottom lip, bringing a smile to Rafe's lips at her impatience. He raised his head and watched her with his dark eyes for barely a moment before cupping her chin, pulling her mouth open and claiming hers in a kiss that could only be described as blatantly carnal.

Noelle had been kissed before. She was not a virgin. There had been the usual experiments with sex in college, but none of those experiences had proven so earthshattering that she'd been in any hurry to repeat them. The result being that there had been long stretches in her adult life when she'd forgone the complications of a relationship. Since she was not interested in one-night stands or casual hookups, her sex life over the past few years could only be described as dismal. She had a feeling that was about to change to a degree she wasn't completely certain she was prepared for.

As if sensing her hesitation, Rafe drew back to whisper against her lips and capture her dazed glance with his, "No regrets, my love. It is much too late for second thoughts now."

Noelle shook her head, trying to stay ahead of the torrent of emotions swimming through her veins. "No, never," she assured him, then reached up her hands to thread her fingers through his hair, and already missing the feel of his lips on hers, pulling him back towards her.

As if he'd needed that final confirmation of her willingness to be with him, one strong arm circled her waist and pulled her away from the car and against his hard masculine frame, where she came up intimately against the evidence of his desire for her. Rafe's lips left hers to trail down the length of her throat, across her chest to descend to where the tops of her breasts peeked out of the plunging neckline of her gown.

"You have tormented me all night in this gown," Rafe assured her, as his tongue dipped beneath the neckline to taste her flesh.

Noelle was losing this battle with herself. The one where she promised herself she was going to savor every moment, let each tantalizing caress be imprinted on her memory to take out at a later date and relive each erotic touch. Her mind tried to hold onto the memory of her promise to herself long enough to remind her of her intent, but it soon abandoned the unequal struggle. How was she supposed to link two thoughts together when Rafe's lips were stealing away every rational thought, even when the occasional valiant stray one managed to climb above her disorientation long enough to make its presence felt?

She leaned back against his car, uncertain if her legs would continue to support her. She wasn't certain how she remained upright in her high heels. She wasn't used to teetering around on five-inch spikes any more than she was accustomed to this feeling of teetering on the edge of a cliff, as if a fierce gust of wind would cause her to fall. She was very much afraid once she toppled into the abyss there would be no going back. She could only pray her weightless, uncontrollable flight would be a long one, because she was not looking forward to coming abruptly face to face with the hard earth that awaited her at the end of the dizzying descent.

Who was she kidding? She'd taken that dive, not cautiously, but gleefully, the moment she failed to protest Rafe's destination when their glances met across the close confines of his car. The speculation in his expression had been joined by another darker intent that he was through playing the gentleman, that if she didn't want things to progress to the next natural step between them she would have to be the one to stop things.

'Just say no,' her rational mind had urged her, reminding her of her grandmother's confessed devastation at the hands of Rafe's grandfather. Are you so anxious for that particular history to repeat itself?' Her cautious side had silently taunted her.

But of course, she hadn't. She just met Rafe's glance with a certainty that even cloaked by the fierce blush she was unable to prevent creeping up her cheeks, he had no trouble interpreting the conviction he read within its depths. A conviction Noelle could only be grateful she'd had the courage to stick to, now that she was here, a live participant in the fantasies she'd been indulging in with increasing regularity lately.

144

"Noelle," Rafe's husky voice against her lips gathered her dazed thoughts enough to force a reply through her lips.

"Yes?"

She felt his lips curve against hers at her hushed, hesitant response. She urged her heavy lids open to meet his glance, aware of the shadows hidden there, even as he reached up one hand to gently brush the stray stands that had escaped the sophisticated chignon at her neck away from her face, letting his touch linger on her skin, caressing her.

"We need to go inside."

"Why?"

His grinned flashed in the uncertain light. "Because tonight, at least, I have no intention of making love to you in the front seat of my car."

Noelle couldn't stop the erotic fantasies that flooded her thoughts at his pronouncement. "I don't think there's enough room."

"We shall put your theory to the test another day," he promised and Noelle could only sigh in response.

"All right."

At her ready agreement, which Rafe apparently took as evidence she wasn't about to get cold feet over her daring leap into the arms of the devil's descendent, one strong hand reached for hers and began tugging her towards the garage elevator. When they entered the harsh light of the lobby, Noelle caught sight of her reflection in the glass doors and hastily straightened her gown and smoothed her hair, bringing an amused smile to Rafe's lips, even as the doors opened and he pushed her into the empty elevator.

She must be as unbalanced as he believed her to be. Was she really going through with this? Was she about to spend the night with Rafe? Didn't she have enough going on in her life right now without complicating things between them? What if sleeping with him changed things between them? What if he wouldn't help her anymore?

He was supposed to take her to the bank on Monday. He'd informed her Thursday morning after their return to Paris that his security people had identified the bank and branch belonging to the safe deposit box key her father left her. What if he changed his mind? What would she do? Who would she turn to for help? Who would keep the bad guys at bay for her?

The elevator dinged, signaling their arrival at Rafe's door. Noelle all but jumped out of her skin.

"Noelle, what is going through that complicated head of yours?" Rafe asked on a sigh, seeing her reaction.

"What if this is a mistake?" She asked a little desperately.

"I cannot speak for you, but it certainly would not be a first for me," he replied drily.

Noelle's lips twitched, but she exclaimed, "I don't want things to become awkward between us. We still have to find out what my father left me in that safe deposit box."

Rather than address her concerns, he took her hand, pulled her along behind him out of the elevator, and then sent the elevator back to the lobby. He unlocked his front door, stepped aside so he could nudge her inside then shut it with a definitive click Noelle found unsettling. He pushed her back against the door and caged her there with his hands on either side of her. "Things will not become awkward between us. There is a bond between us, Noelle that is more than your regret in the morning over a night's intimacy between us can erase."

"You mean because of our families?" Noelle replied in a near panic at the look in his eyes, skimming over her face, her hair, meeting her glance briefly before dipping to where her breasts rose and fell rapidly with the pace of the breath she was desperately trying to slow while she tried to pretend she was as nonchalant about the prospect of the two of them becoming lovers as he appeared to be.

"Our families have nothing to do with tonight," Rafe told her.

"You forgot to mention your own regrets in the morning," she reminded him breathlessly.

"I don't intend on having any."

"Me, neither." Her words escaped on a husky sigh, as Rafe picked up where they left off in the garage, with his lips sliding along her throat. This time though, his hands did not remain safely caging her in. Instead, one hand gripped her hip and drew her closer, while the other wrapped around her and drew the long zipper of her dress down her back. Since the gown was strapless, there was nothing holding it in place. Released from its confinement against her perfumed flesh, it simply slid to the floor on a whispered sigh and settled around her feet that were still encased in her high heels.

At Rafe's sharp indrawn breath, Noelle raised her glance to his, trying not to blush at the realization she was all but naked while he was still formally dressed in his black tuxedo and crisp white dress shirt.

"You're beautiful," he murmured, his lips closing her eyes, as his hands caressed her naked flesh.

"So are you," she whispered, reaching up one hand to trace his jaw, already bearing the evidence of the morning beard he would be wearing when she woke in his bed after a night spent in his arms.

"I'm not going to make love to you against my front door either. At least not tonight." Rafe informed her, not without regret.

"You seem obsessed with getting me into your bed."

"Yes, the prospect has certainly been a growing obsession of mine since the night we met."

"Mine too," Noelle admitted recklessly.

Rafe chuckled at her confession while at the same time he swept her up into his arms and carried her through his enormous and tastefully decorated apartment to his bedroom.

Noelle sucked in her breath.

"Last chance," Rafe warned her, seeing her renewed uncertainty in the nervous glance she lifted to his face.

Remembering Carina, and the legions of women who had no doubt been there before her, Noelle blurted out, "I don't want to disappoint you."

Rafe's lips curved in a tender smile. "Ah, my sweet Noelle, how can you harbor such a worry?"

Before she could explain just how she could harbor such a worry, Rafe's lips bent to claim hers, chasing every rational thought from her head.

Maybe he really was the devil's descendent, Noelle thought wonderingly as his hands skimmed over her naked flesh giving rise to a dark craving within her. It had never been like this for her before. Granted, she was relatively certain none of her previous lovers (pitifully few as they were) could claim Rafe's legendary experience, but it was more. What was happening to her was more than she had even dared to fantasize it was possible for her to feel. How could this be happening to her? What was she doing in the bed of Raphael Lucien? And why, oh why, had she wasted so much time getting herself here? Her grandmother was right. The experience itself was worth an ocean of any resulting awkwardness between them in the morning.

She congratulated herself on not making the same mistake her grandmother had. She was definitely not in love with Rafe. He couldn't break her heart. Which meant she could simply enjoy the ride. Her lips curved in an amused smile at her self-congratulatory thoughts.

Seeing her lazy smile, Rafe asked, "What are you smiling about?"

Shrugging slightly, Noelle admitted, "I get to have this night with you and not wake up with a broken heart in the morning. It's a win-win from my perspective."

Chuckling, Rafe replied, "Mine, as well, that I don't have to worry about the prospect of facing you in the morning with a broken heart."

Curious, Noelle asked, "Does that happen often?"

"No. I do not make a habit of breaking a young woman's heart."

"Is that why you've been so careful with me?"

"Partly, yes."

"I can guess the other part."

"I imagine you can. "

"You're still not quite convinced are you? That I won't wake up tomorrow morning nursing regrets along with a shattered heart. You're still trying to protect me from my own impulsiveness. I don't want you to worry about protecting me tonight. I want to be with you. I want you to want to be with me. I don't want either of us to worry about what happens tomorrow."

He leaned over her, his glance holding hers, testing, probing the conviction behind her claim. "It is true I am being very careful not to give rein to the demands inside of me, urging me to take what you are so artlessly offering. I suspect you have very little idea just what I'm capable of demanding of you tonight, and I keep telling myself to go slow, to be mindful of your innocence."

"I'm not a virgin," Noelle felt compelled to confess.

His lips curved upward slightly, "And you think that makes my fear invalid?"

Thinking of the differences in their experience levels, Noelle sighed and admitted in a whisper, "Probably not, but I don't want you to be careful with me, Rafe. I want this. I've dreamt of this so many nights…just this…lying here with you…seeing you above me the way you are now…hearing your voice whispering erotic promises against my flesh…knowing I would be crazy to let you get this close, but knowing with even greater certainty I would be crazier to deny myself the opportunity to share these precious moments with you. You're right about there being a bond between us that can't be explained away by our long family history. Let's not waste it."

As if her pleading finally convinced him, Rafe held her glance for one long, penetrating moment, stripping her bare with his probing eyes, before releasing the hold on his will that had kept him from revealing to her the extent of his need for her. He'd played the part of a gentleman. Since that very first night. Denying himself. Denying them both what he suspected they could give each other, what they could be together.

He was done playing the knight-errant to her damsel in distress. There was no one threatening her now…no one brandishing guns and demanding she accompany them to God only knew what end. No, the greatest threat she faced tonight was from him. Noelle just didn't know it yet. She lay there staring up at him with wide uncertain eyes, denying her innocence, when even a blind man would have to be aware of it, in her voice, in her hesitancy; in her every surprised gasp as he touched her, as he drove her up…and they were just getting started.

He would take things slow, be careful, show her, give her a taste of what they could be together. He promised himself he would be happy with this one night. That once he'd taken her, once he'd possessed her in the way only a man can possess a woman, he would be satisfied, his curiosity appeased, and she would stop haunting his dreams so that he could return to his former uncomplicated life.

No, Noelle Dominique was definitely not in the running to become the future Duchess of Lucien, and damn Carina for putting that thought into his head. Not that his grandfather had been subtle about his own feelings on the matter. Enough! Enough speculation, enough wondering, enough procrastination and trying to protect Noelle from the consequences of her own recklessness. If the woman could go head to head with an archangel, then she didn't need his protection. God knew he was no angel.

His conclusion he would be satisfied with only this single night with her began to fray as he let himself take, as he watched Noelle let herself take. Her untutored response to his every touch was giving rise to feelings inside of him he'd never known before. He'd never been a particularly possessive lover. When one of his companions tried to rouse a jealous response in him by making sure he knew she'd been frequenting the company of another man, he simply wished her well and moved on. There was no shortage of fish in the sea, and he had no particular attachment to a single species. He loved women. Their softness, the way their minds worked, the way they walked, the way they fussed with their hair...every feminine thing about them fascinated and appealed to him on a purely masculine level.

From the beginning though, Noelle had been different. He'd been fighting it since that first night, while at the same time he had tried to convince himself she was simply a novelty. He'd been bored, growing restless with the course of his life, not understanding the cause. Into the gathering darkness surrounding him enters Noelle all bright and shiny and with a freshness about her that drew him to her like a man who'd known too much darkness.

The cynicism that gripped him had been building slowly over months, years even. His growing conviction that his life lacked true purpose. Like most members of his family, he made money with ease. He anticipated little difficulty following and adding to his father and grandfather's reputation for being a skilled and nimble businessman. The truth was while he busied himself with the family businesses and sought out new opportunities to expand them when the mood struck him, there was little true challenge in the endeavor, as so far they had all ended up predictably and often wildly successful. It was almost as if there was a hint of truth to the legends about the Luciens being descended from the devil himself. One that had more than once led an unwary opponent to conclude bitterly that the devil takes care of his own.

Then Noelle pops into his life like so much manna from heaven and presents him with this wonderfully intriguing and complicated puzzle for him to unravel. Of course, the fact that the puzzle was encased in such a pleasing, feminine package only added to its appeal. Everything about her attracted him on the deepest most masculine level... her beauty, her untutored femininity, and her uncertainty of her own appeal. Even his part of playing knight-errant to her whole damsel in distress drama was a surprisingly pleasant change from his usual casual, completely predictable interactions with women. Noelle was the first woman who'd ever penetrated the wall he kept around his relationships with the fairer sex. The barrier that ensured his relationships remained separate from his family and his heritage. He thought it sneaky, though admittedly unintentional, that she'd attacked his most stalwart defenses from inside the walls of his stronghold.

Noelle was desperately trying to convince herself her heart remained safe and separate from the rest of her body. There was no need for her to be concerned at the way it seemed to melt beneath Rafe's skilled hands, at the sound of his voice against her ear telling her how beautiful she was, that he would never hurt her, how much he wanted her, what she was doing to him. The more he demanded the more she gave until there was no longer any separation between them, until she was having trouble keeping her heart safely locked away, until she was no longer quite so certain of her claim that she could and would wake in the morning with her heart intact and still solely her own, that a single night, no matter how sexy, no matter how erotic lacked the power to change that.

The problem with her line of reasoning was that with Rafe it wasn't just a single night. There was a bond between them, yes, one perhaps rooted in their long family history, but one that had already begun to throw off shoots of its own. She was kidding herself if she truly believed anything could be casual between them. Certainly not this, not this overwhelming need to merge with him, to become one with him and give more of herself than she had ever dared risk with another man. She was inching along dangerous territory, but the feelings he roused in her made it impossible to draw back, to even consider drawing back.

Rafe had been right about one thing. It was far too late for second thoughts. If a broken heart was the price of this night with him she would face that inconsolable loss in the morning. For now, she was going to savor every impossible, unbelievable moment. When he rose over her their eyes met in the dark. She suspected he saw more than she wished he could, but she didn't flinch away from the questions she read in his.

"No regrets," she whispered even as she spread her legs and felt him probing her slick entrance, even as he parted her and drove within, slowly, giving her time to adjust to this deeper intimacy.

He pushed. She retreated. He pushed harder against the last of her shredding defenses, until she abandoned them completely and let go of her sense of caution urging her to cling to her hesitancy and her resolve to not let him all the way in. She couldn't stop herself from responding to his kiss when his lips claimed hers, from opening herself, lifting herself, wrapping her legs around him and drawing him deeper, closer, as she rose higher and higher until desperate for release she sobbed his name, her glazed eyes seeking his in the gathering madness, needing something to cling to in her suddenly reeling world.

"Noelle..."

The whisper of her name on his lips sent her careening over the edge of the very steep precipice they'd been scaling. The one they'd been dancing around since that first night when he followed her onto the terrace at her grandmother's party. Hadn't she known then he would be dangerous to her peace of mind? Hadn't she sought a moment's privacy on the terrace to escape the relentless assault of his eyes on her, moving over her face, her breasts, her legs, until she felt like a wild animal must feel when it was being stalked by a professional hunter.

Nothing in her mostly sheltered life could have prepared her for Rafe to come crashing through her carefully drawn boundaries. She closed her eyes and savored the feel of his lips sliding over hers, coaxing her own apart, to taste, to tantalize, his own curved in a slight smile at her lazy willingness to surrender so readily what had until tonight been a constant battle ground between them. He began the slow climb again. Noelle was barely aware of what was happening to her until that sense of urgency rose within her again.

How could he do this to her? It was as if he knew her own body better than she did. She was clinging to his sweat slicked arms, as he drove harder, faster. She met each thrust, crying out at the pleasure building within her, taking its own control over her scattered will until she couldn't stop herself from plunging over the edge even as Rafe dove with her, and then collapsed on top of her, their hearts rocketing in unison, their breaths coming in sharp, relentless gasps.

When hearts and breaths slowed to a more normal rhythm Rafe propped his weight on his elbows and stared down into Noelle's flushed face. His eyes roamed over her wide eyes and tangled hair with an appreciative smile filled with pure masculine satisfaction. She allowed her own lips to curve upward in a slight smile and reached up one languorous hand to thread her fingers through his hair and brush it away from his face. He turned so his lips brushed her palm.

"I have to admit that was worth the wait."

She laughed, feeling ridiculously pleased with herself and her sense of daring. Her life had certainly taken an interesting turn since her return to France. Despite all the questions dancing around her purpose in returning, she couldn't regret her one act of sheer recklessness in allowing herself to fall victim to the legendary Lucien charm. Rafe bent to capture her parted lips with his, distracting her from her happiness in the moment. When he raised his head again, an audible and satisfied sigh passed through her still parted lips.

"Well, my sweet Noelle, are you going to wake in the morning in my bed with the weight of regret for your impulsiveness weighing on you?"

He was still trying to protect her. Wasn't that sweet. No matter how hard she tried, she just couldn't seem to pin a predictable label on Rafe. He kept wriggling around her attempts to do so, surprising her with his sweetness, his rock solid reliability. She smiled up into his probing glance and shook her head. "No, I can never regret tonight."

"How about tomorrow night?" He teased and she grinned back up at him, absurdly happy at the thought that tonight might not turn out to be a one- time deal after all.

The following morning Rafe woke up with his arms full of soft, perfumed flesh, and his fingers tangled in long, silky strands. He kept his eyes closed. If this experience was going to turn out to be just another dream, or erotic fantasy he was in no hurry to bring about its inevitable, unsatisfying conclusion. Instead, he lifted his head somewhat to breathe in the feminine scent of the woman who lay sprawled across his chest, her head tucked under his chin, and her lips just touching his neck, as her rhythmic breath teased across his naked flesh. He leaned back against his pillow, sighing with contentment, and let his hands wander over the soft flesh beneath the hair his fingers had been unconsciously smoothing the tangles from.

He supposed it should concern him somewhat that the prospect of waking up in a similar fashion for the remainder of his life was not enough to send him scurrying from his own bed to the adjoining bath where he could return to his senses beneath the icy jets of a deliberately cold shower. Instead, he lay there, enjoying the peaceful aftermath of a night of passion. Noelle was still dead to the world. He supposed he couldn't blame her, and was in fact, in no hurry to wake her. He'd kept her up quite late after all.

Contrary to his rather naïve assumption a single night with her would be enough to satisfy his curiosity and growing fascination with the woman herself and the tantalizing mystery surrounding her, he was already plotting how to keep the lovely, intriguing, and at times, amusingly dramatic Noelle close by his side and in his bed. He found himself ironically rather grateful for their current circumstances, which gave him the perfect excuse to do so without delving too deeply into his feelings for her.

He recognized they were a complex mix of family duty, his enjoyment of the chivalrous role he got to play in the drama being played out around them, and the purely understandable joy and gratitude of enjoying the beautiful Noelle in his bed. She stirred in his arms and raised her head to catch him watching her. A slightly embarrassed blush rose in her cheeks.

"How long have you been watching me sleep?" Without giving him a chance to answer she added, "You should have woken me."

"Why? I assure you it is no great hardship to wake up with you soft and clingy in my arms."

When she would have pulled away, he swiftly switched their positions so she lay beneath him. He propped his weight on his elbows and stared down into her wary eyes. He supposed it was some masochistic tendency on his part that found her wariness around him charming. He reached out a gentle hand to smooth a stray dark strand back from her face.

His intent gaze watching her every expression playing across her beautiful face, he couldn't deny himself the opportunity to satisfy his curiosity. "What are you doing in my bed, my lovely Noelle? Carina assures me it is not because you have fallen desperately in love with me."

"God no!" Noelle confirmed vehemently.

Rafe grinned at her heated denial and then prompted her, "You haven't answered my question."

"Actually it was something my grandmother said," Noelle admitted, remembering that morning she'd returned from finding Carina answering Rafe's door and confessing all to her grandmother.

"Your grandmother?" Rafe echoed incredulous, his intent glance searching hers.

"Yes, something about the experience itself having its own compensation for whatever embarrassment or regret I suffered the morning after."

"I believe I would have liked to have been e a fly on the wall for that discussion, as I cannot begin to imagine how it came about." Rafe replied mystified. As he tried to picture the circumstances surrounding the conversation he had indicated he would have liked to have been a silent witness to, his lips kicked up at the corners, then his shoulders started shaking, until moments later he erupted into full-blown laughter.

Noelle's lips curved at the sight of Rafe's hilarity. She supposed she shouldn't have said anything about what her grandmother told her. Maybe it was one of those woman-to-woman things she should have kept to herself.

"And do you believe last night was accompanied by its own compensation for whatever embarrassment or regret you are laboring under now?"

"I can't think of any complaints at the moment," Noelle replied with a grin.

"You will let me know if you have any suggestions for our future nights engaged in a similar manner."

"You'll be the first to know," she assured him.

Rafe laughed at her saucy response, then rolled off of her and rose from the bed. He seemed completely lacking in any notion of self-conscious hesitancy about parading around his room naked in front of her. Noelle only wished she could mimic Rafe's lack of concern. As it was, she couldn't help inching up the sheet a little higher to cover her breasts, painfully aware of her own naked state underneath.

Rafe returned to the bedroom moments later after having disappeared into his walk-in closet. He was now crossing the distance between them carrying an elegantly wrapped box. Curious, Noelle wondered incredulously if Rafe presented all of his lovers with a morning after gift following their first night together. She couldn't deny she was fascinated at the prospect of what the box contained. It was too large to be jewelry. She couldn't begin to hazard a guess at what kind of gift Rafe might deem appropriate for such an occasion. At least, she mused, she should feel grateful that the box didn't appear to contain a thick wad of Euro notes.

Rafe stood by the bed watching each fleeting expression dance across Noelle's lovely face. When she finally lifted her gaze to his in askance, he handed her the gift he held in his hand. "As promised," he remarked, bringing fresh surprise to the curious, and somewhat offended expression she was regarding him with.

"What is it?" Noelle asked warily. Rafe wasn't the least bit surprised when she failed to reach for his gift for her.

"Open it and see."

"Is this some kind of bizarre morning after ritual you conduct with your lovers? How many of these boxes do you have stacked up in there anyway?"

Rafe only laughed at her affront and motioned for her to open the box.

Since Noelle could think of no other way to satisfy her curiosity except by doing what he suggested, she reluctantly accepted the wrapped package from Rafe's outstretched hands. With more wariness than eager anticipation about what she might discover within its depths, she unwrapped the elegant paper and cautiously lifted the lid. She placed the lid on the bed next to her then unwound the tissue to see what was inside. Laughing with delight at his surprise, she raised her wide eyes to meet Rafe's amused glance. Then she reached inside the box and lifted out the contents...an abbreviated, sapphire blue, silk robe.

"You remembered," she exclaimed, and then pushing the box off of her lap, she scrambled out of bed, robe in hand and dashed naked to the bathroom to try it on. She slid into the sinfully soft silk and tied the robe, noticing it certainly qualified as scanty. The bottom of the silk barely reached her thighs. But the material was wickedly soft, the color nearly an exact match for her eyes, and wearing it, she felt sexy and beautiful and daring. She turned away from her own reflection to model it for Rafe, who stood outlined in the bathroom door. His eyes lit with masculine appreciation, amused indulgence at her reaction to his gift, and something more she wasn't certain she could put a name to. "I love it. Thank you."

"I'm glad, and you're welcome," he replied as he stepped into the room. He kept coming until he had her backed up against the vanity.

"So," Noelle began, a little breathless at his nearness. "You never told me how many of these boxes you have stashed away in your closet."

He smiled down at her and tugged on the loose belt with one hand. The robe fell open and his eyes roamed appreciatively over the display of soft, bare flesh beneath. "You are the only woman I have ever purchased a scanty, silk robe for," he confessed, his lips gliding along her skin.

Sighing, not sure she could believe him or not, she whispered, "I'm glad." Then she gave herself up to the flood of emotions he gave birth to in her.

CHAPTER TWENTY THREE

Noelle could tell the bank manager was a little bit awed to find Raphael Lucien in his establishment. Rafe had promised when he took her back to her grandmother's townhome the morning after the President's Ball that he would pick her up the following morning to take her to the bank where her father's safe deposit box was located. Noelle didn't know if she was surprised or not to discover it was in the heart of Paris.

"All right. I guess I'll see you tomorrow." She'd replied somewhat hesitantly to his offer to escort her to the bank.

Sensing her anxiety, he gripped both of her hands and raised one to his lips. "Yes, you will see me tomorrow."

Noelle sighed, nodding, and retrieved her hands from Rafe's possession, causing an amused smile to curve his lips at her continued need to put some distance between them, even after their shared intimacy of the night before and the morning that had already begun wearing away towards noon. The reminder of their search for the safe deposit box her father had left her the key to brought her head out of the gauzy clouds she'd been basking in since the previous night. She sighed again, accepting not for the first time, that reality had a way of smacking her in the face and clearing her head of the daydreams she was inclined to lose herself in when given the chance.

"Noelle?"

She nodded and let her gaze drift up to meet Rafe's probing one. "I'm fine. It was nice to have a break from all of this, wasn't it? Last night already seems like a dream, but I guess it's time to wake up now."

Rafe's expression darkened at her rather depressing conclusion. He gripped her arms and yanked her towards him. "Last night was no dream, Noelle," he insisted then kissed her, hard, reminding her of what they had shared.

He pulled back before she could catch up to his mercurial moods, leaving her dazed and uncertain as to the message his little possessive display had been intent on delivering. "I'll pick you up at ten tomorrow morning."

She'd only nodded, unable to get her words of gratitude passed the blockage in her throat. Maybe it wasn't fair of her to let him get involved in all of this, but Rafe didn't seem too concerned about whether it was fair or not, and she was so happy to be able to confide her secrets in someone and not be alone anymore, that she didn't raise even a token protest to his proclamation. She had to admit, her grandmother was right about one thing. The Lucien arrogance did indeed have its moments.

Rafe hadn't made an appointment at the bank, not wishing to give prior notice of their plans in case whoever had tracked her down at Mont Saint Michel was somehow able to monitor their movements. As disturbing as the thought was, Noelle didn't question Rafe's tactics. She could only be relieved he was taking charge of their plans to retrieve the contents of her father's safe deposit box and was happy to go along with any safety precautions he deemed necessary.

The truth was she was shaken by the memory of almost being kidnapped by two strange men with weapons, more than she'd been at the time of the actual events. Those same strange men, who according to Ari Lucien's sources had turned out not to be members of France's military police, after all. Then to discover her father had left her a mysterious inheritance in the hands of a man he'd barely known, relying on their families' long history and his close friendship with his mother to ask such a favor of him just added to the bizarre puzzle she'd somehow ended up in the middle of.

"M. Martin may I present Mademoiselle Noelle Dominique. She would like to access her safe deposit box."

"Mlle Dominique it is a very great pleasure. You have your key I presume?" The man asked.

Noelle smiled politely and launched into the excited, totally made-up story they'd come up with to explain her delay in retrieving the contents of the box. Again, Rafe's idea, but she was determined to do her part. "Yes, of course, but there's no number on it. I am not certain which box is mine. It was set up for me by my father shortly after I was born. My mother told me the two of them rented the box and enclosed letters they both wrote on the day of my birth and a gift from them for my twenty-first birthday. This is my first visit to France since I came of age and I wanted to retrieve their memories for me."

"Of course, of course. Such a tragedy, your father's accident. Let me look up the box number for you and I will take you back to the vault."

He stepped behind his desk in his office where they had been led to immediately upon Rafe making his identity known to bank personnel. M. Martin sat down in his chair and turned his attention to the computer screen in front of him. Noelle could tell the bank manager was much affected by her rehearsed story regarding the box's contents. She was actually pretty pleased with it herself. If there really were eyes everywhere as Rafe assumed, they might just believe her heartwarming story of the former duke and his young American wife leaving a time capsule in the form of a safe deposit box for their newborn daughter to claim on her milestone birthday. Noelle was willing to half-believe that was all the box contained. A surprise gift from the father she barely remembered.

M. Martin tapped on a few of the keys, and then lifted his gaze to her anxious one. "Ah, here we are. Your box number is 813." He stood once more and added, "If you are ready, Mademoiselle, I'll take you back to the vault."

He held out one hand indicating they should precede him through the door. Noelle rose and smiled her thanks, exchanged a quick glance with Rafe, who she found watching her closely, then passed through the door into the hallway. M. Martin had apparently missed Noelle's startled gasp when he revealed the box number, but she was quite certain Rafe had not. He'd evidently decided to wait until they were alone to question her about its significance.

They followed the bank manager down the hall and into the vault, where he stopped in front of a long row of safe deposit boxes. Turning to Noelle, he instructed kindly, "If you will insert your key, Mademoiselle."

Noelle did so with a hand that shook slightly, suddenly very nervous about what she would discover inside. The manager inserted his own key and turned it, before pulling the long metal box out of its appointed slot. He carried it for her over to a nearby table where they could retrieve its contents.

Turning to Noelle with a kind smile, he told her, "I will leave you now. Please take all the time you need. I will see to it you are not disturbed."

"*Merci.* You've been very kind," Noelle replied, holding out her hand, which he grasped warmly in his.

When they were alone, Rafe turned to her. "What is the significance of the box number?"

Noelle was staring down at the box, suddenly hesitant to discover its contents. At Rafe's question, she turned to him and explained, "August thirteenth. That was the date of my first visit to Mont Saint Michel."

"But your father died before you visited," Rafe pointed out.

"Yes, I know."

"Was your trip planned in advance around a special occasion? Your birthday? Your parents' anniversary?"

"No, not to my knowledge. My birthday is in May. My parent's anniversary is in December." Seeing Rafe's disbelieving look at the incredible coincidence, she added, "Neither of my parents or my grandmother's birthday is in August."

"You don't find the coincidence in the box number and your initial visit to Mont Saint Michel somewhat disturbing?" Rafe wondered at her easy acceptance.

"I'm beyond being disturbed by such minor coincidences, as you call them. You are only disturbed by them because you are trying so desperately to find a rational explanation that would explain everything that has happened in the past few weeks."

"I would think you would be just as anxious to find the same explanation."

"I already know who's responsible so there's no need for me to obsess over such inconsequential details."

Rafe opened his mouth to argue, then quickly closed it again, and offered instead, "Perhaps we should proceed to the matter at hand."

"Yes, all right," Noelle agreed, but made no move to open the box.

"Noelle," Rafe prompted after a few silent moments.

162

Noelle shook off her lingering hesitation to discover the box's contents and reached out with hands that were noticeably trembling and lifted the lid all the way open until it rested on the table. Inside was a small velvet pouch secured with a thick thread, alike yet unlike the leather pouch her father had left the safe deposit box key in. This one appeared richer, the material purple, the thread gold. There was a faded seal embroidered on the outside, but it was so old and faded Noelle couldn't make out the design.

"This is old...very old," she whispered, struck by the ancient aura that emanated from the silk pouch. She was no expert, but a master's degree in church history had given her some knowledge of such things. "It's the kind of covering pilgrims used to safeguard sacred relics. Purple is the color designating royalty."

"Yes, I know. How do you?" Rafe asked curious.

"I have a master's degree from Georgetown University in church history." At Rafe's raised brow, she shrugged and confessed, "Just another one of my delaying tactics to keep from obeying Michael's summons to return to Mont Saint Michel."

He nodded, then added reflectively, "Perhaps he thought such knowledge might come in useful on your current quest."

"Maybe."

Gently, reverently she lifted the pouch, surprised to discover its weight, and examined its covering more closely. Unwilling to confront the suspicion forming in her thoughts she almost dropped the pouch and its contents back on the table. Only Rafe's swift reflexes prevented her from doing so.

"What is it?" He demanded, holding her hand clutching the pouch.

She held up the pouch for his inspection. "Can you make out this seal?"

His swift indrawn breath confirmed her suspicion. "That's the papal insignia."

"Yes, two keys, one gold and one silver, bound by a red cord."

Their eyes met over where their hands were clasped, the heavy pouch resting in Noelle's palm.

"I think we'd better discover exactly what your father left you."

Nodding, Noelle grasped the thread and untied the knot, but then stopped in the process of turning the pouch over to allow the contents to spill into her hand, when Rafe squeezed her arm meaningfully. "I think this is not the place for such a revelation. Let us take this back to my apartment and away from the prying eyes of the bank's security cameras."

At the reminder they were not the only ones likely interested in what the pouch contained; Noelle nodded and held out the pouch to Rafe.

Surprise at her trusting gesture lit his eyes before he shook his head and accepting her offering, quickly tucked it in her purse before handing the purse back to her. Noelle clutched her purse against her chest as if it contained an unexploded grenade that she feared any slight disturbance would detonate. Rafe closed the empty safe deposit box, lifted it back to its place in the vault and turned Noelle's key, relocking it. Turning back to where Noelle stood watching him with wide, anxious eyes, he gripped her arm and led her towards the exit.

The bright sunlight assaulted Noelle's eyes as soon as they left the bank's dimly lit interior. From where they paused momentarily to allow their eyes to adjust to the bright light, she caught sight of the spires of Notre Dame Cathedral in the distance. A feeling of unease swept over her and she clutched her purse tighter against her chest. "We need to leave now," she whispered urgently, in a voice she barely recognized as her own.

It was a voice with that faraway quality Rafe was growing disturbingly accustomed to. Keeping a tight grip on Noelle's arm, he led them swiftly away from the entrance to the bank. When they entered the lobby of a luxury hotel a few blocks away, Noelle turned to him and demanded haughtily, "What are we doing here? We don't have time for a leisurely three hour lunch."

Despite the seriousness of the situation they found themselves in, Rafe grinned at Noelle's obvious disapproval, but declined to explain the reason for their detour. Instead, he pulled her along at his side towards the front desk in the lobby.

"M. Lucien. Forgive me, Sir, were we expecting you?" The awed desk clerk inquired.

"No, Jacques, I am here to pick up a package that was left for me here."

"Oh, of course, let me get it for you."

The man seemed relieved he could accommodate Rafe's routine request. The clerk disappeared through the open door behind him and returned a few moments later. "Here you are M. Lucien," he offered, as he passed a padded, business sized envelope into Rafe's waiting hands. "Is there anything else I can do to assist you this morning?"

"No, *merci*," Rafe replied, and turning away from the desk, he tucked the envelope in his jacket pocket. He smiled slightly at the confused expression Noelle knew she must be wearing, and then he grasped her arm again and led them back across the lobby and through the exit, where he paused to retrieve the envelope from his pocket and tore open the seal.

"Rafe, I really don't think now is the time for you to be dealing with some trivial business matter," Noelle protested at the further delay, uncomfortably aware of the pouch in her purse she still had tucked close against her chest.

His eyes flashing with amusement, Rafe regained possession of her arm and directed her to the hotel's small street level parking area where he stopped near a Ferrari convertible. Before Noelle could question why they were stopping in front of the unfamiliar car, Rafe reached inside the envelope he had been given by the lobby clerk, retrieved a key, unlocked the car, and held the passenger door open for Noelle.

Stunned, admiring, Noelle slid into the front seat and waited for Rafe to join her in the close confines of the car's luxurious interior. When he settled in beside her, he made no move to start the engine. Instead, he turned to Noelle and suggested, "Let's see what's in that pouch."

Nodding, Noelle retrieved the pouch from her purse, untied the string, and then after only a momentary hesitation turned it over and allowed the contents to drop into her palm. Despite its age, the gold ring gleamed softly in the dimly lit interior of the car. Raising her glance to Rafe's she picked up the ring and turned it over so they could both see its face.

"That's a papal ring," Rafe whispered, awed.

"Maybe it's a replica, a clue my father thought would help me unravel all of this," Noelle countered hopefully, denying the evidence she had recognized immediately when it dropped into her hand.

"I don't think so, but there's one way to find out," Rafe countered.

"What are we going to do, go to Rome and knock on the front door of Saint Peter's and ask Pope Francis if he's misplaced his papal ring?"

Rafe grinned at her sarcasm, and then turned his attention to starting the car, while Noelle waited impatiently for him to explain his plan to her. Ignoring her expectant look, Rafe activated the car's Bluetooth and pressed a number stored in its memory. Noelle listened to the echo of the phone ringing on the other end before it was answered in Italian by a deep male voice, the meaning of his greeting lost to Noelle after the initial, *Ciao, Raphael.*

She supposed she shouldn't be surprised when Rafe replied in equally fluent Italian, given the lovely Carina's ancestry. *"Ciao, Gabriel….."*

After a brief conversation, Noelle could only translate a few words of; Rafe disconnected the call and turned to her, his eyes reflecting his amusement at the disgruntled look she sat regarding him with.

"You speak fluent Italian." For some reason she felt the need to point out the obvious.

"Obviously," Rafe confirmed, his lips twitching.

"Is everyone in your immediate circle named after an archangel?"

"I never considered the matter." Was Rafe's only response to her ridiculous question.

Ignoring his amusement at her expense, Noelle waited in silence for Rafe to navigate the tight parking lot and pass through the security gate and onto the busy street. Despite her determination not to give in to the urge to demand an explanation, thus making herself a further source of amusement to her secretive companion, she couldn't help but notice that they were now driving in a direction that was taking them away from both her grandmother's townhome and Rafe's apartment.

"Where are we going?"

Smiling at her obvious suspicion, Rafe announced, "Rome."

Noelle sat beside him in astonished silence for a moment, suspecting him of teasing her. Just to make sure, she confirmed, "I was only joking about knocking on the door of Saint Peter's."

"It wouldn't do us any good even if we did. That ring doesn't belong to the current pope."

"You really think this is an authentic papal ring? Aren't the rings destroyed when a pope dies? Wouldn't we know if one had gone missing somewhere along the way?"

"Not necessarily. I doubt that's the kind of detail the church cares to make public, that one of their own stole a papal ring from a dead pope and likely sold it off."

"I suppose that's true, but how in the world did this ring come into my father's hands?"

Rafe turned to her with a considering look and suggested, "Perhaps Michael would be willing to shed some light on that particular mystery."

"Very funny."

"It would save us considerable time," he pointed out. When she only rolled her eyes at his teasing, he suggested, "You might call your grandmother and let her know we'll be away for a few days."

"A few days? How am I supposed to explain that? Aren't we flying to Rome?"

"No, driving."

"How long does it take to drive from Paris to Rome?"

Rafe shrugged. "About fourteen hours. We'll spend the night in Switzerland."

"And we are driving because?" Noelle wanted to know, thinking perhaps she needed to remind Rafe that she was the one in charge of whatever was going on. Then she remembered her grandmother's claim of dealing with the Lucien arrogance for decades and her own recognition of its uses earlier. Noelle swallowed her protest before giving voice to it, but tacked on silently to herself, 'Just because the Lucien arrogance had its uses, didn't mean it wasn't extremely irritating at times.'

Rafe drew her back to the present with his response to the question she'd almost forgotten she'd asked. "Because commercial flights keep records of their passengers, and even a Lucien pilot has to file a flight plan with the authorities. I would rather not have the Lucien named linked to a spur of the moment flight to Rome the same day a certain Mlle Noelle Dominique visited a bank and retrieved an inheritance left in a safe deposit box there by her father who died two decades ago."

Distracted, Noelle asked, "A Lucien pilot? How many do you keep on staff?"

"I am not entirely certain." Rafe admitted, his confusion over the turn their conversation had taken, silencing her sarcasm for the moment.

"What am I supposed to tell my grandmother?"

"That the safe deposit box your father left you contained an old ring that points to Rome. Given our time constraints with the anniversary of your initial visit to Mont Saint Michel approaching, I wanted to consult a friend in Rome immediately as to its source."

"All right," Noelle assented with a resigned sigh. "But she's going to have questions."

"Yes, but likely she won't risk asking them until our return, hopefully with answers to the questions you refer to."

CHAPTER TWENTY FOUR

The bank manager followed the direction of the departing couple through his office window fronting the street as Raphael Lucien and Noelle Dominique hurried away from the bank entrance. Once they passed out of sight, he turned his attention to retrieving the security films of their visit. Unfortunately, they were of little use as they only covered the vault area and did not reveal what the lovely Dominique heir retrieved from the safe deposit box her father had procured for her more than two decades earlier. It could contain anything, a piece of jewelry, a family heirloom, even a digital record of the time capsule from her parents that Noelle Dominique had claimed she'd come into the bank that morning to retrieve.

It could also contain the answer to the mystery they sought. He found it infinitely frustrating to be so close and at the same time prevented from taking direct action to satisfy his curiosity as to the contents of the box. He could only watch impotently as Raphael Lucien returned the box to its designated place in the vault.

When he lost sight of the couple along the crowded sidewalk, he sat for a moment at his desk considering all he had witnessed and what it meant to their cause. Was Michel Dominique's beautiful daughter a friend or foe? There was no way of knowing. It appeared they would just have to let things play out. Fortunately, he and his compatriots were possessed of a seemingly unlimited reserve of patience. After all, they'd been on the trail of the elusive relic for more than a millennia.

CHAPTER TWENTY FIVE

The drive to Switzerland was long and scenic, but mostly silent. Noelle recognized both she and Rafe were each busy with their own thoughts. Since Rafe didn't appear in any mood to enlighten her as to their plans upon reaching Rome, and she suspected pestering him to disclose them wouldn't put a dent in his stubbornness, Noelle took the opportunity to catch up on her sleep. There had been precious little of that commodity in Rafe's bed the other night...for either of them. It was hard to believe that she'd woken up in his arms barely twenty-four hours earlier. Her memories of that night were already beginning to fade just as if it had indeed been a dream she'd conjured to escape the harshness and growing fear of the reality she faced.

When she woke from her nap, Rafe was pulling the car to a stop in front of a charming, picturesque inn, presumably somewhere either on their way to or already in Switzerland. She wasn't certain how long she'd slept, but from the stiffness in her limbs and the way the sun was beginning to dip in the horizon she'd guessed it had been for several hours.

Rafe cut the engine and climbed out of the driver's seat, and then walked around the front of the car to assist Noelle out of hers. She was grateful for his assistance as her legs still felt half-asleep. His glance was gentle as it met hers. He gave the hand he retained possession of a reassuring squeeze as he led them towards the entrance to the inn.

She stood silently by Rafe's side while he interacted with the innkeeper and noticed that while the innkeeper had greeted them in French, Rafe had replied in Italian. Noelle couldn't help but suspect he had done so deliberately so she wouldn't be able to follow their conversation. The innkeeper replied in turn, seemingly equally comfortable conversing in either language.

Moments later, Rafe reached for his wallet and pulled out several large Euro notes rather than the credit card she assumed he would use to pay for their stay. At the speculative glance the innkeeper covertly cast in her direction, she blushed slightly, suspecting the man had recognized Rafe. He had no doubt concluded the reason M. Lucien was checking into a private, independent inn and paying for his brief stay with Euro notes, was because they were trying to hide their affair from either her mythical husband, or one of the no doubt legions of potential future duchesses of Lucien.

"Do you do this often?" Noelle asked as Rafe, concluding his business with the innkeeper, turned to grip her arm and lead her to their room.

"Do what often?" Rafe countered, puzzled. "Check into a hotel?"

"Check into a hotel under an assumed name and paying with cash."

Rafe's lips twitched. "You are very observant."

"Are we hiding our tryst here from my clueless husband or your hapless wife?"

Rafe chuckled. "Since I suspect the innkeeper almost certainly recognized me, I believe the former is his most likely conclusion."

"Great. Hopefully my picture won't end up on the cover of some sleazy tabloid under the headline of the devil's descendant and his new mistress enjoy a secret getaway in the Swiss Alps."

Rafe laughed at her sarcasm. "Unlikely. The innkeeper is well aware his business relies heavily on his professional discretion."

"So I take it we won't be dining in the hotel restaurant tonight?"

"No. The room service here is rumored to be exceptional."

"You've never stayed here before?"

"No."

Noelle wasn't sure she believed him. "Is there a list posted somewhere of discreet inns where one can conceal an affair from an unsuspecting partner?"

Lips still twitching, Rafe admitted, "Gabriel mentioned this hotel was a convenient and discreet place to spend the night."

"I see," Noelle replied on a resigned sigh. "I can't wait to meet this friend of yours."

"You'll like him," Rafe predicted with a confidence she found surprising given the circumstances. At her raised brow, he added with a smile, "Women invariably do."

Noelle didn't bother responding to his claim of his friend Gabriel's predictable effect on women since she suspected he was teasing her. Silence fell between them again; until they reached the room they'd been assigned. While she waited for Rafe to unlock the door, memories of the night they spent together intruded on her thoughts, making Noelle extremely self-conscious at the thought of what stood behind the door they faced. The same door Rafe was even now standing aside and holding open for her to precede him into the room.

She kept her glance averted as she passed through the threshold. Then couldn't suppress her excited gasp at the sight greeting them on the other side. A delighted smile lit her face as the light from the fading sun danced across the canopied bed set on a platform two feet off the ground. She turned to Rafe, her previous anxiety forgotten for the moment.

"It's just like a fairytale. Can't you just see Rapunzel or Princess Arora sleeping in a bed exactly like this?"

Not waiting for his reply, she crossed the room, climbed up on the platform, turned her back towards the bed, and with her arms outstretched, she let herself fall back into the thick, down comforter covering the bed. She felt herself sink half a dozen inches to the mattress. Sighing with contentment, she turned her head to smile at where Rafe still stood by the door, watching her. "Maybe you're right about your friend. This place really is amazing."

Rafe's lips curved at Noelle's innocent enjoyment of the gauzy bed. She looked right at home there, like a child princess secure behind the thick walls of her father's keep. In her innocence, she apparently had no conception that the danger she should be fearing was already within its massive walls meant to keep that very same danger out. He'd been aware of her nervousness at the thought of sharing a hotel room with him. The pace of her breathing had quickened along with her anxiety until it was all but audible when they stood together on the other side of the door. Did the innocent truly believe he intended to force himself on her?

Gathering his composure and swallowing his increasing affront at the insult she'd offered him, he informed her stiffly, "My room is through the adjoining door. Perhaps once you are settled you would like to browse through the shops in town. Neither of us, I believe, is prepared to spend a few nights on the road."

"You have your own room?" Noelle echoed, climbing back into a seated position, all of her earlier joy squelched from the stunned expression she turned on him.

Rafe swore audibly beneath his breath. Now she was regarding him with a bruised look in her blue eyes as if he'd somehow managed to wound her gentle heart. He'd assumed she would be pleased he was willing to act the gentleman and not force her to share a bed with him simply because of the circumstances they found themselves in, on the run, and trying to stay one step ahead of whoever else was pursuing the answer to the mystery Noelle had stumbled into the middle of when she was just a little girl.

Her averted face forced him to acknowledge that Noelle did not seem exactly pleased by his show of chivalry. How was any man supposed to keep up with the mysteries of the female psyche? Sighing his frustration, he crossed the room to stand before her in front of the platform where she sat in the bed with her eyes downcast and her hands clasped together in her lap.

"Noelle?"

"Yes, of course." She rushed to cut off any further discussion of their sleeping arrangements. "I would very much like to browse through the shops in town. I'll need at least a change of clothes and some toiletries."

He ignored her obvious and rather desperate attempt to change the subject. "I didn't want you to think I expected you to share a room with me simply because of the somewhat unusual circumstances we find ourselves in."

"That's very considerate of you."

She still wouldn't meet his glance. He reached out with a deliberate hand beneath her chin and lifted her face so she could no longer avoid his probing gaze. "Would you prefer we share a room?"

Noelle felt the blush creeping up her cheeks. How was she supposed to respond to his blunt, less than romantic question? Maybe their night together hadn't meant anything to him. Maybe she had been a disappointing lover. Maybe…

"Noelle?" Rafe couldn't begin to hazard a guess at the contents of the thoughts spinning through her busy little mind but with every silent moment that passed between them without an answer from Noelle, he could see her distress deepening in the succession of vivid expressions ranging from embarrassment to dismay crossing her features. She blinked back telling tears before she raised her glance to meet his.

Resigned at the evidence of distress on her lovely face, and his apparent susceptibility to it, he smiled slightly and reached for her hands to pull her up off the bed and fold her close against his chest. She didn't respond to his embrace. Instead, she merely stood still in the circle of his arms keeping her glance averted from his face. When he bent to kiss her she turned her face away, leaving him to slide his lips up the soft skin along the side of her neck to whisper in her ear, "*Mon amour*, if you don't tell me what is upsetting you, how am I to guess?"

It was hard to argue with Rafe's very reasonable question. She supposed she was just going to have to brazen through her embarrassment. "Do you want to share a room with me?"

His lips curved into a smile along her ear, even as he pulled back and raised her face to his, forcing her to make eye contact. "Surely, after the other night you cannot honestly need me to answer your question."

"I would rather you did," she admitted, finally gaining the courage to meet his glance.

Instead of answering her, he took a step closer. She instinctively retreated, her legs coming up against the bed. He stepped closer. His intent glance holding hers was making her nervous. There was no place left except the bed for her to retreat to.

"I would rather show you," he told her, letting his knuckles trail along the side of her face.

"I thought we were going shopping," Noelle reminded him a little breathlessly.

"If you wish, I will take you, but let me now ask you a question."

"What is it?"

"Will you share this bed with me tonight? Or would you prefer I sleep in the adjoining room?"

She sighed, noting how neatly he'd turned the tables on her. She supposed it didn't matter who gave in to who. She thought she'd gotten her answer in the intent focus of his eyes holding hers. "I want you to stay with me," she whispered.

"Because you're afraid to sleep alone in a strange place?" He countered, and Noelle suspected he was only half teasing her.

"No, of course not. I want to be with you. I want you to want to be with me."

He held her glance for another moment, and then let his lips slide into his usual easy smile. "I don't think you need to concern yourself with the latter, my love. The fact that you appear so uncertain about my wanting to be with you does concern me a bit. Apparently I will have to do a better job of convincing you of my desire for you than I did the night we spent together."

She wasn't any good at this. She could have been in this same situation a million times and still not be as good at this as Rafe. On that rather depressing conclusion, she decided to keep her mouth shut, rather than risk putting her foot in it and making an even bigger fool of herself.

Smiling at her obvious discomfort, Rafe dropped a too quick kiss on her lips, then reaching for her hand, tugged her back towards the door. "Come, my sweet Noelle, let us put some distance between us and temptation or we will never make it to the shops."

CHAPTER TWENTY SIX

Noelle was in the midst of another nap to catch up on her missed sleep from the previous night when they passed into Rome. She woke as Rafe was turning into the entrance of the palace, or the Italian palazzo, she supposed was the only word grand enough to describe the elegant estate rising out of its tranquil setting seeming so out of place in the heart of the ancient city, where they were apparently meeting Rafe's friend, Gabriel.

"Your friend lives here?" Noelle asked astonished, as her wondering gaze took in her surroundings.

"Yes," Rafe confirmed smiling at her stunned expression.

"It's like a scene out of one of those movies about the decadence of Rome in the Renaissance era."

Rafe laughed and, looking around as if testing the validity of her conclusion, replied, "The Lazio family history could rival that of the Medici's."

"Really?" Noelle countered her eyes wide with astonishment.

"Yes, really."

Noelle fell silent for a few moments, than mused aloud, "If I remember my church history correctly, the Medici family can count four popes occupying a few of the branches along its family tree."

"Yes. Your memory is correct."

"And your friend's family history is similar?"

Rafe shrugged, explaining. "Gabriel is a devout Catholic. The Lazio family has always maintained a close relationship with the Vatican. One that dates back centuries."

"Are you going to show him the ring?" Noelle asked, not sure how she felt about including even a friend of Rafe's in their small circle. She really didn't think she was up for explaining again her part in all of this and having that look come into Rafe's friend's eyes when she told him about her experiences with Michael.

"No. I merely informed him that you were interested in tracing the history of an inheritance your father left you."

"And the next morning we're showing up on his doorstep? He's going to suspect something's going on," Noelle insisted.

"Undoubtedly, but Gabriel is much too polite to inquire as to its nature if we are disinclined to confide in him."

"Oh, that's a nice quality in a friend."

Smiling, Rafe turned in her direction and reached for her hand and brought it to his lips. "It is indeed."

Rafe had been right about her liking his friend, Gabriel. She couldn't imagine anyone not being charmed when their host set his mind to the task. Obviously he'd set his mind to charming her, though for no reason she could discern. He greeted them on the steps of his beautiful home where terraces lined with colorful pots overflowing with greens and flowering plants provided a welcome contrast to their grand and somewhat intimidating surroundings. Noelle suspected the statues and sculptures lining the walks and placed strategically around the formal gardens were original, priceless works of art. They were displayed in the seemingly artful, casual way only the Italians could pull off while ensuring the end result appeared neither ostentatious nor pretentious.

When she was finished gaping at the magnificent fresco works gracing the three-story entrance, she turned to exchange an awed glance with Rafe who was grinning at her reaction to his friend's home. The friend, whose eyes had met hers with a truly welcoming smile when Rafe introduced them. His manner since could not have been more gracious. Noelle had to assume Gabriel Lazio had been bred to be hospitable to guests in the same manner that Rafe had been bred to take over Chateau Lucien when his time came.

There was no discussion as to the purpose of their impromptu visit, at least in her presence, so Noelle was able to relax and enjoy herself. They dined on the outdoor terrace overlooking the glittering city skyline, on the offerings of their host's truly excellent chef. She allowed her lips to curve in a contented smile when her two companions were momentarily engaged in a conversation about a mutual friend. She gazed out on the impressive view, watching the fading light of a setting sun dance across it, giving the entire scene an ethereal halo. Her lips curving in a contented smile, she silently concluded she had very little to complain about at the moment, despite the potentially dangerous circumstances that sent Rafe and her on a wild goose chase to Rome.

After all, she had two gorgeous men seemingly intent on charming her and succeeding quite nicely, thank you very much. She congratulated herself on her good fortune and put aside for the moment the worries trying to intrude on her thoughts. Reality would make itself felt soon enough. For now, she was determined to relax and enjoy herself.

With that in mind, she replied only with a somewhat hesitant, *Grazie*, when their host reached over to refill her wine goblet. She couldn't help but notice it was a very fine crystal goblet, with nude cherubs circling the bottom. They appeared to be having a fine time gorging themselves on grapes and wine. She was so intent on studying the cherubs she missed the amused glance Gabriel exchanged with Rafe over her distracted head.

True to her intent, Noelle enjoyed the evening immensely. It was surprisingly late, and Noelle was admittedly a little tipsy on the delicious wine that had flowed in a seemingly unending stream from their host's wine cellar, before they rose from the table to say goodnight to Rafe's friend. As if sensing her uncertainty, Rafe helped her from her chair, and then wrapped a strong arm around her waist to steady her steps. Noelle could only be grateful for his solid strength. She leaned against him, hoping to clear her head, which was swimming in an unfamiliar and highly disorienting fashion.

She looked up at Rafe and shook her head slightly in an attempt to clear it, before admitting in a stage whisper, so that Gabriel wouldn't overhear her embarrassing admission. "I think I'm a little drunk."

Smiling, his dark eyes laughing, Rafe bent down to brush his lips across hers and whispered in reply, "I believe you are more than a little drunk."

Noelle wasn't so inebriated that she wasn't somewhat mortified by her condition. "I'm so sorry. I hope I haven't embarrassed you in front of your friend. I didn't realize how much wine I was drinking. I don't think I've ever been drunk before."

"No?" Rafe countered with a grin.

"I don't think so," Noelle confirmed, her brows drawing together in concentration. "I would have remembered something like that, wouldn't I?"

Rafe met his friend's amused glance over Noelle's head and nodded at Gabriel's comment in Italian.

"What did he say?" Noelle asked in another loud whisper, not daring to look back at their host. "Did you tell him I'm sorry?"

Rafe joined in the masculine chuckle from behind them that erupted at Noelle's fear. "He said you were charming and congratulated me."

"Why would he congratulate you on having a drunk dinner guest?"

Rafe grinned down into her puzzled expression, made another comment in Italian to his friend, and then replied evasively, "It's an Italian tradition."

Their host laughed. Noelle braved looking back and meeting Gabriel's smiling glance. Then looked back up at Rafe. "That's odd."

"Yes, it is."

CHAPTER TWENTY SEVEN

Noelle slept like a baby. She woke, stretching, rested, in a strange room and...naked, in a strange bed. She lifted the sheet she was wrapped in just to make sure. Yes. She was definitely naked. She didn't remember taking her clothes off the night before. She didn't remember much after Rafe helped her up the stairs after dinner. Where had Rafe slept? Where was he anyway?

The bedroom door opened as if in response to her curiosity. Rafe appeared on her threshold in all of his typical masculine perfection, showered, dressed and with no apparent after effects from the heavy liqueur she had a vague recollection of indulging in after dinner the previous evening.

"What was that?" Noelle asked, a little irritated at the perfect picture he presented at whatever ungodly hour of the morning it was.

"What was what?" He asked, grinning when Noelle pulled the sheet up around her neck. He thought her modesty a little late; given the fact, he'd helped her out of her clothes the night before. As soft and appealing as she'd been in her tipsy condition, he had merely tucked her into bed and pulled the sheet up around her. She'd been fast asleep before he reached the door to his adjoining bedroom.

"That drink after dinner. It was lemony."

"Ah, I believe you are referring to the Limoncello. It is a traditional Italian after-dinner liqueur."

"What's in it?"

Rafe shrugged, "Lemons, alcohol? You'll have to ask Gabriel."

"I'm not having any more Limoncello. I'll apologize to your friend this morning for drinking too much last night."

Rafe laughed at her guilty expression and obvious discomfort. "You might as well save yourself the embarrassment such an apology would obviously cause you, as I have no doubt Gabriel would deny noticing that you were even the least bit tipsy last night."

"I'm naked," she blurted out her other worry.

"I am well aware of that," Rafe replied, his glance descending to where she had a death grip on the sheet near her throat.

"How did I get this way?"

"I performed the service for you last night as you seemed incapable of doing so for yourself. I assumed you would prefer my assistance to one of the servants."

"Infinitely. Thank you."

Rafe raised a brow in surprise. "Aren't you going to ask me where I slept?"

"No. Even if you slept next to me, I know nothing happened. You would never take advantage of a woman who was so obviously at a disadvantage."

"No I would not. I slept in the adjoining room," he confirmed, then added curious. "Was last night really the first time you've ever been drunk?"

She nodded. Then shook her head testing. "Yes, but I have to admit I had a really good time and no hangover. I was expecting the worst."

Rafe laughed. "The Lazio cellars are considered among the finest in Europe, if not the world. A hangover would be an insult to our host."

Noelle laughed, appreciating his humor. "So what do we do now? Did you ask Gabriel about the ring, or research, or whatever the excuse you gave him to explain our sudden visit?"

"Yes. We have an appointment at the Vatican at noon. It's past ten. If you want breakfast, you'd better get dressed. We need to leave a little past eleven so as not to be late for our appointment."

"It's past ten?" Noelle echoed shocked. "We have an appointment at the Vatican?"

Rafe simply nodded in response to her astonishment, then backed out of the door, closing it firmly behind him. Did the woman truly have no idea of her own appeal? She greeted his appearance at her bedroom door as if it was an ordinary occurrence and then thanked him for undressing her and putting her to bed. Did she really believe the silk sheet she had a near death grip on at her throat offered adequate defense against his memories of what lay underneath? Memories that had haunted him all night as he tossed and turned in his empty bed only a room's width away, while she slept the night away like an innocent child wrapped in her mother's arms.

He'd checked on her more than once when she didn't come down for breakfast, telling himself if she was awake, he could indulge them both with the fantasies that had haunted him in the deepest hours of the night. Gabriel had smiled knowingly the first time he excused himself from their rather evasive discussion about Noelle's inheritance. The smile had turned into an amused grin the second time Rafe had climbed the stairs to Noelle's bedroom to check on her.

He didn't want her to wake disoriented in a strange room with him nowhere in sight was the excuse he used the third time. Gabriel had laughed outright at his weak rationale because they both had known by then there was no time for Rafe to indulge his amorous plans for the morning.

CHAPTER TWENTY EIGHT

"Captain Fils. Welcome back. Did you enjoy your holiday?"

"With my wife's family?" Jean countered at the man's cheery greeting, an incredulous brow raised in the direction of his young assistant. "Let us just say I am happy to have had an excuse to cut my visit short. I am quite grateful for my job this morning, which I suppose is the true purpose of holidays in the first place."

The painfully new recruit to the gendarmes laughed appreciatively at Jean's sarcastic wit. Sighing, remembering his retired assistant's merciless efficiency and intimate knowledge of Jean's every mood, he added distractedly, "Did anything happen around here I should know about?"

"No, nothing urgent. With the holidays, it was relatively quiet. Though there was one incident I believe you'll be interested in."

"What is that?" Jean asked, only half-listening to the other man's response to his obligatory question while he leafed through the paperwork on his desk that had accumulated in his absence. Taking his brief response as encouragement, his painfully eager assistant launched into a rambling account of the day-to-day happenings in the department during Jean's absence. At the same time, Jean bemoaned his former assistant, Claude's retirement, for perhaps the hundredth time. His attention was only partially focused on the younger man's rambling account until Jean thought he heard something about Mont Saint Michel buried within its depths.

"*Pardon*, could you repeat that?"

"Yes, Captain, I knew you would be interested. Apparently, Ariel Lucien called the head of security at Mont Saint Michel and demanded to know why two of our gendarmes had accosted a guest of his at the site."

"What?!" Jean's distraction was cleared in a breath and replaced with intent attention on the younger man's airy response.

185

"Yes, I believe your dismay exactly mirrors that of M. Denard," the young Charles commented with a wide smile. "You can imagine his frantic call to our office demanding to know what we were about assigning gendarmes to the site without the courtesy of informing him. Worse, he demanded to know what two of our men were doing accosting a guest of the Duke of Lucien."

"Why wasn't I notified?" Jean demanded, struggling to maintain his professionalism in the face of his assistant's mystifying smugness. Claude would have known to call him. Claude would have remembered his near obsession, no matter his attempts to conceal it, with all things associated with Mont Saint Michel.

His current assistant was too new to his position to recognize the dangerous tone to Jean's voice. If he did, he would not have launched into his breezy explanation with an unconcern that gave rise to serious concern on Jean's part that the young man could be so completely clueless. "It was all a misunderstanding, Captain. We didn't have any gendarmes assigned to Mont Saint Michel the morning of the incident when the duke's guest was offended and I was quite relieved to be able to pass that information along to M. Denard."

"Did you ascertain that none of our men were actually at Mont Saint Michel at the time?" Jean inquired, stifling the urge to wrap his hands around the younger man's neck and shake some sense into him.

"No," Charles responded, somewhat hesitantly, gaining a sense of his captain's concern. "I checked the schedule for the day and saw none of our men were assigned to Mont Saint Michel and assumed the incident must be some teenage prank."

Jean bit back the scathing rebuke that leapt to his lips and instead inquired stiffly, "Did Ariel Lucien inform M. Denard as to the identity of his guest? And the details of what transpired?"

"I don't believe so, or at least M. Denard didn't offer many details. He was in such a panic at the thought of having offended the duke's guest and clearly hoping he could pass the blame for the incident along to us. Believe me; I was quite happy to be able to report that it wasn't one of our men who accosted the duke's guest. The Lucien patriarch has a somewhat unpleasant reputation."

Jean bit down so hard on his bottom lip it was a wonder he didn't draw blood. "Get me Jacques Denard on the phone. I will get to the bottom of this. And call Commander Willet. Ask him to stop by my office if he's available at eleven."

"Yes, Sir."

Jean congratulated himself on the exquisite control he displayed in not leaping from his chair to wrap his hands around his young assistant's neck and squeezing the last breath from the idiot's lungs. He was still reeling from the rather casual way the idiot in question had announced that two gendarmes had accosted a guest of the Duke of Lucien. The very same idiot who had not even bothered to check if any of their men happened to be at Mont Saint Michel that day, regardless of whether or not they were there on official duty.

He would get the details from Jacques Denard, but Jean was very much afraid that the guest who had been accosted at the site would turn out to be the lovely Dominique heir. He knew she was in France. He would bet she either already had or would soon make her way to Mont Saint Michel. Given the recent incident there, and the close relationship between the Dominique's and Lucien's, Jean didn't think it was much of a leap to connect the two. Which meant that whatever had begun twenty years ago at the ancient abbey had been resurrected by Noelle Dominique's return. Swallowing the acrid taste of fear in his mouth, he reached for the phone.

"Jacques? It's Jean."

A brief chuckle was the only response to his rather abbreviated greeting. "I've been expecting your call, my friend. In fact, I'm surprised I haven't heard from you earlier."

"I've been visiting my wife's family. My new assistant neglected to inform me about the call from Ariel Lucien until a few moments ago."

"Ah, that explains it. I imagine it is at times like these when you truly understand Claude's value."

Jean sighed at the other man's sympathetic teasing. "There are no words, my friend, to voice the depth of my regret over Claude's retiring to the south to be closer to his grandchildren."

Jacques laughed appreciatively. "How may I assist you?"

"Do you have the security tapes from the day the Lucien's guest was accosted?"

"Yes I have them," he confirmed, then obviously couldn't resist poking a little more fun at Jean's expense, "I offered them to your assistant but he informed me you would have no use for them since none of your men were scheduled to work the site that day." He paused to chuckle at Jean's vivid curse. "Yes, I was quite certain you would feel that way so I had copies made. I can have one of my men deliver them to your office this afternoon."

"Thank you, but if you don't mind, I believe I shall come and collect them myself. I'd like to renew my acquaintance with the site. Can you arrange for me to view the tapes this afternoon?"

"Of course, my friend. I am at your disposal. I assure you I am as anxious as you are to get to the bottom of this. The last thing I need is Ariel Lucien breathing down my neck and making a call to my superior complaining about the treatment his guest received during her visit to Mont Saint Michel."

Later that afternoon, Jean sat with Jacques Denard in his office, reviewing the security footage from the day in question. It was as he suspected. Noelle Dominique was the Lucien guest in question, though why the old autocrat had neglected to mention his grandson's presence at the site that day as well was a mystery to him. He slowed the progress of the replay of the tapes to bring the two men dressed as gendarmes into clearer focus.

"Do you recognize either of them?" Jacques inquired.

"Regrettably not, but their uniforms appear genuine. I will contact a friend of mine in personnel and see if he can ascertain if either of these men are current or perhaps past members of the gendarmes. That would make our job of finding them a lot easier."

"I would certainly be interested in learning what prompted them to approach the young woman, what they said to frighten her, and why Raphael Lucien would feel it necessary to run from two men who presented themselves as gendarmes."

"Yes, I wondered the same thing. Either the couple suspected the two men were not the genuine article, or they had reason to fear coming to the attention of the authorities," Jean speculated.

"Let us hope it is the former because I do not believe either of us would welcome the prospect of informing the Lucien patriarch that his grandson is involved in something illegal."

"God forbid," Jean agreed.

"Either way, I can console myself with the thought that if the latter turns out to be the case, that dreadful duty would likely fall on you, my friend, and not me."

"A circumstance, I can assure you, I am painfully aware of," Jean replied with feeling.

After replaying the tapes through another time, Jean leaned back in his chair and switched off the recording. "Do you still have the copies you made? I would like to take them with me and examine them more closely."

"Of course," Jacques replied, reaching behind him to retrieve a bulky envelope from the top of his filing cabinet and passing it to Jean. "You will let me know if you learn anything of interest?"

"You may count on it. Thank you again. I'll be in touch."

Back in his office, Jean sat behind his desk and replayed the tapes again. He evaluated every passing expression on the face of Noelle Dominique and concluded it was confusion that was her initial response to the two men confronting her. Prior to that moment, she seemed completely unaware of their presence almost surrounding her and cutting her off from the other tourists filling the terrace. Certainly, her distracted demeanor was not what one would expect in the company of armed militia if one had reason to fear coming to the attention of the authorities.

Jean then turned his attention to Raphael Lucien. The Lucien heir showed no particular interest in the uniformed men prior to them confronting Mlle. Dominique. His intense focus appeared to be completely absorbed by the woman. No, Jean thought it safe to conclude that neither Raphael Lucien nor Noelle Dominique were particularly concerned about the possibility of attracting the attention of the authorities. Still, he couldn't help but wonder what made them run when one of the men addressed her.

He rewound the tape once again and tried to make out the man's words. He noticed how when the one man gripped her arm, the confusion on Noelle Dominique's face at being confronted by the two armed men, had turned to stark terror. He rewound their interaction again and concluded the fear was not in response to the man's initial request of her. There was no instinctive reaction to flee even when she became aware of the one man's grip constraining her. No, something else sent her running towards the exit. Her movement was so abrupt the two men were slow to react. She was already halfway across the stone terrace leading towards the exit before either man even realized their prey was getting away.

Raphael Lucien had taken one look at Noelle Dominique's face and immediately reached for her hand to lead her away from the men pursuing her. He no doubt wisely concluded that if there was some reason two armed gendarmes had approached his young acquaintance it would be better to confront that reason behind the safety of the Lucien stronghold. The fact that the Lucien patriarch had called within hours of the incident to demand an explanation of the head of security, led Jean to conclude that none of the parties involved feared an investigation by the authorities.

He paused the tape and leaned back in his chair, uncertain whether he should be hoping the two men turned out to be the genuine article or not. The former would make them easier to track down, the latter would at least keep him from having to make an uncomfortable explanation to his superiors as to why two of his men had offended, not one, but two, of the most powerful families in all of France.

CHAPTER TWENTY NINE

Noelle had visited Rome once before when she was a teenager. She had met her grandmother in the ancient city on one of her school breaks. At the time, she'd been too young to truly appreciate the history and grandeur of the city and the way the streets passed from one century into the next in a seemingly endless display of the complexity of Roman history. She'd been more interested in the pizza and pasta than the churches and fountains, but this time, as they made their way across town to St. Peter's Basilica she could only wish they had more time to explore and appreciate the grandeur and beauty of Rome.

"This is amazing. I wish we were here on a holiday and we could spend some time sightseeing," she exclaimed, delighted by everything.

"We can take a few days if you like," Rafe offered, surprising her.

Noelle met his glance and shook her head. "That's very generous of you, but I don't think we can spare the time. The anniversary date of my first visit to Mont Saint Michel is less than a month away."

Rafe reached for her hand and brought it to his lips. "Mont Saint Michel has stood for thirteen centuries. I don't believe another day or two will make any difference."

"But don't you have plans? Work? I'm so sorry for involving you in this, but I'm really glad you're willing to help me," she confessed earnestly.

"There is nothing more important to me at the moment than finding out if there is a threat to you and putting an end to it," he replied earnestly.

Awed, overcome by his fierce commitment, Noelle didn't know how to respond, so she simply said, "I'm really glad I met you."

His lips tilted upward at her admission, his eyes taking in the heightened color staining her cheeks. "As am I."

After they passed through security at the Vatican gate near the basilica, a member of the Swiss Guard escorted them to the Vatican entrance where they were met by a young priest, Father Nuncio.

"Signore Lucien, Signorina Dominique it is a pleasure to welcome you to Vatican City. Conte Lazio requested our assistance in your research. One of my fellow priests has gathered a few resources he believes you might be interested in. Please follow me. I have set them aside in one of the library annexes."

Noelle, her hand clasped securely in Rafe's, followed Father Nuncio along the long corridor. She was distracted by the thought that the long hallway appeared rather ordinary in comparison to the visions she anticipated of the magnificence of the Vatican museums when Rafe announced they had a meeting at the Vatican that morning. Still is was hard not to be struck by the history of the corridor she walked along, the number of priests they passed and the realization that she was likely following in at least one pope's footprints as she walked. Rafe kept a firm hold on her hand, all but dragging her along, as she was inclined to linger and peek around every corner and take in every piece of art on the wall and dotting the corridor.

When they entered the library annex, Father Nuncio stepped aside and gestured to the older man, wearing a priest collar, who was obviously waiting for them. "Allow me to introduce Father Conti. He will assist you further. Please enjoy your visit with us."

After the expected courtesies were exchanged, Noelle focused her attention on the older priest, who she estimated was in his early sixties. "How may I help you?"

At Father Conti's polite offering, Noelle launched into her rehearsed explanation about how she was doing research for her dissertation at Georgetown and how grateful she was for the Vatican's willingness to assist her. Her lies to authority figures were piling up so fast she wasn't sure she could keep track of them.

"Is there a particular topic that interests you?" Father Conti inquired politely.

"I hoped to uncover more detailed information regarding papal rings than I've been able to locate to date."

"Ah, so you are continuing your father's research," Father Conti replied. "You have obviously inherited his love of church history."

"I hope that's true," Noelle replied honestly, hoping her shock at the mention of her father was not evident on her face. "The truth is, I am not certain what I share with my father. I barely have any memory of him."

"Of course, forgive me. Perhaps you will allow me to save you some time?" The priest suggested, and then at Noelle's confused look, added, "Your father's visit was obviously some time ago, just a few months before his tragic death, I believe. He also showed a particular interest in papal rings. When I learned of your proposed visit, I took the liberty of retrieving some of the documents he spent the most time with, but if your research leads you in another direction, please let me know and I will have one of the curators assist you."

"Thank you." Noelle forced her grateful acknowledgement through suddenly stiff lips. Her father had visited the Vatican a few months before he died and sought information on papal rings. She felt an odd sense of connection with him, knowing that they had shared elements of this strange quest she was on.

Taking her silence as confirmation he had guessed correctly the direction of her research, Father Conti led them down another hall through a secure entrance to a small room within the hallowed stacks of the Vatican archives, where several illuminated manuscripts rested on a long table.

Noelle drew in a swift breath at the sight of the ancient works. "These are beautiful." she exclaimed, softly running her fingertips over one ornate cover, struck by the power emanating from it. "Thank you so much for your willingness to share them with me. I am aware they are priceless and irreplaceable artifacts. I promise to be extremely careful with them."

"Indeed, both priceless and irreplaceable, and quite sensitive to light. You can understand why we limit access to such treasures in the interest of preserving them for future generations."

"Yes, it is comforting to know so many treasures of the world's history are in such reverent and capable hands."

Father Conti met her glance and held it, meaningfully, or so it seemed to Noelle. "The church has long been tasked with the stewardship of the sacred here on earth, Signorina Dominique. I believe the church has, with rare exceptions, faithfully executed that stewardship, while remaining mindful of keeping the Lord's will as her guide as to what it is safe to reveal to the public, and when it is in the best interests of mankind to refrain from revealing a sacred truth until a more appropriate time presents itself."

"I don't disagree, Father, but surely not all that is sacred is under the stewardship of the church. To gather such enormously valuable gifts under a single roof would ultimately prove unwise, wouldn't you agree?"

"Ah, Signorina Dominique, you seem to be under the impression that the church has chosen its role as a steward of heaven's gifts to this little world. Surely, you understand it is God who does the choosing. Though to your point, I have little doubt that He has appointed many such stewards on earth. We are but a single instrument of his holy will."

Noelle got the impression there was some cryptic message contained in the older priest's admonition that escaped her. After a moment of continued expectant silence between them, Father Conti nodded in her direction and then turned and left them alone. When Noelle turned to ask Rafe about the priest's odd remark, he silenced her with a gesture and a nod in the direction of the security cameras above them. Sighing, nodding her understanding, Noelle donned one of the pairs of latex gloves left with the priceless manuscripts on the table and then took one of the chairs surrounding it. With a strange reluctance, accompanied by respectful reverence, she reached out to turn the cover of the first manuscript even as Rafe took up a position behind her so he could look down over her shoulder.

"These are incredible." Noelle spoke in an awed whisper as she turned each hand written page. It struck her suddenly that her father had likely mimicked her actions and his eyes had perused the very same pages her own were looking at now. Her eyes filled with unshed tears at the thought, making her feel closer to him in that moment than she had since she lost him so suddenly and so long ago she could barely recall his face.

Distracted from her task, she barely glanced at the pages beneath her hand until a few moments later, Rafe bent down to whisper in her ear, "Turn the pages back, three or four, slowly as if you're going over each page. Be careful not to reveal a particular interest in any of the pages."

Noelle did as he instructed, curious as to what Rafe had seen that she had missed, but she was careful to peruse each page, showing no preference for one over the other while at the same time trying to suppress her excitement as her eyes touched on the third page back, seeing it anew under Rafe's watchful eye.

How had she missed this ring? It was a replica of the one Rafe assured her was safely stowed in the safe at their host's family estate. Rafe believed it would be wiser not to risk bringing the ring her father left her into the Vatican's orbit, less the church officials found the temptation to lay claim to it too much to resist. Since her bag had been x-rayed as they entered the grounds, she could only be relieved by Rafe's foresight.

She forced herself to read quickly even as she continued turning the pages back. The page Rafe called her attention to was the one that detailed the papal ring of Pope Leo III, who served as pope from 795 to 816. The ring disappeared from view as she continued flipping the pages back. At the same time, she wondered what Pope Leo had to do with Mont Saint Michel. He ascended to the papacy nearly a century after Bishop Aubert was visited by Michael and ordered to build a church on the site. If her father had been trying to send her a message by leaving her Pope Leo's ring, she was missing its significance.

She wondered if Pope Leo had any particular connection to Mont Saint Michel or Bishop Aubert. Perhaps there was a familial connection? Bishop Aubert would have likely asked Rome for permission to construct a church on the site, and perhaps requested assistance with funding the construction. The pope at the time would very likely have been the one to grant his permission or withhold it, but what possible significance could a pope that served a century later have? She could only guess her father had stumbled over the same information and thought it significant enough that he'd left the ring in her care. What she didn't understand was why he hadn't immediately returned the ring to the church. It was, after all, by rights, the property of the church.

They spent the remainder of the afternoon perusing the other manuscripts Father Conti had pulled for them, but nothing else of a useful nature sparked their attention. By late afternoon, the writing on the pages was beginning to blur beneath her eyes. Noelle was no longer certain she had escaped her over indulgence the previous evening without penalty, as the beginning of a headache was working its way across her temples to settle into a pounding rhythm there.

Carefully closing the manuscript they were paging through, she removed her latex gloves and rubbed her temples in an effort to relieve the pain. "I think I've seen enough for one day. The pages are all running together. It's time for a break."

"Agreed." Rafe reached for her hand to assist her from the chair.

Noelle gathered her notes and allowed Rafe to lead her from the little room, where a guard informed them that Father Conti had been called away and had asked him to escort them to the exit when they were finished for the day.

They both waited until they were safely seated back in Rafe's car and pulling out of the Vatican parking lot and onto the busy streets surrounding St. Peter's square before breaking the long silence between them. "Did you note the dates?" Noelle asked anxiously

"Yes. Our ring appears to have belonged to Pope Leo III who became the pope nearly a century after Bishop Aubert would have sent his clerics to Italy in search of relics for Mont Saint Michel."

"Yes. But what does it mean?" Noelle lamented, rubbing her fingertips against her throbbing temples.

"It means we're getting closer," Rafe assured her.

"Do you really think so? I wish I shared your optimism. To me, it feels like we're wading deeper into the mud. It also means my father discovered what we did and he was dead a few months later."

"Your father's death might very well have been the accident everyone believed it was as the time."

"I know, but the coincidences keep piling up, don't they?"

"Yes, which is why I asked Gregory Jacobs to look into the circumstances surrounding your father's death," Rafe informed her.

"What did he find?" Noelle asked, holding her breath for his answer, fearing what she might learn.

Rafe reached for her hand. "Nothing as of yet that would point to the possibility that someone has gone to a great deal of trouble to conceal the true cause of your father's death. But he has not yet completed his investigation. These things take time, Noelle. Your father died twenty years ago. Tracking down witnesses, old news accounts, will take time."

Noelle nodded. "Thank you. I know I keep saying that, but I don't know how else to convey how much your help means to me."

CHAPTER THIRTY

Jean didn't know whether to be relieved or worried to learn that neither of the two men who had approached Noelle Dominique that day at Mont Saint Michel were either current or former gendarmes. One of the men, however, was indeed known to the authorities. Franc Gilliard was on a terrorism watch list, not as a member of ISIS or another of the Islamic extremist groups plaguing the world lately, but as a member of one of the homegrown variety.

He was a suspected member of the Sons of France. According to Jean's research the group traced its beginnings to the resistance movement during World War II. Hardly surprising, Jean concluded with an audible sigh, considering during the war, under German occupation, the resistance movement was not in a position to be too picky about its membership. Which led to the resistance having been forged from a rather disjointed conglomeration of competing factions. If the first loyalties of those seeking to assist the resistance were to mother France, their other oddities, beliefs and competing loyalties were often overlooked.

Amazingly, The Sons of France, were still active, though not considered an imminent danger to public safety. The group's primary objective was to arm France at all costs. Its members apparently didn't trust France's allies any further than they trusted her enemies. They threw their support behind any politician or political party that supported a *Frexit* from the Euro and increased isolationism. Jean could understand the logic of such movements in places like the United States where oceans on both coasts separated the country from Europe and Asia, but when one's homeland shared borders with eight countries, such a philosophy became much more complicated to implement.

The group had garnered increased attention by authorities lately because of all the rhetoric about closing France's borders, leaving the European Union and putting a stop to all immigration, especially halting the recent wave of Middle East refugees fleeing the civil war in Syria.

Jean decided to place M. Gilliard under surveillance, rather than pull him in for questioning. Jean was happy to have discovered the man's identity but he was not yet ready to move against him. He needed to conduct further research about this group calling itself the Sons of France. He wanted to know what they were up to. In particular, he wanted to know if they had ever directed any specific threats against Mont Saint Michel, or the surviving members of the disbanded French nobility.

CHAPTER THIRTY ONE

The following afternoon, Jean took a seat in the proffered chair before the desk of Professor Henri Thomas, a long time faculty member of the history department at the Sorbonne. He counted himself fortunate he had caught the man in his office when he tracked him down the previous week. Most academics would have scattered to their country homes this late in the season. A little research into the Sons of France had turned up the professor's name, and wasn't the Internet a wonderfully useful tool for a man in his position.

The professor sat now behind his cluttered desk, in his dimly lit office, with none of the distracted air so often associated with an aging academic. "How may I be of assistance, Captain?"

"First, thank you for seeing me, Professor. I was hoping you could provide some background information on a group calling themselves the Sons of France."

The other man nodded. "I will tell you what I know, of course, but it's a pity you are asking me about this particular group now."

Jean leaned forward in his chair. "Why is that?"

Noticing Jean's intent focus, Professor Thomas quickly waved his hand in a dismissive gesture. "Forgive me. I didn't mean to alarm you. I was only thinking that a former colleague of mine was considered somewhat of an expert on such fringe groups, but he left the department last spring."

"Where did he go?"

A Gallic shrug, accompanied by an amused chuckle, preceded the other man's response. "You may find this difficult to believe, but he moved to Rome to enter the seminary."

"He's studying to become a Catholic priest?" Jean asked astonished.

"Your surprise falls far short of my own reaction and that of his other colleagues here in the department. Nicholas had been on the

201

faculty here for over thirty years. Then one day last spring, out of the blue, or so it seemed to those of us who worked side by side with him for decades, he strolls in and announces that he's leaving the university and moving to Rome. He insisted he'd been called by God to serve in the priesthood."

"That's somewhat odd, don't you think?"

The other man laughed. "More than somewhat, in my opinion, particularly given Nicholas had never seemed particularly religious. I never even knew he was Catholic, though of course in France, most of the populace still identifies with the church, if they have any religious affiliation at all."

"Yes, of course. I am a lapsed Catholic myself, but I can't imagine what would make a man up, quit his job of thirty years, and haul himself off to Rome to study to become a priest. Didn't he have a wife, a family?"

"Yes and no. Nicholas is a widower. He actually has a son and a couple of grandchildren. They live in Nice."

"I wonder what his son's reaction was to all of this."

"According to Nicholas, his son and his family were surprisingly supportive." As if still mystified by the entire incident, the professor shook his head and then brought the conversation back around to the reason for Jean's visit. "Well, as I said, I am happy to tell you what I know of the Sons of France, but if you seek answers beyond a surface level of understanding, you would do well to reach out to my former colleague."

"Thank you. I don't believe it will come to that. Could you share with me what you know? I understand the group had its beginnings in the resistance movement in World War II."

"They were active in the resistance, certainly, but it is a common misconception that the group was born out of the resistance to the German occupation. It is in fact far older, but like most fringe groups, they have often found war a convenient breeding ground to recruit new members to further their cause."

"How far back do the group's beginnings go?"

Professor Thomas shrugged. "There is no definitive agreement on that. The name, Sons of France, was believed to have been adopted during World War II, which is why historians argue about whether this was an entirely new group, or merely a new incarnation of a far older group. Most historians adhere to the latter. The majority of that contingent believes the group was formally established at the time of the French Revolution, but there are a number of historians who would argue that even the group that emerged at that time was merely a new manifestation of a far older congregation. In the 1780's they referred to themselves as the Brotherhood of France, mimicking the church's use of the term Brothers."

"Still some experts claim the group itself has been in existence dating back to the time of the Gauls and that they have continually morphed into a new incarnation in keeping with the times. Always though they have stood for the sovereignty of France and its militarization. The group took the quick fall of the French army before the German onslaught in World War II as a catastrophe of no small matter, and it's believed the easy collapse of the French military at the time turned the group towards a more extremist ideology."

"How extremist?"

The professor shrugged. "That interpretation historians are inclined to leave to the authorities in charge of judging whether or not a particular group poses a true threat to the populace or whether they are simply posturing."

"Then how extreme is their posturing?" Jean persisted.

"I am afraid such groups are not a particular study of mine. Again, my colleague turned seminarian might prove a better resource for you. I have never been a student of such movements and know what little I've told you only because Nicholas was so passionate about them. You would be amazed at the number of extremist groups that populate history. Today it's radicalized Islam. Eighty years ago, it was the rise of Adolph Hitler and the Nazis. Are you aware the term terrorism was first used in France following the French Revolution to describe the government's violent and bloody crackdown of the counter-revolutionaries? So it goes on and on through the violent chronicle of men's often loathsome history."

"I recall there were two circumstances that most surprised my friend Nicholas in following the history of such groups, particularly in regards to the motivation behind their forming and rising. They invariably had their roots in the eternal struggle of good versus evil. Second, the groups had a much longer history than anyone suspected. It was not so much that they died out or disbanded at the end of a particular time of crisis in world history. Instead, he concluded that such groups were apt to go dormant from time to time. When their purpose was achieved they went underground, retreated, bided their time and then when the opportunity presented itself, they rose again to influence the course of world events."

"That is a rather frightening way of looking at things," Jean remarked.

"Yes, indeed, terrifying," the professor readily concurred.

"Do you think your former colleague would be willing to speak with me?"

"Oh, without a doubt. As I said, the study of such groups was a passion of his. Of course that was before he found his new calling, but I cannot imagine he wouldn't be willing to share his knowledge with you. I don't believe it's forbidden or anything."

"Would you mind contacting him and asking him?"

"Of course. I would be happy to. Leave me your contact information."

CHAPTER THIRTY TWO

"There's nothing here that I haven't read before," Noelle offered dejectedly from where she sat on the second floor terrace that connected her and Rafe's suite of adjoining rooms. A bottle of wine from the very excellent Lazio cellars sat nearly empty between them. The attentive servant had just cleared their dinner and dessert plates, with the dangerous Limoncello on its promised way. Gabriel had excused himself from dinner that evening, indicating he had a previous obligation he was unable to excuse himself from. Not surprising, given the abruptness of their unannounced visit.

"What does it say?" Rafe asked.

Sighing, Noelle read from her tablet screen. "Mont Saint Michel, a UNESCO heritage site was founded in 708 by St. Aubert, Bishop of Avranches. Legend holds that the Bishop was inspired to construct a church on the site by the Archangel Michael, who appeared to him in a dream on three separate occasions. It goes on about the history of the site, and how the monks were ejected during the French Revolution and that Mont Saint Michel was turned into a prison for political offenders." Noelle paused in her recitation and turning to Rafe, commented, "I bet Michael was not happy about his home being turned into a prison."

Rafe merely grinned in response, then asked curious, "There's no mention of Pope Leo III's involvement?"

"No, he's not even mentioned here."

"So how did it go from being a prison to a national treasure?"

"It says the government took over the site in 1872 to begin a long overdue restoration after some influential citizens objected to its use as a prison. The prison was actually closed in 1863. For a few years the abbey was leased back to the Bishop of Avranches before the government took it over."

"Hence Michael's insistence that they give it back."

"I suppose so, though the author does praise the skill of the restoration and how the government's commitment and investment saved the site from ruin."

"But Michael apparently was not mollified by France's commitment and fine restoration of his home," Rafe commented smiling.

"Apparently not," Noelle confirmed with a sigh, unsure if he was mocking her or not. "Where do we go from here?"

"Does it say what happened to the records kept at the site when the monks left? Were they destroyed in the Revolution?"

"It says it's believed the records were taken by the last monks in residence at the time of the revolution to the Diocese of Avranches, which became part of the Diocese of Coutances in 1802."

"Then I think that's our next stop," Rafe suggested.

"Why are you doing this?" Noelle asked abruptly, unwilling to risk meeting his glance.

Rafe reached across the table for her hand. "How can you ask me such a question? Prince Charming would never abandon a romantic quest and leave his lady love to the designs of evil men."

She raised her glance to his, was aware of the gentle mockery reflected there. She supposed she couldn't blame him. If someone had come to her with the same story of an angel warning of the coming destruction of the White House or some other American national treasure, she would be every bit as disbelieving as Rafe was. Certainly, she wouldn't have set off across the continent on some crazy quest for answers with the person involved.

She accepted part of Rafe's motivation was the close ties between their two families, and his concern for what those two men were after. On top of that, she thought maybe he really was enjoying playing knight-errant to her damsel in distress. When this was over, though, one way or the other, she needed to remind herself that he would return to his previous normal life. She wasn't sure where she would go, as she'd never had a normal life to return to.

"What are thinking, my lovely Noelle?" He prodded at her long silence.

She shrugged. "I was just wondering what I was going to do when this is all over. This huge threat has been hanging over my head for as long as I can remember. I'm not sure who I'll be when it's gone."

Smiling gently, Rafe stood from where he sat opposite her at the table. Still holding her hand, he pulled her up from her chair. His glance holding hers, he urged her, "Let it go for tonight."

"That's easy for you to say," Noelle's protest came out as a breathless whisper.

"Perhaps, but not I think as easy as you seem to believe it is for me to ignore any threat to you."

CHAPTER THIRTY THREE

"Thank you for seeing me, Father Delacroix," Jean offered as he shook the older man's hand, where he'd waited for Jean's arrival on the library steps of the seminary he attended.

"No, no, I am not a priest," the older man quickly protested. "I am only a year into my studies. Please, call me Nicholas."

"Thank you, Nicholas. Did Professor Martin explain my reason for asking him to arrange this introduction?"

"Yes, he indicated you were interested in the history of the Sons of France."

"Yes, that's right."

"Well as my former colleague, Henri, no doubt told you, the Sons of France, is just the current name for an organization that dates back to before the Middle Ages."

"Professor Martin indicated there was some uncertainty about that among historians."

The older man dismissed Jean's comment with a sweeping gesture of his arm. "Not among those who have studied these groups as extensively as I have."

"I see, please forgive the interruption. I am interested in anything you can tell me about them."

The former professor turned seminarian took him at his word. "Let us take a walk, shall we?" He suggested, setting off down the steps without waiting for Jean's agreement, as if he feared their discussion would be overheard. Jean quickly caught up with the surprisingly swift pace the older man set. For the next fifteen minutes, Jean listened while the aspiring priest lectured him on the various extremist groups active in France at some point or another during his country's long history. He could see why his former colleague had called the man passionate about the subject.

"Were any of these extremist groups tied to Mont Saint Michel?" Jean interjected when the older man paused to draw a breath.

Surprised by the abrupt change in subject, Nicholas' eyes probed Jean's as if he suspected Jean was hiding something from him. "As a matter of fact, several of them, including the Brotherhood."

Jean felt an icy cold trail up his spine. "Why? What would their interest be in an old abbey?"

The older man lifted his brows in askance. "Mont Saint Michel is not now, nor has it ever been, simply an old abbey, as I imagine you know very well, Captain. Did the French government spend hundreds of millions of dollars to restore an old abbey?"

Jean wasn't sure what the old man was implying. "What do you mean? Mont Saint Michel is a national treasure."

Nicholas seemed amused by Jean's insistence. "France has many such national treasures. The efforts to preserve Mont Saint Michel have been extraordinary, wouldn't you agree?"

The truth was Jean had never given the matter much thought. It never occurred to him to question why the French government had taken over the site.

"How much do you know about the history of Mont Saint Michel?" Nicholas asked.

Jean shrugged, "As much as any primary student who's had a course in history."

The older man chuckled. "So you are aware of the legends of St. Aubert, the Bishop of Avranches, being ordered to build a church on the site by the Archangel Michael."

"Yes, of course."

"And how the religious order was evicted at the time of the French Revolution and the site turned into a prison for political prisoners, and remained such until the prison was closed in 1863."

"Yes." Jean could barely contain his impatience. He was beginning to think the priesthood was an ideal new profession for the former professor of history. In the cloth, he could lecture his audience from the pulpit to his heart's content.

"And were you aware the site was then leased, note I said leased, back to the Bishop of Avranches for a few years, before the French government took over the site in 1872?"

Jean supposed he'd heard the history before, but now it struck him as odd. "Why?"

"Why what, Captain?"

"Why did the French government take over the site in 1872?"

"Publically, it was to begin the restoration work that would preserve the site for future generations. Mont Saint Michel is after all, a national treasure, is it not?"

"What aren't you telling me?" Jean demanded.

"Why did the French government take control of the site?"

"We just went over this," Jean replied, growing increasingly frustrated with the man's evasive tactics.

"Were you aware that there are legends that hold the archangel deliberately chose such a remote spot for his church, on an island that was easily defended, for a specific reason? Furthermore, these same legends hold that Mont Saint Michel was built to resemble more of a fortress than a church because it was constructed specifically to protect something?"

Jean was aware of the icy finger on his spine again. "Protect what?"

"Unfortunately that part of the legend has been lost. But that has not stopped one extremist group after another for over a millennia from setting off in search of it. Did you think the battles over the site between Normandy and Brittany were motivated purely by geography?"

"You're implying the government evicted the religious order because they didn't want whatever was hidden at Mont Saint Michel to fall into the hands of the church."

"Whatever was hidden there had always been in the hands of the church, at least until the government took over the site by force during the revolution and evicted the last remaining clergy."

Jean brought to mind a four-year-old Noelle Dominique staring up at the statue of the archangel and holding her ears and screaming, "Give it back, give it back. He says they have to give it back."

"Does the church have it?" Jean demanded.

"If they do, they're not admitting it, certainly not to me."

"What was hidden there?"

The former professor shrugged. "No one knows, but what records I have been able to piece together suggest it was a relic of great power and that Michael feared, as did the church that it would fall into the wrong hands."

"Wouldn't the Vatican have taken possession of it when France outlawed the church during the revolution?" Jean asked, fascinated by the puzzle unfolding before him.

"Yes, if they could, or even if it was still there at the time. Whatever was hidden at Mont Saint Michel, and keep in mind there's no definitive record indicating that anything ever was, that knowledge was lost centuries before the revolution."

"Even to the church?" Jean asked.

"Regrettably, yes, it appears even to the church," Nicholas replied with a sigh.

"You sound remarkably certain of that."

The older man shrugged once more. "As certain as I can be. The church of course is aware of my interests in such matters, and frankly, my expertise. My superiors have encouraged me to continue my research into ancient relics, particular those reputed to possess a supernatural origin. You can imagine my excitement at the prospect of being granted access to the Vatican archives in order to continue my research."

"I imagine, to a man of your passions, that might even be enough of an inducement to enter the seminary," Jean speculated.

Nicholas laughed off Jean's speculation. "No, no. I assure you the two are unrelated, though you are not the first to assume that was part of my motivation in leaving the academic world to enter the seminary. But that would have been extremely foolish on my part, as any serious researcher would know quite well that it is no easier for an ordinary priest to gain access to the Vatican archives than it is for even the most renowned expert in his field. Quite the contrary, I assure you. The latter has a far better chance of accessing certain documents than a priest who is simply satisfying his curiosity."

"But you are conducting research with the blessing of your superiors, so one assumes you have been granted access to the Vatican archives," Jean protested.

"Hm, true," Nicholas acknowledged, "but the access you refer to is extremely limited. They are letting me in inch by painful inch. I doubt I have enough years left to uncover any real secrets," he tacked on good-naturedly. "Not that I am sorry for their caution. Some secrets are too dangerous to be revealed to the public. I am quite happy not to be the one called upon to act as their steward."

A considering silence fell between the two men. It was Nicholas who broke it. Eyeing Jean directly, he asked, "So, Captain, now that I have answered your questions to the best of my humble ability, I hope you will satisfy my curiosity."

"In regards to?"

"I cannot help but wonder what has propelled you to track down a retired history professor in Rome and question him about some obscure fringe group and its connection to Mont Saint Michel."

Jean hesitated only briefly, before recognizing he might very well need to call on the assistance of the former professor again. "A man with connections to the Sons of France attempted to kidnap the heir to a prominent French family. The attempt occurred at Mont Saint Michel."

"Ah, how distressing. I can certainly understand your interest. I only wish I could have been more helpful."

The Captain understood he was being dismissed. "On the contrary, you've been very helpful, Nicholas, and most generous with your time. I hope I might call on you with any follow-up questions I might think of?" Jean asked.

"Of course, of course, Captain. I am at your disposal."

CHAPTER THIRTY FOUR

The Duke of Lucien leaned back in his chair and regarded Jean with an unreadable expression in his eyes, even to one for whom reading people was a critical element of his job. Jean held the old patriarch's searching glance, at the same time acknowledging the old man had acquired his reputation for intimidation not without good reason.

"So, Captain, let me make certain I understand you. One of the men who accosted Mademoiselle Dominique at Mont Saint Michel is connected with an extremist group that goes by the name of the Sons of France. According to your research, this same group may be convinced that there is some hidden relic at Mont Saint Michel that would aid in their cause. Furthermore, they believe that Noelle is in possession of some knowledge that will lead them to this item they seek?"

"In a nutshell, yes," Jean replied, ignoring the old man's incredulous tone. He very much suspected Ariel Lucien was not as astonished by Jean's account as he should be. Which meant the other man knew something he very likely was not about to share with the captain of the local gendarme unit.

"I see, that is of course a matter of some concern," the Lucien patriarch replied and rose from his chair, signaling their interview was at an end. "I thank you for your visit, Captain, and for your efforts in uncovering a motive for the potential threat to Mademoiselle Dominique, astonishing as such a motive might seem to the uninitiated. No doubt, that's why the authorities consider such groups extreme. I will speak with Noelle. I cannot fathom why she would have attracted the attention of such a group. As I'm sure you're aware, Noelle grew up in the United States. This is actually her first visit to France in almost twenty years."

Jean rose from his own chair in front of the massive desk in Ariel Lucien's personal office at his magnificent chateau. He understood the game they were playing, and suspected Ariel Lucien was far more adept at it than he was, but he wasn't ready to concede defeat quite yet.

215

"Perhaps, these men believe there was a reason for Mademoiselle Dominique's return after so long an absence. Twenty years ago Noelle Dominique was just a child. Now that she's an adult, she would have come into possession of her inheritance from her father's estate. Maybe they believe she inherited something valuable to their cause from her father." It was a shot in the dark, but Jean suspected he had struck a nerve by the hooded expression that came over the older man's face. Still, Jean couldn't help but admire his composure. He hoped he never sat around a poker table with Ariel Lucien. He was very certain he would lose his shirt before he was able to rise from it.

With a slight dismissive shrug, the older man replied, "I cannot imagine what that would be. As you are no doubt aware, the Dominique and Lucien families have been close for centuries. Had there been any talk of a valuable relic being in possession of one of the Dominique's I would have heard of it at some point, but I will certainly put the question to both Noelle and her grandmother."

"Thank you. I won't take up any more of your time. I only wanted to put you on your guard. I hope I made the right decision in bringing this matter to your attention. I was reluctant to deliver such news to the duchess."

"Captain, I applaud your discretion. There is no need to upset the duchess over this unpleasant business. It would only worry her. After the incident at Mont Saint Michel with Noelle and my grandson, Raphael, I alerted our head of security. He assures me he has taken the appropriate steps to ensure Noelle's safety for the length of her visit."

"You relieve my mind."

CHAPTER THIRTY FIVE

Noelle found herself back at Chateau Lucien, listening astonished to Rafe's grandfather's account of his meeting with Jean Fils, the captain of the local gendarme unit.

"This group calling itself the Sons of France believes there is some kind of supernatural relic buried at Mont Saint Michel of a military nature? Like a weapon?"

"Apparently, yes." Ariel Lucien confirmed.

"And he thinks they approached me that day because they believe I know where it is and I can lead them to this mythical relic?" Noelle persisted incredulous.

"That was the essence of the captain's report."

Noelle turned her astonished glance to where Rafe sat opposite her around the intimate table in the family dining room.

At the astonished silence his companions greeted his disclosures with, Ariel Lucien continued, "I believe the captain knows more than he relayed to me about this group calling themselves the Sons of France, but I really can't blame him for being less than completely open with me as I was less than forthcoming with him. However, the interview was not without benefit from our point of view. He has provided us with a name and several avenues for us to follow up on."

Turning to Rafe he added, "I think another trip to Rome is warranted. I believe you should follow-up with this retired professor who suddenly discovered a calling to become a priest. Before you meet with him, I think it would prove useful if Jacobs did a little digging into his background. Such a religious calling is not unheard of for a man in his sixties, but this Sons of France group would no doubt find it quite useful to have one of its members granted access to the Vatican archives. Particularly, if they are indeed searching for whatever relic was rumored to have been sent by the church to Mont Saint Michel for safekeeping."

"You believe this former professor entered the seminary in order to discover a clue to the location of the secret relic this group believes is hidden at Mont Saint Michel?" Rafe asked, incredulous at his grandfather's implication.

"I am merely suggesting the possibility. I find it rather odd he chose to enter a seminary in Rome when he presumably lived his entire life in France. I believe it would be wise to find out as much as we can about him. When you meet with him, I suggest you avoid confiding any more than necessary. Certainly, there is no need to reveal to him Noelle's unusual inheritance from her father. Captain Fils has conveniently provided us with the perfect excuse to follow up with the former professor. The two of you will simply identify yourselves as the members of the prominent families in France who were the victims of the attempted kidnapping."

Noelle exchanged an anxious glance with Rafe, who was quick to suggest, "There is no reason for you to accompany me back to Rome. I can meet with Professor Delacroix alone."

Noelle shook her head. "No. I would like to go with you. If this man knows something about the history of this group, and believes they have a connection to Mont Saint Michel, maybe he can tell us more about the religious orders who were housed there and what happened to their records when they left Mont Saint Michel at the beginning of the French Revolution."

"Even if he knows something about the fate of such records, I'm not certain we can risk engaging in such a conversation with him. If he is connected with the group who attempted to kidnap you at Mont Saint Michel then we might as well just admit we're on the trail of the same relic they're after."

Sighing, Noelle nodded, "You're right, but maybe there's someone else we can ask that question of while we're in Rome."

Rafe nodded. "Father Conti," he said, and then added with a smile, "Since you possess that master's degree in church history and you're considering focusing your doctoral dissertation on the popes of the Middle Ages."

"Noelle, I had no idea you were considering returning to school for your doctorate," her grandmother interjected.

Blushing, Noelle turned to her grandmother. "I'm not, Meme. We lied to Father Conti to get access to the church's records of the papal rings so we could see if we could identify the one Daddy left me in the safe deposit box."

Ari and Rafe exchanged an amused grin at Noelle's guilty expression.

Her grandmother replied with an admiring smile, "Your father would be proud of your cunning."

CHAPTER THIRTY SIX

In the end, Rafe convinced Noelle to remain behind in France while he made a second visit to his friend's home in Rome. There were things he needed to discuss with Gabriel that he couldn't broach in Noelle's presence. Noelle hadn't been happy about being left behind, but Rafe hadn't given her a lot of choice in the matter.

He now sat opposite his old friend on the same terrace where Noelle had gotten drunk for the first time in her young life on the offerings from the very fine Lazio cellars. His lips curved in a reminiscent smile when he recalled Noelle asking him why their host had congratulated him on having a drunk dinner guest. He had understood immediately the reason for Gabriel's felicitations even though his old friend's presumption was irritating at the time. It still was for that matter.

"Ah, you are still fighting the inevitable, I see," Gabriel commented into the lengthy silence that had fallen between them while Rafe sat lost in his thoughts.

Rafe drew his attention away from his musings and lifted his glance to meet his friend's amused one. "What are you talking about?"

"The lovely Noelle, of course. I presume old Ari is thrilled."

"Again, what are you talking about?"

His friend laughed at Rafe's visible frustration. "Why are you continuing to wage this losing battle with yourself?"

"You are laboring under a misconception. Noelle and I are…friends. Old Ari asked me to keep an eye on her during the course of her visit with her grandmother. You remember how close our grandparents are," Rafe explained, irritated at both himself and his friend that he felt the need to offer an explanation, and at his own discomfort in doing so.

"Friends? Not lovers? You surprise me. You are right; I was laboring under the misconception that your relationship was one of a more intimate nature. Now that you have set me straight, what brings you back to Rome? What is it? Twice in less than a week? Don't misunderstand me. I am always happy to welcome an old friend into my home. I just don't remember you ever seeking my company so eagerly in the past."

Rafe reached for his glass on the table, abused the wine it contained by downing it in a single swallow and bit down on the sharp retort that sprang to his lips at his friend's teasing. "Fine. Noelle and I are more than friends. I have no idea how it happened. Because I was very much aware of old Ari's delight at the prospect of his old friend's granddaughter becoming the future Duchess of Lucien, I was determined to stay away from her."

Gabriel refilled Rafe's wine goblet from the bottle the two of them were sharing, topped off his own, and replied, "That was both understandable and admirable of you considering the source of the temptation presented."

"Yes, well, my admirable intentions were all for naught."

Gabriel laughed. "I assure you, I had already figured that out for myself."

"She's in trouble. I need your help," Rafe confessed on a sigh.

"You may count on it, of course. I assume the trouble she's in is what prompted your visit last week and the appointment you had me arrange for the two of you at the Vatican?"

"Yes."

"It will be easier for me to assist you if you tell me what we're dealing with," Gabriel commented drily, aware of Rafe's reluctance to confide in him and not a little insulted by it.

Rafe recognized his friend's annoyance, understood its cause, but there was no denying the truth of his statement. Gabriel could hardly help unravel the mess Noelle was in if he didn't confide in him. "Do you believe in angels?"

Gabriel's expression mirrored his shock at the abrupt change of subject. He sat silently regarding Rafe from across the table and then shrugged slightly. "I don't believe I've ever considered the matter closely. I am a man of faith…a devout Catholic, as you know. So yes, I suppose I do believe in angels."

Rafe nodded. "That's a plus, because the trouble Noelle's in apparently began when she was a little girl and the Archangel Michael spoke to her while at a visit to Mont Saint Michel."

"You're joking," Gabriel protested, searching Rafe's face for any sign of amusement at his expense.

"No, I wish I was."

"Perhaps you'd better start at the beginning."

"I'm prepared to do so, but before I do, I need you to consider your offer of assistance in light of your family's close ties to the Vatican," Rafe replied in a serious tone, holding Gabriel's stunned glance.

"Are you saying the Vatican is somehow behind this trouble Noelle fell into when she was a child and believes the Archangel Michael spoke to her?" Gabriel demanded incredulously.

Rafe released an audible sigh and thrust a frustrated hand through his hair. "I don't know, but Noelle's father was in Rome conducting research in the Vatican library a few months before he died."

"I assume you realize you are implying that the Duke of Dominique's research at the Vatican somehow resulted in his death."

"I cannot completely dismiss the possibility," Rafe admitted reluctantly. "Though when Noelle raised the question, I assured her the connection was just a coincidence and her father's death was a result of the tragic accident everyone believed it to be."

"But you are no longer convinced of that."

"No."

"And you believe the Vatican had a part in the duke's death?" Gabriel echoed, stunned.

"I don't know what I believe. Certainly I don't think someone at the Vatican had the duke killed, but it's very possible his research led to his death."

"I think you'd better tell me exactly what is going on. It's clear you need my help. Had you confided in me last week I would not have sent you in blind to your appointment with Father Conti." At Rafe's continued hesitation, Gabriel added impatiently, "You may trust me to keep your revelations between us."

"Noelle's life may very well be at stake. I need to know that I can trust you with it and that you'll put her safety before your loyalties to the church."

His friend's disbelieving gaze held Rafe's for long, intense moments. Rafe understood what he was asking. His friend was not only a man of faith. He was a devout Catholic. His family's ties to the Vatican hierarchy went back centuries. Which was why his assistance would prove invaluable in resolving the mystery Noelle had fallen into. Even so, Rafe was reluctant to put one of his closest friends in the position of having to choose between their friendship and his faith.

"You have my word I will not reveal the contents of what you confide in me without your permission," Gabriel declared finally, his expression serious.

"I'm sorry for dragging you into this. If there was anyone else I could trust, who could provide the insight and the connections we need, I wouldn't have. But Noelle's in danger."

"And you're in love with her," Gabriel completed what Rafe left unsaid.

"Yes." Rafe confirmed with a reluctant sigh, abandoning his efforts at denial. He was in love with her. It didn't matter how it happened. It didn't matter that his grandfather would be thrilled. The only thing that mattered was removing the threat to the woman he loved.

"Congratulations. I envy you."

Rafe laughed. "I imagine there is no shortage of feminine applicants for the *Contessa de Lazio* position."

"Yes, well my mother is not anxious to relinquish the role," Gabriel commented drily.

"No doubt. I imagine she has not yet vacated the Florence estate and taken up residence in the dowager house?"

His friend's laughter this time was not completely devoid of bitterness. "No. I believe my mother considers her continued residency at the historical seat of the Lazio family the least compensation she is due for the embarrassment she suffered in light of the manner in which my father left this world."

"Leaving you behind to clean up his mess, as was his usual custom in life," Rafe pointed out, and then added, not without sympathy. "You're going to have to reclaim your property eventually."

"Yes. I am aware of that, but I would prefer putting off that unpleasant scene until it is absolutely necessary. My mother is still young enough to remarry. I am hoping she will eventually abandon the martyr role she's adopted and get on with her life. Certainly, there are no shortage of family properties scattered across Europe for her to take up residence in. It baffles me why she would want to remain in the property my father brought her home to as a young bride, and the one in which he more likely than not violated those wedding vows before the very fine champagne served at their wedding went flat."

"I imagine she chooses to remain in residence at the family seat because it's her way of saying fuck you to your father's memory."

"Succinctly put," Gabriel agreed drily, and then on a drawn-out sigh suggested. "Perhaps we should return to the matter at hand."

Rafe reached for the bottle between them and topped off Gabriel's glass. "Trust me. You're going to need it," he remarked at his friend's raised brow, before launching into an accounting of the events over the past few weeks that led him to his friend's door. When he was finished, Rafe made no effort to pressure his friend for the response he could see he was struggling to frame. While the silence extended between them, Rafe watched Gabriel reach for his wine, swallow it in a single gulp, mimicking Rafe's earlier gesture and then set the glass back down on the table.

He opened his mouth to speak once, twice, before shaking his head, reaching for the now empty bottle between them, and then seeing it was empty, rose from his chair to go in search of another. He returned with a bottle of brandy and two glasses. He measured out two generous shots, handed one of the glasses to Rafe, held up his own in a mock toast and then downed it in a single swallow.

"You're telling me, Noelle's father left her an authentic papal ring. One that you believe you've identified as belonging to Pope Leo III. The very same ring you stored in my safe while the two of you danced off to the Vatican to continue her father's research."

Rafe's lips curved slightly at his friend's incredulity. "We didn't exactly dance off to the Vatican, and we didn't know we were continuing the duke's research until Father Conti mentioned it."

"But one of the volumes he had already pulled for your visit contained the illustration of the pope's ring that Noelle still has in her possession, I trust. Just tell me you didn't bring it back with you to Rome."

"No, I thought it best to keep it as far away from Rome as possible, especially considering the coincidence you just mentioned of Father Conti pulling out the very book that depicted it and mentioning the duke's interest in papal rings at the time of his death."

"Presumably Noelle's father had the ring in his possession at the time he sought the Vatican's assistance in identifying it."

"Presumably."

"What a mess. You're saying Noelle still believes the Archangel Michael spoke to her that day at Mont Saint Michel."

"Yes."

"She was just a child."

"I know. I assure you I have pointed that fact out to her on numerous occasions."

"What in the world did those two men want with her? And how did they know she would be there that day? Who the hell are the Sons of France? I've never heard of them."

"All excellent questions. Unfortunately I don't have the answers, except what the gendarme captain told my grandfather about the Sons of France."

"What do you know about this captain?"

"I had our head of security look into him. He appears to be exactly what he claims to be, a concerned public servant who wanted to put us on our guard about a possible threat to Noelle."

"He seems to have gone to a lot of trouble for such a simple motivation. He interviewed this former professor-turned-seminarian personally?"

"Yes."

"So this singular incident at Mont Saint Michel sent him off on a wild goose chase across the continent to track down a retired professor, who at the age of what…sixty … up and decides to quit his job at the university and enter the seminary in Rome?"

Rafe nodded, feeling the need to point out, "The Dominique and Lucien families would not be ones a public servant would wish to be deficient in his attention to if there was indeed a probable threat from some extremist group in France."

"Nevertheless. Don't you find it a little too convenient that this professor-turned-seminarian just happened to have information about this extremist group that a professional law enforcement officer, tasked with keeping a handle on such groups had never heard of? Then this same former professor directed said officer right back to Mont Saint Michel with his speculation that some kind of ancient relic had been buried there in the eighth century. He also hints that this same group might be on the trail of this mysterious relic. Which finally leads the gendarme captain to conclude that Noelle knew what or where this relic is and that was the reason members of the group attempted to kidnap her that day at Mont Saint Michel."

"You don't trust the former professor-turned-seminarian."

"No, I do not. I think it likely he's a member of this Sons of France and he's using the Vatican archives to track down the relic they're searching for. He sounds like a fanatic. I can only hope he has not been allowed access to the more secure areas of the archives."

"So if we can't knock on the door of St. Peter's and ask if the Vatican knows what a papal ring was doing in the safe deposit box the Duke of Dominique left for his daughter, and we can't risk returning to the Vatican library to continue the duke's research, or question the professor-turned-seminarian ourselves, where does that leave us?"

Gabriel did not immediately offer a reply to Rafe's questions. After a considering silence, he commented, "I believe I will pay a visit to my Uncle Antonio."

Rafe's lips kicked up. "That would be Cardinal Lazio?"

"Yes. I'm curious to know if he's ever heard of a legend surrounding Mont Saint Michel being the repository for some ancient, sacred relic related to the Archangel Michael." At the concerned look that entered Rafe's eyes, he added, "I will merely relate that you came to me for help after the captain of the local gendarme unit near Mont

Saint Michel alerted you to a possible threat to a close family friend from a group of fanatics calling themselves the Sons of France. Trust me; my uncle does not want to be in the position of possessing information regarding the reappearance of a lost papal ring that's been missing for twelve centuries."

CHAPTER THIRTY SEVEN

With the promise to his old friend that he would be in touch after he spoke with his uncle, Gabriel set off the following afternoon on a scenic drive to his uncle's diocese in Northern Italy. The drive would take several hours. Though he could have cut his travel time significantly by flying rather than driving, he was looking forward to the silence of long hours on the highway to be alone with his thoughts. There was too little time for that lately, at least since his father's untimely death, three years earlier and precious little while his father remained alive.

Rafe had been right when he pointed out that he'd been cleaning up his father's messes since he was old enough to understand what kind of man he was. Gabriel wasn't certain which he loathed more: whitewashing his father's spectacular excesses, usually involving much younger women, or dealing with his mother's complaints about the untenable position his father had thrust her into when he insisted on recognizing that conniving little bastard, as was his mother's way of referring to Gabriel's now teenaged half-sister, complements of one of his father's particularly public affairs with one of his young administrative assistants. That particular spectacular scandal had occurred when Gabriel was still of an age when he for the most part could delude himself into believing that his father was worthy of the larger-than-life hero worship Gabriel had thrust upon him since he was a young boy.

The same hero-worship that was destined to die a painful, but still drawn-out death when one of Gabriel's school friends had confronted him with the details of one of his father's more sordid affairs with a much younger, married woman, whose husband happened to work in one of the Lazio businesses.

Bringing his attention back to the present, Gabriel turned off the highway and took the exit leading to his uncle's home. Many might consider the estate and vineyard surrounding it too luxurious for a servant of the Lord. There had actually been an article about the estate written by a foreign member of the press looking to expose the church's excesses, complete with pictures of the acres of vines and the glorious Renaissance era villa that sat at the heart of the property. His uncle had even graciously consented to give the author of the story a personal tour of the property and had given his permission for the idiot to take as many pictures as he wished.

There was quite a splash when the story first aired. The reporter had gotten what he wanted out of the expose'. Gabriel believed he'd even made a few rounds on the daily talk shows, going on and on about the waste at the highest levels of the Vatican hierarchy. The following week, a small local paper printed another story about Cardinal Lazio that was scooped up eagerly by those looking for more dirt on the Cardinal and his wealthy family whose close ties to the Vatican were well documented.

The article detailed how the small town near the Cardinal's residence was on the verge of bankruptcy after the factory that employed the majority of the town's citizens shuttered its doors. The article went on to say that Cardinal Lazio, after being elevated to the position of cardinal had elected not to take up residence in the traditional residence in one of the diocese' larger and more-well known cities. Instead, Cardinal Lazio had moved into one of his family estates located just outside the boundaries of the suffering town.

At the same time, the cardinal had decided to renovate the aging villa and estate and insisted on using local labor and materials whenever they were available to perform the work. Since the estate was owned by the family, the cardinal insisted on paying for the renovations to the estate from his personal wealth. He'd even insisted on paying for the repairs and much needed renovations to the local parish church with family rather than church funds. Since these repairs included a new roof and heating and air conditioning system, the parishioners of the small parish, many of them elderly, could not have been more pleased with Cardinal Lazio's assignment to their small diocese.

Once the renovation of the estate was complete, the cardinal had turned his attention to the grounds. Again, he hired local gardeners to bring the former formal gardens back to life and then expanded the small vineyard surrounding the estate until it became a thriving commercial venture that now employed more than the number of locals who lost their jobs when the factory outside of town had closed. The end result was that the little town was now once more thriving, and the writer of the article in the local paper was quite vocal about giving all of the credit for saving the town to Cardinal Lazio's generosity.

As Gabriel remembered, the article was picked up by the Associated Press and enjoyed its own splash in public attention, thus bringing more welcome notice to the little town. The increased publicity gave the town a boost as a weekend tourist destination and for day-trips for city dwellers to explore the charming countryside. The prospect of an afternoon at the Cardinal's vineyard, which by then hosted a restaurant and daily wine tastings, was an added incentive to attract tourists to the region. During the summer months, there were concerts featuring Italian musicians and performers. The last time Gabriel had visited; there was talk of displaying the work of local artisans and setting up a gift shop on the grounds of the vineyard.

As he approached the estate, Gabriel could see the long line of cars snaking their way towards the vineyard entrance. Smiling, Gabriel shook his head in wonder at his uncle's generosity and generally good-natured acceptance of the inconveniences and responsibilities of running a now thriving business with dozens of employees, in addition to his primary responsibilities to the church. Duties he knew his uncle took seriously.

His uncle offered Mass at a different parish church in his diocese every week. He still baptized the newly born and wedded young couples who sought the blessing of the church. He officiated at funerals, comforted the grieving, counseled the doubting, visited the sick and dying and kept up a work and social schedule that would exhaust a much younger man. At the same time, Gabriel was in a position to know his uncle was quietly and mostly anonymously generous with the needy in his district, and used his influence for the benefit of those without a voice.

Gabriel found it hard to believe his uncle and father were brothers raised in the same household. Though as young men the two had often been mistaken for twins, their natures had always been diametrically opposed. Gabriel's father, with his quick wit and engaging manner was always in the spotlight while his younger brother, Antonio, was the more reserved of the two.

As the traffic slowed near the entrance to the estate, Gabriel was grateful to be able to turn off at the private entrance leading to the villa. His uncle greeted him at his door with a welcoming smile and a speculative expression as to what crisis had compelled his nephew to seek him out in the middle of the week. The two men embraced and regarded each other with the easy familiarity of family and similar outlooks on life. A bond that had only been strengthened by grief and the various threats to the family reputation over the years, most of those a result of the carelessness of a man both men had loved until the day he died.

Pulling back, Gabriel greeted his uncle with a smile, "Uncle, do I kiss your ring?"

"Ah, well, we can see to the formalities later. What brings you to my door, Gabriel? I can see it is not for merely a pleasant, overdue visit with your uncle."

Sighing Gabriel nodded, not surprised his uncle could read him so easily. "I feel the need to unburden my soul. You will act as my confessor, I trust?"

A new seriousness entered his uncle's expression as he led them inside. "Of course. Would you prefer this reconciliation with our Lord to be conducted in the privacy of the confessional or is a face-to-face accounting acceptable to you?"

"I would prefer a face-to-face accounting, preferably over a glass of wine; and dinner would not be despised," Gabriel replied in all seriousness.

His uncle laughed at Gabriel's frankness. "I will see to it. I am ever a servant of our Lord. Whatever I can do to make the penitent more comfortable in their desire to seek a more perfect union with the divine will. As his humble servant I will spare no effort in bringing such a reconciliation about."

Laughing, Gabriel followed his uncle through the house.

After a pleasant dinner on the terrace overlooking the vineyard, during which they studiously avoided any potentially unpleasant and or controversial topics, they strolled through the formal gardens, assuring themselves of privacy for their discussion. "So, my son, shall we proceed with your reconciliation?"

"Bless me, Father, for I have sinned. It has been some time since my last confession," Gabriel began the process of reconciling himself to God with the sacrament that was as old as the church itself. He had insisted that his conversation with his uncle be held in the confines of the confessional, because such conversations were sacrosanct in the church and were protected in most civil courts around the world. His uncle could not be forced to reveal what was said in the confessional by any authority, whether it be in the church hierarchy or civil authorities. Not that he would mock the sanctity of the sacrament by deception. There was no shortage of sins weighing on his soul for him to confess, but he preferred to work his way up to the unpleasant task of baring his soul, by first seeking assistance from his uncle with the mystery at Mont Saint Michel that Noelle Dominique had unfathomably fallen into.

"You are saying this group calling itself the Sons of France believes there is a sacred relic connected to the Archangel Michael that is buried at Mont Saint Michel?" His uncle was asking, his expression mirroring Gabriel's own incredulity when Rafe confided in him.

"Yes, that is what I was told," Gabriel confirmed.

"And that members of this group attempted to kidnap the Dominique heir because they believe she possesses information in regards to its location?"

"Yes. Presumably they believe her father left her something important to their cause."

"And did he?" The cardinal asked drily.

"I believe you would prefer I not answer that question."

"I see." His uncle replied with a heavy sigh. "So presumably there is some evidence to support this fantastic notion that Mont Saint Michel has acted as some kind of repository for a relic of the Archangel Michael."

"I don't know how you want me to answer that."

"Given Michael's role as the Prince of the Legions of Heaven, and this fringe group's interest in it, it would not be too great a stretch, if this relic does in fact exist, for it to be of a nature that provides some kind of military advantage. A weapon of a supernatural origin perhaps."

"God forbid," Gabriel exclaimed.

"Yes, well, while I agree with your sentiment I very much doubt the Almighty will involve himself in the matter. Free will and so forth being what it is."

"Surely Michael would not trust mankind with a weapon of a supernatural origin?" Gabriel persisted, his dread and astonishment growing in equal measure at the absurd and frightening direction their conversation had taken.

"How am I to know the motivation of an archangel? Perhaps he is aware that mankind will be requiring such a weapon in the not too distant future, and he wanted us to be prepared."

"What are you suggesting? An alien attack of some kind?"

His uncle laughed. "Aliens? No, I hadn't considered that possibility. Actually, I was thinking of an opponent Michael is likely far more familiar with."

Gabriel hesitated, then offered, his voice dropping an octave, "You refer to Lucifer?"

His uncle shrugged. "It is mere speculation on my part, as I have never heard a whisper of any sacred relic of a supernatural origin being held in safekeeping at Mont Saint Michel." The two men fell silent for a moment, each busy with their own thoughts. Then his uncle raised his glance to Gabriel's, probing it with an intensity his nephew found unsettling. "What in the world have you fallen into, Gabriel?"

"I wish I knew. I came here prepared for you to tell me the entire legend was nonsense and it was ridiculous for anyone to believe the Vatican would have any knowledge of such things. Just one more example of the ignorant inventing some crazy conspiracy theory with the church at the middle of it. You have instead left me with the opposite impression, Uncle."

"Unintentionally I assure you. Though I must admit, I am fascinated by the possibilities such a story gives rise to. However, I have little doubt the legends you speak of will prove to have no evidence to support their fantastic claims. They are likely the remnants of exaggerated stories passed down by word of mouth over the years, particularly the mouths of those fond of such tales and not averse to embellishing them along the way to the next set of ears. You will remember much of man's recorded history was lost during the dark ages. As is the way of such times, suspicion and superstition were quick to fill the vacuum created by the absence of true knowledge. Many of these kinds of legends surrounding sacred artifacts and relics believed to be from the time of Christ, and even earlier biblical times, originated when the light of truth dimmed and chaos reigned in its place."

Just as Gabriel was beginning to feel relieved by his uncle's reassurance, the older man added in a considering tone, "Still that does not mean Noelle Dominique's experiences at Mont Saint Michel can or should be immediately dismissed as fantasy. There are more than a few largely accepted claims in mankind's history, and I am not only referring to the Catholic Church's history, of angels speaking to mortals. I will make some discreet inquiries in regards to church legends concerning Mont Saint Michel and about this seminarian who, I agree, seems to be a little bit too conveniently in place to direct the course of the official investigation, or at a minimum to be kept apprised of its progress."

"Thank you. I need not emphasize, I am certain, the need for the utmost discretion in this matter," Gabriel replied.

"No, my Gabriel, you certainly do not need to emphasize the importance of discretion to a priest. Now if we may proceed to your reconciliation with our Lord. Is your mother tormenting you again? Or is it that minx of a half-sister your father plagued you with?"

"They are both challenging, but I can excuse my half-sister's antics to the excesses of youth, and the fact that she is being raised by her mother without the least bit of concern for developing even the smallest modicum of self-discipline. No, as usual, it is my mother's refusal to move on from the circumstances surrounding my father's death that I find insurmountable."

"She was humiliated in the worst possible way by those very circumstances you refer to," his uncle reminded him gently.

"Surely she knew what he was when she married him," Gabriel responded bitterly.

"Perhaps, but a woman in love often deludes herself that she will be the one to change the leopard's spots."

"I am not certain she ever loved him."

"Which makes it more difficult for you to deal patiently with the manifestation of her grief now."

"My father died three years ago in his usual spectacular fashion in the bed of his current mistress who was barely twent at the time. Any delusions my mother retained of my father's fidelity to his marriage vows should have died with him."

"I understand your frustration, Gabriel, and applaud your patience in your dealings with both your long-suffering mother and that troublesome half-sister of yours, who unfortunately appears destined to follow in her mother's footsteps. I assure you, our heavenly Father must surely be pleased with your patience with those who depend upon your generosity and restraint."

"Thank you, Uncle. Perhaps you could suggest to our heavenly Father that it is time he sent someone else to take-over the role of trustee of both my mother and step-sister's inheritances, and of their persons apparently, as the incumbent is quickly losing the patience he is hopefully so pleased with."

His uncle laughed. "I will pass along your suggestion in my evening devotions. Now for your penance may I suggest an hour spent in quiet meditation with our lord and two Hail Mary's to our lady as your current difficulties are feminine in nature. Perhaps she will intercede with your request to our heavenly Father."

"Her assistance would be most appreciated." Gabriel replied, causing his uncle's amused chuckle in response. Then Gabriel bent his head while his uncle made the sign of the cross over him and murmured the prayer absolving him of his sins.

CHAPTER THIRTY EIGHT

The improbable head of the Sons of France sat behind his desk in his personal office in his home. He was careful not to keep any evidence that would tie him to their cause in his workplace. Ironically, he understood his position in a city that had experienced more terrorist attacks in recent years than any other city in the west made him the subject of intense scrutiny from supporters of the majority if not all of the political parties in France who hoped to gain influence in the upcoming elections.

France seemingly was the battleground of the immigration debate. The ruling coalition in neighboring Germany was dealing with its own fall-out over its open door policy. Why any political figure tasked with keeping its citizens safe would open its doors to millions of refugees with too little concern for the security risk presented by terrorists masquerading as refugees was beyond him. He applauded their Christian values, which motivated their generosity and provoked their sympathies, but shook his head over their inconceivable innocence.

Returning to the matter at hand, he slit open the envelope the courier had just delivered from one of the group's lesser members and retrieved the neatly typed report. He stood from his desk to recover the current code for Sons' communications from his wall safe.

His hand trembled with anticipation as he translated the contents. They were close. Closer than they'd ever been, in his lifetime, certainly. He was quite certain Noelle Dominique was the key. It had been a mistake to attempt to take her. One that was crudely executed and that had resulted in the kind of spectacular failure one expected from such a foolish maneuver. He had been too anxious when the brother in place at Chateau Dominique had informed him the young Dominique heir intended to return alone to Mont Saint Michel the day after the duke's daughter had visited with his mother, the duchess.

The day had not been a complete loss. Noelle Dominique's diary was now in their possession, compliments of the same brother. They had yet to recover anything useful from it, but their experts continued to attempt to decipher it. He'd seen copies of the pages, but he'd been unable to make any sense of them. Clearly, they were written in some kind of primitive, even childish code. He put the mystery of the diary aside. Once they recovered Noelle Dominique, she would unmask the contents for them.

He returned his attention to the report on his desk. The Luciens' involvement was unfortunate, but not insurmountable, and could be made to work to their advantage. The Luciens' had connections, particularly in Rome, that the Brotherhood did not. Despite their efforts over the centuries, they had never managed to climb beyond the most mediocre administrative levels of the Curia.

The Lazio's influence, on the other hand, reached to the highest levels of the Vatican hierarchy. Raphael Lucien and Gabriel Lazio were old friends. The Lucien heir's recent trip to Rome, accompanied by Noelle Dominique, shortly after they had retrieved the contents of a mysterious safe deposit box left to her from her father presented all sorts of interesting possibilities.

It might make more sense to allow Mlle Dominique, with the aid of Raphael Lucien, to retrieve the relic for them, and simply take possession of it after they had done so. As much as he would like to be the one credited with locating the archangel's lost relic after all this time, he rebuked himself to keep his focus on the end game.

The relic was the key to returning France to her former glory in world affairs. Once it was in their possession, France would never again suffer the embarrassment his homeland endured in World War II or the inconceivable losses of a generation of young men in World War I. Nor would she be forced to pay homage at the altar of America's military dominance, nor accept with barely a murmur of protest America's insufferable arrogance on the world stage. Nor, he swore silently, his eyes burning with intensity, would the extremists and jihadists shouting their allegiance to their Allah ever again defile France's soil with their disgusting acts of violence against the innocent.

CHAPTER THIRTY NINE

"What did Gabriel say?" Noelle asked anxiously as she flung open the door to her grandmother's home in Paris. Apparently, she'd been watching for his car and was too impatient, in typical American fashion, to wait for Bernard to perform his duty and open her grandmother's door to guests.

Rafe wasn't certain why he found her inability to do so charming, rather than irritating. So much for his plans to put off any discussion of the reason for his visit to Rome until after they had dined. "I will tell you what he said over dinner. How have you been entertaining yourself for the past two days?"

"I've been doing some research trying to connect Pope Leo III to Mont Saint Michel."

"Did you discover anything interesting?" Rafe asked as he settled Noelle into the front seat of his car. He'd returned from Rome earlier in the day and went straight to his office to catch up on a few urgent matters he'd neglected in his pursuit of answers to Noelle's mystery, but his afternoon had not been a productive one. Thoughts of Noelle, of her beauty, of her innocence kept invading his concentration until he'd finally abandoned the effort at proving to himself he was more than capable of keeping his distance, that he had not fallen victim to her charming femininity and become a predictable cliché of a man in love.

Noelle waited to reply to Rafe's inquiry until he was settled in the front seat next to her in the close confines of his convertible. "I will tell you what I discovered over dinner."

Rafe grinned at her impudent reply and reached over to wrap one hand around the back of her neck and pull and her towards him. "Did you miss me?" He teased, their lips a breath apart.

"Maybe," Noelle whispered.

"Just maybe?" Rafe countered. "Then let me remind you of what you missed."

He closed the slight distance separating them and captured her lips. Noelle allowed herself to be reminded. She closed her eyes and let Rafe draw her under. Who was she kidding? She was quite certain Rafe hadn't been deceived by her less than truthful reply about missing him. She was very much afraid she was destined to share her grandmother's fate at the hands of another Lucien male. She was falling in love with him. Maybe she already had fallen. How would she know? She had never before in her life felt these intense feelings rushing through her.

After the *maître d'* seated them and the sommelier delivered the requested wine, Rafe leaned back in his chair and asked, "So, what did you discover in your research while I was away?"

Noelle hesitated, wanting to hear first what Rafe had discovered from Gabriel, and then accepted it would be quicker to reach her ultimate goal by just telling Rafe what he wanted to know, rather than argue with him over who reported their progress first. With a resigned sigh, she detailed the results of her research for Rafe.

"Well, Michael apparently had no shortage of devotees among the powerful figures in France over the past millennia or so. In the year 813, Charlemagne placed himself under the archangel's protection by ordering Michael's feast day be celebrated throughout the Frankish empire. King Charles VI and VII were both ardent admirers and one of them declared Michael a royal saint. Even Joan of Arc, who was burned at the stake and who later became a saint herself after she was martyred, seemingly had her own delusions of Michael speaking to her. According to my research, she reputedly believed Michael instructed her, "I am Michael, the protector of France. Rise up and go to the aid of the King."

"Over the years the abbey's unlikely ability to hold off English assaults gave further credence to Michael's role as the protector of France. Even after the revolution and the oppression of the church in France, the archangel remained an important symbol for the people of France. He was called upon to assist France in their battle against the Germans nearly a century after the French Revolution."

Noelle paused on a sigh, and added discouraged, "Which is all very interesting but it doesn't explain where Pope Leo III fits in to all of this."

"Were you able to discover anything about Pope Leo?" Rafe asked, fascinated in spite of himself.

Noelle shrugged and began sharing what she'd been able to uncover about the pope whose ring her father had incredibly come across and left her in his safe deposit box. "As you know Pope Leo ascended to the papacy nearly a century after Bishop Aubert would have responded to Michael's urging and built the church at Mont Saint Michel. My father must have believed he was connected somehow, but I haven't been able to uncover anything suggesting he was. If Pope Leo had no connection whatsoever to what's going on at Mont Saint Michel, I can't imagine why my father didn't simply return the pope's ring to the church."

Shrugging, her recitation of her research complete she turned to Rafe and challenged, "Your turn."

"My visit was not as fruitful as yours. At least not yet," he added at Noelle's disappointed expression. "Gabriel has connections that we do not have access to, but if we want him to be discreet, his inquiries are going to take a little time. He promised to call when he learned anything of interest."

Sighing, Noelle nodded. "All right, that makes sense. I hope you thanked him for his willingness to help us. I would rather have gone with you," she tacked on, not completely concealing her frustration at having been so summarily left behind.

Rafe grinned. Reaching for her hand he brought it to his lips and offered, "I can assure you I would also have rather had your company, especially at night, but Gabriel would not have been as forthcoming in your presence. As I explained before, his family has strong ties to the church hierarchy at the Vatican. Before I confided in him, I needed to make certain I wasn't putting him in an untenable position of having to choose between our friendship and his faith."

"Oh, oh, I never thought of that. You didn't tell him about the ring did you?" Noelle asked anxiously.

He squeezed the hand he still held. "It would be somewhat difficult for him to assist us if I was not completely forthcoming with him."

Noelle released an audible sigh. "You're right, I know. I'm sorry for putting your friend in such an awkward position. Did you tell him about Michael?"

At the slight shrug Rafe greeted her anxious question with, Noelle heaved another audible sigh. "What did he say when you told him?"

When Rafe merely responded with a gentle smile, she shook her head. "Great, now your close friend, Gabriel, thinks I'm delusional."

"My close friend Gabriel thinks you're charming," Rafe countered.

Expelling a resigned sigh, Noelle concluded, "Fine. I'm a charming nutcase."

Rafe laughed.

He didn't take her back to her grandmother's. Noelle wasn't aware of her anxiety that he might, but Rafe must have been, because he reached for her hand, drawing her gaze to his and asked, "I hoped you would share the night with me. Would you rather I take you back to your grandmother's?"

Sighing, a little discomforted that he seemed so in tune with every little thought of hers, she met his glance and responded honestly, "No. I want to share the night with you, too."

Holding her glance, he raised the hand he held to his lips, then lowered it but retained possession of it, as he steered them back to his apartment.

Much later, she lay in his arms, with her head resting against his chest and his fingers running lightly over her naked flesh, beneath her long hair. On the verge of sleep, she whispered, "I'm so glad you're back. I know this sounds crazy, and I'm sure it's only my imagination, but I can't help wondering what happened to my diary. I feel like I'm being watched all the time...even at my grandmother's. I feel safe here. You make me feel safe."

Noelle was aware of the break in the rhythm of his gentle stroke on her skin at her confession, but the tender caress resumed a moment later. He lifted his head to kiss the top of hers where it rested against his chest. "Sleep, *Mon amour*, you're safe. I will never let anyone harm you."

Comforted by his promise, Noelle abandoned herself to the seductive lure of sleep.

Rafe, feeling her surrender to his soothing caress, forced himself to continue the gentle motion of allowing his fingertips to play against the silky skin of her back. He knew it would be a long time before he was able to find the escape of sleep. Noelle's confession that she felt as though she was being watched had robbed him of the languor of spent passion. In its place, the cold thrill of fear was working itself up his spine.

The reminder of her missing diary forced him to confront the unpleasant possibility that the Sons of France had long ago penetrated the Dominique household. Which made him re-evaluate his initial feelings of relief at Bernard's assurances that there were no new employees at either of the duchess' residences. He would have Jacobs begin looking into the backgrounds of the duchess's household staff in the morning.

The thought that someone was in a position to know Noelle's every movement was more than disconcerting. He'd dismissed her encounters with the archangel as a childhood fantasy, but it was proving infinitely more difficult, in the face of mounting evidence, for him to dismiss the idea that there was someone, or a group of someones, stalking her every breath. His grandfather had been right to suggest Noelle remain at Chateau Lucien until they solved the riddle they were tangled up in. He would broach the subject with her in the morning.

CHAPTER FORTY

"You want me to move in with your grandfather?" Noelle echoed incredulously where she sat next to Rafe in the front seat of his car in her grandmother's driveway. "Surely, you're joking."

Rafe's lips twitched at Noelle's obvious dread at his proposal. "Do I need to remind you your diary went missing from Chateau Dominique? I think we have to consider the possibility that a member of the staff was responsible for its loss."

"But Bernard said there weren't any recent additions to the staff at Chateau Dominique," Noelle protested.

"Yes, I'm aware of that, which leads to the possibility that someone has been in place for a long time to watch your grandmother's movements and to wait for you to return."

"That's ridiculous," Noelle protested, then added with a desperate attempt at humor, "You're beginning to sound like me. Maybe my delusions are contagious." Rafe's lips curled in a smile for her efforts, but his amusement didn't reach his eyes. "You really believe it was someone on the staff who took my diary?"

"Do you have a more plausible explanation?"

"Not really," she admitted. Chateau Dominique was a modern day fortress. It wouldn't have been easy for a stranger to gain access to the chateau, let alone her suite on the second floor.

"I'll call my grandfather this morning and make the arrangements."

"No, not yet. I've been thinking I should return to Chateau Dominique."

"Absolutely not," Rafe insisted.

"No, listen. Michael said something about me being my father's heir. Whatever this is has been going on for a lot longer than a single generation. How did my father get involved in all of this? Doesn't it make sense, that this task or responsibility, or whatever it is I'm supposed to do has been passed down generation by generation through the Dominique bloodline? Don't you see? Maybe my grandmother doesn't know anything about all of this because she wasn't born a Dominique. She married into the family. Maybe that's why my mother doesn't know anything either, and why my father passed the pope's ring directly to me. Even though I was just a little girl when he died, he made certain it came to me, and only to me, when I was old enough to take his place."

Noelle was relieved when Rafe didn't immediately dismiss her conclusions as fantasy. She was onto something. She felt it in her heart. "As much as I hate to admit the possibility that this mystery surrounding Mont Saint Michel has been passed down to the Dominique heir for generations, it does fit with the circumstances of neither your grandmother or mother knowing anything about any of this."

"Don't you see? I have to go back to Chateau Dominique." When Rafe would have protested, she cut him off. "There have to be family records there going back centuries, at least. It makes sense that Chateau Dominique, a property that's been in the family since its beginnings would be the repository of such records. Maybe my father found some documentation there that set him off in pursuit of his own answers. Maybe he came into an inheritance from his own father. Or my grandfather left my father the pope's ring and that sent him to the Vatican in search of answers. My mom would know. Maybe she remembers an attorney representing my grandfather's estate visiting my father. I remember my grandmother saying they died in quick succession…that my father was killed in that accident before she even had a chance to recover from my grandfather's loss. It makes sense, don't you think? I'm going to call my mother today and see if she remembers my father mentioning a visit or a legacy from his father that was separate from the normal estate proceedings."

Rafe, aware of the rising excitement in Noelle's voice, reached out to grip her hands in case she decided to run off and call her mother before she even made it inside. "Let's not involve your mother in all of this just yet," he cautioned.

The excitement Noelle had been feeling at the thought of finding some real answers fell flat at Rafe's gentle caution. "You're right. I can't risk involving my mother, but it makes sense for me to ask my grandmother about where the Dominique family records are kept."

"Agreed. I have some commitments at the office today, but I'll drive you back to Saint Malo in the morning," Rafe promised.

Noelle shook her head. "I appreciate the offer. I really do, but this is something my grandmother and I can do. You've been spending almost all of your time helping me unravel this mess. I'll be fine. We'll be fine. I promise not to return to Mont Saint Michel without you. We're just going to go through some old family journals and bibles. It's probably a dead-end, but it will make my grandmother feel better that she can do something productive to help us."

Noelle held Rafe's probing glance without flinching. She could tell he was trying to decide if he could trust her not to get into any trouble while they were apart. "You will not, under any circumstances, return to Mont Saint Michel...no matter what you uncover in the family records at Chateau Dominique?"

"I promise we won't leave the estate. If anything feels off, I'll have my grandmother call your grandfather. Or better yet, we'll flee to Chateau Lucien at the first sign of trouble. Your grandfather's home is barely half an hour away from Chateau Dominique."

She could tell he didn't like the idea of her going off with just her grandmother to keep an eye on her. She bit down on her smile at the thought that Rafe would be more comfortable with a big strong man to accompany them. "Bernard will drive us. The two of you already took care of beefing up my grandmother's security, right?"

"And yet you still feel as though you're being watched," Rafe reminded her of her regrettable late night admission.

"Well, maybe it's just the stress of all of this and the memory of those two men chasing me. I'm sure it's nothing. Probably just my imagination," she tacked on soothingly.

"Your imagination?" Rafe echoed incredulously. "You insist you're on speaking terms with an archangel, but at the sign of a true threat, you're willing to concede you might be imagining things?"

Blushing, Noelle admitted, "Well, yes, I can see where that might appear to be a contradiction, but you have to remember, I've been living with Michael's voice in my head since I was four years old. Men with guns only started chasing me in the past few weeks."

She could tell she'd made a mistake reminding him about their mad sprint to escape the two men dressed as gendarmes at Mont Saint Michel, but she didn't have any intention of returning to the site. "We won't leave the estate. You need to catch up on your work and I need to keep tugging at every possible thread that might provide the answers to the message my father was trying to leave me with the pope's ring. There's probably nothing but a bunch of dusty books and papers back at the chateau, but I don't have anything better to do at the moment. I can't go to your office and watch you work. Let me do this. I promise not to get into any trouble."

Rafe released one of her hands to thrust his own through his hair. "Trouble seems to have a way of finding you whether you intend to attract it or not. Fine, you and your grandmother may conduct your family research at Chateau Dominique. Bernard will drive you. You will not go anywhere alone."

Lips twitching at his autocratic tone, she nodded smartly, barely restraining the urge to salute. "Yes, Sir. I'll report in if we find anything of interest, Sir."

Clearly not pleased by her teasing, he gripped her chin and pulled her towards him. "That is not amusing. And see that you do." Then he brushed her grinning lips with his before releasing her to climb out of the car to open her door.

Later that afternoon, Noelle was seated on the floor of the imposing library at Chateau Dominique with her grandfather's family bible open between her legs. Imposing because every wall in the room was covered by floor to ceiling bookcases, all of which were filled with books. There had to be thousands of books neatly lined up on the shelves. Apparently, her Dominique ancestors were dedicated readers. Fortunately, her grandmother knew where the family journals and other family papers were kept, so they didn't have to face the daunting prospect of searching the stacks column by column.

While Noelle sat on the floor with small piles of books surrounding her in a semi-circle around her outstretched legs, her grandmother sat at the desk near the large window overlooking the formal garden, a stack of far older bibles and journals in front of her.

Noelle was working her way from the most recent records backwards. Her grandmother had taken the oldest records and was working her way forward. So far, neither of them had found anything of particular interest to their cause.

"Did Daddy not have a family bible?" Noelle asked, more to break the silence, than because she thought the omission odd. Her father was still in his twenties when he died, not much older than she was now. She didn't have a personal bible to keep a record of important events in her life. She was too young to have had many important events in her life to keep a record of. She guessed the closest thing she had was her missing diary. It saddened her to think she might never see it again. At the same time, she couldn't imagine what anyone else would want with it.

"No, not to my knowledge. Your father left home so young. He was educated in the United States and many of his business pursuits kept him there. Then of course, when he met your mother, well, he rarely came home except for abbreviated visits. Not that we blamed him, of course. Once we got over the initial shock of their elopement, we were genuinely pleased he'd found someone who made him so happy."

"You were?" Noelle confirmed.

"Yes, of course. A parent's fondest wish is for their child to be happy. You and your mother were the center of Michel's life, as you should have been."

Nodding, thinking she might pass along her grandmother's assertion the next time she saw her mother, Noelle returned to the heavy bible in her hands. She noted the carefully inscribed dates inside the front cover, of her grandparents' marriage and the birth of her father. There was also a brief family tree that had the names of both of their parents and grandparents. She noted her father's marriage to her mother had also been noted, as well as the date of her own birth. She traced her fingertips across the writing, feeling a connection to the grandfather she'd never known and the long history she'd become a part of when she was born. Her eyes fell to the bottom of the page where a faded watermark appeared at the right hand corner. Struck by a familiar chord the image brought to mind, she bent over the book, but in the dim light of the library, she couldn't make it out clearly.

"What is it, Noelle? Have you found something?" Her grandmother asked, noting Noelle's sudden distraction.

"I don't know. This watermark looks familiar, but I can't quite make it out."

"Bring it to the desk. You'll be able to see it more clearly under the light," her grandmother suggested.

Noelle rose somewhat awkwardly from her cross-legged position on the floor and carried her grandfather's bible over to the desk. She placed it directly beneath the light of the lamp and pointed to the bottom of the page on the inner front cover.

"See this mark. Do you recognize it?"

Her grandmother bent closer to examine the watermark, then lifted her head and turned to Noelle. "No, it's not familiar at all. It's so faded; I can barely make out the image. It looks like two crossed swords."

"Of course, no wonder it looked familiar," Noelle breathed out, and then bent closer. "We need a magnifying glass. Do you have one?"

Her grandmother reached inside the top desk drawer and handed the magnifying glass she retrieved there to Noelle. "What is it, Noelle? Do you recognize this image?"

Noelle didn't answer her grandmother's anxious question immediately. She wanted to be certain her imagination wasn't running away with her. After examining the image for long, silent moments, she raised her head. Turning to her grandmother, she passed her the glass. "Look again and tell me what you see."

Noelle waited with a knot of both anxiety and rising excitement hardening in her stomach while her grandmother examined the watermark beneath the magnifying glass. "Oh, I don't believe the image is of two crossed swords, after all. It appears more like two crossed keys with a string or ribbon binding them together."

"Yes, that's what I see," Noelle replied in an awed tone.

"But what does it mean?" Her grandmother asked, mystified.

"Two crossed keys with a red thread binding them together is the papal insignia."

"There must be some mistake," her grandmother insisted, incredulous at Noelle's disclosure.

"I don't think there is. This same insignia was on the pouch Daddy left Pope Leo III's ring in. I think it's significant. This was Granddad's bible. Did his father keep a journal or a bible?"

"I honestly don't know. Let's see."

While her grandmother began combing through the books on the desk, Noelle returned to the pile spread out in a circle where she'd been seated on the floor. "Here it is," she exclaimed. With a sense she could only describe as reaching for her destiny, she opened the front cover. She was almost afraid to glance down at the bottom right hand corner, but of course, she did. "It's here. Look!" She exclaimed jumping up and carrying the heavy book over to her grandmother.

"But what does it mean?" Her grandmother repeated.

Shaking off her grandmother's question, Noelle asked instead, "Do any of your records have this same seal? I think we should check all of the family papers we have. If we find anything with this insignia I think it's safe to assume it's significant to our search."

Her grandmother nodded and the two of them returned to their places and began leafing through the journals, bibles and documents they had pulled from the family archives. Noelle discovered something interesting in her search. Her grandfather and his father's family bible's each bore the watermark of the papal insignia, but her great-great grandfather's did not. Then the next generation it appeared again, but for two generations beyond there was no sign of it. Possibly, there were other records or journals of the same time that they were not in possession of that did bear the mark, but Noelle thought it more likely that for whatever reason, not every generation was tasked with resolving the Mont Saint Michel mystery.

'Your father was an evil man and truth be told, your brother is reputed to be worse,' the sound of Mother Superior's remembered voice drifted through her thoughts, when she'd been a young novitiate named Sister Marie. There were evil men in the world at every time of human history.

Turning her attention to her grandmother, she asked, "Did you find any more records bearing the papal insignia?"

"Yes, but only family bibles. None of the other records have the mark and not every bible has it either."

"Yes, I found the same thing. I think the lack of the mark implies that not every generation was considered trustworthy enough to share the secret."

"That makes sense, but how does this lead us any closer to whatever it is that is supposedly hidden at Mont Saint Michel?"

"I don't know," Noelle admitted, "but at least now we know whose papers and records we should concentrate on in our search."

"True, there's that consolation. I suggest we take a break. My head's beginning to spin with all of this."

"You're right. Why don't we take a stroll through the gardens to clear our heads? Is there a family cemetery nearby? After all of this, I feel the need to pay my respects to my ancestors."

"That's a wonderful idea. I'll show you where your grandfather is buried. Your father of course was buried in Washington."

Though her grandmother made the comment in a neutral tone, Noelle couldn't help but wonder if she wished her only son was buried here on the estate of his family home. Noelle didn't ask. Although she could see her grandmother's point, she couldn't fathom broaching such a sensitive topic with her mother.

Just as they entered the garden, her phone rang. She reached in her pocket but didn't recognize the number. Exchanging a puzzled look with her grandmother, she answered it a bit hesitantly, "Hello."

"Hello." Rafe's familiar voice came across the line causing her to release the breath she was holding in a rush.

"Oh, Rafe, hi." She noticed the knowing smile that came over her grandmother's face before she drifted off down one of the garden paths to give Noelle privacy for her conversation with Rafe.

"Hi. I haven't heard from you. Does that mean you haven't found anything interesting, or you forgot your promise to report to me if you uncovered anything?"

"Neither. We actually did uncover something, but I didn't have your number to reach you."

"Now you do," he pointed out, and then added, "What did you find?"

"I was going through my grandfather's bible and you won't believe what I found there."

"I certainly won't believe it if you don't share it with me."

"Ha, ha."

"Well?"

"There's a watermark of the papal insignia in the bottom right hand corner of the front cover."

"That's interesting," he replied, noncommittal.

"It's more than interesting. It can't be a coincidence after the pouch Daddy left Pope Leo's ring in. Plus, the same watermark is in a number of the family bibles, but not in all of them. It's like the pope of the time, or Michael, didn't think some of my ancestors were worthy to share in the secret the others knew."

Her conclusion was greeted with silence on the other end. "Rafe?" she prompted him.

His sigh was audible. "I'm not saying you're wrong, but of course we have no way of knowing what it signifies."

"My grandmother said the same thing, but I think for now we can concentrate our research on the papers of the men whose bibles have the mark."

"That's not a bad idea. Now that you have my number you'll keep me posted on what you find," he reminded her.

"Of course, but I don't want to interrupt you at work," she qualified, then added silently, and she definitely didn't plan on reaching out to him in the evenings, just in case he wasn't alone.

After she ended her call with Rafe, she found her grandmother seated at one of the benches in the flower garden. "I love these gardens. They bring me such comfort. I think I spent most of the first three years of your life here, mourning first your grandfather, and then your father."

Noelle sat down next to her and grasped her hand. "I don't have any memory of my grandfather. Perhaps you could re-introduce us?"

"Yes, that's a lovely thought," her grandmother assented. "He was so thrilled to have a granddaughter. We didn't get to see you often that first year, but whenever we did, I remember he always looked at you as if you were an angel sent straight from heaven."

Noelle laughed and arm in arm they left the gardens and headed in the direction of the family cemetery. "This is your grandfather's grave."

Noelle stood staring down at it for long silent moments. Then she made the sign of the cross and offered a prayer for her grandfather's eternal soul. She bent down to brush some stray leaves away from the stone at her feet. Near the bottom of the stone, she discovered a carving of an old-fashioned key. "Meme, what does this key signify?"

Her grandmother knelt at her side and traced the key with her fingertips. "I have no idea. I was informed it was a Dominique custom when I was making your grandfather's funeral arrangements, so I just went along with it. You'll notice several of the former duke's graves are marked with the same symbol."

"But not all?" Noelle wondered.

"No, I don't believe so. I remember noticing the discrepancy one day when I was spending a lot of time here visiting with your grandfather, but no one could explain why some of the duke's graves have a key on their stones and some don't."

"I wonder if the dukes with the keys on their graves are the same ones whose bibles bear the papal insignia," Noelle mused.

"That's a fascinating possibility. Why don't we find out?" Her grandmother suggested.

Noelle retrieved her phone from her pocket and noted the graves of the former dukes with the key emblem carved into the grave markers. Then they returned to the library to confirm her suspicion. 'Don't tell anyone about its existence, Marie. Take it with you when you leave. Your father was an evil man. Your mother told him you were stillborn and secreted you here to the convent.' The words played around and around like a recording in her mind.

"Noelle...Noelle. Are you all right?"

Noelle shook herself free of the disturbing memory and smiled reassuringly up into her grandmother's concerned face. "I'm fine, just tired. It's been a long day. We were right about the keys and the signs in the bibles; either the dukes' graves and records bore both marks or neither. There's not a single case where a duke's bible was marked with the papal insignia but his grave lacked the symbol of the key, or vice versa."

Still concerned, her grandmother gripped her arm and led her towards the library's exit. "Let it go for tonight. We'll return to our research in the morning and see if we can discover the significance of the key symbol."

Noelle nodded her agreement of her grandmother's plan, but she didn't need to do anymore research to discover the symbol's significance. She recognized the key. It was the same one Mother Superior had thrust into her hands, and with her dying breath, had admonished her to keep it safe and secret.

CHAPTER FORTY ONE

Noelle's sleep that night was fitful and her dreams unpleasant. Either Rafe and the lovely Carina played a starring role, or men chased her with guns demanding she give them the key. She finally abandoned all pretense of sleep and sat up in bed in the dark, almost wishing Michael would make his presence known and just tell her what he wanted her to do so she could get it over with once and for all.

Her entire life he'd prodded her to return to Mont Saint Michel. She'd done that. Ever since he'd given her the order to run from those two men dressed as gendarmes, he'd been frustratingly silent. Maybe her return was all that was necessary to set things in motion again. What those things were she couldn't fathom a guess, but she was now fairly certain the key would prove an important element of her appointed task. Perhaps she was supposed to locate it, but even if she did miraculously discover its whereabouts, what then? She still had no idea what the key opened and why her father thought Pope Leo's ring would be helpful to her in resolving this mystery.

Clearly, he was somehow involved with all of this. Why else would her ancestors mark their bibles with the papal insignia and their graves with the symbol of the key? Hadn't Saint Peter been handed the proverbial keys to heaven by our Lord? And wasn't he the first pope? She accepted she was reaching, but she didn't dismiss her logic out of hand. The popes on earth were entrusted with the keys to heaven. The popes were called the successors to Saint Peter, the Bishop of Rome, and the leader of the church on earth. Did Saint Peter have anything to do with Michael?

Frustrated she thrust her hands through her hair, distracted by the tinkling sound of her charm bracelet. She examined it now, noting the key to her missing diary was still in place. She guessed whoever took her journal had simply smashed the lock to get at the contents. She felt a disturbing violation of privacy at the thought of some stranger reading all about her childhood discussions with Michael. Then brushing aside the unpleasant notion she let her eyes linger on the other charms, recalling the significance of each one.

She reached out to clasp the little locket charm her mother had given her for her sixteenth birthday. Her mother had always worn the locket around her neck. It contained a picture of Noelle's parents in front of the tiny rural church where they'd run off and gotten married. Her mother had the locket converted into a charm for Noelle's milestone birthday. Noelle guessed it was her mother's way of saying goodbye to her husband, but as far as Noelle knew, there had never been another serious relationship in her mother's life.

She sprang the catch to reveal the picture of her parents. Her father was a few years older than she was now, her mother a few years younger. Her lips curved in a smile at their obvious joy in each other. She traced the smiling faces with the tip of her finger then raised her finger to her lips to kiss it, and then press her kiss back against the picture of her parents. When she would have snapped the locket closed, her eyes skimmed the intricate design etched into the inside of the cover.

Her head was already shaking back in forth in denial even as she reached over to turn on the bedside lamp for a closer look. There was no mistaking the design. Two crossed keys bound together with a ribbon, but there was one small but significant difference from the papal insignia copied into the family bibles. In the symbol in her locket, an old-fashioned key was standing on its hilt between the two crossed ones and was secured to them by the ribbon.

Noelle sat staring at the locket for a long time, her thoughts stuck in her head, refusing to form any conclusions about the evidence staring her right in the face. Her mother knew something about all of this. Even if she didn't know she knew, the locket was a sign. Her father had entrusted part of the answer to the mystery they were chasing to the stewardship of his mother's close friend, Ari Lucien. The key to a safe deposit box he'd opened in his only child's name…his heir's name.

The other half of the answer to the puzzle, she was now quite certain her father had left with his wife. She thought she knew what that other half was. The only way to find out was to confront her mother. Had she known? Had she known all this time? Noelle couldn't be certain, but it was time she and her mother had the discussion both of them had been avoiding for the past twenty years.

Since she knew sleep would continue to elude her for the remainder of the night, she began making tentative plans for her return to Los Angeles. Rafe would never agree to allow her to return alone. That was going to be a problem, because she was quite certain her mother wouldn't speak openly in Rafe's presence. It was less likely she would speak openly in her mother-in-law's. No, Noelle knew her best chance of getting her mother to open up and confide in her about her father was to confront her alone.

If she'd fled both France and the east coast in an attempt to protect her only daughter, than Rafe's presence and his insistence on secrecy and additional security measures would only make her mother deny knowing anything that would help them in their quest for answers. She was her mother. There may have been some awkward moments between them, but there was no doubt in Noelle's mind that her mother's first loyalties were to her only daughter. She would not risk putting Noelle in danger, no matter how many popes and future dukes and archangels compelled her cooperation.

Somehow, Noelle needed to convince her mother that finding the answer to her father's legacy was the only way to ensure her daughter's safety. Only when the mystery was resolved would Noelle be able to go on with her life without looking over her shoulder in fear that someone was watching her.

Of course convincing Rafe or her grandmother, for that matter, to agree with her line of reasoning was not going to be easy. More like impossible. Perhaps it would be better to apologize for her sin of slipping out of the country without telling either of them, than to try to convince them hers was the best way to get the answers they sought. An attempt which she already knew would prove to be a futile one, at least when it came to Rafe. The Lucien reputation for stubbornness was well earned, as she could attest to from previous personal experience.

So, though the idea of deceiving both Rafe and her grandmother didn't sit well with her, she was pretty certain doing so was the only way she was going to be allowed to return to Los Angeles alone. It wouldn't be difficult. She could just tell her grandmother she was spending the day with Rafe and vice versa. Hopefully by the time either of them figured out she was lying, she would have already called from Los Angeles to tell them where she actually was and that she was on her way to speak with her mother and would return as soon as she got the answers they sought.

Then hopefully it would be over…or at least they would be one-step closer to its being over. Noelle mulled over her options and decided it was worth the resulting consequences and smoothing of hurt feelings and injured pride she would have to go through upon her return to France.

She spent the following day with her grandmother going through the journals and bibles of her most recently deceased ancestors. A call to check-in with her mother that morning had confirmed she was at home and had no plans over the coming week that would take her away from home. When Rafe called later that evening, she gave him a vague response to his question about whether she and her grandmother had made any additional progress on their research of the Dominique family records. She was surprised by the ease with which he accepted her answer. She couldn't help but notice he appeared distracted. Noelle tried not to torture herself with thoughts of the potential source of that distraction. He was a busy man after all. It was probably just some work crisis that made her feel as if he was only half-listening to what she was telling him.

Still, she couldn't believe her good fortune when he informed her business would take him to London for the next few days but that he would return by the weekend. Smiling at the lucky coincidence, her earlier dejection at the possibility he might not be sleeping alone in his plush Paris apartment pushed aside for the moment, she wished him a good trip. He didn't even inquire as to how she was going to spend the next few days, apparently assuming she would continue her research with her grandmother, so she therefore wasn't forced to lie to him about her plans. Though Mother Superior considered a sin of omission to be in the same league as a sin of commission, Noelle wasn't inclined to see it that way.

Seizing her opportunity, she went on-line and booked a direct flight to Los Angeles from Charles de Gaulle airport for the following day.

She mentioned to her grandmother over dinner that she would be returning to Paris in the morning, as she had a date with Rafe. Her grandmother had merely nodded her smiling assent, and indicated she would remain at Chateau Dominique for a few more days to continue their research. If Noelle had no objection, she might engage her good friend Ari to assist her.

Noelle was only too happy to grant her consent for Ariel Lucien to assist her grandmother. With Rafe out of the country and her grandmother happily engaged with her old friend, there was less likelihood anyone would even notice she was gone, at least for the first twenty-four hours or so. By then it would be too late for Rafe to interfere with her plans.

CHAPTER FORTY TWO

Her escape had proven surprisingly easy, Noelle concluded as she took her seat on the jet for the slightly less than eleven hour flight. Maybe she had a future in clandestine work. She'd even upgraded herself to business class at the last minute, justifying her indulgence with all of the stress she'd been under lately.

By the time she landed in LA, she had reconsidered her future as a spy. Her conscience about lying to both Rafe and her grandmother, considering how generous they'd both been in helping her resolve her problem with Michael was eating her up inside. She would call them as soon as she had passed through customs, she promised herself, a knot of anxiety already forming in the pit of her stomach in anticipation of Rafe's reaction to her deception.

Customs was mercifully efficient, or so she was quite certain her fellow travelers considered it so. To Noelle's mind, it was a little too efficient. She wouldn't have minded an excuse to put off her conversation with Rafe for a few more minutes. Since she didn't plan on staying for more than a couple of days at her Mom's, she hadn't checked a bag.

Putting off confronting Rafe a little while longer, she decided to wait until after she was in the rental car. She thought it would be best if their conversation was held in as private a location as possible. So, she took the shuttle to the rental car facility, saw her name and the location of her rental car posted on the board, and with dragging steps wheeled her carry-on bag behind her as she made her way to the car.

The door was unlocked, and LA summers being what they were, sweat was already beginning to bead on her forehead and dampen her blouse. She stowed her luggage in the trunk, climbed into the driver's seat and started the engine, turning the air-conditioning to max. She sat for several moments waiting for the car to cool, and then gathering her courage; she turned the fan down and reached for her phone to dial Rafe's number. With the eight-hour time difference, it would be late evening in London. Hopefully he'd been pre-occupied with a dinner party and hadn't attempted to reach her in the past several hours.

Just to be sure, she checked the face of her phone and found no less than a dozen missed calls and several increasingly urgent text messages from Rafe. "Damn," she muttered under her breath and pressed the send button on the last, near frantic text. She didn't bother listening to the voice mails. She suspected they were all from Rafe.

"Noelle? Where are you? Why the hell haven't you answered any of my calls or messages?" Rafe's frantic voice rushed out before the first ring was even complete.

"I'm sorry, I'm sorry. My phone was turned off." Her apology was automatic, as was her instinct to avoid confessing the full truth before it was absolutely necessary.

"Your phone was turned off?" Rafe echoed incredulously. "I've been frantic. Where the hell are you? You're certainly not with me which was the lie you gave your grandmother."

"Oh no, you spoke to my grandmother?"

"What choice did I have when I couldn't reach you? Where are you?" At her continued silence, he demanded, "Answer me!"

"I'm in Los Angeles," Noelle offered meekly. Then braced herself for Rafe's reaction. It wasn't long in coming. A string of vivid, angry curses erupted from the other end of the line. When silence fell between them, Noelle tried to explain, "I know you're angry..." Rafe cut her off.

"Angry? You think I'm angry? Trust me, anger doesn't begin to cover what I'm feeling at the moment. How dare you? Do you have any idea what I've been through for the past several hours not being able to reach you, and your grandmother telling me you were supposed to be meeting me. I thought you had been taken and were in the hands of that extremist group."

"Oh God, I'm so sorry, it never occurred to me you would think that," Noelle rushed to explain.

"It never occurred to you I would think that?" Rafe echoed incredulously. "Do you think this is some kind of game? Two men traced back to a militant extremist group attempted to kidnap you just weeks ago and you decide to take a trip home to visit your mother without informing anyone of your plans? What the hell was I supposed to think? Was this some kind of a test? Did you deliberately want to make me go out of my mind with worry?"

Tears streaming down her cheeks, Noelle protested desperately, "No, no of course not. I didn't think…I wasn't thinking. I knew you wouldn't let me come alone and I knew my mom wouldn't speak openly in front of you. I'm not even sure she'll speak openly with me. But I had to come. I had to try. The answer's here, Rafe. My father left half of the answer with your grandfather, the clue to lead us to the pope's ring, but he must have left the other half with my mother. It's the key, Rafe. My mother either has the key or knows where it is."

"So you believe your father found the answer to the mystery of Mont Saint Michel and you went off blindly to claim it. Alone, damn it, without a word to any of us…even your grandmother. Have you forgotten your father died just months after his visit to the Vatican? Have you forgotten someone is likely watching your movements and tracing your every step? Did it ever occur to you they might follow you to Los Angeles, especially as you've now given them the perfect opportunity to get you alone and unprotected?"

Noelle's hands were trembling so violently she could barely hold the phone to her ear as Rafe continued to berate her. When a stark, empty, bitterly cold silence finally descended upon the distance separating them, Noelle could only offer another whispered apology. "I'm sorry. I'm sorry you're so angry. I'm sorry I deceived you."

"So am I," Rafe declared bitterly. "Enjoy your visit with your mother."

Rafe disconnected the call. Noelle was convinced he was so furious with her he wouldn't particularly care at the moment if a hundred extremists surrounded the car and took her away. She carefully placed the phone on the seat next to her and reached up with trembling hands to brush her tears away. It was too late for tears now. What was done was done. There was nothing she could do to undo the damage she'd wrought with what she had assumed would be a relatively innocent deception on her part, so she might as well get on with the purpose of her visit. She hoped Rafe would give her a chance to help him forgive her, because if she lost him over this, she was quite certain she would soon discover just what her grandmother had meant when she'd assured her, that those who claim a heart can't truly break could never comprehend the devastation of those whose had because there's had never been broken.

She wasn't quite certain how it happened. She'd been so determined to protect her heart against him. She'd assured herself she could have a wildly, reckless, dashing affair with Rafe and not suffer the consequences. Too late, she discovered she'd been deceiving herself. She had fallen victim to the legendary Lucien charm and good looks, just like so many others before her. She was in love with Rafe and the thought that she had just ruined any chance of being with him was a crushing blow to the confidence she'd begun her plan with just hours earlier.

She raised her hands and impatiently brushed away the fresh tears blinding her vision. Then she put the car in gear and backed out of her space in the rental car lot. Just to top off her day she was just moments behind a multiple car pile-up on the interstate, so rather than the drive taking the forty-five minutes it should have taken, it took her almost three hours to reach her mother's oceanfront home in Laguna Beach. Fortunately, her rental car was full of gas when she picked it up, otherwise she would be calling a tow truck to rescue her and her stranded car from the highway.

Dusk was turning to night by the time she pulled into her mother's driveway and climbed wearily from the front seat. Not bothering to retrieve her luggage, she barely took note of the tangy sea air and light breeze blowing inland off the Pacific as she trudged on heavy steps to her mother's front door. She didn't bother knocking. Her mother never locked her door. Something about the whole laid back west coast outlook on life, as if the evil in men's hearts checked itself at California's sunny border. As suspected, the front door opened easily under her urging.

"Mom, it's Noelle...Surprise!" She offered half-heartedly by way of explanation for her unannounced visit.

The response she received was not uttered in her mother's excited, surprised voice. Instead, the voice that replied to her airy greeting was male, and somehow menacing, and it froze her blood to the bone.

"Mademoiselle Dominique, please come in. Join us. We've been expecting you. I suppose you were delayed by the traffic on the Interstate. I was beginning to wonder if you were one of the unfortunate victims."

Shocked, disbelieving, her flight or fight instincts urging her to flee, that there was still time to escape, Noelle instead stood rooted to the floor. They'd followed her. Just as Rafe had predicted they would. She'd put her mother at risk. All of a sudden, the mystery at what was hidden at Mont Saint Michel lost all importance. If she had in her possession whatever relic they were looking for she would hand it over without a moment's thought. "Please God," she whispered in the silence of her frozen mind, "Just don't let them hurt my mother."

The owner of the menacing voice made no move to meet her at the door. He knew as well as she did that she wouldn't leave her mother to the unlikely mercy of fanatics. More terrified than she'd ever been in her life, and cursing Michael for his failure to warn her, and for allowing her mother to be put in danger, Noelle forced her feet to take one halting step forward and then another. When she reached the great room, with its wide wall of sliding doors fronting the view of the moon rising over the Pacific, while the last of the sun set beneath the horizon, she heard her mother's anguished, muffled voice calling her name. Noelle turned at the sound and her glazed will took in the sight of her mother tied to one of her kitchen chairs, a gag covering her mouth.

Behind her bound mother stood a strange man with a gun. By the way he handled it; Noelle concluded fearfully he was as comfortable holding the weapon as she was with a book in her hand. The coldness in his eyes scared her more than the gun. She had no doubt he would not balk at using the weapon, or whatever means he deemed necessary to get what he wanted.

CHAPTER FORTY THREE

Rafe disconnected Noelle's call and sank down on shaking knees into the chair behind his desk. She was safe. She wasn't in the hands of madmen, being tortured, sexually assaulted, drugged, whipped or on the receiving end of every other evil a deranged fanatic could inflict upon another human being, particularly an innocent like Noelle. She'd simply left…without a word….without a moment's consideration of what he might think if he discovered her deception.

He wasn't entirely convinced it had been only naivety on her part that had put him through the past several hours of hell. He'd called her earlier to let her know he'd concluded his business in London early. He thought she would be pleased to hear that he was returning to Paris that night and would drive out to St. Malo in the morning to assist her and her grandmother with their research into the Dominique ancestors with family bibles bearing papal insignias.

A part of him suspected her of just what he had accused her of. Maybe she'd been testing him. Perhaps she thought to force his hand by making him realize how much he cared for her. If that had been her intent, Noelle had badly miscalculated. He was still shaking with rage at her deception and even her tearful, too little; too late apology had done less than nothing to diminish it.

After another moment of sitting there immobile and impotent, he reached for his phone again. He at least needed to inform the duchess that Noelle was alive and unharmed, and had simply decided to pay an impromptu visit to her mother, thinking her husband might have left a further clue in her possession. He called his grandfather's number. He knew in a crisis of this magnitude, with Noelle missing, the two would be together.

"Raphael, have you heard anything?" His grandfather's anxious voice answered before the phone even rang, or so it seemed to Rafe.

He wearily thrust a hand through his hair and admitted in a quiet, deliberately unemotional voice, "Yes. Noelle just returned my call. Apparently she's in Los Angeles visiting her mother."

"I don't understand," his grandfather confessed, then turned from the phone and repeated to the duchess, "Michel, Noelle is fine. She's in Los Angeles."

"What? Los Angeles? Is her mother all right? Is she safe?"

"You heard?" Rafe's grandfather asked.

"Yes and yes, Noelle's in Los Angeles. As far as I know, her mother is fine and Noelle is safe. She believes her mother is in possession of some clue that might lead to solving the mystery surrounding Mont Saint Michel."

"What was she thinking? Why would she worry her grandmother…all of us, in such an incomprehensibly inconsiderate and cruel manner?"

"I don't know. I imagine she guessed I would never have agreed to allow her to go alone," Rafe responded wearily.

"Alone? She's alone? Has she lost that idiot brain of hers? Does she not remember she was almost kidnapped barely weeks ago?"

"I cannot comment on the state of Noelle's mind at the moment. My own is not functioning particularly clearly. I will call you if I hear anything more."

"Yes, do that. And see to it that Noelle calls and apologizes to her grandmother for causing her needless worry."

After informing her grandmother she was safe, Rafe rose from his chair to gaze out over the Paris skyline, taking in its glittering night-lights from his living room window. His raging fury at Noelle's senseless risk and as his grandfather had termed it; incomprehensible cruelty had left him feeling drained and empty. How could he have been so mistaken about her?

CHAPTER FORTY FOUR

They were running out of time. He felt it deep in his soul. If they didn't reclaim the relic soon they would risk losing the opportunity of taking possession of it for another millennia. It was this gathering darkness closing around his psyche that prompted him, albeit reluctantly, to grant his permission for their agent to confront Noelle Dominique in Los Angeles, where she was inexplicably travelling alone. The opportunity to discover what her father had left her in that safe deposit box twenty years earlier, and what she was unable to uncover in Rome that prompted this sudden trip to her mother's home was too great for them to pass up.

Of course, he was well aware that the Dominique heir would not surrender the information they sought voluntarily. She was her father's daughter after all. Her mother's presence would prove a valuable aid in loosening her tongue. He only hoped Mlle Dominique saw the wisdom of cooperating with their agent. The man was not known for his patience. Nor was he likely to be swayed by the young Mademoiselle's beauty and innocence.

No, the most prudent course of action for the lovely and surprisingly enterprising Dominique heir was to surrender all she had and all she knew in connection with the relic to the brother who was trailing her. The man was unquestionably loyal to their cause, but he was possessed of a somewhat regrettable tendency towards violence.

CHAPTER FORTY FIVE

Ari Lucien disconnected the call with his grandson and turned to enfold a trembling, tearful Michel close against his chest. "She's fine, Michel. She's safe," he assured her, aiming for a gentle voice, when every nerve ending inside of him was screaming with outrage at Noelle's thoughtlessness. If she had not considered his grandson's feelings on the matter, she might have at least considered the effect on her elderly grandmother if it was discovered she was missing and no one could reach her.

Michel had been beside herself for the past several hours...ever since Rafe called looking for Noelle. And every endless moment since had stripped away his beloved friend and lover's confidence, the assurance with which she greeted the world, her faith in a loving God, her generally sunny outlook on life despite the grief she'd endured over the years, losing her husband and her only child in quick succession. And Ari had simply stood there, helpless to do anything to shield her from the pain of her loss, of her unfathomable pain at the thought of what her only granddaughter must surely be suffering at the hands of men without a conscience...men who wouldn't hesitate to strip Noelle of her innocence and violently abuse her to achieve their ends.

The fact the little innocent was still alone and without protection from the very same threat they'd tortured themselves with over the past several hours was slow to penetrate, but it did eventually break through his wall of outrage. He was tempted to leave her exactly as she'd left them for the past several hours...swinging in the wind. But, he wouldn't. If not for his own sake, he would never forgive himself for hurting Michel again so grievously when he had the means to prevent inflicting such a wound. So bending to kiss the top of her head, where it rested against his chest, he pulled back and led her to the chair opposite his desk.

They were in his private office at Chateau Lucien. As soon as they realized Noelle was missing, they'd retreated there, unwilling to risk being overheard by whoever had penetrated the ranks of the household staff at Chateau Dominique. The other reason he'd insisted they leave Michel's home was because he couldn't bear the thought of whoever was behind Noelle's disappearance feasting on the evidence of Michel's grief.

He pushed her down into the chair opposite his desk, very aware of the dazed, questioning glance she raised to his. Swearing softly under his breath he walked over to the shelves against the wall, retrieved the brandy snifter, and poured out two generous shots. He turned back and handed one to Michel. "Drink it," he ordered, when she would have simply placed the crystal snifter on the edge of his desk untouched.

Nodding, she threw back the shot, replaced the glass on his desk, and raised her hopeful, but still disbelieving glance to his. "Are you certain she's safe?"

"Rafe spoke to her from the airport parking lot."

"There must be some explanation, Ari. Noelle doesn't have an inconsiderate bone in her body."

"I know you would like to continue believing that *Mon amour*, but I am not in the mood to listen to your defense of her at the moment, particularly after what she put you through this afternoon, and what she put my grandson through."

Michel opened her mouth to protest, thought better of it, and closed it again.

Ari reached for the phone.

"Captain Fils, please. Yes, this is Ariel Lucien." Ari waited for the captain to pick up the line.

"M. Lucien how may I be of assistance, Sir?" The captain's familiar voice came over the line a few moments later.

"I have a favor to ask, Captain. I assume the gendarmes maintain relationships with their American counterparts?"

CHAPTER FORTY SIX

Ignoring for the moment the man with the gun, Noelle rushed over to kneel at her mother's feet and reach for her hands, after she removed the tight gag covering her mother's lips. "Mom, Mom, I'm so sorry. Are you all right? Did he hurt you?"

"No, he was waiting for you. Noelle? He says you have something that belongs to him. What is he talking about? If that's true just give it to him," her mother pleaded, her voice breaking.

"I suggest you follow your mother's excellent advice, Mademoiselle. As touching as this family reunion has been, I need to be on my way."

"I don't know what you're talking about," Noelle denied, defiantly meeting his glance.

"Please, let us not play games. I want the key."

"Key? What key?" Her mother interrupted, confused.

"I don't have it. I have no idea where it is," Noelle told him truthfully.

"I will warn you one final time, Mademoiselle. Hand over the key or I will put a bullet in your mother."

The coldness in his voice and the ease with which he made his obscene threat made Noelle accept he wouldn't hesitate to do as he threatened. Her mother was pleading with her desperately, "Noelle, Noelle, what is he talking about? Just give him whatever he wants. Do you have this key?"

Noelle squeezed her mother's hands. "Mom, he's after a key he thinks Daddy left me."

"A key? Why would your father leave you a key?" Her mother echoed confused, distracted for the moment from the menace of the threat hanging over them. "A key to what?"

Noelle sighed, holding her mother's glance, and admitted tearfully, "I don't know what it opens, but I think it has something to do with Mont Saint Michel."

"Mont Saint Michel? You're joking. What is this all about? How would your father know anything about what happened that day at Mont Saint Michel?"

Noelle shook her head, trying to get through her mother's dazed shock, feeling the impatience of the man who held them captive increasing with every confused denial out of her mother's stunned lips. "It didn't start that day, Mom, when I was a little girl. I think Daddy knew something about whatever's going on at Mont Saint Michel."

"Going on at Mont Saint Michel?" Her mother echoed incredulously, and then protested, "You were just a little girl, Noelle, and imagined you heard the statue of the angel speaking to you. Your father was already gone by then. How could he know anything about what you thought you heard that day?"

"Mom, did Daddy leave anything with you to give to me when I was older?" Noelle asked desperately, ignoring her mother's questions.

Her mother shook her head in confusion. "Leave anything? You signed the papers for the trust your father left you when you turned twenty one."

"There wasn't anything else? Jewelry? Maybe a family heirloom he didn't want to leave with the estate attorneys?" Noelle pushed, becoming more frightened with every passing moment as the realization settled in that her mother didn't have the key and didn't know where it was. Terror rose in the pit of her stomach and blocked her throat… stark, unadorned fear at what the man would do to them when he realized they couldn't give him what he came for.

"Family heirloom? Noelle, surely your grandmother would know more about that kind of thing," her mother protested, fearfully lifting her eyes to the man intently following their conversation.

"She doesn't have it," Noelle replied bitterly, then braved lifting her glance to the man standing over them. "My mother doesn't know anything about this. Let her go."

"I think not, Mademoiselle. Your mother might not know where the key is, but you obviously came here for a reason."

"I thought my father left something, some clue with my mother," Noelle explained, releasing one of her mother's hands to push her hair back from her face, "but I was wrong. I don't have the key. I don't know where it is. Maybe my father never found it either."

"He found it, Mademoiselle, but he managed to hide it before we caught up with him."

Noelle's eyes widened as her reeling thoughts took in the implication of his revelation. "You killed him. You killed my father for the key!" Unthinking of the danger they were in, Noelle jumped up and slapped the man in the face. "You bastard! I hope you rot in hell for all of eternity."

The man's eyes burned as they drove into hers. "We need you, Mademoiselle, but you are right. Your mother apparently cannot help us locate the key."

Too late, Noelle realized her mother had just become expendable. She read his intent in his eyes a moment before he raised the gun and aimed it at her mother's heart. Noelle launched herself at him. The gun erupted. Noelle screamed. Her mother screamed. Blood erupted in a terrifying fountain and spattered Noelle's skin, even as she latched onto the killer's arm and struggled for control of the gun. Time stood still. Noelle forced everything she had, everything she was into gaining control of the gun, or at least keeping the man wielding it from killing her mother.

After what seemed to Noelle endless moments engaged in a primitive, no holds barred contest for her mother's life, her attacker gained the upper hand. He swatted her aside like an annoying pest and flung her away from him. At the same time, he aimed the gun at where her mother sat bleeding, whimpering and frozen with terror. Noelle's temple connected with the sharp corner of the coffee table. Dazed, she heard the blast of another shot echoing in the air around her. More blood splashed over her, momentarily blinding her. Terror filling her heart, she wiped the blood from her eyes with trembling hands and began crawling towards where her mother sat slumped in her chair. All her eyes could see was red. It was red everywhere; as if the gunshot had rocketed her into some kind of bizarre alien universe where even the air was red.

CHAPTER FORTY SEVEN

Two uniform patrol officers cruised by the elegant beach house their captain had ordered them to check out. The palm trees out front stood still, without the slightest breeze to disturb the perfect picture they framed. It almost seemed as if they were made of wax and had been placed there by a photographer looking for an iconic photo of elegant but breezy west coast living. A pale yellow bungalow with the moon rising over the Pacific even as the sun began to set provided the backdrop for the unmoving palms. The bungalow had wide windows looking out over the street, with white trim and plantation shutters, and flower boxes beneath the windows. A whimsical old-fashioned porch swing hung from two thick chains that had been painted white so as not to impose the slightest imperfection on the scene. Painted pottery jars and vases generously overflowing with their colorful offerings lined the steps and crowded the porch, spilling over onto the walkway. More flower-filled painted pots were clumped around the bases of the palm trees.

"Nice place," Officer Tim Delaney remarked admiring as his partner slowed to take in the closed garage door with the rental car parked in the driveway. "Looks like she's got company from out of town."

"Probably the daughter from France. I don't see any signs of trouble but we'd better check it out just to make sure."

They parked the car and Tim climbed out of the front seat, giving the front of the house an experienced once over. He turned back to his partner, who was climbing out of the driver's seat. "Call it in. Just to be safe. The front door's ajar."

Mike nodded and did as his partner suggested. The two officers approached cautiously, staying out of the line of sight of the windows across the front of the house. "Probably nothing," Tim whispered as they climbed the first step. "Daughter was probably so excited to be home and see her mother she didn't realize she left the front door open."

"Probably," Mike agreed as he joined his partner on the porch, and slowly eased the front door open.

"Police, Ms. Hanson, are you all right?" Tim called out, but he was quite certain no one inside the house heard his greeting, because chaos erupted at the same time the words were leaving his mouth.

He heard Mike yell, "Shot fired," followed instantly by anguished feminine screaming and the muffled sounds of a violent struggle. Instinct took over. Instinct and years of training to flee towards the source of danger, rather than run for cover, as any sane person would do at the sound of a gunshot.

Tim took in the scene in the living room in a fraction of a second. The woman, about his age, covered with blood struggling with the man holding the gun. The woman tied to the chair, slumped over, bleeding profusely from her midsection. He raised his own gun.

"Police, drop the gun!"

Neither of the combatants involved in the life and death struggle playing out before him paused. He was certain the man with the gun heard him, but the woman was locked in, every ounce of attention focused on keeping the man from killing her mother. The man finally gained the advantage; he freed himself from the younger woman's desperate grip and in one swift, trained motion turned to confront the greater threat. For a moment, their eyes locked. Tim pulled his own trigger just a hair of a second faster than the gunman did. But, a hair of a second was fast enough. The man got off his own shot. Tim felt his vest absorb the hit before he was flung backwards by its force. He heard Mike's weapon fire almost simultaneously and saw the shooter fall, his forehead taking his partner's shot, the assailant's chest already stained bright red from his own.

CHAPTER FORTY EIGHT

The head of the Brotherhood stared unseeing down at the face of the burner phone, absorbing the news he'd just received through it. He very deliberately unclenched his tight grip on the phone, and then just as deliberately he drew a deep, steadying breath. Then just as slowly, just as deliberately he drew another. Control was everything to a man in his position. The fanatics, the hot heads would never rise to it for the simple reason they lacked it and the ability to mindfully contemplate the future course of the movement beyond the heat of the moment, the hour, the decade or the current millennial. No, causes like the one they were engaged in required leadership who were students of man's violent past. Those who understood when it was time to fold a losing hand and retreat from the table with enough funds to play another day.

He quickly ran through in his mind the events of the past few weeks, and came to a few shiningly apparent conclusions. First, it was clear they'd underestimated Noelle Dominique. He acknowledged his mistake even as he recognized his irritation with himself at falling victim to such an obvious error. He'd let himself fall victim to her youth and stunning beauty in very much the same way Raphael Lucien had seemingly done, forgetting that greater men than either of them had been led to their doom by a beautiful, feminine face. Look at the lesson of Helen of Troy…the face that had launched a thousand ships.

His lips curved in an amused smile. He was somewhat relieved he was still capable of falling victim to a woman's wiles. It had been some time, since his wife's death, that he'd given the matter even the most cursory attention. Returning his focus to the matter at hand, he reminded himself that he was a man who rarely made the same mistake twice. He would not underestimate again the surprisingly deft opponent the Dominique heir had turned out to be.

The second conclusion his evaluation of their current circumstances led him to was that it was not yet time to fold his hand

and retire from the table. They were close. Noelle Dominique was obviously still a step ahead of them but she clearly had access to resources they did not. He reconsidered his earlier proposal and discarded strategy of simply allowing her to retrieve the relic for them, then relieving her of it after she had accomplished the task.

There were more than a few risks with that particular strategy which is why he'd given his reluctant approval to intercept her at her mother's. He resisted the urge to chastise himself too bitterly over the disastrous outcome of that decision. Had Noelle Dominique not proven more resourceful than any of them had counted on, the key would already be in their possession. Instead, she had mystifyingly come out the victor in a very dangerous game with a professional fixer...a man whose chosen career path in life had been to handle similar problems and then make those problems disappear for men like him.

His lips tilted up at the corners and he gave a slight nod of acknowledgment in the direction of the absent Mademoiselle Dominique. He hoped her mother survived. He was a man with a great deal of familiarity with grief. It would be a shame to lay such a burden on one so young.

He was not particularly troubled by that emotion at the loss of the fixer. The old cliché' about the man who lived by the sword perishing by it had become a cliché for a reason. The man had known the risks going in. He had obviously been as guilty about underestimating Noelle Dominique as he had been. He could regret though that they'd lost their eyes on her current whereabouts. The thought did not concern him overly much. With her mother's life hanging by a thread, he was quite certain the young mademoiselle wouldn't be leaving Los Angeles any time soon. There was plenty of time for them to pick up her trail.

No, no. It was not yet time for them to retreat from the field of battle. A pawn had been sacrificed but their queen stood unchallenged and soon it would be time to call the rook into play.

CHAPTER FORTY NINE

"Yes, *Grandpere*, what is it?" Rafe asked, unable to completely swallow his impatience when he recognized the number on the face of his phone.

"Raphael, where are you?"

"Where do you think I am?" He countered, in a voice laced with self-mockery. "I'm in a plane on my way to Los Angeles."

"Good, that will save time. Noelle wasn't hurt…" His grandfather assured him before beginning to explain the reason he felt the need to offer the reassurance in the first place…and in the past tense.

Rafe cut him off instantly. "What happened?"

"They were waiting for her when she arrived at her mother's home," his grandfather replied cautiously. "Her mother was shot. She's in surgery, but the officer in charge assured Captain Fils that Noelle is unhurt."

Rafe felt his heart start beating again in his chest. He would have sworn it stopped for a moment when his grandfather said the words, 'they were waiting for her when she arrived at her mother's home.' His mind reeling at the realization of Noelle's narrow escape, Rafe asked in a strained voice, "How did Captain Fils get involved?"

"I called him."

"Of course you did," Rafe concluded bitterly at his own lack of foresight. His mind had no trouble leaping into action again at his grandfather's admission and torturing him with what might have happened to Noelle if his grandfather hadn't reached out to the authorities. She would even now be in their hands…at their mercy…the victim of ruthless men…

"Rafe?" His grandfather drew him mercifully from his preoccupation with Noelle's narrow escape.

"Where is she now?"

"They took her mother to Mission Hospital. Noelle's there under police guard waiting for news of her mother. They'll both have to make a statement. God knows how we're going to explain all of this."

"I'll take care of it."

"I know you will. Please keep us informed. As I'm sure you can imagine, Michel is beside herself with worry."

"Yes, I'll make certain Noelle calls her grandmother as soon as I see her. I trust you will extend our gratitude to Captain Fils for his assistance."

"I have already taken care of the matter," his grandfather assured him, then added, with some hesitation. "Raphael, if I might offer you a little unsolicited advice."

"What is it?"

"I can tell you're still in a rage, and rightfully so, but Noelle's just been through a terrible ordeal. Her mother was shot in front of her. This isn't the time to lose control of your temper no matter how justified your anger with Noelle is at the moment."

"I'll take your advice under consideration. Thank you for involving Captain Fils. You likely saved Noelle's life."

"You're welcome, always."

CHAPTER FIFTY

Noelle sat alone in a small waiting room at the hospital, with police standing on the other side of the closed door. Her hands felt sticky and were stained with her mother's blood, and that of the man who'd traumatized her, aimed a gun at her and shot her without a moment's pause, without a breath of hesitation. The coldness of the act…the casual way he'd simply aimed the gun at her mother and pulled the trigger, not particularly caring how much damage he inflicted, as long as it wasn't lethal, shocked her to the point of immobility.

With the initial shot, Noelle understood, the man planned to use her mother's agony to extract information from Noelle about the key's whereabouts. Once he realized her mother didn't know anything to help his cause, he planned to kill her. The next shot, Noelle knew would have proved fatal. With his experience, and at that distance, he certainly wouldn't have missed his target. Then he would have taken her with him, away from her mother's house, to somewhere he could have dealt with her slowly, tortuously, until he'd extracted every piece of information from her and they'd gone after everyone else she loved in pursuit of the key.

Noelle didn't think it was bravery on her part that impelled her to leap to her feet and launch her full weight at the arm holding the gun pointed in her mother's direction. No. She was quite certain it had been terror for her mother, but also for herself, for Rafe, for her grandmother. She had fully expected her opponent to win their unequal contest. He was, after all, a trained killer.

She had been certain when he flung her away from him, and she'd been dazed from the side of her head connecting with the corner of the coffee table that the next shot she heard had killed her mother. Still, she'd crawled in her mother's direction, tears filling her eyes and spilling down her cheeks, not only for her mother's loss, but from the terror of knowing she was alone and at the mercy of the man who killed her.

Noelle didn't remember the police arriving. She hadn't seen the killer fall, or heard the other shots fired. She didn't know she was safe until she was forced to crawl over him on her way to her mother, but even then, she couldn't figure out what he was doing on the floor at her mother's feet, covered with the stain of his own blood. Noelle had just climbed over him, still on her hands and knees, until she reached her mother. Crying hysterically, she desperately attempted to stem the blood pouring out of the wound in her stomach.

"Mom, Mom, please don't let go. I'm here. We're going to get help. I'm sorry, I'm so sorry. I love you. Please don't die, please don't die..."

"Noelle?" Her mother's labored voice had breathed her name, but before Noelle could answer, strong arms lifted her up and away from her mother.

"Miss? Miss? Let go. We've got her," they had assured her. "Are you hurt?"

'Was she hurt?' Noelle thought that was the funniest thing she'd ever heard. 'Was she hurt?' The laughter bubbled up inside of her and erupted in full-blown hysteria. 'Was she hurt?' No. Hurt didn't begin to cover the damage she'd inflicted on herself that day... and on everyone she loved. She'd been a one-woman wrecking ball and she was going to have to live with the consequences.

Her mother was in surgery with a bullet in her middle fighting for her life because of her. The man she was desperately in love with...well, she could still remember the coldness in Rafe's voice when he'd rebuked her. He'd been incredulous at her thoughtlessness, at the careless indifference with which she'd treated him and her grandmother when she'd dashed off on her foolish trek half way around the world. She couldn't even remember why she'd thought it so important to sneak away without telling anyone.

It already seemed like the events of the day before had happened a million years ago. She didn't even remember who she'd been then. She wasn't certain she knew who she was now. She just knew in the space of a heartbeat she had been irrevocably changed...her innocence shattered beneath the explosion of a bullet racing out of the shaft of a gun and speeding gleefully towards her mother's terror, its aim to inflict as much damage to her soft, fragile flesh as possible.

Her brows furrowed in concentration. She guessed the events that replayed relentlessly through her thoughts, over and over without rest, had occurred the day before. She had no way of knowing. The face of the clock above the door, where she could see the back of the head of the police officer standing guard outside it, read three twenty three. Was that three twenty three am or pm? Was it the same day her former self had been so proud of her own cunning when she'd settled into her business class seat on the direct flight from Paris to Los Angeles? Or was it a new day? That seemed more likely and infinitely more fitting, because one person couldn't possibly have inflicted such damage, could not possibly have been altered as she had been in the space of less than a single day. Could she?

Maybe she could, because time now moved with agonizing slowness as she sat and watched each second tick away on the clock. It seemed like hours for the second hand to make its tortuous way around the face of the clock and for the click of the minute hand to echo in the silence indicating a single minute had passed. An hour might as well have been a decade to Noelle's way of thinking.

They asked if there was anyone they could call for her. She had only barely restrained the almost overwhelming urge to surrender to the full-blown hysteria bubbling up inside her once again. Who would she tell them to call? She had effectively destroyed her relationships with the only other people in the world she could reach out to in a moment of crisis. And what did that say about her? About her life leading up to the sound of that gunshot that still echoed around and around inside her head?

She thought she would even welcome Michael's condescending voice in her head, but he was gone too. He'd deserted her at the time of her last visit to Mont Saint Michel, right after he'd warned her to run from those men with guns. There'd been nothing since, not even the hint of his presence in her thoughts. Maybe she had imagined him, after all, as everyone insisted she had.

She glanced up at the clock again. Three twenty four and forty four seconds. What was taking so long? Why wouldn't someone tell her what was going on with her mother? Was she dead? Were they waiting for someone, whose job it was to impart such news to the grieving family, to come and tell her she'd killed her own mother? Maybe, given her near hysteria when they'd asked if there was anyone they could call to come sit with her, they were afraid to tell her. Maybe they were even now looking into her background for other family members, or friends even, anyone they could find so there was someone to take charge of her when they delivered the crushing blow of her mother's loss.

She let her head drop into her hands, and hunched over, her elbows resting on her knees. Her hands were still sticky with blood, and she could only imagine what her face must look like. She could feel the matted blood in her hair and her clothes...well, her clothes were a mess. They'd offered to bring a hospital gown for her to change into, but she'd just stared at the kind nurse and mutely shook her head. It was stupid, she knew, but somehow her mother's blood staining her clothes, her skin, meant she could cling to the fading hope that her mother was still alive.

She raised her head to glance again at the clock. Three twenty five and sixteen seconds. Was it am or pm? Why didn't they put that critical piece of information on the clock somewhere? And what day was it anyway? Why weren't they telling her anything?

CHAPTER FIFTY ONE

Rafe took the elevator to the fifth floor where he'd been informed Noelle could be found. When the doors slid open, he strode impatiently down the long, antiseptic corridor until he saw the two police officers standing in front of one of the doors at the end of the hall. He felt the breath of a pause in his step at the sight of them. One was a young officer. Rafe guessed he was a recent addition to his chosen profession. The man standing next to him was older, clearly in charge, but still in uniform. A man, Rafe guessed, who'd spent a lifetime patrolling his city's too often violent streets.

What was he going to say to her? He was reminded of his grandfather's warning, and accepted he was right, but Rafe was having limited success getting his still hot, blazing wrath at Noelle's thoughtless deception under control enough to allow him to feel any sympathy for what she'd suffered at the hands of the deadly man who'd shot her mother. She'd brought this on herself.

How could she have been so careless and so damned inconsiderate? Her grandmother was an elderly woman. Had Noelle given no thought to the duchess' terror if she believed Noelle had gone missing? And what about him? Did she trust him so little? Did she have so little regard for his feelings that she would put him through the hell of the hours he'd suffered; frantically trying to trace her steps when he realized she'd lied to her grandmother about spending the day with him? He stopped in front of the two policemen. The older man looked askance in his direction.

"I'm Raphael Lucien. I'm looking for Noelle Dominique."

Raphael was aware of the increased tension that had come over the two men at his arrival, the way their eyes took in and assessed him for any signs of a threat to Noelle. He sensed they were aware of his own tension, and in the way of law enforcement professionals everywhere, their instincts were picking up that he did indeed represent a threat to the woman under their protection.

"Do you have any identification, Mr. Lucien?" The older man inquired. Apparently, he'd been advised of Rafe's impending arrival.

Rafe reached into his jacket pocket for his passport, slowly, aware of the two men's eyes intently following his movements. He just as slowly retrieved the passport and handed it over to the older officer for his perusal. The other man examined it, then nodding, handed the passport back to Rafe.

"Thank you. We were told you'd be stopping by," the man informed him.

"May I see Noelle?" Rafe asked, trying not to let his impatience spill over into his voice, guessing antagonizing the two officers would only delay him.

His lips flirting with the glimmer of a smile, the older man replied frankly, "I can see you are not too happy with Miss Dominique at the moment."

Rafe abandoned all pretense of attempting to hide his current mood. Apparently, it had been a futile attempt on his part. "I'd like to strangle her," he admitted freely, bringing a sympathetic chuckle to the officer's lips.

"We haven't had a chance to question her, but considering the call from the French authorities alerting us to a possible threat to Miss Dominique, I have to assume she also had reason to believe there was a possible threat hanging over her head."

"Indeed," Rafe replied without elaboration.

"And she ignored it," the officer filled in the blanks Rafe left unsaid.

"Yes, and neglected to inform anyone of her impulsive decision to visit her mother halfway across the world...alone, without taking the least precaution for her safety, or for her mother's for that matter," Rafe loosed a little the leash on his straining frustration.

"I can see you're furious with her, and not without good reason. I have five daughters, Mr. Lucien, so you have both my sympathies and my complete understanding of your frustration at the moment, but I'm still going to give you some unsolicited advice."

"I'm listening."

"That young woman in there," he began, motioning with his head towards the closed door behind him, "has been through hell in the past twenty four hours. Maybe it's a hell she's partially responsible for bringing down upon herself and her mother, but that doesn't change the fact that she's been terrorized by a violent, professional killer, witnessed her mother being tied up and shot in her own home, and engaged in a life and death struggle with the same violent, dangerous man to save her mother's life. She's sitting alone in that room waiting for word of the outcome of her mother's surgery, blaming herself, knowing she'll be at least partially responsible if her mother doesn't make it. She's covered in blood, has a knot the size of a robin's egg on her head where the man threw her into a table so he could finish the job on her mother, and she's barely holding herself together. So, before you go in there guns blazing, you need to swallow that rage I can see shooting sparks off of you at the foolish risk she took with her own safety and that of her mother's. I'm not saying I won't let you inside if you can't, but speaking from experience, I'm telling you you'll regret adding to her pain, today of all days."

Rafe held the other man's intent glance as he lectured him, then released an audible breath when the man fell silent. "My grandfather gave me the same advice," he admitted, his eyes glancing over the man's broad shoulders to catch a glimpse of Noelle, but the two men's broad shoulders blocked his view through the small glass opening in the door.

"Sounds like a wise man."

"Yes, yes he is," Rafe admitted, thrusting a hand through his hair. "I know you're right. I know you're both right, and I'll try to resist the almost overpowering urge I'm wrestling with to shake some sense into Noelle when I see her, but it will not be easy."

"Again, you have my sympathies," the officer replied with a slight smile.

"Thank you, Officer...?"

"McGarry. Jack McGarry and this is Officer Ted Stevens."

Rafe shook hands with both men. "Thank you. I'm in your debt."

Office McGarry stepped aside from his stance in front of the door and motioned for the younger officer to do the same. Rafe stood in front of the closed door for a moment before steeling himself to reach for the handle and turn the knob.

CHAPTER FIFTY TWO

Noelle, so attuned to even the slightest sound in the heavy silence she was encased in, looked anxiously towards the door at the slight click of the turning of the knob and the sound of the door being almost silently pushed open. Expecting to find a doctor, robed in a white cloak and wearing a serious expression standing on the threshold, she was beyond stunned when she saw Rafe's somewhat disheveled appearance there instead. Neither spoke, nor did Rafe make any effort to step away from the doorway and close the door. They both remained motionless, rooted seemingly where they were, staring at each other.

Noelle guessed her endless hours of watching the seconds tick by on the generic hospital clock had enhanced her powers of observation, because she noticed all kinds of things about Rafe, she knew she would have missed prior to her experience of the past twenty four hours. His hair was mussed somewhat. She guessed he had thrust his hands through it numerous times waiting for word of her whereabouts. It was a gesture she recognized as one he succumbed to under stress.

The expression in his dark eyes was not filled with the slightly amused indulgence he generally regarded her with. No, this time beneath the shock in his glance at her own less than coiffed appearance, was an icy coldness, tinged with a hot rage she could tell he was having trouble keeping in check. She guessed his hesitation to step further into the room and bridge the distance separating them was due to his uncertainty that he would be able to control the rage shimmering just below the surface of the iron will he'd slapped over his baser instincts.

Noelle recognized she would have to take the first step to begin bridging that distance that was now more than a physical gap separating them. No, the chasm they regarded each other across was filled with anger and hurt and stunned incredulity that she could be so careless with both the feelings and the physical safety of those she professed to love. She'd created that breach. It would be up to her to navigate the minefield of unspoken accusations and savagely suppressed feelings separating them. She urged herself to stand and begin the process, but her body refused to respond to her mind's urging. She opened her lips to speak, to begin the task of explaining, of apologizing, of making things right between them, but the words refused to form in her throat.

For his part, Rafe stood rooted in the doorway, shocked beyond words, beyond his driving fury, beyond his outraged affront at the appearance Noelle presented covered in blood, her hands and face still stained with it, her hair matted with it, her clothes bearing the evidence of the violent encounter she'd been a part of. Officer McGarry had claimed 'that she'd engaged in a life and death struggle for control of the gun that had been used to injure her mother, and whose owner's intent was to kill her. Noelle bore the evidence of that desperate struggle in her clothes, on her flesh, in her hair, but mostly in the vacant, deadened eyes she was regarding him with out of her bloodstained face.

He was afraid to approach her...afraid to frighten her further. Scared that at even the most gentle of greetings from him she would simply shatter beneath the pressure. So, he waited for her to say something, to acknowledge his presence. To scream at him, to rage, to stamp her feet, to break down in desperate sobs of worry for her mother's life...anything but to just sit there regarding him with that dazed, blank expression on her face.

He waited silently as she seemed to force herself to stand. The small act appeared to require an enormous amount of will on her part. She tried to thrust her fingers through her hair, but her fingers got stuck in the knotted mass of blood and tangles, so she simply swept what she could away from her face. She took a cautious step towards him; he stood absolutely still, not wanting any sudden movement on his part to send her fleeing in the opposite direction, or screaming for the police, who still stood guard outside the door.

He watched her take another halting step towards him, saw the tears fill her eyes and trickle down her cheeks, carving out rivulets of unstained flesh, washing clean her bloodstained face with her own tears. As the trickle became a flood, her steps quickened, until with an agonized cry she was running towards him, sobbing his name, her breath escaping in desperate, frantic gasps. He opened his arms and she leapt into them, wrapping her legs around his hips as he drew her close and pressed her head down on his shoulder, her face resting against the bare skin of his neck.

He made no effort to dam the tide of tears, or the hushed, breathless apologies. He simply held her in his arms, whispering soothing words against the top of her head, while his hands stroked her back and threaded through her long hair, slowly beginning to work the matted tangles free. When the sobs began to slow, he walked with her back to the sofa beneath the windows and took a seat, still holding her trembling form in his lap.

With an effort, Noelle slowly pulled back from the warm cocoon of Rafe's strong arms, wrapped tightly around her, keeping her safe. She reached up her hands to clasp his face between them, and held his intent, probing gaze and began the long task of undoing the damage she'd done. "I'm sorry. I can't undo what I did. I can only say, stupidly, I didn't think you would figure out I was gone before I landed in L.A. and called to let you know where I was. I know that doesn't mean much now and doesn't make up for the worry I put you through. Is my grandmother all right?"

"No, but I promised you would call her as soon as I saw you." Rafe replied, deliberately emotionless, because now that she was here where he could touch her, hold her, his temper was straining against his will to stifle it. There was no denying Officer McGarry's point. Noelle had already been through hell. She had already paid a high price for her reckless little jaunt and might yet be forced to pay an even higher one, depending on the outcome of her mother's surgery. Now was not the time to unleash his own resentments given her currently fragile state.

Noelle couldn't detect any forgiveness in Rafe's flat response or in his empty glance probing hers. She couldn't detect any emotion at all in his voice. His eyes, the tension in his stance told its own story. She would have to face that…deal with it, but now she needed to call her grandmother and assure her she was safe.

"You're right. I'll call her now," she responded belatedly to Rafe's comment. "I don't know where my phone is. Can I borrow yours?"

She waited for Rafe to reach into his pocket and hand her his phone. She just stared at, making no move to dial her grandmother's number, puzzling over what she was going to say to her, and how she would begin to explain. Rafe finally grew impatient with her delaying tactics. He took the phone back from her unresisting grip, slid his thumb across its face and pressed send, before handing the phone back to her.

"Rafe? Have you seen Noelle?"

Noelle froze at the sound of Ariel Lucien's anxious voice on the other end of the line. Sighing impatiently, Rafe once more took the phone from her hand, and replied for her. "Yes, she's right here. She wants to speak with her grandmother."

Rafe placed the phone back in her hand, and Noelle stared at it almost incomprehensively, until her grandmother's voice broke through her daze, "Noelle? Noelle? Are you all right? Did that bastard harm you?"

"Meme? Meme? Yes, I'm fine. He shot her. He shot my mom. It's all my fault. I'm so sorry, I'm so sorry I worried you. I'm so sorry for everything," Noelle was sobbing and gasping for breath as the words suddenly poured out of her at the sound of her grandmother's worried voice.

"It's all right, Noelle." Her grandmother assured her, and then asked, "How is your mother?"

"I don't know, I don't know. She's still in surgery. They won't tell me anything. They said her injuries weren't life threatening, but it's been so long and she lost so much blood. Maybe something happened. Why is it taking so long? Why won't they tell me anything?"

"Try to stay calm, Noelle dear. I know you're scared, but I'm sure your mother's going to be fine. Is Rafe with you?"

"Yes, yes he's here," Noelle confirmed, and then glanced in the direction of the door when she caught sight of someone standing in the doorway. "Meme? I have to go. The doctor's here. I have to go."

"All right, dear. Call me as soon as you hear anything about your mother. I'll be praying for her."

"Thank you, Meme. I'll call you soon." Noelle disconnected the call and then climbed awkwardly from her perch on Rafe's lap. Their glances met for a moment, and he helped her to regain her feet. Then he stood next to her, and together they approached where the doctor, in surgeon's garb, waited for them near the door. As they crossed the distance to hear the results of her mother's surgery, Noelle reached for Rafe's hand. After a moment's hesitation, he threaded their fingers together and gave hers a reassuring squeeze. No one spoke until they stopped in front of the doctor and Noelle raised an anxious glance to her face.

"Miss Hanson?" The woman, who looked not much older than Noelle asked before continuing, "I'm Doctor Rodgers. I performed your mother's surgery."

Noelle shook her head, stupidly correcting the woman. "No, actually it's Dominque. My mother reverted to using her maiden name after my father died and we moved out west. And, I'm sorry. You don't need to know that. I'm Ms. Hanson's daughter, Noelle. Is she all right?"

The other woman regarded her sympathetically, her expression revealing her surprise at Noelle's disheveled appearance. She glanced over her shoulder to where Rafe waited silently standing behind Noelle. With her newly enhanced powers of observation, Noelle caught the swift passage of expressions across the surgeon's face, surprise that the mess of a woman standing in front of her could attract the attention of the man at her side, a purely instinctive feminine admiration, followed swiftly by a return to her best professional manner, as if she was annoyed for allowing herself to become distracted by an attractive man. She met Noelle's anxious glance with a reassuring smile.

"Your mother's surgery went very well, Miss Dominique. I don't foresee any reason why she won't make a complete recovery."

Noelle only half listened as the other woman continued to explain about how they would have to keep a close eye on her mother for the next twenty-four hours, about the ever-present risk of infection, and that her mother would have to stay in the hospital for a few more days. The surgeon's pronouncement that her mother would make a complete recovery just kept reverberating around and around inside her head. She raised trembling hands to her face and would have collapsed to the floor when her knees gave out but for Rafe's swift reflexes. His hands encircled her waist and pulled her back against him.

She allowed herself the indulgence of leaning against his strength for a few moments, then forced herself to pull away and rely on her own, depleted as it was at the moment. She offered her hand to the woman who saved her mother's life, too late realizing it remained bloodstained. Embarrassed, she swiftly attempted it to draw it back. Dr. Rodgers, no stranger to blood, grasped Noelle's hand before she had a chance to tuck it out of sight and then released it.

"Thank you. Thank you for saving my mother. Can I see her now?" Noelle asked her voice husky with emotion.

"She's in recovery, but if the officers at your door have no objection, I don't see any reason why you can't wait for her there."

"Thank you."

When the doctor turned back to speak with the officers, Rafe, who had been a silent witness to their exchange, wrapped his arms around her middle and pulled her back against him. He bent to brush his lips against her bloodstained hair. Noelle turned in his arms and lifted her embarrassed gaze to his. "I'm a mess."

"Yes, you are," Rafe agreed with a slight, gentle smile, then reached for her hand and raised it to his lips. "But you're alive, and though I'm still furious with you for sneaking off the way you did, I can share your joy at the news about your mother."

"Thank you." He nodded, and Noelle added, "No, not just for now...for everything...for caring...for dropping everything and flying out here...for being with me through all of this. I don't deserve you, I know, but I'm not letting you go."

His lips twitched and for a moment, the stark icy rage in his glance was replaced with a glimmer of humor. "You're not?"

"No. I'll figure out a way to make all of this up to you. When this is over and well... you can look at me again and not want to strangle me."

Amusement flashed in his glance again, giving Noelle hope. "Apparently I'm not as successful at concealing my emotions as I've always assumed I was."

Noelle shrugged. "Usually you're really good at it. Today though I keep waiting for the bomb to drop. It's like I'm trapped in a locked room with an unexploded grenade, knowing eventually it's going to go off and just hoping that when it does, I'll somehow survive the devastation."

He grinned and grasped her chin with his hand. "I never kick a lady when she's down, but I'm glad you realize there's still some unfinished business between us."

Noelle shrugged and with a slight smile, responded, "I can take comfort from that."

He chuckled, slid his phone out of his pocket, and handed it to her. "Call your grandmother. I will speak with the officers and see if we can convince them to allow you to wait in recovery with your mother."

CHAPTER FIFTY THREE

Noelle sat beside her mother's bed in the private room the police no doubt insisted upon. Her mother had regained consciousness for brief moments in recovery; enough to assure herself Noelle was alive and well. Then she'd lapsed back into a deep, more restful sleep. Noelle dozed fitfully throughout her long vigil, exhaustion winning the battle with her will to watch carefully over her mom and be there for her the moment she woke. She was aware of Rafe standing behind her near the window, which she knew was what allowed her to put her fear to rest long off to drop into fitful sleep.

Her mother's hand stirred in hers, bringing Noelle instantly awake. "Mom? Mom? Can you hear me? It's Noelle."

"Noelle?" Her mother answered in a labored whisper. "Are you all right, honey? He didn't hurt you?"

"Oh, Mom, no, no. I'm fine. He didn't hurt me. He tried to kill you," Noelle replied in an agonized voice, sitting up and leaning over her mom, staring into her drug-glazed eyes.

"But he didn't. I come from tough mid-western stock. Takes more than a madman with a gun to take me out."

Noelle laughed weakly at her mom's attempt at humor and summoned the expected response, "Guess we showed him."

"Damn straight," her mother whispered back, closing her eyes and squeezing Noelle's hand reassuringly.

The next time Noelle woke was to the sound of an anxious, deep male voice, calling out, demanding to know where her mother was. "Jeanie? Can you hear me? Tell these officers to let me in."

Confused, Noelle raised her head from where it rested on top of where her hand still lay clasped with her mother's limp one.

"Jimmy, is that you?" Her mother called out weakly, but loud enough to attract the attention of the officers, who stepped aside and allowed the bull of man, with a ruddy complexion and a patch of marine-short, greying hair, wearing a worried expression on his strained features to pass through the door.

"Jeannie," her mother's name came out in a rush in a voice filled with obvious relief. Noelle looked between her Mom and the strange man who'd rushed to her mother's bedside and gripped the hand Noelle wasn't holding and who reached out to brush a tender hand across her mother's cheek. "Jeannie, honey, what in God's holy name happened to you? I was frantic when I couldn't reach you. I finally flew out here and drove by your home. I swear the police tape in front of your door damn near stopped my heart in my chest."

In her dazed, exhausted state understanding was slow to dawn, but finally a slight smile played around Noelle's lips when she asked her mother, wonder in her voice, "Mom, are you dating Jimmy?"

While her mother blushed and searched for words to answer Noelle's teasing, Jimmy interrupted, "Dating? Young lady I'm on the wrong side of fifty so it seems a little silly to waste time dating at my age. I've been trying to convince Jeannie to marry me for the past six months, but she's as stubborn as she is pretty. You must be Noelle. I'm glad to finally meet you, but I can't believe this is what it took to bring the occasion about."

Noelle sat up and stretched her hand across the bed. "It's nice to meet you too, Jimmy, and yes I'm Noelle." Jimmy accepted her hand and shook it, for the first time taking a good look at her.

"No offense, Noelle, but if it's possible you look even worse than my Jeannie here." He cast a glance beyond her shoulder to where Rafe was silently watching the introductions. He stretched his long arm over the bed in Rafe's direction and offered, "Jim Holzinger."

"Raphael Lucien," Rafe replied equally briefly, accepting the other man's hand.

When an awkward silence fell between them, Jim added, "Is someone going to tell me what the hell is going on?"

When no one made an effort to fill the silence, Noelle offered dejectedly, "It's my fault."

Her mother instantly protested, "Noelle, don't be silly. None of this is your fault."

302

To which Jim added, his brow raised, "You shot your mother?"

Smiling slightly, Noelle replied, "No, of course not, but the man who did was there because of me. I led him to Mom's house. It's my fault she almost died."

"It's because of you she's still alive," Rafe commented quietly from where he still stood near the window.

Noelle swung around to meet his serious glance and shook her head. "No, that's not true."

Rafe turned his attention to her mother and Jim and explained, "Officer McGarry told me Noelle struggled with the gunman when it was clear he was going to kill you. She bought enough time for the police to get inside and eliminate the threat. That knot on the side of her head is from where the intruder threw her off of him and into the corner of a table."

"Oh, Noelle, honey," her mother cried, reaching out to run her fingertips gently across the bruise on her temple.

"Thank you, young lady, I owe you," Jimmy added seriously.

"No, no. It's my fault he was there in the first place. Mom, you almost died because of me," Noelle protested.

"Don't be silly, Noelle. You were in trouble and you came home," her mother argued, thinking to assuage Noelle's feelings of guilt, but Noelle could only imagine Rafe's reaction to her mother's claim.

"That's not true," she protested quietly. "I've been in trouble for weeks, ever since I returned to France. I didn't tell you. I didn't want to drag you into any of this. Rafe's the one who's been helping me."

"But you didn't run to me when you were in trouble," he reminded her bitterly.

"I didn't know I was in trouble...or at least that they would find me so quickly. I thought I could end this. Instead I almost got my mother killed."

"And you were almost taken," Rafe pointed out.

"Yes. I screwed up and made a mess of everything. I get that and I'm sorry for it, but I have to finish this. We both know they're not going to stop. They'll go after my grandmother next, and then you and your grandfather until they've threatened everyone I love. I can't let that happen. I have to find that key and turn it over to the authorities or

303

do whatever Michael wants me to do with it. I have to end this once and for all, or none of us will ever be safe again."

"*We* have to end this," Rafe corrected.

"I think it would be better if you just stayed away from me…at least until this is over," Noelle replied in a dejected whisper.

"You don't want to go there," Rafe warned her.

"Noelle, what are you talking about? That's what that man wanted. He kept asking you where the key was. I think it's time you told me, in Jimmy's words, what the hell is going on."

"It's better if you don't know any more than you already do, Mom."

"Screw that!" Her mother protested, wincing when she tried to sit up in bed. Noelle watched Jimmy reach out to help settle her mother back against the bed and couldn't stop the smile that curved her lips at the big man's obvious concern for her mother. "You always did keep every little thing to yourself. For the most part, I did my best to respect your privacy, but we're a long ways beyond that now. I'm your mother and I'm part of this now. I should have been part of this all along. I've taken a bullet for my part in it so I think I'm entitled to an explanation. This has something to do with your father and what happened at Mont Saint Michel that day when you were a little girl. I've pieced that much together. Now start talking."

Noelle held her mother's glance for a long moment, then turned behind her to meet Rafe's slightly amused one. "She's your mother. They've already no doubt figured out she doesn't know anything to help their cause. I think she's entitled to an explanation."

"It's because she's my mother I don't want her involved in this," Noelle protested.

"She's already involved," Rafe pointed out.

"Because of me. Because I brought this to her door," Noelle countered bitterly.

"They would have likely eventually come here anyway." Rafe raised his hand when Noelle would have interrupted. "If you managed to piece together that your father left a clue to the key's whereabouts with his wife and came here looking for it, they would have eventually reached the same conclusion."

"He's right, Noelle. If you explain to me whatever clue you believe your father left with me, it would make it easier for me to help you," her mother insisted.

Noelle turned back to her mother, letting her eyes roam over her. She looked so pale and small lying in the hospital bed with tubes in her wrists. She thrust her hands through her hair and replied quietly, "I have to think about this. I'm so exhausted I can't even string two thoughts together. Daddy obviously thought to keep you safe by not involving you in any of this. His intention obviously worked for the past twenty years. I'm the one who led them to you and put you in danger. I'm not sure pulling you in any deeper than you already are is the right thing to do, even if I do owe you an explanation for your home being broken into and for you being terrorized and shot by some deranged fanatic on the trail of an ancient religious relic he thinks I have or I can lead him to. I need a shower. I need clean clothes. I need to sleep and I need to think about what's best for everyone involved. So, I'm going to leave you in Jimmy's obviously capable and caring hands and I'm going home to put your house back in order and to wash the blood out of my hair and fall into bed and sleep. The police have been very patient, but I realize I'm also going to have to come up with some kind of convincing explanation for all of this that won't have them concluding that I'm the one who's deranged. So if there's nothing you need from me right now, I'm going to go back to the house and try to figure out how not to hurt anyone else I love more than I already have."

"Noelle, honey…" Her mother began and then let her voice trail off. Noelle saw her exchange a glance with Rafe over her shoulder.

Noelle swung around to meet Rafe's speculative glance. "Will you come with me? I need your help."

Brows raised at her surprising admission, he corrected, "You need me."

Nodding, she agreed, "Yes."

CHAPTER FIFTY FOUR

At least they could remove the police tape, Noelle thought, tugging at it blocking the entrance to her mother's pretty little front porch. Rafe had confirmed with the officer outside her Mom's hospital room that the police were done with the house, but that both she and her mother still needed to make a statement.

Noelle stood at the front door, fumbling for her key to her mother's house in her purse, surprised by the knot of fear that was forming in her stomach. Her hands were shaking so badly when she tried to insert the key in the lock, that Rafe finally put his larger hand over hers and steadied her. He helped her turn the handle and push the door open.

"Thank you," she whispered, refusing to turn around and meet his gaze she could feel watching her. "I know this sounds silly, but I'm afraid to go inside. Imagine how my mother's going to feel. This is her home. I've stolen that away from her."

Rafe's hands descended on her shoulders and he bent to brush his lips across the top of her head, but he didn't deny her dejected conclusion. "You need to reclaim your mother's home from the violence that was done here. Your doing so will make it easier for her to return."

"You're right. Thank you for being here with me," she replied and turned to face him. They were barely a breath apart. All she wanted was to lean into him and feel his strong arms come up around her and hold her close, but she could tell, helpful as he was being, that he was still having trouble getting over her deception. She took a deliberate step back. He made no move to stop her. Turing swiftly around so he wouldn't see the shimmer of fresh tears in her eyes, she took a cautious step inside the house.

It didn't look all that different from where she stood in the entry. There was no obvious evidence of the violence that had been done there. She could hear the echo of the intruder's voice, calling to her, "Come in *Mademoiselle*, we've been expecting you. I guess you were held up in that accident on the Interstate. I was beginning to think you were one of the unfortunate victims."

She forced herself to take another step further into the house, aware of Rafe following silently behind. When she stood at the opening to the great room, she gasped, fighting the onslaught of memories of her mother sitting slumped over the blood-stained chair. The white carpet was more red than white now and the furniture was still exactly as it had been that morning. The chair and table lay askew and blood-stained. Some of the books and knick-knacks that were knocked over in her violent struggle with the intruder lay scattered around the floor.

"I don't even know where to begin," Noelle whispered, turning to face Rafe.

His eyes clashed with her hesitant ones she raised to his face and she could see he was having trouble controlling his temper all over again. She wished he would just get it over with it, so they could hopefully, begin moving beyond it. She was beginning to believe the anticipation of waiting for the explosion to break over her head was worse than living through the experience itself.

But, of course he didn't yell at her. He was too much of a gentleman to kick her when she was already down. Instead, he reached up a gentle hand to brush his fingertips across the bruise to her temple. "It's taking everything I am right now not to shake some belated sense into you."

"I know and I appreciate your restraint. I kind of wish though that you would just get it over with. The anticipation is killing me," she confessed in a whisper.

Rafe's lips curved slightly. "I'd rather wait for you to recover your strength. Then I won't have to concern myself with pulling any punches."

"There's that I suppose," Noelle acknowledged dejectedly. Then she turned around and took a step into the room, as much to prove to herself she could, rather than because she had any actual plan for dealing with the mess. "The rug and chair are total losses. The table is salvageable. I think I can get the blood off the wood and glass."

"No," Rafe objected immediately. "I don't think you want your mother to picture you flying into the edge of that table every time she looks at."

"You're probably right. Do you think her interior designer could help with some of this? I met him when she bought this house. She had so much fun decorating it. She said it was like a dream to be able to live on the ocean. I always thought she'd go back to the mid-west once I went off to school, but instead, she moved out of the suburbs and bought this place."

"Yes, I think calling your mother's designer is an excellent idea. Then go upstairs and take a shower, find something clean to put on and sleep."

"You need to sleep too," Noelle pointed out.

"I know. I will, after I've made a few calls. This house looks large enough to have an extra bedroom I could use."

Noelle nodded at the obvious implication he wasn't particularly interested in sharing a bed with her. She tried not to be hurt by it. He was furious with her. They would get passed this, she promised herself. They had to. "Yes," she forced the words through the blockage of tears in her throat. "There's a guest suite on this floor down the hallway to the right." She pointed in the direction of the guest suite.

"Thank you."

"I'll call Jerry and see if he can come over and take a look at things."

"Have him come in the morning. You need to sleep."

Upstairs in the bathroom of the suite her mother decorated for her even though they both knew at the time Noelle would likely never take up residence there, she turned the water on as hot as she could stand it and stood under the pulsing jets for what seemed like hours. Her discarded clothes were already in the bathroom trashcan. She finally summoned the effort to reach for the shampoo and scrub her scalp until it was finally clean, then used the washcloth to remove all evidence of blood stains from her skin. She was so tired by the time she was finished, she stumbled out of the shower, towel dried her hair and skin, then stumbled naked into bed.

She woke dazed and confused, not immediately recognizing where she was or how she'd gotten there. Then the awful memories returned in a rush. Her breathing quickened and she had to forcibly remind herself it was over. She was safe. Her mother was safe. Her lips curved at the reminder that her mother apparently had someone to look after her now. She was happy for her.

At the reminder she had her own Prince Charming waiting downstairs for her Noelle forced herself to climb out of bed and go in search of something to wear, as she'd left her suitcase in the rental car. After brushing her hair and teeth and donning an old sundress she found in her closet, she went downstairs to see what surprises this new day had in store for her. She was hoping one of those surprises included a meal. She discovered she was starving and puzzled over when was the last time she ate. It was before she left France, but she'd lost track of the time since then and didn't know if she arrived at LAX yesterday, the day before, or the day before that.

She followed the sound of voices into the great room and saw Rafe standing in the middle of the room speaking with Jerry, her mother's designer. The two men looked up at her entrance. Noelle was aware of Rafe's eyes sweeping over her, evaluating her current emotional and physical state, even as Jerry rushed over to hug her, exclaiming, "Noelle, look at you. It's such a relief to see you. Mr. Lucien was telling me that your mother is recovering? I've been worried sick ever since I saw the news."

"Hi Jerry." Nicole greeted the older man about her height, his concerned glance meeting hers, returning his gentle hug. "Thanks so much for coming on such short notice. Yes, Mom's doing better. I want to clean all of this up before she comes home."

"Yes, of course. I know what she likes. Why don't you let me take care of this for you?" He suggested.

"That would be wonderful, thank you. The floors might be stained beneath the rug and…"

He cut her off. "Let me do my job. I know exactly what needs to be done here in order to restore your mother's house to the way she likes it. You'll let me do this for her…for both of you."

"Thank you."

Leaving Jerry to work his magic, Noelle left with Rafe to return to the hospital. He pulled into a restaurant along the way

At her raised brow, he informed her, "You need to eat."

"Yes, thank you. I'm starving."

"When did you last eat?"

Noelle hesitated before continuing the already awkward conversation. She was quite certain, Rafe wasn't going to be pleased with her answer. Then sighing, she responded honestly, "I'm not sure. Before I left France. When was that by the way? I've lost track of the days."

Noelle could tell from the tightening around Rafe's lips that he didn't like her answer, but he merely said in reply, "You left France on Tuesday. Today is Friday."

"Friday?" Noelle echoed incredulous. "No wonder I'm starving."

With that inauspicious beginning, the day didn't get much better from there. Rafe sat opposite her at the restaurant, counting every morsel she placed in her mouth, or so it seemed to Noelle. When she pronounced herself full after barely half a sandwich and a few chips, she could see Rafe wanted to say something but managed to bite his lip in time. Noelle thought Rafe's lips must be bleeding on the inside given the number of times he must have bitten down on his bottom lip since he caught up with her to prevent some scathing comment from erupting through them.

It was a relief when they made it to her mother's hospital room. Her mother smiled her greeting. Noelle was aware of her mother's experienced mom eyes running over her, seeing more than Noelle hoped she would. When silence fell over the room after the obligatory greetings were exchanged, her mother asked the two men to leave them alone…that she needed to speak privately with Noelle.

Noelle could tell neither man liked the request, but given the circumstances, they could hardly refuse.

"So, I can see your Raphael is a little upset with you," Her mom commented when they were alone, a glimmer of amusement in her eyes.

"That's putting it mildly," Noelle agreed on a sigh, and then was quick to add, "but, he's not my Raphael."

311

"But you'd like him to be," her mother countered, her glance probing Noelle's.

"Yes, but I don't see that happening. At least not after everything that's happened this week."

"Don't be too sure of that. A man doesn't drop everything and fly halfway around the world to chase after a woman he's not serious about."

"Maybe," Noelle acknowledged, "but I messed up with him, Mom. I snuck away and didn't tell either Rafe or Meme where I was going. They thought I'd been kidnapped by those men. He's still furious with me for deceiving him. I don't know how we'll get passed that."

"You could start by apologizing for worrying him."

"Done and done and done. It doesn't seem to be working."

"Then keep apologizing until it does," her Mom recommended, and then added, "You're in love with him."

Blushing, Noelle admitted, "Yes."

A pleased and at the same time, reminiscent smile curved her mother's lips. "The same way I loved your father …madly …recklessly …crazily. A woman loves like that only once in her life. Trust me, I know. I've been looking for those same feelings since I lost your father. I was so young. I just assumed I'd fall in love again as easily as I fell for your father. It never happened. I accept now that it never will. So don't be so quick to give up on what you have with Rafe, thinking another Rafe will come along for you. He won't."

"Is that why you've never married again?" Noelle asked curious. It was the first time she could remember her mother ever speaking so openly about her relationship with Noelle's father.

"Yes. As the years passed, I accepted I never would." There was a wistful note in her mother's voice, Noelle found a little disconcerting. It was almost as if she was looking in the mirror at her own relationship with Rafe. He probably wouldn't die suddenly, but if Noelle couldn't fix things between them, the ending of her once in a lifetime love affair would have the same lonely ending.

"How did you meet Jim?"

She watched her mother's lips curve at the memory. "He was visiting the beach with his daughter and her husband and grandchildren." She laughed. "He was like a fish out of water, literally, but he was trying so hard to get this enormous kite in the air for a little blond haired girl. It brought to mind how your father did the same thing for you one evening on the beach. Neither of them were particularly successful at it." She sighed, smiling at her memories. "The next day Jimmy showed up at my front door clutching a few dozen tulips. I guess you could say we've been dating ever since."

"Are you going to marry him?" Noelle asked.

"I'm leaning in that direction. He lives in Montana. He has a ranch there, but he's agreed we can split our time between the beach and the ranch. That was an enormous concession for him…and for me frankly, to leave the ocean for half the year. It's funny, how fond I've grown of it. I think I was fifteen when I saw the ocean for the first time. Now I can't imagine living anywhere else." She paused and met Noelle's glance. "He's a good man, Noelle. And I've stopping clinging to the notion that I'm going to find again what I found with your father. Maybe I can't love Jimmy the way I did Michel, but I do love him. He makes me happy. He's the only man who's made me laugh since Michel. I don't want you to worry he's after my money. He's a wealthy man. He has no need of mine. In fact, he's very insistent I set aside the bulk of my wealth in trust for you before we marry."

"It's your money, Mom. You know better than anyone how generous Daddy was to me. I hope you keep your money and do whatever makes you happy with it."

"Thank you. I just want you to know I wasn't deliberately keeping my relationship with Jimmy from you."

Noelle laughed. "And I wasn't keeping mine with Rafe from you. It's none of my business, Mom. I'm so glad you found someone to make you laugh, and who makes you happy."

"Me too, and likewise, even if your Rafe's a little upset with you at the moment."

Noelle rolled her eyes at her mother's gargantuan understatement, bringing fresh laughter to her mother's eyes. Then she watched her mother's expression turn serious. "Now I've been thinking about that key you're looking for and won't tell me anything about. It's a long shot, but I think I might know where your father would have hidden it."

"What? You're joking," Noelle exclaimed incredulous.

"We'll see if I'm right or not, but I think it's worth a look," her mother demurred, and then asked in an abrupt change of subject. "When you moved back to the townhome in Georgetown did you change the room you slept in when you were a little girl?"

Noelle shook her head, a little embarrassed to admit her reluctance to cling to her childhood. "No. I couldn't bear to. I loved it so much and all of my memories of us as a family are in that house, in that room."

Her mother smiled her understanding. "You loved that room. You were every Disney princess there."

"Don't keep me in suspense, Mom. What made you ask about my old room?"

"After you left yesterday I began thinking about those months before your father died." She paused, and added resigned, "I guess we know now his death wasn't an accident. I'm glad you slapped that bastard." Her mother added with feeling. At Noelle's surprise, she added, "I remember that part. It's only after he shot me that things get a little fuzzy." She held up her hand to stop the apology forming on Noelle's lips. "No, Noelle. You were right to come to me. I'm your mother. It doesn't matter how grown up you get; I'll always be your mother. It's my job to keep you safe from the evil in this world. I guess I didn't do a very good job of it the other day, but now I think you're right. If someone has been after this key for centuries, as you implied yesterday, and they killed your father for it, you need to put a stop to this. Not alone. You take Rafe and all the help you can get."

"I will. I'm done playing the role of heroine," Noelle promised bitterly.

"Good. Now, about your old room. For about six months or so before he died, your father and I had been discussing moving you out of the crib and into a toddler bed. We were planning on having another child."

"Oh, Mom." Noelle squeezed her mother's hand in empathy.

"I know, honey. It still hurts, but it was a long time ago. Time heals. The hurt fades." Noelle nodded, but waited silently for her mom to continue her story. "We'd never gotten beyond the planning stage until one day your Dad came home after a trip to Europe. All of a sudden he was possessed to get working on your new room. He insisted on having the bed custom made, with all of that intricate woodwork. You really were just like a fairy princess in that bed."

"Mom, are you implying you think Dad hid the key in my bed?"

"I know it sounds crazy, but do you remember the cupola where all the gauze came together over the canopy? The way it was secured to the ceiling with that metal ring at the top, almost like the hilt of a key? It might be nothing, but I just remember how after months of talking about it, your father was suddenly obsessed with the idea of moving you out of the nursery and into that bed in one of the larger bedrooms. It's not like he wasn't a busy man and he was just filling time. For all of his inherited wealth, your father worked incredibly hard."

"Did Daddy keep a family bible?" Noelle asked, curious.

"Not to my knowledge. Your father was Catholic and insisted our children be raised in the faith as you know, but I honestly don't remember him ever reading the bible or any other religious scripture. Why do you ask?"

Noelle hesitated, then sighing admitted, "Because Daddy's father and grandfather had a special mark in their family bibles, and their graves are marked with the symbol of a key."

"And you think those marks and the key symbol are significant."

"Yes."

"I can see you're reluctant to tell me anymore, and I won't push you, but I confess I'm curious. When this is all over, promise me you'll come back and tell me the whole story."

"I promise, Mom, but I can't leave you...not like this," Noelle protested.

"Don't be silly. Jimmy's dying to take me back home and keep me safe. We're not going to deny him that, after worrying him the way we did. You'll let Raphael keep you safe from the bad guys too,"

"He's probably wishing he could find a replacement Prince Charming to take his place, but he won't. In his mind, I'm sure he figures he's stuck with the job until this is over," Noelle admitted dejectedly.

"Then you have a little time to help him forgive you."

"Yes, there's that I suppose."

CHAPTER FIFTY FIVE

"Are you going to tell me what your mother told you?" Rafe asked, while they walked back to the hospital parking lot.

"Yes," Noelle replied without hesitation. "No more secrets. She thinks she knows where my father hid the key."

"What?" He demanded incredulous, stopping abruptly his swift strides, and gripping her shoulders to turn her to face him.

"We need to go back to the townhouse in Washington to see if she's right."

He nodded, and then tacked on, curious. "Your mother?"

"Mom insists it will make Jimmy happy to look after her."

Lips curving in a slight smile, Rafe agreed. "Yes, I believe it will. So we're leaving?"

"Yes, I confirmed with Officer McGarry that I could leave the country. Will you come with me?"

"Yes," he confirmed simply.

"All right. I know you're still mad at me. I don't know how to fix that," she confessed, searching his gaze.

"Nor do I. So why don't we just take the next step and see where it leads us?" He suggested practically.

"Yes, all right."

They didn't fly directly to Washington. Instead, Rafe directed the pilot of his private Lucien jet to take them to New York where they checked into a hotel, had dinner, and planned to spend the night. Rafe thought it would be wise to take the precaution of not heading directly to Washington. In fact, his plan was for them to remain checked into the New York hotel, rent a car in the morning, and drive to Washington.

Noelle wasn't particularly surprised, when after dinner in the elegant dining room where they had studiously avoided any discussion of their search for the key, or the dismal state of their personal relationship, which made for an awkward, uncomfortable evening, Rafe elected to sleep in the second bedroom in the suite he procured for them. Rather than question their sleeping arrangements, Noelle just whispered a soft good night when Rafe left her at her bedroom door with the admonition that she should go right to bed, try not to worry, and catch up on her rest. She guessed she was back to being the somewhat irritating younger cousin or niece his grandfather had asked him to keep an eye on and make sure she didn't fall into any trouble.

He'd made no move to kiss her goodnight, or to join her in her bed, which had more than ample enough room for both of them. Deflated, she'd turned from him and headed to the bathroom to get ready for bed. The big Jacuzzi tub was just sitting there. She couldn't help but notice that it wasn't just the bed that was big enough for two. Since the hotel was generous enough to supply bath oils for soaking in the tub, Noelle decided to take advantage of them.

She turned on the water as hot as she could stand it, and then stripped out of her clothes while the tub filled. She removed her makeup and brushed out her hair, and teeth, all the while eyeing herself critically in the mirror. The bruise on her temple stood out vividly on her fair skin. In the past day, the scar was beginning to close from where her head split open after being slammed into the corner of the coffee table, but the swelling hadn't subsided much, and now the entire area was an ugly, brownish-purply color. No wonder Rafe was no longer attracted to her.

'Right Noelle, like all this new tension between the two of you is going to miraculously disappear when your bruises are healed.'

Sighing at the depressing rejoinder, she used a hair tie and some hairpins, (also, thoughtfully provided by the hotel) to put up her hair so it wouldn't get wet, then strode over to the tub and cautiously stepped down into the almost too-hot depths. She poured the entire bottle of scented oil into the water and pressed the knob to turn the jets on. Sighing audibly, she sank down deeper, leaned her back against the tub and closed her eyes, only just remembering to turn off the water before it splashed over the sides of the tub.

She took a deep breath and let the hot, scented water wash away the tension of the past days and weeks. She lay there so long the water began to chill. For a moment, she considered emptying the tub and refilling it, but since she'd already used the entire bottle of scented oil, she decided she would be better served climbing out of the tub and crawling into bed.

Mission accomplished, she slid naked between the sheets and lay on her back staring up at the ceiling. There was enough light from the busy New York street below to allow her to see clearly the ornate plaster medallion above her. She couldn't help but wonder if Rafe was doing the same thing or if he'd he already drifted off to sleep. Tears stung her eyes at the depressing prospect that he might never forgive her.

Her mother's reminder drifted back through her thoughts, about how a woman only gets one mad, crazy, reckless love affair in a lifetime and that Noelle shouldn't give up on hers without a fight. Noelle didn't know what she was supposed to do to make Rafe change his mind. She reached up to pull the pins and hair tie from her hair and then scooted herself up so she could rest her back against the pillows and the headboard. 'Carina would know what to do,' Noelle told herself dejectedly. A woman like that would just sashay into Rafe's bedroom in her scanty, silk red robe and make Rafe forget all about being mad at her.

Noelle was aware of the incipient plan taking shape in her head, but quickly dismissed the idea as ridiculous. Maybe she had a little more experience in that department than she had when she arrived in France, courtesy of Rafe of course, but she was no Carina. There was no way she could pull off such a maneuver without making a fool of herself. Rafe would probably laugh her right out of his bedroom. She didn't even own a scanty blue one.

…but she did own a scanty blue silk robe. She even had it with her. At the last minute, she'd thrown it in her suitcase, as a sort of substitute for Rafe's presence in her bed. Not much of a substitute, she acknowledged, but she'd reasoned it represented some small connection to him.

Maybe he would see it that way too. A reminder of happier times they'd shared together...when he still wanted her. "…don't give up on what you have with Rafe without a fight..." her mother's advice drifted through her thoughts again.

What difference did it make if she made a fool of herself and he tossed her out of his bedroom? Things could hardly get any more awkward between them than they already were.

Was she actually considering this? Was her brilliant plan to seduce Rafe? The Rafe of the legendary reputation with women? As if he wouldn't see through her little ploy before she even got passed his threshold.

She spent another ten minutes arguing with herself over the foolishness of her plan. Then deciding even if she couldn't seduce Rafe into bed, at least she might break through the wall of self-control he'd encased himself in since he caught up with her at the hospital. She didn't think she could stand four long, tension-filled hours in the front seat of the car with him on their drive to Washington. The uncomfortable cross-country flight in his private Lucien jet had been bad enough. The prospect of repeating that dreadful experience in the morning on the drive to Washington was enough to get her out of bed and scrambling for the scrap of blue silk in her bag.

She retreated to the bathroom. Hands trembling with both anxiety and anticipation, she brushed her hair, applied a light spray of perfume, and a fresh sweep of body lotion over her freshly soaked skin. Daringly, she even added a little color to her lips, and then spoiled the effect by running her tongue over her bottom lip in an instinctive nervous gesture. Self-consciously, she pulled her hair forward to hide the bruise on her temple, then giving herself a bracing lecture beneath her breath, she turned away from the mirror and took a wary step in the direction of the lion's den...and then another...and another until she had talked herself as far as the living room of the suite. Even in the shadows, she could see Rafe had left his door open. Probably so he could hear any hint of a disturbance in the night. She was grateful for that small blessing. At least she didn't have to knock on his door and ask if she could come in, like a repentant child standing at her parents' closed bedroom door seeking forgiveness for some minor transgression.

Was she really going to go through with this?

319

Her answer was to take another silent, dragging step forward and then another until she was standing framed on the threshold of Rafe's bedroom.

"Noelle, what is it? Is something wrong?" Rafe demanded in an urgent voice, obviously concluding nothing short of a catastrophe would have brought her to his room.

Noelle could just make him out in the shadows, sitting up in bed, naked...at least from the waist up.

"Yes, something is wrong."

"What is it?"

"You're in here. And I'm over there." Noelle was quite sure Carina could have come up with a more seductive opening, but it was taking all of her nerve to simply stand there and force the words through her lips.

"Noelle, this isn't the time for this conversation."

She felt his eyes roaming over her in the dark, even though she couldn't see his face clearly in the shadows. She took a step into the room and tugged on the belt of her robe. It fell open. The silence from the bed was audible now. Heart pounding she reached up, slipped the robe off her shoulders, and let it fall to the thick carpet at her feet. It didn't make a sound as it hit the ground, but Noelle heard the audible catch in Rafe's breath even across the distance separating them.

She walked naked to the bed and stared down into his intense dark eyes probing hers. She lifted the sheet and climbed into bed, straddling him, her hands clasping his face and said huskily in response to his greeting, "That's all right. I'm not really here for conversation."

She sensed his indecision in the way his hands were suddenly fisted in the sheets...in the way his eyes raked over her naked breasts...in the way he was holding himself so stiffly beneath her she thought he might snap in half with any sudden movement on her part. So she moved over him slowly, running her fingers through his hair, letting her lips slide along his face, closing his eyes, and then trailing down to tease his open. Her fingertips danced across his chest, tugged on the mat of hair they found there, then moved down towards his flat, tense stomach.

One strong hand suddenly reached out to grasp her wrist, halting its slow descent. She pulled away, so she could see his face, meet his blazing glance.

"Just remember this was your idea," he warned her in a voice that was no longer so controlled, but nor was it filled with that flat, icy emptiness he'd used with her since finding her in the hospital waiting room. Given the choice, she'd take her chances with this version. The grip he had on her wrist was just over the edge of painful.

"No problem," she agreed, her lips curving slightly at the realization Rafe did not intend to toss her out of his bed.

He moved abruptly, switching their positions so Noelle found herself flat on her back, with Rafe looming above her, her hands above her head, her wrists secured with one of his hands.

"I'm not going to be careful with you tonight," Rafe warned her.

"I hope not," Noelle made no effort to hide the longing in her voice.

"Be careful what you wish for."

"Shut up, Rafe," Noelle commanded in a whisper.

He chuckled, then holding her glance for another intent, silent moment, be bent his head to trail his lips along her bare flesh.

"Thank God," Noelle whispered, as his free hand began moving over her, until her whispered prayer was cut off abruptly by a moan of longing as his mouth closed over her breast.

That was her last rational thought. Rafe was suddenly everywhere...his hands, his mouth taunting, tugging, tantalizing until she was writhing with longing.

"I'm still furious with you," he made certain she understood his position against her lips.

"That's all right. You can go back to not speaking to me in the morning," Noelle agreed swiftly, struggling to free her hands from his grip above her head. She needed to touch him the way he was touching her. She needed to sink her hands into hair, his hot flesh, and pull him towards her, make him stop teasing her. He was driving her crazy.

Maybe it was because of the recent distance between them that being with him like this meant so much. Or maybe it was because of her mother's warning that she would never love like this again, but every glide of his hands, of his lips against her bare flesh was drawing her towards what she recognized would be the point of no return.

She couldn't halt her dizzying descent. She'd known her heart was in danger. She'd understood she'd been on the verge with Rafe of the kind of love affair her mother had with her father…that once in a lifetime kind of feeling, that no man would ever be able to take his place in her heart. She'd been dancing giddily along that sharp, narrow edge since their first night together, after the President's ball.

She recognized they'd been dancing together all along…intricate steps of a rhythm as old as time, as old as life itself. They drew together and then stepped apart, hands and glances holding, even when fingertips barely touched. It wasn't as if she'd gone into this…whatever this turned out to be with Rafe…blindly. No. Eyes wide open; she'd cautiously skirted the edges of the pool, experimented with dipping a toe in the water to test the temperature, to see if she could survive in its depths. Sensible caution had given way to the dizzying brilliance of falling in love. She'd taken that first dive rioting back and forth between hesitancy and gleeful abandon in Rafe's arms, enjoying the fruits of her own recklessness even as her more cautious side warned of the less than gleeful consequences she would be forced to face when she awoke from the fantasy she'd wrapped herself in. The fantasy that she would never have to wake up. That she could dream forever, this wonderful, amazing precious time with Rafe locked in their own private world where no one could reach them, where no one threatened everyone and everything she loved.

The veil of her dreams had been torn violently from her eyes when a deranged fanatic had calmly pointed a gun at her mother and pulled the trigger, forcing her back to reality in a blood-spattered instant. Tonight, with Rafe, she was forced to confront another uncomfortable truth. She wasn't just indulging in a reckless love affair, enjoying Rafe's legendary prowess with women. No, she'd been deluding herself about the true depths of her feelings for him, just as she'd been deluding herself that the quest they were on to solve the mystery of Mont Saint Michel was a game, as though they were all engaging in some kind of grown-up treasure hunt. There was no real danger in playing a game,

322

just a hint of it lurking in the shadows to make the contest more interesting.

The events of the past few days had effectively stripped away all of her delusions...about the true nature of whatever or whoever lay behind the man who followed her to her mother's and about the true depths of her feelings for Rafe. She was in love with him...wildly, crazily, recklessly...forever. There would never be another man who could ever move her the way he did, who could make the breath catch in her throat with just a glance, or a glide of his fingers along her skin. Even now, the beauty of his touch, his lips sliding along her sweat-dampened skin brought tears to her eyes. How would she live without this? How could she ever go back to not having him in her life? She didn't even remember what that life looked like anymore.

"Noelle?" Rafe's husky whisper brought her out of her musings.

"Yes?" She met his glance in the shadows, blinking back the betraying tears she could feel filming her eyes.

"Why are you crying?" He asked, capturing a tear just as it pooled on her lashes and would have slid down her cheek.

"I'm such an idiot," she whispered, turning her lips to caress his palm.

"If you're expecting an argument from me, I'm going to have to disappoint you," he remarked, reminding her there was still an uncomfortable discussion looming over her head.

"Well, that too, but that's not what I meant," she told him, her glance clinging to his.

"Then what did you mean?"

"Do you remember when I said I would never making the colossal mistake of laying my heart at your feet?'

"Vividly," he responded with a grin.

She shrugged slightly beneath his restraining hands and explained tearfully. "I messed up. I fell in love with you. I guess I never really had a chance and now my heart isn't mine anymore. It's yours. I wasn't careful enough with it and somehow it fell out of my chest and landed at your feet. Now you're so angry with me and I don't know how to fix it. I don't know how to fix us."

Her tear-filled glance clung to his intent one, probing hers, as if testing the sincerity of her claim. She could sense his indecision, knew he was still outraged at the risk she'd taken, the memory of how she'd simply dismissed him in such a casual, thoughtless manner. She saw too, though, a glimmer of a smile in his eyes, of delight at her fall, that was contesting against the anger and resentment he wasn't ready to give up on yet. In the end, he compromised.

"*Mon amour* now is not the time for such a discussion." He told her and kissed her, silencing her questions and doubts and any further attempt at a serious discussion between them.

The following morning she woke disoriented, wonderfully rested and warm with a rhythmic beating in her ear. It took her a moment to figure out where she was and that it was Rafe's heart that was responsible for the rhythmic beat beneath where her head rested on his chest. She kept her breathing slow and steady, feigning sleep as she was in no hurry to confront the reality morning would bring along with it.

She supposed she should be dreading the look of mocking triumph she would no doubt see in Rafe's eyes this morning, at the depths of her stupidity for letting herself fall in love with him, but she could not, would not regret sharing her feelings with him. If they weren't destined for a future together, she could live with that. She supposed she would have to somehow learn to live with that, as her mother had after her father's loss. But, she didn't think she could live with the regret of keeping her heart and her feelings tucked away, locked in a safe place and never sharing them with Rafe. Realizing that's what she was doing by continuing to pretend to be asleep, she lifted her head from his chest and met Rafe's startled glance at her sudden movement.

"I love you." When he would have spoken, Noelle reached up to place her fingers across his lips. "No, you don't have to say anything. No explanations, or cautions necessary. I don't expect anything from you Rafe, nor do you owe me anything. I just need you to know how I feel. I know I was careless with you and my grandmother...worrying you the way I did. It was stupid and I'm sorry. I don't even remember why I felt it was so important to sneak away the way I did, so I can't even offer you a reasonable explanation for why I did it. I just want you to know I'm not careless with people's feelings, especially people I love. It wasn't some kind of test, like you implied that day. I hope you don't really believe I'm capable of that. I don't want things to be awkward between us. Even if you don't or can't feel about me the way I feel about you, we still have to finish this. So if you'd rather we went back to just being family friends…you know … without benefits, I can live that. It's not what I want, but if it would make things easier for you…"

He finally put a stop to her rambling recitation by placing his fingers over her lips to still them. He shifted their positions so she was now looking up at him with her back on the mattress, his weight propped on his elbows. A slight smile curved his lips when he bent to whisper in her ear, "Noelle?"

"Yes?"

"Shut up."

When she woke again it was to the sound of voices in the outer room and the heavenly aroma of fresh coffee and eggs and bacon and all of those other wonderful breakfast aromas. She suddenly realized she was famished. She sat up in bed, looked around the room for her robe, located it on the floor near the door, then smiling widely at the memories of the night following her daring infiltration of Rafe's stronghold, she climbed out of bed and crossed the room to retrieve it. She slipped down the hall to her own bath, and brushed her teeth and hair, loosened the tight knot on the belt around her waist, and tossed her hair in an effort to emulate Carina's tousled gorgeous morning-after-sex look. After a moment or two of practicing in front of the mirror, she abandoned the effort since it only made her appear ridiculous and desperate, and left her room in search of both Rafe and breakfast.

He looked up from the table when she entered the room, his admiring glance roaming over her, bringing a blush to her cheeks. He stood when she approached the table and surprised her when he pulled her into his arms and gave her a very nice, more than just a brush against her lips, morning after kiss.

"I believe what we shared last night, you Americans call make-up sex," he teased, pulling away slightly so he could watch the expressions chase themselves across her expressive face. "I have to say, it's almost worth having the argument in the first place."

"Does that mean you're not mad at me anymore?" She asked, unable to hide the eagerness in her voice.

"It will take me a lifetime to get over being mad at you for taking such a risk."

"All right," Noelle replied with a happy smile. "That means we get to have lots of make-up sex, right?"

"I admit that was a critical element of my devious plan," Rafe agreed, kissing her again, letting his warm hands slide beneath the loosely knotted robe.

Noelle sighed with regret when he pulled back again. "You need to eat," he admonished, pushing her gently down into the chair opposite his at the small dining table. "You've lost weight."

"I have?" Noelle asked, surprised by the turn their conversation had taken. "How can you tell?"

The old familiar amusement flashed in his eyes before he assured her seriously, "I notice everything about you. Now eat."

CHAPTER FIFTY SIX

The drive to Washington proceeded without incident. They drove through the picturesque streets of Georgetown, to P Street where Noelle's house was located. The boughs of the old trees lining the street were green and lush, and the tips of the trees on either side almost reached across to touch the tips of their siblings on the opposite side of the street. Noelle directed Rafe to pull into the garage through the alley in the rear of the house. Then they entered through the back gate. She was pleased to see the company she had hired to keep her lawn cut and weeded was doing its job.

"You live here alone?" Rafe asked, looking around curiously, as Noelle unlocked the back door and they entered the two hundred year old brick row house through the kitchen.

"Yes. It's the house we were living in when my father died, so all of my memories of us as a family are here. I can understand why my Mom doesn't want to come back, but I don't think I'll ever be able to let it go."

"Your mother believes your father hid the key in your old bedroom?" Rafe asked, reminding them of the purpose of their visit.

"Yes, upstairs."

She led Rafe through the narrow house and along the hallway to the second bedroom in the front. She met Rafe's smiling glance as he joined her in the doorway and took in every little girl's dream bedroom. It was all done up in pink and white. Unicorns pranced along one wall on their way to a romantic castle, complete with an iron-gate and moat to protect the princess from the evils besetting her. Stars were painted on the ceiling. A large bow window looked out over the street front.

"I can see why you were so excited about the bed at the inn we stopped at in Switzerland," Rafe commented with an indulgent grin.

Noelle shrugged. There was no reason for her to be embarrassed. She'd been barely three years old when her parents had the bedroom designed for her. She pointed to the top of the canopy. "See the metal piece securing the canopy in place? My Mom thinks my Dad might have hidden the key there. If not there, she was pretty certain, that if the key's in this house, it's somewhere in this room."

"Why was she so sure?" Rafe asked, curious.

Noelle shared with him her mother's memories of their father's sudden drive to move her into this room, after he'd returned home from one of his trips to Europe, and his insistence that the furniture be custom made.

Rafe look around and nodding said, "Makes as much sense as anything else we've tried. Do you want to do the honors or shall I?"

Noelle felt a pang of regret at the thought of dismantling the bed. It was silly, but real. "Do you mind doing it? Somehow, it seems wrong to me after my father went to so much trouble to create the perfect room for me."

Smiling, Rafe squeezed the hand he held, and then releasing it, approached the bed. He removed his shoes, and then stood on the bed, testing his weight first, and reached for the metal piece securing the canopy. "I don't suppose you have tools tucked away somewhere? A screwdriver would be nice." He asked over her shoulder, after struggling to release the screws securing the metal piece for several minutes.

"Yes, they're in the basement. I'll be right back," Noelle assured him and hurried towards the door.

She returned a few minutes later with her father's old toolbox in hand. She retrieved a screwdriver and handed it to Rafe. She watched with both growing excitement and anxiety as Rafe loosened the screws holding the circular metal piece in place. She was beginning to think her Mom might be right. It did appear as if it could be the round hilt of an old-fashioned key. "Can you get it?" She asked, unable to contain her anticipation.

"Yes, but I don't think it's the key," Rafe informed her, still concentrating on the task at hand.

"Why not?" Noelle called up, approaching the bed, so she could get a better look.

With the last screw freed, Rafe pulled the clasp away from the ceiling. The white, gauzy canopy floated down towards the bed. Noelle ignored it, peering instead at the round metal piece that had secured it to the ceiling. Unfortunately, Rafe was right. It wasn't a key. Just an ordinary piece of round metal with a hole in the middle to secure the canopy to the plaster ceiling.

"Oh," Noelle exclaimed, disappointed. "I was so certain my Mom was right."

"Just because the key wasn't securing the canopy doesn't mean it's not in this room," Rafe pointed out.

"You're right," Noelle agreed, then looking around, asked doubtfully, "Where do we begin?"

Even though the room was quite small, the task confronting them was still daunting. The furniture had been custom made. Her father could have instructed its makers to carve out a tiny hiding place in any of the pieces and then conceal it. A key didn't take up much room.

Shrugging, meeting Rafe's glance, Noelle began rifling through drawers and closets. She saw Rafe begin to do the same from the other side of the room. When they met in the middle, they both sat side by side on the small bed. "I hate the thought of tearing this furniture apart, but it occurs to me, my Dad wouldn't have hidden the key in a drawer. My mother or our housekeeper would have been bound to come across it when they were cleaning in here."

"Good point. Let's take a closer look at this woodwork. Maybe there's a latch somewhere that will trip open revealing a secret compartment," Rafe commented.

Noelle grinned. "A secret compartment? Do you realize how crazy that sounds?"

"It doesn't sound any crazier than an archangel instructing little girl to warn France to give back his home," Rafe pointed out in response to her teasing.

"All right, I guess you've got a point," Noelle conceded. "But I have no idea what I should be looking for."

"A small lever, or opening in the wood. Something that doesn't quite match the pattern," Rafe told her.

"Do you have experience with this type of thing?" Noelle asked, unable to completely disguise the sarcasm in her voice.

"I grew up in a thousand year old chateau. So, yes of course, I have experience with this type of thing."

Since she had no rejoinder to contest Rafe's excellent point, she merely mimicked his actions and began carefully examining the intricate woodwork on the bed. No matter how many potential levers she thought she discovered, or how many heads of mythical beasts she tugged on, attempting to turn them in her hand, or separate them from their background, she had no luck discovering her father's hiding place.

Dejected at their failure, they came back together on the bed. "Maybe your father never found the key," Rafe offered into the silence.

"No, he found it," Noelle contested, remembering the intruder's conviction.

"How can you be so sure?" Rafe demanded, curious.

After a moment's hesitation, Noelle admitted, "Because the man who shot my mother told us my father had found the key but was able to hide it from them before they could recover it." She lifted sad eyes to Rafe's face. "They killed my father. They killed him for a stupid key."

Rafe gathered her into the comfort of his arms and kissed the top of her head where it lay against his chest. "I'm sorry, Noelle. Is there any place else you think your father might have hidden the key? Did he keep an office in the house?"

Noelle didn't answer Rafe's question. She never heard it. She was squirming in her father's arms, her small child's hand pressed tightly against her lips to suppress the excited, hushed giggle trying to escape. She felt her father's strong arms give her a warning squeeze. "Sh," he cautioned as he carried her out through the back door and into the cool evening air. Night was just beginning to fall. Mommy was napping on the sofa in the living room.

Her father carried her all the way to the back of the yard, where a small statue of an angel guarded the secret iron-gate that no longer led anywhere. He set her down on her feet. Noelle could see his eyes, exactly like her own, holding her gaze intently. The seriousness of his expression and the way his hands descended on her shoulders so she would stand still while he instructed her, took away some of her excitement about the secret they were keeping from Mommy.

"Noelle, you must never tell anyone what I'm about to show you," her father cautioned her, in his deep, slightly accented voice.

"Not even Mommy?" Her younger self asked breathlessly.

"No one. Not even your mother. You must promise me, Noelle. And you must keep this promise forever."

"All right, Daddy. I promise," she heard her younger self repeat solemnly.

"Noelle? Noelle?"

Rafe's voice finally broke through the wall her memories of that night had erected around her. She raised a dazed glance to his and whispered, "I know where it is."

"What? How?"

"I remember. Daddy made me promise not to show anyone or tell anyone about our secret…even Mommy."

"You're going to tell me," Rafe proclaimed in a hard voice.

"What?" Noelle echoed, then shaking her head to clear it, she added, "Yes, yes of course. If it's still here, it's in the back yard. Maybe we should wait until it gets dark, in case anyone's watching us."

"No. We're retrieving it now before anyone catches up with us. Let's go," Rafe insisted and Noelle nodded, rising on shaking limbs to her feet.

She led them out of the room, down the stairs to the first floor and then out the rear door. Reaching for one of Rafe's hands, she pulled him along the stone path to the garage, but before reaching it, veered off to the right back corner of the yard. There a miniature statue of Michael stood guarding the iron-gate, just as she had remembered. At Rafe's swift indrawn breath, she turned to him and whispered, "It's a replica of the fleche at Mont Saint Michel."

"Yes," he confirmed then squatted down to inspect the marble statue.

"The key's hidden in a box beneath the statue. There's a shovel in the garden shed. I'll get it," Noelle offered and set off in the direction of the shed.

Moments later, she returned and handed the tool to Rafe. On the third sweep of the shovel, he hit metal. Exchanging a glance, both trying to contain their excitement in case their discovery turned out to be another dead-end, they bent together to see what Rafe had uncovered. Brushing away the damp earth, he retrieved a small steel combination safe, not much larger than his fist.

Turning to her, he asked, "You don't happen to remember the combination, do you?"

Noelle nodded. "You know it too."

"What do you mean?"

"Eight.one.three. August 13th the day of my first visit to Mont Saint Michel. Eight.one.three the safe deposit box number my father left me."

Holding her glance, and then shaking his head in wonder, Rafe tried the combination. When they both heard the distinct click of the lock being released, he lifted the top of the tiny safe. Inside, was another velvet pouch, purple with the papal insignia stitched across its front. Rafe lifted it from its resting place in the safe and held the pouch out to her. Noelle accepted it, then holding her breath; she opened the pouch and retrieved the contents. As soon as she touched the metal, Mother Superior's voice echoed through her thoughts, "Take the key, Marie. Don't tell anyone …."

"Noelle?" Rafe prompted at her hesitation.

She drew the key from the pouch and held it up for his inspection. He drew in a sharp breath and their glances met.

"This is what we've been searching for. I don't know what it opens, but I know it's the same key Mother Superior passed to me with her dying breath."

Rafe didn't bother raising an objection about her surety concerning the key's provenance.

"Well done, Mademoiselle. Your father is pleased and proud of your efforts, but it would be wise to leave now. Evil was only delayed by the incident at your mother's house, not defeated."

Nodding to the echo of Michael's familiar voice in her head, she raised her glance to Rafe's. "We need to leave now. Michael says the evil that hunts this key was only delayed at my mother's house, not defeated."

His glance holding hers, intent, probing, Rafe rose to his feet and drew her up with him. He used the shovel to replace the dirt he'd disturbed and reset the statue on top of it. Then he returned the shovel to the garden shed, locked it and came back to stand in front of Noelle.

"Do you need anything from the house?" He asked.

Noelle shook her head, returning the key to the pouch and the little safe and clutching it close to her heart. "No, but they'll come here won't they?" She asked in a whisper.

"Yes, likely sooner rather than later," Rafe conceded.

"I don't want them in my house, searching my things," Noelle admitted, distressed at the thought of violent men in her home, pawing through her clothes and possessions.

"I'll call Jacobs and have him secure your home."

"All right. Thank you. I don't want anyone else hurt because of this. We need to finish this. How do we find out what this key opens?"

Rather than answer, Rafe grasped her hand and began tugging her in the direction of the garage where they'd left the rental car. "I don't know. We'll go over everything we've learned once we're back at Chateau Lucien. I'll reach out to Gabriel. Maybe he's discovered something that will help us identify what the key opens."

CHAPTER FIFTY SEVEN

The four of them huddled around Ariel Lucien's desk in his private office. Noelle noticed her grandmother kept checking every few moments to make certain Noelle was still there, and that she was safe. Noelle reached out and squeezed her hand.

"It's almost over, Meme. I don't know how I know that, but I can feel we're close. Maybe closer than anyone has ever been to solving this mystery. The key is the key...sorry, you know what I mean."

"Michel told you where he hid it before he died?" Her grandmother confirmed incredulous. At Noelle's confirming nod, her grandmother added, "But you were so young. How did you remember after all this time?"

Noelle shrugged slightly. "It came back to me when I was sitting on the bed in the room I slept in when I was younger and Daddy was still alive. He told me I must never tell anyone, even my Mom. I never did. After my father died, I guess my subconscious suppressed the memory until I went back to my old room."

"But how do we discover what the key opens?" Her grandmother persisted, as anxious as any of them to put this behind them.

Rafe interjected, "Noelle and I are returning to Rome in the morning. Gabriel said he might have discovered something of interest in his research, but he didn't want to discuss it over the phone."

"I'm coming with you this time," Noelle announced.

"Yes," Rafe readily agreed. "I'm not letting you out of my sight again until this is finished."

"Good, then I don't have to let you out of my sight either," Noelle announced with a satisfied air.

Rafe decided to risk the flight to Rome. They were running out of time. The anniversary of Noelle's initial visit to Mont Saint Michel was less than a week away. Gabriel greeted them at his door with a relieved, if serious expression on his face. He gripped Noelle's chin and examined the still vivid bruise on the side of her temple.

"I pray you will not take another foolish risk. I don't believe my good friend would recover. How is your mother?"

Touched by his concern, Noelle replied, "She's recovering. I think she's safe now. There's no reason for them to go after her again. She doesn't know anything, but even so, she assures me Jimmy has her safely ensconced in his twenty thousand acre ranch in Montana and that it would take an army to penetrate his security."

"*Buona.*" Gabriel nodded. "Did you bring the key with you?"

"No, Rafe thought it would be safer at Chateau Lucien," she responded and then added anxiously, "Rafe said your research discovered something that might help us?"

He shrugged, his eyes apologetic, "Perhaps, but it is doubtful. I may have exaggerated what my research uncovered because I wanted to ensure you accompanied Raphael so I could see for myself he hadn't done you any grievous injury for driving him mad with worry."

Grimacing at the reminder, she risked a glance over her shoulder to meet Rafe's pointed expression, and then turned back to Gabriel and admitted, "No, he's restrained himself until now, but I can assure you it was touch and go there for a while."

"I am frankly amazed at his self-control. I trust you have no undisclosed plans that would test it again in the same manner," he both chided and asked at the same time.

"No, I've learned my lesson the hard way," Noelle confirmed.

"Good, then let us go inside and perhaps we can piece together what this key of yours opens."

"It's not my key," Noelle protested vehemently.

Gabriel grinned, and shrugging, replied, "Fine, let us see if we can piece together what this key you have been granted hopefully brief stewardship over unlocks."

"Yes, please the briefer the better, as far as I'm concerned."

Their host led them through his impressive foyer, down a long hall, and into an expansive room Noelle concluded acted as both an office, and an occasional conference room. There was a large table on one side, with no less than a dozen chairs arranged around it. A few books were stacked in the corner. The light streamed in from the large windows with a view of the river.

Rafe filled Gabriel in on the events of the past few days. Gabriel turned to Noelle and asked, incredulous, "You remember your father showing you the location where he buried the key? You were what, a child of three or four?"

"Yes I guess I blocked it out until we returned to the house where we lived when he died. When I sat on the bed, I remembered his voice admonishing me in a serious tone, "Noelle, you must promise me you won't tell anyone what I'm about to show you." I was so awed at the idea that we were keeping a secret from Mommy, and so excited to see what it was," she tacked on in a wistful voice.

Gabriel exchanged a glance with Rafe, and added hesitantly and as tactfully as possible, "Raphael also mentioned you believe you remembered receiving the key before."

She turned to glare at Rafe, who shrugged and gave her an encouraging nod. She turned back to Gabriel, "I had a vision…I guess you would call it…of being a novitiate and being called into Mother Superior's cell. She was dying and she wanted to say goodbye. She told me my mother had given her the key to keep safe and secret…that my father and brother were evil men and could never know of its existence. I was to keep it safe and secret, but she died before she could tell me what it opened."

"Do you remember anything else?" Gabriel asked.

Noelle sighed in relief. "You believe me?"

He shrugged, "After all that's happened, yes, I'm inclined to give credence to all of your memories regarding the key, the relic, Mont Saint Michel."

"There was one other, but it didn't have to do with the key," she began hesitantly.

"Go on, "Gabriel encouraged her, exchanging a glance with Rafe over her head.

Noelle swung her head around, "I didn't tell you about this one," she warned him, uncertain of his mood.

"Because my nature is not as accepting of such things as Gabriel's," Rafe remarked holding her glance.

338

She shrugged, "At the time…it was in the beginning…when I first returned to Mont Saint Michel with my grandmother…I didn't want you to think less of me than you already did."

He reached out his hand to smooth her hair and cup her chin. "Then I will accept the blame for your reticence, since I have a vague memory of being less than accepting of your claim that Michael spoke to you."

"That's an understatement," she replied, rolling her eyes.

He grinned, and squeezing her chin in warning, he suggested, "Perhaps we should return to the matter at hand."

"Maybe, you'd like to take a break of something, while I relate this story to Gabriel," she suggested hopefully.

"No, I would not," Rafe, replied.

She heaved an audible sigh and capitulated, "Fine, but just stay back there where I don't have to see that look come into your eyes."

"What look is that?" he teased.

"The look that says… what was it you called it? Oh, right, the one that says I'm confused and prone to dramatics."

Gabriel chuckled and grinning, suggested a second time, "Perhaps we could return to your memory when you first returned to the site."

Reluctantly, Noelle nodded and began hesitantly, "I didn't make the connection, until recently. I've been wondering about the discrepancy with the family bibles and the graves…"

"What discrepancy?" Both men interjected simultaneously.

Noelle turned to Rafe, "I told you about the family bibles."

"You mentioned that some of your ancestor's family bibles bore the mark of the papal insignia on the inside cover, while others didn't."

"What?" Gabriel interjected. "I don't remember hearing about family bibles bearing the papal insignia. Whose family bibles are we discussing?"

Noelle turned back to answer Gabriel, "The Dominique dukes." Then turned back to Rafe and protested, "I told you about the dukes' graves bearing the mark of the key. The same ones that had the papal insignia in their bibles."

"No, you did not. This is the first I'm hearing anything to do with the duke's graves bearing the symbol of a key."

Noelle shook her head, confused. Gabriel interjected gently, "Perhaps you could tell us again about the Dominique family bibles and the graves of the dead dukes."

Noelle nodded, thrusting a hand through her hair, she began tentatively. "I don't remember now what led me to research the family records back at Chateau Dominique. I think it was because I realized that my father had passed this task, for lack of a better word, to me, his heir. I wondered how my father got involved in all of this. I thought maybe his father had passed the same duty to him. So I thought maybe we could find something to help us in some of the old family records."

"That was very perceptive of you," Gabriel said, impressed.

Noelle shrugged away his praise. "By that point I was grasping at straws. My grandmother and I returned to Chateau Dominique and divided all the records we could find in the library. I found a watermark of the papal insignia in one of my ancestor's bibles. I figured, given my father's legacy to me, that it could be significant. So we checked all the family bibles and the other books and records and found that not all of the dukes' bibles were marked with the insignia, and that no other journals or ledgers bore it." She turned to Rafe and insisted, "I know I told you about this."

He nodded, confirming, "Yes, you told me about the bibles, but you never mentioned anything about the graves."

Noelle thought back to that day. "I remember now. My grandmother and I were taking a break in the gardens when you called to check up on me. We hadn't discovered the keys on the graves yet. After our conversation, I asked my grandmother to take me by my grandfather's grave, so she could re-introduce us. I was feeling the weight of all this family history and I wanted to pay my respects."

"And that's when you discovered the keys on the graves?"

Noelle nodded, "Yes, my grandfather's grave was marked with the symbol of a key. I asked my grandmother what it symbolized, but she didn't know. She said when she was making my grandfather's funeral arrangements; she was told that it was a Dominique tradition, so she just went along with it. I wondered if there were any other previous dukes whose graves bore the same key symbol. Like the bibles, we found some of the graves had the key symbols and some of them didn't. I wondered if maybe the graves of the dukes with the key symbol were the same dukes whose bibles bore the papal insignia."

"Did they?" Rafe asked.

"Yes. We returned to the library and checked each bible with the papal insignia against the list we made of the graves that bore the key symbol. They matched. There was never a case when a bible had the insignia but the grave didn't have the key, or *vice versa*. Then I remembered Mother Superior telling me that my father and brother were evil men, and that my mother hid both her infant daughter and the key at the convent for safety."

She was too caught up in her thoughts to notice the look exchanged between the two men over her bent head.

"Was that what sent you to your mother's?" Rafe asked in a surprisingly neutral tone given the disastrous consequences of that singular decision, bringing her focus back to the present.

Noelle shook her head, and then turned to lift her gaze to meet his. "No, it wasn't the graves. It was the locket on my charm bracelet."

His glance dipped to the bracelet on her arm, then lifted back to hers. "I don't understand."

Noelle held up the locket her mother made for her. "My mother wore this as a locket for as long as I can remember. On my sixteenth birthday, she had the locket made into a charm for my bracelet. See, it has a picture of my parents inside." She opened the clasp on the locket so he could see the picture.

He nodded, and then met her gaze again. "I still don't see why this caused you to rush off to your mother's."

"Look at the other side," she suggested softly.

Rafe reached for her arm to hold it steady so he could examine the inner side of the locket clasp. A moment later, he swore softly under his breath.

"What is it?" Gabriel demanded urgently.

Rafe met Noelle's glance again, then at her assenting nod, held out her arm to Gabriel so he could see the design on the inner covering.

"That's the papal insignia with a key, almost as if it's standing guard, in front of it," he whispered stunned.

"Yes, that's what sent me to my mother's," Noelle admitted softly, "The realization that my father had given this to my mother and that she never took it off until she had the charm made and passed it to me. I realized my father left half of the clue to solving the mystery with Rafe's grandfather, and he left the other half with my mother."

"The key," Gabriel concluded.

"Yes, only my mother didn't know anything about the key," Noelle explained bitterly. "And I almost got her killed."

"But you saved her in the end and she remembered enough to lead you back to the house in Washington," Gabriel pointed out.

Noelle nodded, but she was distracted by her memories of that fateful day when she almost lost her mother, and by everything that had happened since that led her to the key. For a moment, she could hear her father's voice inside her head again, making her promise not to divulge to anyone their shared secret. Her lips curved in a reminiscent smile. Then her father's voice was replaced by Mother Superior's strained whisper as Noelle bent over her frail form in her simple cot she rested in.

"Your father was an evil man, Marie, and truth be told your brother is reputed to be little better." Their graves probably weren't marked with the sign of the key, Noelle concluded with a slight nod of satisfaction. Michael would not have been fooled. He would have seen them for what they were. Just as he would have known what kind of man, her father had betrothed her to. I bet her father's grave didn't carry the key symbol either.

"Of course," she whispered, drawing the two men's attention.

"What is it?" Rafe demanded.

"Sister Marie and Noelle. We were all Dominiques. The men in our lives were either unable to complete the task assigned them, or were deemed unworthy of it. In each case, the key came to me. I bet he saved me that day, and the price of Michael rescuing me was to either locate the key or safeguard it from my father and brother."

"What do you mean Michael saved you that day? The day the two men dressed as gendarmes approached you?" Rafe asked, puzzled, his expression echoing Gabriel's mystified one.

"No, a long time ago," Noelle contested with an audible sigh, and then offered a brief summary of her memories from that first day she returned to Mont Saint Michel. She studiously avoided meeting Rafe's glance, when she was relaying her story, then turned to him pleading, when a heavy silence fell between them at the conclusion of her recollections. "I know you don't believe me…that you can't understand what it's like for me, but it's all connected. It must be. The family bibles, the graves, my connection to Mont Saint Michel and why I was so drawn to it…why I went there when I was in trouble. I knew he would help me. They were Dominiques. They had to be. The site was close enough for my mother to have convinced my father I was stillborn and to have spirited me to the convent at Mont Saint Michel, along with the key. She sent us both to the convent so the key would be protected by the church and remain beyond my father and brother's hands."

Rafe held her glance and finally released the breath he'd been unconsciously holding in an audible exhale. "I'm not saying I don't believe you, but I don't see how all of this gets us any closer to finding what the key opens."

Listening to their exchange, Gabriel interjected, "I think we're missing something."

"What?" Noelle demanded, quite proud of herself she had everything figured out.

"Where does the number 813 fit into all of this?"

"What do you mean? The safe deposit box, the combination we found the key in, even the day of my first visit. It's part of every clue my father left."

"Exactly. So there should be something to do with 813 that leads us to what the key opens," Gabriel pointed out.

"Maybe you're right," Noelle sighed. "But where do we begin?"

"Maybe it would help if we knew what happened in the world in 813?" Rafe suggested.

"All right, let me check." Noelle turned her attention to her tablet and typed in world events in the year 813. When that didn't turn up anything interesting, she tried other variations of the same search words. Finally, giving up, she sighed and admitted, "Apparently not much interesting happened in history in the year 813."

At the two men's slightly amused smiles in response to her resigned conclusion, she sighed. "The funny thing is I remember something about 813 in my earlier research. Let me see if I can find it." She fell silent for a few minutes as she read back over the research she'd collected and saved. "Here it is," she announced with growing excitement. "In 813 Charlemagne proclaimed Saint Michael's feast to be observed throughout the Frankish empire. He became king of the Franks in 768 and King of Italy in 774. Listen to this... *He was a staunch supporter of the papacy and reached the height of his power when in the year 800 he became the first Holy Roman Emperor in three centuries.*" She looked up and met Rafe's interested glance. "He was crowned Emperor of the Romans by Pope Leo III on Christmas Day at old St. Peter's Basilica."

"He was crowned by Pope Leo III?" Rafe repeated.

"Yes and by 813 he had issued the demand that his subjects celebrate the feast of Saint Michael."

"Did Charlemagne ever visit Mont Saint Michel?"

"It doesn't say," she replied with a sigh.

Silence fell among them while they each busied themselves with their own thoughts. Noelle finally broke it, offering from the research she was perusing, "Did I tell you that Joan of Arc is said to have credited the Archangel Michael with inspiring her to go to the aid of the king? Apparently, he referred to himself as the protector of France."

"Maybe it wasn't France he was worried about protecting," Rafe suggested.

"Maybe, he helped her," she suggested.

"Perhaps he gave her something to assist her with her task of defeating the English," Gabriel interjected.

"That would point to there being something of importance being hidden at Mont Saint Michel," Rafe admitted with some reluctance.

"Well, as much as I hate to admit it, the idea's not as crazy as it first seemed. And I can't help but take note of the fact that the names you mentioned, those closely connected with the Archangel Michael, Charlemagne and Joan of Arc were at the head of armies." Gabriel commented.

344

"You think there's a possibility that the professor who left the university to enter the seminary is correct? That the relic the Sons of France is after is one that confers some advantage in battle?" Noelle asked.

"Charlemagne, known as the Father of Europe, and Saint Joan of Arc? That's pretty elite company in military circles," Gabriel replied.

"Wait a minute," Noelle responded with growing excitement. "813. Charlemagne issued the order to celebrate Saint Michael's feast day in the year 813."

"Yes, so?"

"Was Leo III still the pope in 813?" Rafe asked.

She checked her notes. "Yes, it says here he was the pope until 816."

Gabriel interjected, "There is a reliquary in the Aachen Cathedral that depicts Emperor Charlemagne flanked by Leo III and Bishop Turpin."

"Where is the Aachen Cathedral?" Noelle asked curious.

"In Germany. It's the oldest cathedral in northern Europe constructed under the order of Charlemagne in 805. He was buried there after his death in 814."

"He died in 814?" Noelle asked, stunned.

"Yes."

"That was the year following his order to celebrate St. Michael's feast day," Noelle reminded them.

"So?" Gabriel asked, not following her.

"So, Joan of Arc was burned at the stake shortly after the coronation of Charles VII."

"I'm still not sure I understand the connection."

"Maybe when Michael's finished with his messengers, well…"

"Well?" Gabriel echoed incredulous. "Do you realize what you're implying? You believe he disposes of them?"

She shrugged, but her anxious glance met Rafe's.

Rafe, smiling slightly at his friend's reaction to Noelle's suggestion that the archangel dispatched his recipients of his assistance, proposed, "Perhaps they didn't outlive their usefulness. Perhaps they decided they no longer needed his assistance."

"The relic," Gabriel expelled in a hushed whisper.

Then Noelle added in an equally soft voice, as if fearing someone could eavesdrop on their conversation, "Maybe they refused to give it back. Maybe they liked the power it gave them over their enemies and decided to use it for their own ends."

"Crazy as it sounds, that makes sense," Gabriel replied. "I imagine Michael would not be too pleased with anyone commandeering his sacred relic for their own ends…even those who had previously proven to be faithful servants of the divine will."

"Okay, well that's a relief," Noelle released the breath she'd been unconsciously holding in an audible sigh.

"Why is that?" Rafe asked, his lips curving in a smile.

Noelle turned to him and related, "Because I have absolutely no intention of or interest in keeping or using whatever this relic is for my own ends. I just want to give it back to Michael or return it to wherever he wants it returned to and get on with my life….my nice ordinary, non-supernatural life."

"I hate to dampen our enthusiasm, but I have to point out this is all conjecture on our part," Gabriel said.

"True," Rafe conceded, then added, "but I'm beginning to think the professor-turned-seminarian's conclusion that the relic we're all on the trail of is one that confers a military advantage is not as preposterous as I originally assumed it was.

"So where does that leave us?" Gabriel asked.

"We have to return to the site. Whatever the key opens has to be at Mont Saint Michel," Noelle declared with growing certainty.

"Unless it just leads to another clue," Rafe pointed out.

"No, I don't think so," Noelle protested.

"What makes you so sure?"

"My father was killed once he found the key. If it were just another clue, they would have let him lead them to the next revelation before killing him. They must know what the key opens and that the key is everything. We have to go back."

"As much as I dislike the idea of returning to the site, I tend to agree with you, but you'll recall the site is huge. We can't just wander around looking for a convenient keyhole."

"All right, that makes sense, but the buildings were constructed over the course of centuries weren't they?" Noelle pointed out.

"Yes."

"So maybe we should concentrate on the oldest buildings. Are there any that date back to Bishop Aubert's time or Charlemagne's?"

Gabriel commandeered her tablet to look up the answer. "The oldest part of the site is only open to lecture tours and not the general public. It dates back to the 10th century, the Pre-Romanesque Church of Notre Dame Sous Terre. Listen to this, *"The church of Notre Dame Sous Terre is the oldest and most venerable building on the Mont Saint Michel. It is the abbey's heart, for tradition has it that it stands on the spot of Saint Aubert's original shrine."*

"That sounds promising. Where is Saint Aubert's shrine now?" Rafe asked.

"This article says that Saint Aubert was believed to have been buried at Mont Saint Michel, but that the relic of his skull, with the hole where the archangel is believed to have pierced it can be seen at Saint Gervais Basilica in Avranches" Gabriel replied.

"So if his skull is in Avranches, I imagine the rest of the saint's remains accompanied him there," Rafe speculated.

"You would think so, but apparently, it is generally believed nowadays that the skull at Saint Gervais Basilica is actually a pre-historic relic showing signs of trepanation."

"What the hell is trepanation?"

Smiling, Gabriel turned his attention back to the tablet and related, "It's a surgical intervention to relieve pressure in the brain or to release the evil spirts inhabiting the person in question."

"I think if someone was going to drill a hole in my head, I would prefer it to be done by an archangel," Noelle announced.

"Good point," Gabriel agreed with a grin.

"So, if Saint Gervais doesn't house the remains of Saint Aubert, maybe he's still at Mont Saint Michel," Noelle speculated.

"We can't just start digging up the floors looking for him," Rafe pointed out.

"I don't think we have to. Didn't it say that the church of Notre Dame Sous Terre was the oldest and most venerable building on the site because it's believed it marks the spot of Saint Aubert's original shrine?"

At Gabriel's nod, she retrieved the tablet, read further and announced into the silence. "It says here the walls in the church are almost six feet thick and that the cyclopean wall which was discovered in 1960 behind the altar on the right was for a long time attributed to Saint Aubert, but was later found to have been constructed in the late 10th century. Let me see if I can pull up a picture of the altar." The two men waited in silence, until Noelle swung the tablet around so they could both see the interior of the church of Notre Dame Sous Terre. "See those large, irregular stones behind the altar? There could be a keyhole hidden there. I think it's worth a look."

"I don't like the idea of you returning to the site. They'll be expecting that," Rafe protested.

"Then we don't go alone. I bet the good captain who warned your grandfather of the threat from the Sons of France would be willing to accompany us," Noelle proposed.

"You want to bring in the captain of the local gendarmes into our confidence?" Rafe echoed astonished.

"Why not? I don't think anyone's going to try to kidnap me with him around. Besides, I can't imagine the good captain demanding an explanation. I believe this is where the legendary Lucien arrogance will come in handy."

"She's got a point," Gabriel remarked.

"We're going to have to offer some explanation as to why we are requesting the gendarmes to accompany us back to the site." When Noelle would have offered her lips to speak, Rafe added, "Besides the fact that we'd like their protection because you'd like to return and complete your visit to the site that was interrupted by two men posing as gendarmes attempting to kidnap you."

Noelle brushed aside Rafe's objection to her plan to include an official presence on their return visit and offered, "He already suspects that my father left me something in regards to the relic the Sons of France are believed to be after. We could sort of imply that the clue my father left led us to Notre Dame Sous Terre. That would probably get us access to the church without having to join one of the lecture tours."

Rafe offered no further objection to her proposed plan, but Noelle could tell he had little liking for it. Smiling slightly, she reached across the table for his hand. "We have to finish this. Whatever the key opens is at Mont Saint Michel. I don't believe Michael would have allowed it to leave the site without his permission. If Joan of Arc was in possession of the relic at some point, Michael retrieved it and returned it to Mont Saint Michel for safekeeping."

"How can you be so sure?"

Noelle released a heavy sigh, and explained, "Remember my missing diary?"

"Yes. What about it?"

"I told you, right, why I finally agreed to return to France? Because Michael showed me his plans to destroy Mont Saint Michel?"

"What?!" Gabriel interjected.

Rafe ignored the interruption. "Yes, I remember."

"He wouldn't have any reason to destroy it if the relic wasn't there. Remember, he told me that mankind had proven an unreliable steward?" At Rafe's nod, she added, "He wasn't referring to his home on earth. He was talking about the relic. He's not going to let it leave the site. We need to go back before the anniversary of my first visit. That's his line in the sand. Eight, one, three. August thirteenth. If we don't find what the key opens by then, I don't think it will matter anymore after the anniversary has passed."

"Do you realize what you're implying?" Gabriel demanded, aghast.

"I'm not implying. I'm telling you with certainty. If we can't solve this in the next six days, Michael will take matters into his own hands."

CHAPTER FIFTY EIGHT

They crossed the bridge in Captain Fils official vehicle. They climbed out of his car and stood looking up at the imposing entrance. Noelle wasn't sure what excuse Rafe used to compel the captain's cooperation but she could feel the older man's tension where he stood silently to her left. Rafe's grip on her arm was just short of painful, giving testimony to his own tension at the thought of her returning to the ancient abbey.

"They're here," Noelle announced softly.

"Who's here?" Rafe asked, disturbed by how quickly she'd fallen back to that faraway place he couldn't reach.

"The others. The ones who hunt the relic for their own ends."

"We are prepared for any such attempt," Captain Fils pronounced confidently.

Noelle shook her head, unconvinced. Turning to the captain, with a slight, vague smile curving her lips, she informed him, "The gendarmes have long since been compromised, as has the security at Mont Saint Michel. Just like Chateau Dominique. They've had men in place for decades in order to be kept apprised of our progress in locating the relic."

Before either man could respond, they were joined by another man who the captain introduced as M. Denard, head of security for Mont Saint Michel. After the niceties were completed, M. Denard filled the awkward gap, "Captain Fils has informed me that your interest is with the Church at Notre Dame Sous Terre."

"Yes, thank you."

M. Denard led the way. Their small company followed him. Captain Fils, watchful, even more so after Noelle's proclamation about the gendarmes and Mont Saint Michel security having been penetrated brought up the rear of their small, compact group. Jean couldn't prevent himself from casting an appraising look in his counterpart's direction, wondering just how far up the security at Mont Saint Michel had been penetrated. It would be convenient indeed for the Brotherhood to have infiltrated the security at the highest level of the presumed resting place of the relic they were after.

They filed in silence behind M. Denard as he led them to the entrance to the church. He had closed the structure to tours for the morning so they wouldn't be disturbed. There was a different aura here, whether it was because they were entering the most ancient part of the site or if the change was due to another reason, Noelle couldn't be certain, but she bowed her head at the entrance, and genuflected in the direction of the altar, making the sign of the cross, before regaining her feet with Rafe's steadying grip beneath her arm. She noticed the head of security and the captain of the gendarmes had stepped aside at the entrance, apparently deciding there was no sign of a threat and allowed her and Rafe take the lead.

Lifting her glance to Rafe's, at his encouraging nod she took a hesitant step forward, only now becoming aware of the light surrounding the altar. She looked around curious, searching for some sign of discreetly hidden lighting and found none. There were candles set up on the altar as if in preparation for Mass, but they were unlit. Disturbed by the oversight, she walked with more confidence down the aisle towards the altar. She paused again to genuflect then ascended the steps and used the modern lighter she found there to illuminate the candles. Satisfied, she backed away to rejoin the others where they waited for her at the foot of the steps.

Rafe was regarding her with a gentle expression and a slight smile playing around his lips she found odd, given the circumstances.

"What do we do now?" She whispered, reluctant to reveal to their official companions that they were grasping at straws and more likely than not wasting their valuable time in this endeavor.

"Why did you light the candles?" He asked, his intent glance probing hers.

A little embarrassed by her boldness, Noelle shrugged, blushing. "I'm not sure. It just seemed right. This church is very old," she added with a distracted air. "I remember praying here for the repose of the bishop's soul. It's a sacred place. Can't you feel it?" She added, lifting her glance to Rafe's.

When he merely held her glance and made no effort to respond to her questions, she turned her attention back to the altar and continued softly, "It's the heart. Gabriel was right. This is the heart of Mont Saint Michel. Whatever remains of what was once a place of devotion before the divine emanates from here. It's the repository for the final hope against the consequences of mankind's faithlessness."

Aware of the meaningful, astonished looks being exchanged by the two officials, and of Rafe's encouraging glance holding hers, Noelle turned away and once more climbed the steps to the altar. She knelt in front of it and bowed her head reverently until her forehead brushed the stone floor. Then she rose and stepped behind the altar to examine the cyclopean wall, wondering what purpose it served. She ran her fingers over the stone and felt the life pulsing within. Whatever it was the key tucked into her pants pocket opened she was absolutely convinced it lay behind this massive stone wall.

She had no notion of how to go about proving her conviction however. She doubted Captain Fils or M. Denard was going to stand idly by while she and Rafe took a sledgehammer to the ancient stone. She stepped closer to examine the cracks, seams, and crevices where the individual stones came together, searching for a convenient keyhole, but not really expecting to find one.

So when her finger came across an opening in the stone at knee level where she was crouched down and searching blindly by feel, she barely swallowed her gasp of excitement in time. She was careful not to turn to let Rafe know she'd found it, afraid of alerting their official escort. She kept up her pretense of searching, running her hands in a seemingly random fashion over the stone, while she positioned her body to block the opening. She bent down to examine a stone to her right, drawing attention away from where her left hand slid into the pocket of her trousers and retrieved the key. Hand shaking, she inserted the key into the key hole she'd located and turned it clockwise until she heard a distinctive click.

She couldn't contain her surprised gasp and turned her head to seek out Rafe's gaze, making eye contact, grinning widely. She saw the stunned recognition take shape in his eyes, the slight curve of his lips that they'd actually found it, noted him take the first step forward to join her on the altar. Then without warning, the wall she was leaning against dropped away.

Noelle was so stunned she barely had time to scream and brace herself against the sudden, helpless, headlong rush into the darkness below. Still, she managed to retain enough awareness of her surroundings to notice the opening above her slam shut and the darkness become absolute. Just before she was completely alone in the hidden tunnel she was sliding down, she heard Rafe's panicked shout, the sound of his feet racing up the steps to the altar, then nothing but the sound of her own panicked cries and the answering pounding on the closed wall of the fists of the three men. After a few seconds, she lost even that small connection to Rafe. She could no longer hear his voice.

It seemed to Noelle like she fell a long time, but maybe it was simply the acrid taste of her own terror on her lips that made it seem so. She was aware of the steep descent beginning to level off so her headlong plunge slowed and she was able to control her progress enough for her to regain her feet. She gripped the wall and paused her forward movement to consider her next steps.

Brushing the hair from her face, she tasted blood on her lips. She couldn't see them but she could feel the cuts and scrapes on her palms and fingertips from where she desperately tried to brace her fall. Drawing a steadying breath she looked up at the perch from where she'd fallen and recognized immediately that even if she could find a way to scale the sheer, steep drop there was no way to know if the key worked to both open and close the secret portal.

Portal to where? She wondered, trying to stifle the fear that was closing her throat and interfering with her ability to think. She turned to glance down in the direction her fall had taken her. Though she couldn't see where it led, she could see evidence of a light at the end of the proverbial tunnel. Recognizing her continued descent was as inevitable as when that lunatic held her mother captive and had simply waited for her to come to him, Noelle took a hesitant step forward, grasping the key like a weapon. Astonishingly, she hadn't lost it in the fall. It was gripped tight against her bloody palm.

Even if she couldn't hear him, she knew Rafe would come for her. Even now, she knew he was frantically trying to get the portal open again from above. He wouldn't hesitate to bring every pressure the Lucien name represented upon both Captain Fils and M. Denard to get the help he needed until he could reach her. She just had to live long enough to be reunited with him. Besides, it was unlikely the Sons of France were the ones who waited for her at the end of the tunnel. If the relic they sought was here, and they had reached this place in front of her, they wouldn't have needed her to locate the key for them to open the passageway.

Surprisingly enough the thought did little to ease her fear of what awaited her up ahead. If it wasn't the Sons of France, she doubted it was anyone connected with the French authorities. Had they known about the tunnel in advance, she doubted Captain Fils and M. Denard would have allowed her to so freely search for the opening, if they were intent on keeping their presence at the site a secret.

So, if it wasn't a bunch of fanatics seeking a supernatural weapon to further their cause and it wasn't the police, awaiting her in the opening ahead, where the light was growing stronger, Noelle was at a loss to guess the identity of those waiting for her. The only other person, for lack of a better word, in Noelle's experience who'd ever shown an interest in the events at Mont Saint Michel was Michael. Since she doubted the Prince of the Heavenly hosts awaited her at the end of the passage she was slowly, hesitantly traversing, she concluded the near paralyzing anxiety she was suffering from was well justified.

The dim light grew brighter as she approached the opening. She paused to listen for voices or movement, anything to give her a clue to what she was about to confront. There was nothing, only silence echoing back at her from both above and below. It was as if she was suspended in a kind of purgatory between heaven and hell and neither state seemed inclined to go to the trouble to claim her at the moment.

Chiding herself for her tendency to dramatize, she drew a deep breath and stepped out of the tunnel and into what appeared to be some kind of medieval hall, with broad wooden beams supporting the massive structure. A fire burned in the huge stone fireplace opposite where she stood gazing around her in astonishment. From somewhere she thought she caught the smell of meat cooking and bread baking.

Noelle instinctively attempted to swallow her astonished gasp, but even if she could have managed the impossible feat, it would have been a futile gesture on her part. They were waiting for her. It was as if the wall opening and her undignified descent down the dark, narrow tunnel had set off an alarm of some sort, giving them ample time to prepare for her arrival.

Noelle concluded the greeting party had been expecting someone or something more sinister than a single, unarmed, rather terrified woman. When it became obvious she was alone, an older man standing in the center of the hall gave a silent signal for his companions to lower their weapons, all of them gripped in massive, male hands and aimed at Noelle's heart. She let out a relieved sigh when they complied with the older man's silent command, even though she couldn't help but notice their hands still gripped the hilts of their finely honed broad swords and their intent eyes followed her every breath as it rose and fell in her chest.

While she was still reeling from the sight of no less than a few dozen men of various ages dressed in robes, and steel hauberks, resembling to her grasping mind the knights of Arthur's mythical round table, their leader, wearing a monk's brown robes and rope belt, crossed the distance to the tunnel opening where Noelle still stood frozen in shock. He greeted her with a wide smile and a voice that seemed sincerely welcoming.

"Mademoiselle Dominique. It is a pleasure to finally make your acquaintance. Our mutual benefactor indicated you would be joining us before too long, but I admit, shamefully, I doubted his assurance. It has been so long you see and even a man of faith sometimes falters when he has been so dearly tested."

"Our mutual benefactor?" Noelle echoed confused.

At his slight shrug and knowing expression, Noelle stuttered, astonished, "Michael? You speak of Michael?"

The older monk bowed slightly in acknowledgement. Noelle shook her head, trying to clear it of the confusion sparked by the man's seemingly casual acknowledgment. "Who are you? What are you doing here? How long have you been here, anyway?" She had not failed to take in the significance of their medieval robes, the shoulder length hair and full beards of the men wielding the broad swords but her reeling brain refused to accept the fantastic notion taking shape in her thoughts as one fantastic conclusion collided with another.

"Ah, well, I fear we have little time for extended explanations. Our continued presence here has always been predicated more on secrecy than on the might of our defenders, strong and noble as they are and have been over the long march of years that we have kept watch here. But, our time in this sacred place is drawing to a close. We were ordered to be ready to leave on a moment's notice. Not so small a command, given the length of our sojourn here, but we are ever his faithful servants." The monk explained, then at the muffled sound of loud pounding coming from the tunnel, his lips curved in a slight smile and he added with a sparkle in his eye. "Ah, I believe the Lucien heir is ramming the entrance in his desperation to rescue you from our nefarious clutches."

At the sudden wariness that rose in Noelle's expression, the older man waved his hand in a dismissive gesture. "Please, please. There is no reason for the anxiety I see in your eyes. You have nothing to fear from us. If you will just give me the key, we will retrieve that which we have so faithfully guarded all of these long years and be on our way."

"Be on your way where?" Noelle asked, neither denying nor confirming the existence of the key she still held clutched in her closed fist at her side.

"Wherever our lord leads us." The older man answered, then looking around him, added wistfully, "I cannot say I will be sorry to feel the sun on my face again, or the wind in my hair or see a flower in bloom on a hillside, but there is a part of me that will regret leaving this place. It has served us well. It has served mankind well, but we cannot afford further delay. If your companion breaks through the wall before we are gone, there will be bloodshed. Our benefactor will not risk what is guarded here falling into the hands of the faithless and ignorant."

Noelle held the other man's glance. He didn't shirk from her perusal, nor did he attempt to intimidate or threaten her. They both knew he could have taken the key by force at any time since her arrival in the odd chamber, but he hadn't. She was curious, after all these years, to discover what the key opened and what had been hidden beneath the

356

ancient abbey, but sometimes it was a steward's role to simply fulfill her stewardship and not question or demand answers to the mystery she and her blood had been a part of for centuries. Sighing with only a little regret and disappointment that there didn't appear time to compare notes with the older man as to the nature of their mutual stewardships, she held out her arm and turning her hand over, opened her fist to reveal the key.

There was audible surprise from the men still gripping their swords at their sides and a delighted satisfaction in the monk's eyes. He nodded, as if in confirmation of a voice she could not hear. She felt her own lips curving in a smile and knew she was doing the right thing. This is where the key belonged, in this man's hands, in the stewardship of Michael's most trusted servant. The monk didn't just reach out and grab the key from her outstretched hand, but instead, met her glance, his expression seeking her permission first. Then when she nodded her assent, he gently, and with near reverence closed his fingers around the key and lifted it from her grasp.

"*Merci*, Mademoiselle. The order is forever in your debt. You have rendered mankind a service I think you cannot fully comprehend."

She laughed. "That is understating the matter considerably."

He smiled, his amusement evident in his dark eyes, then bowing slightly he turned and motioned for his knights to follow him. Noelle watched as the monk, followed by the others crossed the width of the chamber. There, against the far wall, he paused and inserted the key into what appeared from where Noelle waited across the distance of the massive room, to be solid stone. Noelle couldn't help but notice that nothing happened. She waited, breath held, wondering if they were missing something, maybe it was the wrong key, maybe there was some clue she missed, some task she'd overlooked.

Then just as true panic began to take hold, a light began emerging from a crack that appeared where the key had been inserted into the stone. The crack grew larger, and the light became blinding. Noelle watched in stunned astonishment, as the opening grew large enough for the older monk and his knights to step through. For a moment she could see a jeweled box, recognized it as the source of the light that even from the distance separating them, she was forced to lift her arm to shield her eyes against its brightness.

Then four of the knights surrounded the chest and each of them lifted one end of the two poles she could see were threaded through the sides of it. She could see, despite their massive strength and size, the men labored to carry their treasure, but they steadied themselves beneath its weight and began walking deeper into the stone, where apparently another tunnel lay hidden behind the wall of rock and granite. The remaining knights gripped their swords and took up a protective posture, surrounding the men carrying the chest. When the older monk fell into step behind them, Noelle couldn't stop herself from calling out.

"Bishop Aubert?"

The older man paused and then he turned around to meet her questioning glance, surprise at her perception evident in his. "Yes, Mademoiselle?"

Even though she'd suspected his identity, the shock of his confirmation almost knocked her over. "What happened to Sister Marie?"

His lips curved in an understanding, if slightly amused smile at the subject of her curiosity. "You would do well to ask the Lucien patriarch for the answers you seek."

Shocked into silence, Noelle could only nod, then watch as the Bishop turned around and once more began following his men down the hidden tunnel. Just before he passed from her line of sight, he turned and nodded once more in her direction. "Mademoiselle?"

"Yes?"

"Our mutual benefactor wanted me to inform you that he considers your debt to him paid in full."

Noelle nodded, speechless, as the Bishop responsible for the construction of Mont Saint Michel thirteen centuries earlier, after Michael visited him in his dreams, turned back and with a wave of his hand, disappeared from view. The opening in the stone closed behind his departing back just as Rafe burst through the opening in the tunnel behind her.

She turned at the sound of his panicked voice, screaming her name. "Noelle! Noelle!"

Their eyes met across the few feet separating them. Noelle saw the relief in his eyes that she was alive and apparently unharmed, followed quickly by rising anger. "Why the hell didn't you answer me? I thought you'd been taken. What happened? What is this place?" He added in wonder, as his eyes left her face and took in the chamber, the huge fireplace, where meat still sizzled in the flames and bread baked in the iron pans.

Before Noelle had a chance to answer, Rafe was followed into the chamber by Captain Fils and M. Denard. Several armed gendarmes rushed in behind them. They stopped suddenly at the strange chamber greeting them and at the sight of Noelle standing opposite them, seemingly alone and unharmed.

"Mademoiselle Dominque? Are you all right?" Captain Fils demanded.

Noelle nodded, but kept her eyes on Rafe's when she responded, "Yes, Captain. Thank you. I'm finished here. We can leave now."

She could tell Rafe was dying to ask her what had happened, what the key opened and how in the world she had come to the conclusion she was finished there, but knew he dared not reveal the existence of the key and the true purpose of their visit in front of the others. He merely nodded, and gripping her arm, led her back towards the entrance to the tunnel.

Remembering the steep descent, she eyed Rafe doubtfully.

"Do you have another suggestion?" He asked, his glance piercing hers.

Noelle looked around the chamber, could see no evidence of where the Bishop and his men had exited through the opening in the stone, and sighing, turned back to meet Rafe's probing glance. "I guess not."

"Mademoiselle Dominique," Captain Fils voice stopped her when she would have placed her hand in Rafe's and head back towards the entrance to the tunnel.

"Yes, Captain?"

"What is this place?" He finally got out, after an obvious struggle to suppress the string of questions she could see backing up in his eyes.

She stopped and let her eyes take in the expanse of the chamber, and shaking her head in wonder, met the captain's suspicious glance and replied honestly, "I don't know."

The patent disbelief in his expression made it obvious he didn't believe her denial. "Did you grow so tired of waiting for us you decided to light a fire and prepare a meal?"

Noelle's lips curved in an amused smile at the Captain's sarcasm. She couldn't come up with an explanation he would accept or believe, so she merely shrugged her response, a sympathetic understanding lighting her eyes, then she turned to Rafe and together they passed back through the entrance to the tunnel leaving the astonished authority figures to make of what they willed of the evidence before their eyes.

Rafe waited until they were out of earshot of the entrance and then demanded in a fierce whisper, "What the hell is that place? What happened? Where's the key?"

Noelle lifted her glance to meet Rafe's intent one, then turned to glance beyond his shoulder just to ascertain their conversation wouldn't be overheard. She met the intense glance of Captain Fils, who had silently followed in their footsteps, no doubt concluding he was more likely to get answers to the mystery he'd spent the past several weeks chasing from the one person who'd been at the heart of it all. Deciding she owed him for her mother's life and for her own escape from the madmen pursuing her, she turned back to Rafe and replied, "The key's back where it belongs."

At Rafe's raised brow, she added with a slight smile, "In the hands of Michael's faithful steward."

"That's who's been living down here?" He demanded incredulously

"Apparently so. The last line of defense against those who would have tried to steal the relic."

"How long have they been down there? How is it possible the authorities never suspected their presence? Where did their supplies come from? Where did they go?"

Noelle shrugged slightly, and then told him what she could. "They left and took with them that which they've been guarding all this time."

"How did they leave?" Rafe persisted.

"Through the wall."

"The same way you did?" Rafe asked drily.

Remembering her sudden, undignified descent through the tunnel, Noelle replied, "Actually, their departure was a little more dignified than my own from the altar."

Captain Fils, who'd been listening intently, but silently until this point, interjected, "There are men surrounding the structure and ships patrolling the bay. They'll never escape."

Noelle turned to glance over her shoulder, reminding him, "No one ever suspected they were here all this time?"

Noelle could see her question was an uncomfortable one for the captain to confront. He held her glance when he asked, "How much time are we talking about?"

"Unfortunately there wasn't enough time for an extended conversation. They were in a hurry to be on their way, but if I had to guess, I would say the monks have been here since the beginning."

"Since the beginning of what?" The captain echoed incredulous.

"The beginning," Noelle insisted.

"You're saying that hall beneath the *Church of Notre Dame sous Terre* has always been there?"

Noelle shrugged. "Obviously I have no way of confirming that, but I think so. A fortress within a fortress. An order within an order to protect what lay hidden here."

"Who told you this?"

"No one. As I said, there was too little time for an extended conversation with the authorities closing in on them. My conclusions are pure speculation on my part, Captain. They have no basis in confirmable evidence."

"Yet there were men…monks you say, waiting for you at the bottom of the tunnel."

"Yes."

"And now they're gone."

"Yes."

Noelle could understand the captain's frustration. He was the one, after all, who was going to have to explain all of this to his superiors.

"How can you be certain the men who met you at the end of the tunnel were not in league with the Sons of France?" He finally demanded, searching desperately for clarity.

361

"There's no possibility of that," Noelle assured him.

"How you be so sure?"

"Because they already had in their possession that which the Sons had been so desperately seeking."

"Seeking for the past millennia?"

Noelle lifted one shoulder in a delicate shrug. "It would seem so."

The older man opened his mouth to speak, to protest the surety of her conviction, and then finally demanded. "The relic. You saw it?"

"I saw evidence of it," Noelle admitted, a bit reluctant to confirm even to a man she believed she could trust that there actually was something hidden beneath Mont Saint Michel. She didn't want to risk a new generation of fanatics setting off in search of it for another millennia.

"What evidence? What did you see?"

Noelle shook her head. "Captain, no disrespect intended, but I believe it would be best if I didn't say anymore. The relic is gone. Safe for the moment from the evil pursuing it. Write whatever you will in reports to your superiors, but I think it would be best if you left out all mention of the relic."

"How am I supposed to do that?" The older man thrust a hand through his hair in a gesture of patent frustration.

"I don't know, but there are some truths too dangerous to be trusted in the hands of a porous bureaucracy, don't you agree?"

He held her glance, but didn't immediately respond to her question. He was a man who dwelt in facts after all, a public servant who had spent his career, his life, acquiring the kind of hard evidence that led to prosecutions and convictions, the kind that kept the ordinary citizens he protected safe from the evil men of this world. The untidiness of the incredible discovery of the hall beneath the ancient abbey had shaken him, had shaken his beliefs, in the natural order of things to a degree he was having difficulty coming to terms with.

Further discussion was cut off for the moment because they'd reached the steepest part of the ascent and all of their focus was needed to claw their way up and out the rough opening that had been hewn open in the stone wall behind the altar through which Noelle had fallen.

362

Seeing the damage done to the ancient wall, Noelle heaved a regretful sigh.

"Don't," Rafe warned her from where he stood directly behind her, making sure she didn't stumble.

She sent him a laughing glance over her shoulder, and then turned to grasp the hand of one of the captain's men being held out to her to assist her through the opening. Rafe followed close behind. She took a final look around the old church and turning to Rafe, announced with a lightness she couldn't ever remember feeling before. "My part in what this was is finished. I can feel it. Whatever bound me to this place is gone. Can we go back to Chateau Lucien? I have a few questions for your grandfather."

"My grandfather?" Rafe echoed. "Why?"

Noelle shrugged. "Something one of the monks said."

"Yes..." Rafe pushed.

"He said I would do well to ask the Lucien patriarch for the answers I seek."

"In regards to what?"

"Sister Marie."

"Sister Marie? How could my grandfather know anything about Sister Marie?"

Noelle smiled at Rafe's obvious frustration. Like Captain Fils, she could tell their conversation was beginning to edge into uncomfortable territory.

"Let's go find out," she suggested grinning.

Nodding, obviously wanting to say more, but apparently deciding to wait until they were alone, he nodded, gripped her arm and began leading her to the exit of the ancient church.

"Mlle Dominique?" Captain Fils' voice halted their progress towards the door.

"Yes?" Noelle responded, turning to face the captain.

"What will the Archangel Michael do to this place now that the monks have gone?"

"I don't know."

"What do you believe he will do?" Unsatisfied with her evasive answer, the gendarme captain pushed back.

"I don't believe he'll do anything. He no longer has any reason to concern himself with the fate of Mont Saint Michel."

"Then what will happen to this place?" The captain persisted, unwilling to let the matter drop.

Sighing Noelle paused and decided to give the captain the honesty he sought from her. "I have no way of knowing for certain, but I think it will simply fade away and become like other old archeological sites. One that was once a place of importance in the ancient world. It will become, as it already appears to those without faith…a collection of rocks and iron and glass. A curiosity, if you will, for tourists."

Jean met her glance, disturbed by the intensity of the blue of her eyes… the Dominique eyes. He'd come across a few of the odd legends about the Dominiques in his search for answers. He had dismissed them as the hysteria of medieval times. Now he was no longer certain there was no foundation of truth in them.

Noelle turned back to where Rafe waited for her, and together they continued towards the exit to the church. Before they passed through the opening, she paused and turned back to where the captain still waited, watching her.

"Captain, if anyone asks, you might suggest whoever is in charge of such things that they consider changing the name of this place."

"Surely you're joking, Mademoiselle," Jean protested. "Mont Saint Michel is a national treasure."

"It may have been at one time, Captain," Noelle agreed with a regretful sigh, before adding, "Now it is merely an old fortress that sells coffee and t-shirts. I don't believe the Archangel Michael would be pleased to have his name associated with it. In fact, I believe he may take it as a personal affront if it continues to bear his name. I don't think anyone wants that. Do you?"

She turned to smile at Rafe and let him lead her away from the depths of the site out into the bright sunlight. "Let's leave this place. It no longer has any hold over me. I can't imagine ever returning here again."

They crossed the bridge and turned for a final look back at the ancient abbey. Noelle lifted a hand in a final gesture of farewell in the direction of the gleaming statue of Michael that stood watch over the ancient abbey. Maybe it was just a trick of the light, but for a moment, Noelle's eyes were blinded. Blinking quickly, she refocused her gaze on the statue only to watch as the replica of the prince of heaven separated itself from the base securing it and fell head first into the bay.

She lifted her gaze to meet Rafe's incredulous one. "I guess Michael is finished protecting Mont Saint Michel."

"God help us all," Rafe remarked with feeling, reaching up to the make the sign of the cross.

Then turning his attention away from the abbey, he caught Noelle's concerned glance watching him and added with a grin, "Let's go see what old Ari has to say about all of this. Apparently it wasn't only your father's legacy to you he's been keeping secret all these years."

They didn't learn until later that the plastic mold standing at the exit, the one that spoke to a little girl twenty years earlier, had shattered into tiny fragments at the same time the statue of Michael fell into the bay from the peak of the structure. The fragments were so small there was no recovering them to rebuild the model. In fact, a swift breeze had swept up the dust and scattered it over the bay.

The End

EPILOGUE...

"Bishop Aubert? As in the dead monk with the hole in his head?" Rafe echoed incredulously.

Noelle turned to grin in his direction, but responded only half-teasingly. "Yes, I know it sounds crazy, but remember Gabriel said the authorities are no longer convinced the body in his tomb is the bishop's. Remember the trepanation?"

"You think the trepanation is the only problem with your theory that you turned over the key to the founder of Mont Saint Michel, a man, who despite the disputed final resting place of his remains, has been dead for almost thirteen centuries?"

Noelle was aware of the astonished glances their grandparents were exchanging at their budding argument, but neither interrupted the lively interplay. She ignored them for the moment. She was too intent on convincing Rafe that she was right. "Don't you see? The monks had to explain the bishop's disappearance somehow. So, they announced his death, found a convenient, if unfortunate body with a hole drilled in his skull to alleviate pressure on his brain or release the evil spirits held there, and buried it in the bishop's place. When the tomb was found centuries later and re-located to the Gervais Basilica in Avranches, everyone believed it was the bishop's because of the hole drilled in the side of his head. In the meantime, the real Bishop Aubert never left Mont Saint Michel. He was guarding whatever it was the key opened in the vault beneath the abbey."

"That's ridiculous!" Rafe exclaimed, thrusting an impatient hand through his hair in a gesture Noelle recognized as a sign of his growing frustration with her "absurd" claim.

"Noelle, sweetheart, you're saying you actually spoke to Bishop Aubert, or someone claiming to be the bishop, at Mont Saint Michel today? And you handed the key to him?'

"Yes, Meme."

"And he used the key you found in the box at your home in Washington to unlock a vault hidden in the wall of a hall beneath the

366

abbey that the authorities never even knew was there? For what? The past twelve centuries?"

"Yes. Isn't that amazing? I hope Daddy knows we solved the mystery. Do you think he does?" Noelle asked.

Exchanging a cautious glance with Rafe's grandfather who had sat silently listening with growing astonishment as Noelle had recounted her experiences that day at the site, Noelle's grandmother reached out a gentle hand to squeeze one of Noelle's and answered reassuringly, "I'm sure he does, Noelle and I'm certain he's so proud of you. But, you haven't told us what the vault contained. What were the…" she paused briefly, then continued, "bishop and his men protecting all of these years?"

Noelle released an audible sigh. "I don't know. It's probably for the best, I know, but still it feels a little like leaving right before the end of an intense movie and never learning what happened. Whatever it was the relic was enclosed in a jeweled chest that took four men to lift. The chest itself gave off the strangest light… or maybe it was the relic it held that was responsible for it."

"Where did they go?" Her grandmother persisted.

Noelle shrugged. "I don't know. When the wall hiding the chest opened, the bishop's men surrounded the chest and used the two poles to lift it onto their shoulders. I could tell it was heavy. It took four men to lift it. Then they just kept walking deeper into the vault and the opening closed behind them."

"Did the bishop say anything to you?"

Noelle nodded, and reached for one of the intricately decorated cookies laid out on the plate of sweets between them. It occurred to her she was starving. She'd been too nervous to eat that morning and in all of the excitement, hadn't had a chance to eat since. She took a bite of the cookie, before admitting, "Yes, he thanked me for my service to the order and then said that our mutual benefactor wanted him to inform me that he considered my debt to him paid in full."

It was her grandmother's turn to release an audible sigh. "Michael."

Noelle nodded, smiling. "Yes, it's finished, Meme."

"Do the men who were chasing you know it's finished?" Her grandmother wondered, her concern evident.

Noelle shrugged. "I have a feeling that word will trickle down to them."

Her grandmother was obviously not comforted by her rather airy reassurance. "Did the bishop have any other messages to relay from your mutual benefactor?"

"As a matter of fact," Noelle began and then pinned old Ari with her intent gaze.

"Yes, my dear?" Ari asked, puzzled by her focus on him.

"I asked him what happened to Sister Marie. He suggested the Lucien patriarch could satisfy my curiosity."

"Ah, I wondered if we would circle back around to the good sister," Rafe's grandfather commented with a smile playing around his lips.

"*Grand pere'*, you know something about all of this? And you haven't seen fit to divulge it before now?" Rafe demanded with growing outage.

Ari gestured for Rafe to sit back in his chair, as in his pent-up frustration Rafe appeared on the verge of jumping over the table and strangling the older man. Releasing a sigh of his own, the older man relayed, "I admit I was shocked when Noelle related her experience as Sister Marie."

"Why?" Rafe demanded, then added, "Beside the obvious reason that she was claiming she remembered a previous incarnation."

Ari chuckled. "Yes, that's a fascinating possibility, isn't it?" Seeing Rafe's dark expression, he continued, "Actually I found Noelle's account so interesting because it brought to mind a story I had read in my youth when I was researching Lucien family history."

"Really?" Noelle interjected, her excitement evident.

Ari rose from his seat around the table and gestured for the others to follow his lead. "Come, I will share with you what I know of Sister Marie. Obviously I have no way of knowing that Noelle's Sister Marie has anything to do with ours, but given recent events, and ah...the bishop's comment, I'm inclined to believe they are one and the same."

Smiling triumphantly, Noelle rose excitedly from her chair, and reached for Rafe's hand to pull him up from his. "I told you, I'm not delusional."

With another sweep of his hand through his hair, Rafe denied, "I never thought you were delusional."

Noelle rolled her eyes in his direction, exchanged an excited, amused glance with her grandmother who was already on her feet, and the three of them followed Old Ari from his personal office where they'd gathered to hear Noelle and Rafe's recounting of the events at Mont Saint Michel. They continued trailing him up the curving marble staircase leading into the main entry foyer, down another long hall, until they reached the portrait gallery. Noelle couldn't resist sending Rafe an "I told you so" glance over her shoulder, to which he merely grinned and shrugged, shaking his head. Then she turned back to follow Rafe's grandfather to the spot where he had come to a stop in front of the portrait of one of the Lucien duchesses from what appeared by the way she was dressed, to be the Renaissance era.

"Sister Marie," Ari announced with an admiring smile in Noelle's direction.

"But how did she end up here? Wasn't she a nun?" Noelle's grandmother protested.

Noelle shook her head. Staring at the portrait, she replied, absentmindedly. "No, she was a novitiate. She hadn't taken her final vows yet." She turned her attention to the man at the duchess' side. "He rescued her. Just like you rescued me," Noelle tacked on, turning around so she could meet Rafe's glance where he stood behind her. "I bet my...*her* father or brother found out that her mother had lied about her being born dead. They must have tracked her to the convent, searching for the key. He rescued her by marrying her. They wouldn't have dared challenge a Lucien duke."

When Rafe couldn't summon a reply to her fantastic claim, Noelle turned back to face the portrait. She felt his hands descend on her shoulders and pull her gently back against him. He bent and whispered in her ear, "It's a nice ending, and if you're intent on believing it I won't argue with you."

In response, Noelle grinned up at him and pushed, "That's because you know I'm right."

EPILOGUE...

The head of the Brotherhood rose from his place behind his desk. He had come to terms with the loss of the relic and after much prayer and self-deliberation; he'd passed the stewardship of their cause to a new leader. For himself, he'd decided on another tactic.

He left his office in downtown Paris dressed in a western suit, but by the time he arrived at the area surrounding the *Arc de Triomphe* where thousands had gathered to mark the anniversary of the 2015 massacre at the offices of the satirical weekly newspaper, *Charlie Hebdo*, he had changed his attire. He now appeared as one of the protestors, even going so far as to don a *Je suis Charlie* t-shirt in commemoration of and in communion with those who were killed in the terrorist attack. He took his place among the other protestors, looking around curiously. He was surprised by the diversity of the crowd, and the number of Muslims marching side by side with their western counterparts, all of them chanting, *Je suis Charlie*. I am Charlie. Their point being of course, that we were all Charlie, all of us were innocent victims of the violence and hatred plaguing the world. And, each of us bore a responsibility to stand in the place of the fallen and be a voice for justice and freedom and basic human rights.

As idealistic and doomed as he believed the cause of those surrounding him, he couldn't help but admire their willingness to embrace it and offer their very lives in pursuit of it. It occurred to him that they were not so very different after all. Their tactics might vary widely, but their goals were remarkably aligned.

The truth was, he was tired of all of the depressing news, of turning on the television and being forced to grapple with the graphic images of a new attack, each more heinous than the last. He was exhausted from the bloody scenes of war...of death...of ceaseless violence and the seemingly never-ending lust for blood, and forever more spectacular scenes of death and destruction...and the all-important media attention resulting from it.

Yes, a change in tactics was definitely in order. Obviously the current ones were not working.

Perhaps, it was time to adopt the advice of the old John Lennon song and "Give Peace a Chance…"

Coming to a decision, he nodded to himself, and joined in the chanting echoing around him…

Je suis Charlie…

Je suis Charlie…

Je suis Charlie…

Printed in Dunstable, United Kingdom

65113155R10221